REDEMPTION IN STONE

A SEVEN FAMILIES NOVEL: WOLF
BOOK TWO

KAT SIMONS

T&D PUBLISHING

Published 2023 by T&D Publishing
Cover design: © 2023 T&D Publishing
Interior book design © 2023 T&D Publishing
ISBN-13: 978-1-944600-62-4 (Trade Paperback Edition)
ISBN-13: 978-1-944600-63-1 (Large Print Edition)

This is a work of fiction. All of the characters, places, organizations, and events portrayed are either products of the author's imagination or are used fictitiously. Any resemblance to actual persons, living or dead, business establishments, events, or locales is entirely coincidental.

First printing T&D Publishing edition: March 2023
For information, contact T&D Publishing: https://www.tanddpublishing.com

REDEMPTION IN STONE

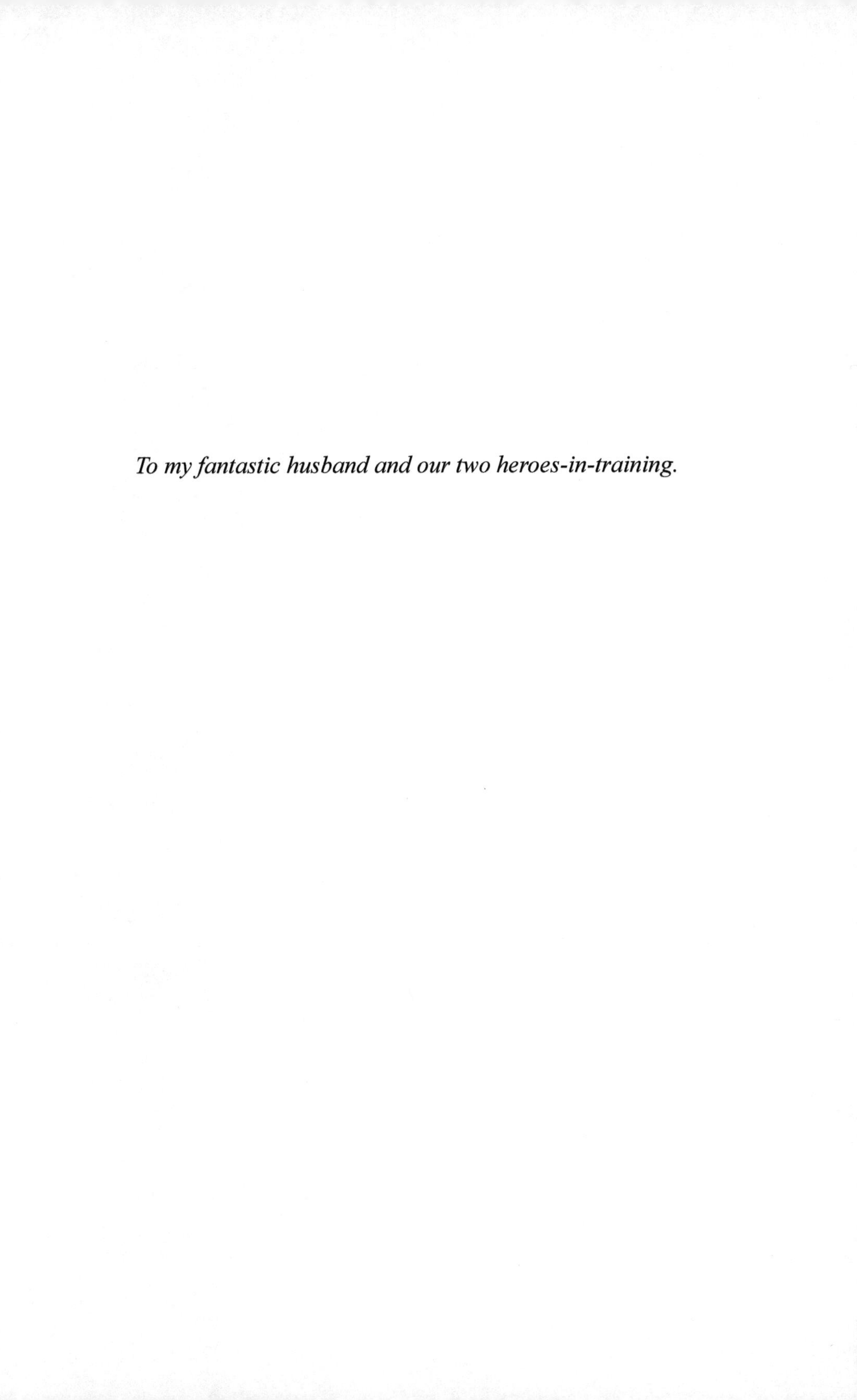

To my fantastic husband and our two heroes-in-training.

CHAPTER ONE

Rebecca Logan crept through the woods, studying the ground, the lines barely visible in the dirt. With the night covering the ground beneath the pines in shadows, she needed every ounce of her heightened eyesight to follow the faint trail.

The monster was close.

She'd been following it through the mountains for two days now. Rumors of mysterious cattle deaths just the other side of the mountain drew her here to the Cascades. Then trails of dead deer, their bodies torn apart in ways that some accounts tried to write off as bear or wolf killings. One story tried to blame a coyote for the slaughter.

But little details had crept into the news accounts. Little signs of "something not right" with the excuse of ordinary animals, even packs of animals, being responsible for the weird slaughters. Things like the dead carrion birds found near the bodies. The bulging round injuries that looked almost like suction cup burns. The fact that none of the teeth marks could be matched to any of the local predators.

And then, the stories of people seeing a "monster" started to show up in less reputable magazines and newspapers. Seeing something with tentacles moving around the edge of property. Something with huge teeth scurrying through the yard.

No humans believed those stories. They were nightmares. Fictions. Things you found in horror books, not in real life. Must have been weird shadows. Something ordinary looking strange in the dark.

But Becca knew better.

Monsters were real. And it was the job of her family to hunt and kill them.

She'd been fighting monsters her whole life. Almost two centuries training and then hunting them down. Destroying them so they couldn't harm En's precious humans. The job was ordained by old gods and came with a lot of responsibility.

A lot of potential danger as well.

The faint trail she followed started to widen. Signs of something large moving through, pushing down the undergrowth, scrapping pine needles into unnatural lines. The smell hit her next. Faint on the wind, but there. An almost salty scent, mixed with the metallic tang of blood, and a faint hint of something like animal feces. She wrinkled her nose. Not only did the fucking things have to be dangerous. An inordinate number of them stank.

She let out a long, slow breath, settling her shoulders. There was a clearing ahead. A good place for an ambush.

Pulling her sword from the scabbard across her back, and dropping the pack she carried from her shoulder to rest against the thick base of a fir tree, she inched silently through the trees, her full attention now on the very faint snuffling noise ahead. So faint, if she'd been an ordinary human, she would have missed the sound. Maybe confused it for a breeze or the ruffle of a night bird's feathers.

Autumn in these mountains was already getting cold enough to feel the approaching winter. Though it was still early in October, a bite of sharp chill kissed her cheeks as she slipped silently to the edge of the clearing.

She took her sword in a two-handed grip and stared at the beast.

An irgotoc. She could hardly believe it. She'd really hoped she was wrong.

Tiny blade-like talons flicked out from the tips of two dozen brown tentacles covering the thing's scaled sides. Its bat-like wings rose and fell, shrunken and useless for flight, but the movements created a wisping sound, like canvas shuddering in an ocean wind. Its four thick crocodile-like legs were squatted down low, putting the monster's belly close to the ground. From her angle behind a tree, she couldn't see the beast's tail, but its flat snout was buried in the remains of…something. Hard to tell what that something used to be.

Two humans had gone missing over the mountains before she'd been able to get here. Their bodies hadn't been found. She very much hoped that wasn't one of them.

Settling her sword more firmly in her grip, she moved out of the trees, approaching the monster at an angle. If it was occupied with its meal, she might be able to get close enough to cut off its head before a real fight erupted.

But irgotoc weren't so easy to sneak up on.

The beast spun, faster than it looked like it should move, whipping its tail around with a snap, the wicked six-inch barbs covering the tail tip hit the ground only a few inches from Becca's leg.

Okay. Fight it was.

The tentacles along its side flailed toward her, forcing her to swing wildly at one before jumping to one side and slashing through another. The creature's acid blood leeched into the ground, making the dirt sizzle.

She hated irgotoc. Acid blood was such a pain to deal with.

Another slash along its side drove it back a few feet, but then it charged again, fast on those squat crocodile legs, two side tentacles flicking at her as its barbed tail swung around again. She leapt back a foot, took a swipe at the beast's side, and scrapped her sword over the rock-hard scales.

Those were tricky to get past. But she didn't need to get her sword through its side. She needed to get her sword through its neck.

Getting at the neck with all those flailing tentacles and that spike-barbed tail wasn't a simple ask.

She dove close again, swinging in wide arcs to dislodge the tentacles. The irgotoc screeched and spun, those short squat legs swinging it around faster even than a crocodile. Moving fast enough to push her into moving faster as well. Her enhanced speed would make it obvious to a human she wasn't entirely human herself, but there were no witnesses this deep in the mountains.

Fortunately. Because she didn't want any humans in danger.

A blur of movement from the side, and she flicked her sword out without looking, the metal tinging against the hard talons tipping the tentacle. Then she dove away as the beast's tail whipped over the top of her head. The whistling sound of those sharp barbs passing close to her hair made her wince.

Coming to her feet a few yards away didn't give her any breathing space, though. The irgotoc charged forward. She took out a tentacle, the severed limb dropping to the ground with a wiggling thud, the blade shaped talons on its tip churning up the dirt.

To her horror, the severed tentacle started to grow back.

What the hell? Irgotocs didn't have limbs that regenerated.

The beast's little vestigial wings beat the air. And while they were small and useless, the movement sent the noxious smell of its blood and natural shit stench over the top of Becca. She gaged and snarled. One of the times her sensitive sense of smell was a drawback.

She slashed and cut at flailing limbs again and again. Diving beyond the beast's tail. Spinning and lunging forward again. Always aiming for the neck.

Two of the severed tentacles regenerated, but a third remained a lumpy, bleeding stub. The anomaly in the irgotoc's physiology was distracting.

Irgotocs weren't new monsters. The species had existed for millennia. They weren't the oldest of the monsters, but they were still old enough that the Families had all their traits and dangers well catalogued.

But the Families had also managed to drive the irgotocs to near extinction. She hadn't personally fought one in…a very long time. In fact, they'd started to believe irgotocs were actually extinct.

Then she'd started seeing those reports of dead animals and the two missing people. She'd expected to find some sort of monster in these mountains. When she'd seen the scat evidence of an irgotoc, though, she hadn't quite believed her eyes.

But there was no denying the monster still existed, when it was right in front of her. And it looked like it had evolved.

Which really really sucked.

She dove to the left as it charged, tail swinging, the wicked six-inch barbs covering the tail's tip barely missing her head again. She took two tentacles in one swing, leaping back to avoid the talons as the limbs flew away from the beast.

A piercing screech erupted from the irgotoc. Wincing, she jumped over more flailing limbs, and used a tree trunk to boost herself in a high jump that landed her several feet behind the monster.

She sucked in a deep breath. Sweat trickled down her back beneath her sweater, despite the cold air kissing her cheeks.

The irgotoc spun again, but this time, instead of charging toward her, it lunged into the darkness beneath the trees.

Shit.

Her most basic instincts urged her to race after it. But her training checked the charge. She opened her senses, listening, scenting the air. Irgotocs were fast monsters, and more graceful than might be expected for that collection of body parts, but they weren't naturally suited to moving easily in the undergrowth.

A shadowed movement to her left. The sounds of scrapping over dirt and detritus.

She rushed toward the sound, the scent of shit and monster getting stronger in that direction.

But another smell, something weirdly familiar, weirdly nice, brushed her senses. Made her stumble a step. Blinking.

What the…?

Before she could analyze the new smell, the irgotoc rushed out of the trees at her, forcing her into defensive sword swings and retreat to gain some ground. Fuck.

She tripped over a branch, dropping hard onto her ass. With another curse, she stabbed her sword toward the irgotoc's face as it raced to overwhelm her. She skewered one of the tiny black eyes above its bloodied snout.

The beast screeched again and stopped the headlong charge. Giving her enough time to roll back to her feet.

Then a second huge shape lunged between her and the monster.

And that weirdly familiar scent brought her up short again.

Oh no.

CHAPTER TWO

Becca had a full second to register the stranger standing between her and the monster, one single second to take in the large shadow of him. The blackness under the trees, hid any distinct features. But she got the impression of wide shoulders and height.

Then the large shape leapt away again.

The irgotoc spun, following the moving shadow, its bloodied snout snuffling the air, its vestigial wings fluttering as it shuffled on its crocodile legs to face the stranger.

A weird sort of panic she wasn't used to filled Becca. Panic that the monster would reach the newcomer before she could kill it.

The odd fear, that pulse of terror, was a distraction she couldn't afford. She hadn't felt *panic* in a fight with a monster since her early years. Why now? Where was the throat-clogging terror coming from?

Whatever it was, the emotion sent her charging toward the irgotoc, desperate to get its attention back on her and away from the stranger.

The monster's distraction worked for her, though. She went right for its neck, able to slide through the still flailing tentacles, slipping past tiny blades, to slice her sword across the thick neck at the base of the monster's round head. No scales here. Nothing to stop the honed edge of her sword.

The monster spun around, tentacles swiping at her, tail a blur of movement. Its acid blood sprayed out with its wild movements, forcing her to leap away, to pull her sword free too soon.

Damn it. Hadn't gotten the head off. And the fuckers just kept moving so long as their heads were attached. Even if only barely.

The shadow that had distracted the monster before charged behind the beast. The irgotoc swung around, its head lolling sickeningly to one side. Becca cursed, pulled the dagger from her boot sheath, and charged the irgotoc again.

Dodging deadly tentacles, slashing at them with both dagger and sword, she tried to work her way back to the monster's neck, looking for an opening. From the corner of her eye, she saw the shadow dart past the back of the beast again, watched the irgotoc's tail whip toward that shadow. She might have screamed a warning. She couldn't be sure. But her own distraction cost her.

A tentacle hooked her ankle and brought her down hard on her ass again.

The irgotoc lunged for her, its snout open to reveal shockingly thick, sharp teeth. Instinctively, she dropped her weapons and reached with both hands to hold the monster's head back.

She realized in that moment, the neck wound she'd already issued was healing. No more acid blood spit out. Good given her position underneath the monster as she struggled to hold the snout and sharp, snapping teeth away from her face. Bad because she still had to get the head off somehow.

And she'd had to drop her sword and dagger.

Desperately, she reached one-handed for her sword, keeping one hand on the irgotoc. But every time she released her hold, the monster pushed forward, and she had to quickly use two hands to hold it back again.

She was stronger than a human woman, by a lot, but the irgotoc was her match. It pushed those sharp teeth at her, making a high-pitched sound like a snuffle and a whine combined. The sound pierced her sensitive ears, breaking up her concentration.

As she struggled, one of the blades tipping a tentacle cut through the thigh pocket of her cargo pants, only missing skin because the pocket carried a water flask.

Her lungs burned and she realized she wasn't breathing through her gritted teeth. She sucked in a breath, gulping foul-smelling air. The creature's rotten smell coated the back of her throat. And where its acid blood had sizzled the soil, that sharp acrid stench stung her nostrils.

She reached for her sword again, only to have to swing back to keep both hands on the snapping beast's head. She needed purchase and a better position. She didn't have any leverage like this. But the irgotoc gave her no room to move, to stand up. And no space to reach her weapons.

A high howl rent the night air.

Suddenly the monster jerked back a few inches. Pulled off of her. Giving her some room to move. Its head swiveled to look at its tail.

And Becca took those precious seconds.

Without looking, she snatched up the closest weapon to hand. Then she thrust her dagger up under the irgotoc's chin into the soft flesh of its neck.

It reared back, releasing another piercing whining screech.

Scrambling away as acid blood sprayed out, Becca snatched up her sword and stood in one movement. Spun. And brought the sharp blade down across the monster's neck. This time severing its head in a single swing.

The head bounced along the dark soil, rolling a few feet away. The body continued to thrash for several seconds, the remaining tentacles groping wildly at the air. Then it collapsed and dark acid blood seeped from its neck to soak the ground.

Becca took a breath. Fucking irgotocs.

She scooted away from the pooling blood and turned her attention to the monster's tail to see what had pulled it off her.

And she realized why the scent she'd caught earlier seemed familiar.

A wolf, twice the size of a normal animal, held the creature's tail in its massive jaws. Black blood dripped from the wolf's mouth, but it didn't let go until the final tentacle lay still.

"Drop it," she said, a little panicky. "Drop the tail. Acid blood. It's burning you."

The wolf dropped its hold and took a step away from the irgotoc. Shook its snout a little, as if to dislodge the blood. Then looked up and met her gaze. Intelligent, glowing yellow eyes stared steadily at her.

There was more awareness in those eyes than there should have been in an ordinary wolf. And that glowing yellow…not just a trick of the night.

She stepped around the monster, approaching the wolf slowly and deliberately. Worried about the acid burns he must have gotten. She didn't want to send him running away without first assuring herself the injuries were survivable. Especially since the wolf had helped her.

She wanted to scan the trees for the human man who'd jumped into the mix earlier—had he been wounded? Had he run away? Had the wolf hurt him?—but with the huge wolf standing only a few feet away, possibly severely injured, she had to focus on him first. And something about the sheer size of the animal, and the color of his eyes…

"That wasn't a very good idea," she said, keeping her voice low and soothing. "This thing's killed a lot of animals. Probably a couple of humans, too. They're very dangerous. You could have been killed."

The almost sardonic tilt of the wolf's head made Becca certain he understood her. And that he was absolutely more than a wolf.

The absence of the human man who'd first jumped between her and the irgotoc started to make sense.

"Thanks for the help," she murmured.

The wolf dipped his head in acknowledgement. Which confirmed her suspicions.

"No ordinary wolf, then." Not like her either. But not just a wolf.

The instant she voiced the realization out loud, the wolf started to change. His body convulsed and expanded as he rose onto two legs. Hair receded. Tail disappeared. Paws turned to hands. Muzzle retracted. Within minutes, the wolf had shifted. And a human man stood in the woods before her.

Wow.

Becca blinked. He was…not what she'd been expecting.

His eyes were still a little yellow, though not as bright as the wolf's had been, and for some reason, she was insanely curious what his eye color without the shifter glow might be. His hair was a shaggy dark brown, almost black, crowning a ruggedly handsome face. Not pretty, but compelling. The sort of face that would make her miss a step if she passed him on the street. Sharp, wide features. Shadows cutting beneath his high cheekbones. A hard mouth that kept drawing her attention—just to reassure herself the irgotoc's acid blood hadn't done him any serious damage, though, she told herself. That was the only reason she couldn't seem to pull her attention from his mouth.

He was naked after his shift, of course, and was nicely muscled. At least in the parts of him she allowed herself to peek at. She knew shapeshifters didn't worry about nudity the way humans often did. But since he'd helped her in the irgotoc fight, she felt like she should afford him at least a little discretion. Keeping her gaze from dipping lower was more difficult than it should have been, though. Something about him…drew her.

So much so, she took another step toward him.

His scent washed over her then. Not just wolf this time, but…*him.*

Recognition hit like a hammer. The panic earlier in the fight after he'd appeared… That distracting terror that had filled her…

Shocked realization left her breathless for several long seconds. Her heartbeat pounded hard in her chest. Her pulse throbbed in her veins. Was this real? Could this be possible? Here? Now?

She met his gaze.

After all these years. One hundred and ninety years of knowing this moment would come. Hoping this moment would happen. Holding the god En's promise in her heart. That this would come before one of the monsters killed her.

And here he was. Just…standing in the woods with her over the carcass of an irgotoc.

He was the one.

The one man who could save her from the curse that haunted very member of her Family—haunted all of the Families. A curse En had promised would be broken when they found their Nam-tar. Their true love. Their destiny.

After almost two centuries, she stood face-to-face with the one person who would change her life forever.

The overwhelming reality crashed down on her, leaving her speechless. Breathless.

A slight movement from below and to her left caught her attention. She reacted instinctively, jumping backward to escape a last, spasmodic thrash of the dead monster's tail. But she wasn't fast enough.

One of the spiked barbs sliced through her leg, tearing open her pants and thigh muscle in one painful cut.

Cursing under her breath to offset the pain, she stared at the wound. Blood oozed down her leg, but thanks to her instinctive reaction, the spike hadn't buried itself in her thigh or caught a vital artery. Still, she needed to bind the wound. Soon.

Amateur move. Letting a dead monster injure her. Not exactly the first impression she'd hoped to make when meeting her Nam-tar for the first time.

She opened her mouth to say something, though what she wasn't sure. Then her vision started to cloud. Black spots danced in front of her eyes. Numbness seeped up her limps. All of it too sudden and pervasive. Not shock. Not just blood loss.

Her heartbeat stuttered, then pounded hard. She sucked in a ragged breath. Glanced at the man.

He took several steps closer, reached for her.

"Oh, this isn't good," she said.

And darkness closed around her.

CHAPTER THREE

Adam Walsh lunged forward, catching the woman seconds before she hit the ground. Cursing as graphically as she had, he lifted her into his arms. He hurried through the trees to his home, leaving the carcass and her weapons for later, a little rueful at having to cross the rough, needle and rock-strewn ground on his more tender human feet rather than well-toughened paws.

He had had shoes on when he left the house, of course. He'd had clothes, too. But once he'd seen the creature attacking the woman up close, he'd stripped fast and shifted. His wolf form was more agile, and the wolf's enhanced night vision seemed like a better option in the moment.

He'd been less happy with his sensitive sense of smell in his wolf form. Whatever that thing had been, it smelled like shit, literally. Worse. It smelled like death. Had tasted pretty horrible, too. He glanced down at the unconscious woman in his arms. She'd said the blood was acid. He'd wondered why the hell his mouth burned when he bit down on the thing to drag it off her. Fortunately, the shift back to his human form had healed the burns.

Not that he'd have done anything different.

Taking the back steps to his two-story cabin two at a time, he elbowed open the door—which he hadn't taken the time to lock—and passed through the kitchen to the living room. He'd take the woman up to his guest bedroom later, if she survived, but all his medical gear was on this floor.

The thought of her not surviving buried something painful and sharp into his chest. He ignored it.

After he laid her on the couch and removed the scabbard still strapped across her back, he retrieved his First Aid kit along with an armful of towels from the bathroom. Gently arranging one of the towels beneath her wounded thigh, he studied the injury through the rip in her pants. A deep gouge in her thigh muscle that luckily seemed to have missed any important arteries. A puncture where the spike had gone in, and a trail of torn skin where the spike had ripped back out.

Not pretty. Needed stitches. And she'd probably have a scar. Nothing he could do about that. But he could suture it and make sure it was clean at least.

He set a compress to the puncture to staunch the bleeding, only then realizing her wound wasn't bleeding as much as it should have been. Frowning, he released the pressure and carefully cleaned around the cut with sterilized wipes. The bleeding had slowed to barely a trickle.

Ordinary humans didn't heal from injuries like this that fast.

So. No ordinary woman.

Since she'd known the wolf hadn't been an ordinary wolf, and he'd shifted in front of her, that was probably for the best. He had enough problems as it was. Last thing he needed was a mundane human knowing he was a shifter.

Though, given the way she'd fought that thing, whatever it had been, and the speed she'd moved during the fight, he should have known she was something more even without the fast healing. What exactly...? Well, that would have to wait until she woke up.

He cleaned around and inside the puncture wound. While the ragged edges of her injury still looked red and swollen, the muscle beneath didn't look quite as damaged as it had earlier. He carefully pulled the wound closed and covered it with butterfly stitches. While she was obviously healing much faster than a mundane human, it never hurt to aid that healing.

He'd learned a lot about fixing up wounds on fast healing shifters under a previous alpha, before his brother had taken over the pack. The previous alpha loved a good fight, was a bully, and didn't have the care for his pack to ensure the ones wounded during the fights got proper help. A broken bone that heals fast but not properly aligned could cause a shifter a lot of pain. And usually had to be rebroken and reset. Shifting with broken limbs only made things worse, even though shifting for most injuries healed them faster.

So he and his brother and sister had taken on the task of medic to the pack out of necessity. At least for a little while.

A tightening in his chest made him shake his head. Even after more than three years, he had a hard time thinking about his family. Hard not to wonder how they were doing. What they were doing. He wondered if Siobhan's boutique in Eirene was growing. How the pack was faring under Gabriel. If Siobhan had finally hooked the wolf she'd been in love with for years. If Gabriel had gotten his own head out of his ass and looked for a mate. So much he was missing out on.

He and Gabriel occasionally snuck in a phone call, and Gabriel insisted on putting money into Adam's bank account regularly, even though Adam wasn't sure the pack could afford it. But for the most part, Adam had had to break all contact with his siblings. And even years later, that still bit deep.

That was even before he considered the loss of his pack.

The panic came on suddenly, predictably, curling in his chest and stomach. His skin tingled and a light sweat broke out on his brow. He tightened his jaw and let out a slow breath, then relaxed his jaw. Closed his eyes briefly and steadied his hands. Other things to think about just then. Like not fucking up the butterfly stitches.

Once he'd finished, he studied the unconscious woman on his couch. The puncture hadn't taken her out like this. He was sure of that. Given the creature had acid blood, he was guessing those spikes had more to them, too. Poison? Possible. He'd never seen anything like that…whatever it was before, even though he'd seen some of the dead animals it had killed—including a fucking black bear. There'd been a smell on those carcasses, which could have been poison. He'd given them a wide berth, not knowing what he was up against. But poison was a real possibility.

Would her ability to heal fast take care of the poison, too? He had nothing here to treat her for a mysterious venom or poison, and he had to assume taking her to a hospital wasn't an option. Not that there was one anywhere near here. The drive to reach one would take hours. And from the animal evidence, he wasn't sure they'd have hours if there was poison involved. Besides, human doctors would probably be more trouble than help.

Still, as he watched, her face tightened and relaxed, sweat beaded her forehead, her breath fluttered in and out of her, faster now. Too fast. None of that seemed good.

The thought of her dying bothered him far more than the death of a stranger should have. Hitting him hard in his chest again. Not that he wouldn't feel sympathy for anyone dying on his couch. But the idea of this woman's death hit a nerve.

Strange.

He shook off the weird feeling and contemplated how he'd bandage her wound. He could do that for her at least. Her pants leg had to come off. Would she be pissed if he ripped the material out of the way, since it was already torn? Or would she be more upset if he removed her pants altogether?

He studied her face as he considered his options. She was an attractive woman. Maybe not stunning, but still the kind of woman who'd have made him turn for a second look. Her long dark hair was pulled into a braid that was falling apart. Her face had interesting angles at her cheekbones and chin, though her skin was probably whiter than normal, given her injury. She was tall, with a curvy figure beneath her cargo pants and black sweater. When she'd looked at him in the woods, her eyes were as dark as her hair. Brushing a strand off her cheek, he found himself hoping to see those eyes again in better light, to see if they were really as dark as they'd looked.

Her scent was as interesting as her face. There was the smell of the monster and fight and sweat on her clothes of course. The blood from her injury was there. Some of that bitter scent he'd gotten from the monster's previous kills—that he didn't like at all. There was also a faint wolf scent, but he assumed that was from him carrying her. But under that, where her natural scent signature was, he picked up an earthy, citrusy smell that made him want to breath deeper, try to pull that scent in so he could better analyze it. Maybe even memorize it.

And her lips… Up to that very moment, he would have considered himself a breast man. But her lips absolutely captivated him. Perfectly shaped, full and lush, beautiful and—he ran a thumb across her bottom lip—naturally rose colored.

When he realized he was gently rubbing her bottom lip, he jerked his hand away. The woman was a stranger and unconscious and possibly dying. He had other things he needed to do for her right now that did not involve falling into an obsession with her mouth and acting like a creep while she was unconscious.

Jesus, he'd been on his own for too long.

With a quiet curse, he returned to the problem of whether to remove her pants or not. Acutely aware that he was still naked, and with the memory of the heat in her eyes when she'd seen him in human form, he decided it best not to remove her clothes. Instead, he ripped away her pants' leg from the tear down, and promised himself he'd replace the pants when she recovered.

As he bandaged the cut, he kept sneaking glances at her face, kept trying to catch the illusiveness of her scent better. Definitely more than a mundane human woman. He could sense the difference, even if he hadn't seen her move with a speed far faster than the average human. Her skill with a sword had been undeniable. And, from her scent when he arrived, he knew she'd had no sense of real fear in the fight with the monster, just frustration.

Until he'd entered the fray. Then there'd been a spike of fear.

But she wasn't a shifter. He'd be able to smell that, sense that. He considered that hint of wolf clinging to her again. Now that he focused on it, he realized that wasn't his wolf. It wasn't strong enough for that even if the smells had been the same. This was a lot fainter. Something else. Mingling with her scent signature. A hint of canine, that was a part of her, but also not. His own wolf had a hard time parsing it out. Yet he was certain, in the background of that earthy citrus that was her…the smell of wolf.

A mystery he'd have to solve later. If she survived. And he really hoped she survived.

When he finished wrapping her injury, he left to get dressed. He still had things to do before he could rest.

Most importantly, he had to burn the carcass. The animals he'd encountered that had been killed by the monster had needed to be burned. What was left of the carcasses had festered with the unidentified poison, and he'd worried they'd infect anything that got near them, especially after he'd found a few dead carrion birds near the bodies. He had to assume the monster's body would do the same. Especially those barbed tail spikes.

He was no chemist, but he wondered if he should keep a spike. See if there was a way to test the poison and maybe even create an antidote? If there were more of those monsters around, having something to counter the poison seemed like a good idea. He didn't know anyone who could help with that, though. Maybe if he still had his pack…

Adam cut the thought off with a sharp curse. Jerking his t-shirt down over his head, he forced himself to breathe. The panic rose again, before he could stop it, and it took long moments to get his pulse back under control. Damn it.

He'd made his choice. And he didn't regret it. But being without a pack… He understood viscerally now why lone wolves went feral.

Shaking off the moment, he padded back downstairs. He paused at the couch, looking down at the woman. He had to remember to collect her sword and dagger, too, after he disposed of the monster. They'd looked like good weapons and he didn't want to leave them just sitting around. If she survived, she'd want them back.

If she survived.

That thought had him hesitating to leave. He had to get the monster's carcass destroyed and buried, but he didn't want to leave her alone while she was still in such a precarious state. Not that there was anything more he could do. If she'd been poisoned, it would either kill her or it wouldn't. He didn't know what she was, just that she was more than human, and he hoped whatever that more was helped her heal. But outside of waiting and hoping, the recovery was now entirely in her hands.

And standing around staring down at her, willing her to live, wouldn't accomplish anything. Still, he hesitated a few moments longer. Actually found the effort to leave physically difficult.

He touched the back of his hand to her forehead. She didn't seem to have a fever. She was resting more peacefully than she had been when he'd gone to get dressed. Still unconscious, but not restless or showing signs of distress anymore. She wasn't sweating. Her breathing seemed normal. Maybe her body had already taken care of the poison.

Brushing his fingers across her brow, tucking some stray strands of hair behind her ear, he let out a quite grunt. He couldn't leave the carcass any longer. The last thing he needed was some midnight hiker or a group of kids on a camping trip stumbling across the thing and killing themselves on its still poisonous extremities, or burning themselves with its acid blood.

He grabbed a shovel from beneath his deck and headed back into the woods, ignoring his discomfort at leaving the woman alone. The pull to return to her side immediately almost overwhelmed him. But this wasn't the first time he'd had to ignore his instincts to do what was necessary.

He made quick work of the process, though.

When he was gathering wood for the fire, he discovered a backpack leaning against a fir tree near to where the monster had been. A quick inspection confirmed the pack belonged to the woman. Her New York driver's license revealed a surprisingly unflattering picture given how attractive she was in real life. And her name. Rebecca Logan. If she lived, he'd have to ask what a New Yorker was doing all the way across the country in Washington. In the Northern Cascades. With a sword. Fighting a nightmare monster.

Again the thought *if she lived* had his gut tightening. And the urge to rush back to her side nearly got the better of him. He forced himself to be thorough, though. He hacked off one of the tail spikes with her sword, used his shovel to set it to one side, just in case it might be useful for analyzing the poison. He cleaned her sword and dagger in the ferns under the trees, using the leaves to rub off any remaining monster residue. Then he threw those leaves into the fire with the carcass.

The stench was overwhelming. The monster itself had been bad enough—a sort of sewer left to rot kind of stink. Shit and horror that made him gage. But take all that and burn it… One of the few times he regretted his keen sense of smell.

He waited, upwind to minimize the effects, ensuring the carcass burned completely. When it was down to ash, he buried the remains and all evidence of the fire. Hard, dirty work. But when he was done, no sign of the monster, or the fight, remained except for the single spike he'd kept.

That, he carefully wrapped in the t-shirt he'd left behind in the woods before shifting. Then, because he wasn't sure how much poison was in the thing and if it would leak or not, he wrapped the pair of jeans he'd left in the woods around the spike, too.

By the time he got home, replaced the shovel under his back porch, and settled the woman's backpack, sword, and dagger against a wall in his kitchen, it was nearly four in the morning according to the clock on his microwave. He set the clothing wrapped spike in a cooler he had tucked under the sink to keep it isolated, leaving the cooler next to her backpack and weapons. Washed his hands thoroughly.

Then he hurried to the living room to check on his patient.

She was still alive, but she was thrashing around on the couch and sweat soaked her clothing.

"Damn it." He didn't even have to touch her to feel the heat radiating off her skin.

With another more graphic curse, he lifted her into his arms and carried her upstairs to the guest bedroom. After settling her on the mattress he got a bowl of room temperature water and a washcloth. He didn't dare give her any drugs, even if he'd been able to get them into her, for fear of their reaction with the poison. Obviously, his hope that her ability to heal would neutralize the poison quickly was in vain.

He mopped her face and neck with the cool water, murmuring nonsense under his breath in the hopes of soothing her. As she continued to thrash and her clothing tangled around her body, he worried about her comfort. She wasn't exactly dressed in pajamas or something soft and comfortable. And her clothes were soaked with sweat now, too.

Giving in to his need to make her as comfortable as possible, he quickly stripped her down to her panties and bra then pulled a loose sheet across her overheated body. That seemed to settle her a little, taking some of the struggle from her movements, but heat still pumped from her skin, the fever turning her pale skin a splotchy red.

He continued to stroke cool water over her forehead and neck, occasionally drawing the washcloth along her arms, refilling the bowl when the water got too warm. Her color went from splotchy red to a sickly white, almost translucent. Her breathing turned shallow and harsh.

For the next two hours, he sat vigil, attempting to cool her fever and sooth her distress. But doubts about her survival plagued him.

Should he just try to get her to a hospital? It wasn't a short drive. He might have wasted too much time already. He wouldn't want to be taken to a human hospital in her condition, because he had something to hide—mundane humans didn't know werewolves existed and he had no intention of given them the proof that shifters were real by going to humans for help. He had a feeling the woman—Rebecca according to her i.d.—Rebecca wouldn't be keen on human help either.

Still, he couldn't just sit here and let her die.

The helplessness made him growl. And his wolf raised its head. Fiercely insistent this woman live. He'd have to think about that impulse later. Something there bothered him. But mostly, he just wanted to *do* something to help her and consequences of that be damned.

He started to rise, intent on getting her into his truck so he could get her to a hospital, when movement under her skin froze him in place. He watched in horror as the flesh across her cheek distorted, like something beneath pressed against the barrier of her skin. Her color went from deathly white to nearly gray. And the movement beneath her skin spread over her entire body, unnaturally stretching areas as what looked almost like paws tried to push out.

And then the movement stopped. Her skin settled. After a few moments, the gray faded back to pale white.

"What the hell was that?"

He leaned closer but was almost afraid to touch her now. Could the monster have released a parasite into her body? None of the other animals he'd seen killed by the creature had shown any signs of parasites. None of them had looked to have something under their skin trying to get out.

He shuddered at that idea. And for some reason, he thought of newly made werewolves, the ones made and not born to it, who didn't get proper training, who didn't have a pack to support them. The ones who didn't know how to control their shift and got stuck mid-way through the process.

Another shudder racked his shoulders.

When several minutes passed without the movement returning, he ran his hands along her torso, searching for evidence of something invasive crawling through her insides. Nothing unusual. Nothing obvious.

But he no longer thought taking her to a human hospital would work. Even if she survived the trip—and that didn't seem likely given how pale she was now—whatever the monster had done to her might spread. He couldn't take that chance.

A third hour passed as he kept vigil, waiting for that movement again. It never returned. After half an hour more, her color turned to a more ordinary pale, losing the translucence.

By the end of the fourth hour, he started to wonder if he'd imagined the whole thing. Her fever-induced restlessness had stilled. She was no longer pumping off so much sweat and heat. Sunrise peaked through the closed curtains, casting a strange dim light through the room. Had that been why she'd looked gray? Strange light as the dawn broke?

Possible. He'd been so focused on her fever he hadn't really noticed the light in the room changing. He hadn't turned on any lights—he didn't need them to see clearly in the dark. So maybe the natural light filtering through the blue curtains and his own worry had conspired to get his imagination working overtime.

The memory of paw-like things pressing against her skin, pushing it out like the paws intended on breaking through, rose again. But…she wasn't a werewolf. She wasn't shifting and she wasn't stuck mid-shift.

That was one of his worst nightmares, one of the things he'd had to bear witness to and never ever wanted to experience. He was probably just projecting his personal fear onto Rebecca and his fear for her had him imagining the worst thing he could think of. But she wasn't a wolf shifter. So she wasn't trying to shift.

By the time the gray dawn rolled into mid-morning, filling the small room with muted light, her fever had broken. Her breathing settled into an even rhythm, and the strain around her mouth and forehead eased as she sighed and rolled onto her side.

The signs of recovery, of peaceful sleep rather than unconscious distress, had Adam dropping back onto his haunches, letting his head sag forward. He rolled his shoulders, releasing the tension coiled in his neck and back. Then he stood and pulled the quilt at the foot of the bed over her shoulders.

He watched her sleep for another hour, making sure the fever didn't return. Fatigue pulled at his eyelids. More than once he found his head bouncing as sleep tried to overwhelm him.

Finally, he allowed himself to leave her bedside for his own rest. Questions about Rebecca Logan followed him down to the pillow, but answers would have to wait.

Sleep took him instantly.

CHAPTER FOUR

Becca woke with the sun warm on her face and the sound of quiet movement shuffling around her. She blinked at the sunlight a few moments, trying to reorient herself. She was on a strange bed. In a strange room. Not sure how she got here. Not sure where *here* was. Her body ached, like she'd been fighting a dozen monsters at once for over a month. But she was alive. That had to count for something.

The sunlight spilled into the room through thin white curtains, the thicker blue curtains in front of them pulled back to let the light in. The bed under her was well-cushioned and comfortably cozy. She was warm, tucked under a soft quilt. And the sheets covering her smelled clean and faintly of… Wolf?

The night before came rushing back to her. The irgotoc. The fight. The werewolf who'd helped her. The barbed spike through her leg after she'd killed the fucking monster because she'd been distracted.

The reason she'd been distracted…

A wash of adrenaline-fueled fear and excitement rushed through her blood. Rolling onto her back, she tried to clear her throat and discovered she was parched. She could barely muster enough spit to dampen her mouth.

"Here, drink this."

A hand holding a plastic cup appeared in front of her face. She sat up and took the proffered cup. A quick, subtle sniff, confirmed it was ordinary water, so she gulped the entire contents in one go. When she was done, she sighed and looked at the helpful water-provider.

The man, the werewolf, who'd joined her fight with the monster stood by the bed staring at her with a slight frown, worry lines creasing his brow and bracketing his mouth. He looked just as handsome in full daylight as he had in the dark. That sort of rough handsomeness that wasn't pretty but still arresting. Dark shaggy hair. A mouth that drew way too much of her attention. And without the yellow shifter glow, his eyes were blue. Very deep blue, rimmed by dark lashes.

Her Nam-tar. Standing right there in front of her. Close enough to touch.

She could hardly believe it.

She swept her gaze over him and another, more heartfelt sigh escaped. "Shame," she muttered.

His frown deepened. "What?"

She waved a hand toward him and said, "You're dressed now."

His sudden laughter filled the small room, startling them both, but making her grin crookedly. He had a good laugh. Deep and easy. A sound that left her breathless.

"Not exactly the first thing I expected you to say, Rebecca," the man said as he sat on the edge of the bed and took the empty cup from her hands.

"Found my pack?"

He nodded.

"I don't suppose you…"

"I burned the…whatever it was, and buried what was left, including the remains of the…prey it had been eating—"

"Human?" she asked, wincing at the possibility.

"No. It was a moose."

She let out a slow breath. Okay. That was something at least. Not another human victim. Or potential victim. She hadn't found any human remains yet. She just wished she'd gotten here sooner, before there were any potential human victims to worry about.

"After I was done," the man finished, "I brought your pack, sword, and dagger back here."

"Thanks." She glanced around the comfortable, cozy little room. "Uhm, where is here exactly?"

His slight grin had Becca's heart beating a little faster.

"My home," he said. "Not far from where the creature was killed. Middle of nowhere in particular I'm afraid."

The scent of his hesitance and worry threaded between them, so she rushed to reassure him. "Thanks again for helping. I really appreciate it." Then she felt compelled to say, "You shouldn't have gotten involved in the fight, though. You could have been hurt. That creature's been killing animals all over the area, and—"

"I know. I've seen the remains."

"And it likely killed two humans recently." At least as far as she could tell from the missing persons reports. But really, it could have killed a lot more people whose absence just hadn't been noticed yet. She'd only noticed the stories that brought her to the Cascades a week ago, and had only been tracking the monster for two days. She only wished she could have gotten here sooner. Before the fucking thing got to humans.

And she still had one more irgotoc to find.

"Do you know what that thing was?" the man asked quietly. "I've never seen anything like it. Never *smelled* anything like it."

She could appreciate his disgust with the smell of the monster. That lingering stench still loomed large in her memories. She glanced toward the window. "Unfortunately." Turning back, she caught his curious expression. "It was an irgotoc." She circled her hand. "A monster."

"You've seen them before?"

She shrugged. "Not in a long, long time. We thought they were extinct."

"We?"

"That wasn't the first time I've fought and killed a monster, though," she said, ignoring his question for now. She'd have to tell him everything eventually. He had to know all of it. But that was a longer, and very different, discussion, and she didn't want it all mixed up with the current monster discussion. "I've seen a lot of monsters," she finished.

"Werewolves."

Her sensitive hearing picked up the undertone of tension in his voice, an element she wasn't sure she would have noticed if she had normal human hearing. "Wolf shifters aren't monsters. I'm talking about *real* monsters. The things nightmares are made of."

"Many would put wolf shifters in that category."

"Not if they'd seen what I've seen."

He held her gaze, and she let him read her sincerity.

Her Family fought real monsters—amalgamations of vicious animals put together into single, deadly creatures by the demon god Ne to terrorize humans. The other preternatural creatures sharing the planet had never been the concern of the Seven Families. If they were problems, they were other people's problems. But if they didn't harm humans, she saw no reason to think them as any more monstrous than she was.

After the silence stretched for another few moments, the man nodded as if accepting her explanation. She released a small sigh, only then realizing she'd been tensely waiting for his response. She needed him to believe her, to believe her sincerity. Starting off with him thinking she considered him one of the monsters would have complicated things.

He stretched out his hand. "I'm Adam, by the way. Adam Walsh. And you, Rebecca Logan, are lucky to be alive."

She gripped his hand, and a shudder went through her. She wasn't sure what she'd been expecting. She'd met other people's Nam-tars, seen the way they were together, the way her parents had been together, the way her sister Judith was with her Nam-tar. She'd known, intellectually, that this moment would rock her world and that this man would change everything. She recognized that this moment, this touch, was important.

And still she hadn't been prepared for the full impact.

Her stomach danced at the feel of his callused fingertips pressing against her skin, the strength in his grip, the way his pupils dilated. The smell of him washed over her, a mix of something earthy like cedar and the musk of his wolf. His nostrils flared, as if catching her own scent. His gaze dropped briefly to her mouth before meeting her gaze again. And the urge to lean into him, take his hands and put them against her skin, feel his breath on her cheek almost overwhelmed her.

"Call me Becca," she murmured, swallowing hard.

She held onto his hand longer than was necessary. Her heart thumped hard. He could hear that. Just like she could hear his heartbeat. Could he smell her desire rising? Most Nam-tar, in her experience, were ordinary humans. Not necessarily mundane humans. But humans nonetheless. She hadn't personally met a shifter Nam-tar before. Did that make things different, change anything?

His sense of smell was as good, maybe even better than hers. Could he scent their connection? Did he know there was more here between them?

Did he believe in destiny?

She finally dropped her hold on his hand when she realized what she was doing. They had a lot to talk about. Better not to rush into the questions about destiny and the future. He had to stay of his own free will to break her curse. Getting to that point would take some time.

The thought that he might not stay, that he might not want her, left her chest tight. And not just because it would doom her to a horrible end when she eventually died.

But that was more than she could think about just yet.

Glancing down to keep him from seeing her expression, she suddenly noticed her state of undress. She still had on her bra, but the blankets had pool in her lap, so her upper body was perfectly displayed. A quick glance under the blanket confirmed her pants had been removed too.

She caught sight of the bandage on her leg and had to hide her soft smile. He'd bandaged her wound.

Looking up, she caught his gaze and raised a brow. "I presume I'm mostly undressed thanks to you?"

To her amazed delight, color rose in his cheeks. "You had a fever. I was trying to make you more comfortable."

She nodded, and finally let that soft smile out. "Thank you. That was very considerate of you." She frowned and looked around the room for a clock. "How long was I unconscious anyway?"

"Nearly two days."

"Two days!" She straightened abruptly. She'd assumed this was the next morning after the fight. That she'd faced the irgotoc just last night. But…

Two days? Fucking hell.

"The first night was the worst," he murmured. "I bandaged your wound, but after I got back from destroying the carcass, you'd come down with a fever. You nearly died."

Stunned into momentary silence, she let that information sink in.

As well as the irony.

Just as she'd met the one person who could end her curse, she'd let herself get distracted by him, been wounded by an already dead monster. And had come close to dying. She might have laughed if it wasn't so absurdly terrible.

It would have been an awful, grisly thing to witness, too, her death. Thanks to Ne's curse, all members of the Families were destined to die horribly. She'd witnessed a few of those deaths in her lifetime. The memories sent another shudder through her.

Her only comfort was that she'd been too fevered and ill to notice or really feel anything. But still, coming that close to dying, now, when she'd finally met her Nam-tar, left her breathless.

"So close," she muttered, not realizing she'd spoken aloud until she felt Adam's soft touch on her cheek.

"You're okay now."

She tried to smile but was afraid the expression was strained.

His fingers brushed across her cheek, teasing the corner of her mouth. It took a great deal of willpower not to turn her face into his touch and kiss his palm. He stared at her mouth for a long moment, and Becca held her breath. There were things they needed to talk about. A lot he needed to know. A lot she wanted to know about him. Hell, they didn't *know* each other at all. She didn't want to rush things, get ahead of themselves, before he understood…well, anything.

But he was her future. She hoped. And in that moment, there wasn't much she wanted more in the world than to kiss him.

When Adam dropped his hand from her cheek, and leaned away, Becca had to suppress a disappointed sigh. She couldn't have expected more. She wasn't even ready for their first kiss so soon after recovering from a prolonged illness.

But she was still disappointed.

"I have to check on dinner," he said, standing. "There's a bathroom down the hall, second door on the left. Your backpack is inside along with towels and a robe. Let me know if you need anything else." He rushed from the room, moving just a little faster than a human man would have.

This time Becca did sigh aloud. "Well, that's not very promising." She was sitting half-naked, welcoming his touch, and he ran away.

She tunneled her fingers through her hair and grimaced. She probably looked horrendous. Now that Adam was gone, she realized she didn't smell the best either. Given he was a werewolf with a sense of smell even more sensitive than hers, she was surprised he hadn't made an escape sooner.

With an embarrassed groan, she threw back the covers and took stock of the wound on her leg. She removed the clean dressing and examined the slice. Frowned. Sutures closed the still healing injury.

Still healing. Not healed.

Under normal circumstances, that wound would not only be gone by now, there'd be no evidence it had ever existed. Two days had passed. And one of the benefits the god En had given members of the Families was the ability to heal quickly. They needed it in their fights with monsters. But her wound was still a lumpy red welt which looked like it could split back open if not for the butterfly stitches.

An effect of the poison maybe?

Except there wasn't anything about that in the literature. In fact, as far as she remembered, irgotocs didn't have poison in their tail spikes. Acid blood, yes. Dangerous spikes that could cause severe injury and make removing their heads difficult, yes. Suction cups on their tentacles that burned? Unfortunately. But poison?

That was new. And it didn't bode well. Irgotocs were not only *not* extinct, it looked like they'd evolved some additional weapons. The ability to regenerate limbs. Poison that actually slowed her healing. What did that poison do to their non-Family victims? There were still two missing, and presumably dead, humans out there somewhere. That she knew of. If the humans found those bodies, they'd run autopsies. If those autopsies revealed a mysterious toxin no one had encountered before, that could be bad.

The Seven Families kept the existence of monsters hidden from the world as much as possible. Some knowledge of the monsters had crept out and occasionally showed up in horror stories, but humans were content to consider those things fiction. And the Families ensured that kind of thinking continued. Having humans realize monsters like the irgotoc were real would just cause chaos. Even if the Families could convince humans to stay out of the way while they did what they did and destroyed the monsters.

The existence of the Seven Families was a closely held secret, too. No one outside of the Families knew they existed. Except, of course, the monsters. And the Nam-tars.

She glanced at the closed bedroom door. Her Nam-tar was just right here. That thought still stunned her. Overwhelmed her. And a combination of joy and terror tightened her gut. She'd been so close to dying. So close to salvation only to die before she could claim it.

Pressing her fingers to the healthy skin beside her wound, she frowned again. She needed to find out what the poison was, why it was slowing her healing, and how to counteract it. And she needed Family help to do that. But…

But Adam had destroyed the monster's body. As he should have. He'd even said he burned and buried the remains. How he'd known exactly what to do with the thing, she couldn't say, but she was both impressed and grateful he'd done the job so thoroughly. The only problem was now they had no way of examining those tail spikes and analyzing the poison. Until she found the second irgotoc. *If* she found it. The bastards had hidden so well over the last century, they'd been presumed extinct. But one undisputable fact about irgotocs, they always came in pairs.

Or, well, they used to. But they were evolving. It was always possible there was only just this one monster.

She doubted she'd be so lucky.

Letting out a long breath, she forced herself up and out of bed. Her legs wobbled so she had to grip the wooden headboard to stay upright. Damn it. She hated feeling weak like this. Normally, she'd just let her wolf out. The transition would let her body heal even faster and, hopefully, clear out any lingering trace of the poison so it would stop complicating the healing. But she didn't dare do that yet. Not here. Not with Adam in the house.

Not until he knew what she was.

Especially since he was a werewolf. The idea of him coming upon a strange wolf in his house, with no explanation… She shuddered. She didn't want to imagine his reaction. And in wolf form, with her human body a stone statue in the corner of the room, she'd have no way to explain things to him.

No. No transitions until her wolf shifter Nam-tar understood what she was.

He could probably already smell the underlying wolf in her, probably better than she could smell his wolf. He had to realize she wasn't a shifter. Hopefully, that hint of her wolf would make learning about her real nature easier on him.

She pushed away from the bed when she felt like she had her balance and took stock. Yeah, too weak. And in desperate need of food. She still couldn't believe she'd been out for two days. In a virtual stranger's home. So close to death.

She started toward the bedroom door, only to have her leg give out on her again, sending her careening. She grabbed for the dresser, slamming against it hard, but managed to keep herself upright at least. "Fuck."

The door swung open, startling another curse from her.

"What's wrong?" Adam. Standing in the doorway looking ready to fight something.

She wasn't sure whether to be delighted by his speed coming to her aid or appalled that he was seeing her so weak. Since he'd tended to her while she almost *died*, she supposed he'd seen her in worse shape.

"I'm fine," she said, trying to reassure him and herself. "Just having trouble putting weight on my injured leg."

He hurried to her and wrapped an arm around her waist. "I didn't think. I'm sorry. The wound started to heal fast that first night, but after the fever, everything slowed down."

"Really?" She frowned. "That's strange."

"And not normal, I take it," Adam said.

No. Not normal. Except she didn't know what normal was with this new poison. She'd assumed it had been slowing her ability to heal from the start. A delayed response to the poison was…odd. A product of her natural healing abilities, or a function of the poison? She wanted to curse again because she had no way to find out now.

Her own damned fault too, for getting injured in the first place. For letting the realization her Nam-tar was standing in front of her distract her. Even dead monsters were dangerous. She knew this. Had been taught this from birth. And now she'd gone and gotten herself poisoned by one *after* it was dead, leaving herself weak and nearly dying. And all in front of the one man in the world who could break her curse.

The situation was just so embarrassing.

She'd have to admit all this to her family eventually. Her brother Eric, the head of the Logan Family now, needed to know all of it. Especially that the irgotocs had evolved and weren't actually extinct. But she was not looking forward to telling any of her siblings. She was going to be hearing about this for centuries.

With her leg aching and weak, Becca let Adam help her limp from the guest bedroom to the bathroom in the hallway. His touch was firm and clinical. Supportive and gentle, but nothing more intimate to it.

And all Becca could think about was the heat of his palm on her bare skin and the fact that she wasn't wearing anything but her underwear and bra.

Now that she was aware of her own pungent odor, though, the call of the shower outweighed the thrill of desire curling in her lower stomach.

She glanced at the side of his face and decided she could risk revealing a bit of her nature. "I guess, being a shifter, you're used to strange things."

He chuckled, his expression sardonic.

She grinned crookedly. "Right. Well, I usually heal fast. Faster than a mundane human woman."

"I'd guessed as much."

"No drug or poison I've come across has ever slowed that down before."

"The wound should have healed by now."

She nodded as he leaned her against the bathroom counter very gently. For just an instant, standing face to face, with his hands at her waist as he ensured she had her balance, she forgot what they were talking about. Hell, she very nearly forgot her own name. Her gaze dropped to his mouth, then jumped back to his eyes. Eyes so blue they reminded her of the shallow ocean over sandy white beaches in the Caribbean.

He broke eye contacted and stepped away quickly, turning toward the bathtub.

She swallowed a sigh, reminded herself she was in terrible shape and he knew it, and tried not to feel too disappointed by his reaction.

To distract herself, she took a moment to examine the room. Not huge, but there was a full bath and shower. Decorated mainly in basic grays and blues. The fixtures were silver, the tiles grey marble, the cabinets and shower curtain a rustic blue. The sink and shower themselves were white and clean. A single toothbrush sat in a container on the counter.

For some reason, that filled her with relief. Though she hadn't realized she'd needed reassurance. But there was no reason for her to assumed he was single. There could be a romantic partner lurking around here somewhere that she hadn't met yet. And wouldn't that just complicate everything. There might still be the complication of a romantic partner somewhere, and she had no idea how she'd deal with that. But at least, right now, it was obvious there wasn't another person living here with him.

How did she bring up the question of him being in a romantic relationship, though, without it sounding strange and awkward? Since she was feeling strange and awkward just standing here leaning against the counter, wearing nothing but her underwear and desperately in need of a shower, she wasn't even sure that was possible.

Adam turned on the bath water, keeping his hand under the flow as he adjusted the temperature. "You'll be more comfortable sitting," he said, his back to her. "You need to keep the wound dry for a bit longer."

She nodded, even though he wasn't looking at her, and glanced into the mirror over the sink. Mistake. Big mistake. She looked worse than her driver's license picture.

What was left of her braid was a tangled mess falling over one shoulder, and the hair around her face was standing out in wild disarray. Her skin was a sickly pale, with splotchy pink patches on her cheeks, and her eyes red rimmed. She ran her tongue over her teeth and grimaced, then tried unsuccessfully to tame her hair with both hands. She looked like she'd been through a war.

"Thanks for…everything," she said as he continued to fill the bathtub without glancing at her. After seeing her reflection, she could hardly blame him. "For bandaging the wound and looking after me while I was sick. Not a lot of people would have done that."

"Yes, they would."

"You knew not to take me to the hospital, though."

His broad shoulders shrugged. "Close call at one point," he muttered. "But I figured you…might not what to go."

Because as a wolf shifter, he wouldn't want to be brought to a human hospital either. The fact that he already moved in the preternatural world, already understood about secrets and strange beings and even monsters, made the conversation they'd eventually have to have a lot easier. He might not know what she was, but he'd have a lot easier time accepting than if he'd just been a mundane human.

Most Nam-tar were just humans. Though many of them had some sort of…quirk or skill. Not all of them did. The man who worked as their butler in their upstate New York mansion was the Nam-tar to one of her cousins who'd since passed away. Gregory had been a perfectly ordinary human when he and Abraham met. He wasn't ordinary any more. But he'd had no idea the world of shapeshifters and vampires and monsters existed. He'd needed time to make the adjustment to that world.

Adam Walsh was a werewolf. He knew this world, at least a part of it, and she hoped that made him open to…their future.

So hard to think of a future in that moment. Still a little shocked she'd finally met him—and then almost died—and feeling like she'd been run over by a truck. Everything in her felt jumbled and edgy, a little frantic and panicky. And really, what she needed in that moment, was the bath he was drawing and some quite time to let her head settle.

But a question nagged at her, one she really needed to ask. Especially if the irgotoc wasn't the only monster in the mountains.

Quietly, she said, "I didn't realize there was a wolf pack in this area." It wasn't exactly a question, but she didn't think he missed her curiosity.

A long silence. Then, "There isn't."

"You're here alone?"

And not just alone as in no romantic partner. Alone as in no pack? That wasn't normal. She was no expert on wolf shifters or pack structure, not by a long shot, but she knew enough to know werewolves were rarely solitary. Wolf shifters almost always had a pack.

"The water's ready." He stood, ignoring her question, and turned toward the door. "You think you can get into the tub okay?"

"I'll be fine."

"Just shout if you need a hand." He finally glanced toward her, though it was a fleeting look. And the grin he attempted looked forced. "I've got good hearing so you won't need to yell too loudly."

She tried to return his half-hearted smile, but he rushed from the room, closing the door behind him. Leaving her staring at a white robe hanging on a hook behind the door.

She'd hit a sore spot with that question. But there was a lot she didn't understand about shifters. Especially wolf shifters. Most of the Families tried to avoid shifters, knowing they'd be able to sniff out the animal sides of the Family members. Obviously, Adam didn't want to discuss his status, pack or otherwise. So her questions would have to wait.

So many questions, too. So much they had to discuss. That thought brought on the jangly edginess again, collecting in her gut, making her nervous and uncomfortable.

A bath. She needed to get clean. She needed to wash her hair. That would help everything.

She let out a near-silent groan as she stripped off the last of her clothes. Her body ached from two days in bed and fighting off the poison. And the grime of sweat and stink clinging to her made her a little desperate to climb into the bathtub.

Carefully, she sank into the hot water, her injured leg on the lip so the bandage wouldn't get wet, and let the warmth sooth her muscles. She forced aside her worries. There was time now. Time for conversation and questions and answers. Time to find the other irgotoc —if there was one—and maybe even find out what this poison was that the monster had evolved. Time to introduce Adam to her world in a less abrupt way.

Time to convince him to stay with her.

So long as she didn't fuck up and get killed first.

CHAPTER FIVE

Adam glanced at the ceiling, then quickly back at the pot of potatoes boiling on the stove. He didn't want to think about Rebecca…Becca naked and climbing into a hot bathtub. He was having a hard enough time keeping his mind off her mouth.

She was still recovering from her injury. She needed time, food, space. And, given his history, his current status, he didn't have much to offer a woman anyway. Better just to help her finish recovering and then let her leave. He was alone for a reason, and it was better this way.

But her acceptance of his nature, her lack of fear, was so damned seductive. She didn't consider him a monster. How rare an experience that was in his current life. Even among other shifters.

Her eyes were brown. Deep, dark, beautiful brown. Fringed by even darker lashes that had looked even longer when they'd fluttered open than resting against her too pale cheek while she was sick. After two days of looking after her, hoping she'd be okay, finally seeing those glorious eyes open and shining in the light of day had left him a little breathless.

He stuck a fork into the pot to test the potatoes. But trying to focus on cooking when there was a much more interesting puzzle upstairs wasn't doing much to distract him.

Becca had secrets. Secrets he'd been considering for two days. What was she, exactly? Not a shifter. Not a mundane human. But what? Not a magic wielder that he could tell. Not a Fae. Not demon. Not another otherworldly creature that he could sniff out. She mostly smelled like earthiness, citrus and that faint hint of wolf. But definitely not a shifter.

She healed fast. She fought monsters. She moved as fast as he did. She swung a mean sword. Her healing speed seemed to be as quick as his, when not slowed by poison.

But she wasn't a shifter.

A mystery.

He'd always enjoyed solving puzzles. And she was one he wanted to solve. He wanted to learn all there was to know about her, from her mysterious nature to what she liked for breakfast and whether or not she liked to read. What was her favorite movie? Would she like his collection of old movies or was she not a black-and-white kind of person? Did she like sports? Romcoms? Cooking shows? Did she like to hike in the woods or swim in the sea? Did she get motion sick or did she have a stomach of iron? Did she like wolves…?

The fact that he wanted to know everything, not just *what* she was but *who* she was caught him off guard. This stranger with the tempting mouth and beautiful brown eyes who'd shown up in his territory. He should be helping her get well and then getting her out of here as fast as possible. The longer she stayed, the greater the chances of dragging her into his troubles. And that was the last thing he wanted to do.

Especially since he'd lied to her about there being a wolf pack in the area. He wasn't part of the newly forming pack, of course, so he'd been answering her unspoken question more than the question itself. Maybe not a real lie, or not such a bad one. She deserved to know he was a lone wolf and therefore someone she needed to avoid. But he had lied about there being no werewolves in this part of the mountain range. The pack to the north was pretty new. And far enough away, he hoped they'd never notice him. But he didn't think he'd get that lucky. If the pack decided to take issue with a rogue wolf anywhere near their territory, that was going to be a problem. A problem he didn't want Rebecca Logan involved in.

He felt a little guilty for that jump in his pulse when he'd realized she wasn't fully recovered and would have to stay with him a little longer. Not just a little guilty. A lot guilty. The impulse was selfish. A desperation for company. He'd been on his own for too long, and for someone not used to being isolated from others of his kind, from other people period, the time had been…difficult. He wasn't naturally a loner. He might have hated the complications and politics of pack life, but the company was…

Well, he only realized how dependent he was on that company, how much a part of his life that constant interaction with other people was and how important it was for him, after it was gone. The panic that rose up when the sense of loneliness overwhelmed him didn't help.

He might almost convince himself that was the only reason he felt drawn to Becca. He was just lonely. He just wanted someone to talk to. Needed some company and companionship after so many years.

But he'd be lying to himself.

There was something more here, something more between them. He couldn't put his finger on it. Attraction, yes. The feel of her body against his as he'd helped her to the bathroom was imprinted on his skin. She'd been warm, no longer feverish—which was a relief—and soft, and she'd felt very right in his arms. Like she belonged there. He'd had to concentrate to keep dispassionate and clinical when what he'd wanted to do was lift her into his arms, whisk her into the bathtub, and tend to her personally, help her bath around her wound, making sure she was safe and comfortable, taking care of her.

He wanted desperately to just take care of her.

That impulse had sent him rushing from the bathroom as fast as he could go. Because it hadn't felt like an impulse or a call to assuage his loneliness. It had felt like instinct. Like something he'd always done for her. Something he was *supposed* to do. Like he had a right to take care of her.

But he didn't even know her.

She was in a vulnerable position, wounded and recovering here with a virtual stranger. Whatever the hell was wrong with him and his reactions to her, he had to keep that in check. Whatever instinct was driving him to think of her as *his* to protect and care for was just fucking wrong. He had nothing to offer her. Nothing he could give right now besides temporary shelter. So he was going to rein in his instincts, help her get back on her feet, and let her go.

He had no other choice.

But for the first time since deciding to leave his pack rather than challenge the alpha, he had qualms about the way he was forced to live. Not that he regretted the decision. Even the panic and loneliness couldn't make him regret his choice. He'd cut off his own arm rather than challenge his brother for a position he never wanted anyway. But he'd sacrificed a lot when he walked away from his pack, more than just the safety and familiarity of family and friends. More even than the balance and structure werewolves needed to stay mentally sane.

And it felt like he was being required to sacrifice more now.

He glanced at the ceiling again and groaned. Not his. Giving her up was not an actual sacrifice. Just a random—though mysterious, intriguing, and tempting—woman who was in his life temporarily while she healed. Nothing more.

Taking the potatoes off the stove, he dumped them into a colander in the sink, then quickly put the drained potatoes back into the hot pot and went to the fridge for milk and butter. Hopefully, Becca wasn't too picky about her food. He cooked for himself but mostly simple fare, nothing that would land him on a cooking show. He found himself thinking of the local diner in Eirene, near the pack's territory. That diner had made Eirene a regular tourist stop, and the wolves starting a few businesses in town had enabled his pack to get back on their financial feet after a bad alpha. The diner was run by a tiger shifter who did most of the cooking, and when he wasn't cooking, he hired outstanding chefs. The food had always been excellent.

Adam found himself wanting to be able to do that for Becca. Make her a truly outstanding meal.

He shook off the thought. Meat and potatoes would have to do for today. He hoped she ate meat. That hint of wolf smell on her—the one mystery he did hope to get answers to—made him think she probably did, but he had some things he could put together if the meat wasn't to her liking.

As he mashed the potatoes, her first words came back to him. Her comment about it being a shame he was dressed had taken him completely by surprise. When was the last time a woman had flirted with him? Had made him laugh? When was the last time he'd laughed period? Or felt like more than an outcast?

The slush of water as her bath started to drain made him look at the ceiling again. She might need help getting out of the tub, drying off, getting dressed…

He sucked in a deep breath and returned to smashing potatoes. Mind on the task at hand. Feed her. Get her healthy again. And let her go back to her life. Nothing else.

He heard her come into the kitchen a few minutes later, despite her quiet movements, but he didn't turn immediately. "How was the bath?"

"Perfect. I feel a lot better now."

"Do you need help rebandaging your cut?"

"No thanks. I took care of it. Not the first time I've had to do it."

Where the hell was that curl of disappointment coming from? He was glad she had a fresh bandage. He did not need an excuse to touch her again. Better she'd done it herself. Better he didn't put his hands on her again at all.

After giving the potatoes one last smash, he finally turned to face her. "I hope you like…"

The words dried in his throat. She was wearing the terrycloth robe he'd left on the back of the bathroom door. Her dark hair was still wet and combed smooth. Moisture glistened on her throat and the part of her chest exposed by the v of the robe. Water droplets on her long eyelashes made her dark eyes look huge. As he watched, she licked her lips in what he was sure was a nervous gesture. But anything that drew his attention to her mouth was dangerous.

She fingered the lapel of the robe. "I hope you don't mind I stayed in this. I was feeling too clean to get dressed in the days old clothes I have in my bag."

Clearing his throat, he said, "It's fine." Before he gave in to the urge to move closer, he turned back to the stove. "I hope you don't mind roast. If you don't eat meat, though, I'm sure I can scrape something vegetarian together."

"Thanks, but I'm definitely a carnivore. Roast is fine. It's kind of you to feed me."

Did she think he'd let her starve? "Have a seat." He gestured to the table at one side of the kitchen. "You must be hungry."

Her chuckle danced along his spine, making him acutely aware of her every movement.

"I could almost eat as much as my little sister. And that's saying something since she can eat as much as four large men."

He smiled over his shoulder, curious about her family, her life. Which was only natural and nothing he needed to worry about. "One sister or more?"

"More. Big family. Eight brothers and four sisters."

Letting loose a low whistle, he put the potatoes into a ceramic bowl and brought it to the table. "You don't see families that size very often these days."

"We do have a large grocery bill."

She fidgeted in her seat, the movement opening the robe over her legs, giving him a tantalizing glimpse of lush, pale skin. He moved back to the oven, keeping his back to her.

After a moment of silence, she drew in a breath. "We need to talk. About the monster."

He nodded as he set out the rest of the food. "An irgotoc right?"

"Right. You've seen its kills. Do you know anything else about it?"

He shook his head.

"Okay." After a pause, she said, "Maybe I should start from the beginning. I fight monsters."

That simple statement made him smile again. "So I saw."

She grinned. "What I mean is my…duty in life is to destroy

monsters. My entire family is dedicated to that goal. To protect humans from the things that are only supposed to exist in nightmares."

The honesty and straightforward discussion surprised him. He'd have assumed he'd need to drag this kind of information from her, slowly, over time. In his world, secrets were vital to the pack survival. Keeping the existence of wolf shifters from the general mundane human awareness ensured the pack's safety. He wouldn't have talked about his nature with someone he didn't know well.

Except she already knew he was a werewolf. Already knew his nature. And didn't consider him one of the monsters.

The fact that she was offering such personal information about herself to him so easily, trusting him with it, was…electrifying.

He ignored the response. "Worthy goal. Why haven't I heard of your family?" He sat across from her and started to dish out food.

"We work really hard to keep what we do and who we are private."

"You're not the only ones. But I still know of the existence of other preternatural creatures and otherworldly beings. And you obviously know about those other creatures since you knew what I was."

"We hide from everyone. Trust me, it's better that way."

"Everyone?"

She sighed. "Our…existence has gotten out, of course. There are people who do know we exist. There are even a couple of books, I understand, though we've tried to confiscate most of them. I think The Bookstore might have a few still. Anyway, we've worked to keep knowledge of our existence as limited as possible, even with the few failures, for…millennia."

"Millennia?" He frowned. Shifters tended to live long lives. If they weren't killed by each other. Some species in the hundreds of years. Others, just longer versions of human lives, but averaging over a century. Millennia was… Well, he wasn't sure even vampires managed to survive that long. They could, in theory, of course. But they always got killed—re-killed?—before they had to really worry about eternity.

There were truly immortal beings, like the Fae, but she wasn't claiming to be Fae. She was…something else.

"Have you lived for millennia?" he asked.

Her sudden grin hit him dead center in his chest, leaving him breathless. The expression was light and amused, and lit up her gorgeous brown eyes, and it would have taken a monster invasion to get him to look away.

"No," she said, chuckling. "The Families have existed for millennia. I haven't." She ducked her head a little and gave him a look. "Wolf shifters live a long time."

Statement. Not question. "We do if we can manage to survive."

"Same," she said. "If we can survive, we live…a while."

"Is it rude to ask how old you are?" He tried to lighten the question with a smile, but he was out of practice and wasn't sure it came off as easy as he'd have liked. Smiling, hell conversation, hadn't been common in his life for the last few years. He was rusty. And grateful they weren't attempting small talk right now. He couldn't remember how to do small talk with a pretty woman anymore.

"Hundred and ninety years old."

He nodded. Wolf shifters, if they weren't killed, could live for two hundred or more years. But she was at the upper end of that timeline. And looked, from a human perspective, in her early to mid-thirties. "How long can you live?"

"My oldest brother is more than three hundred years old. My parents…" She folded her lips in briefly, blinking hard, before saying, "My mother is obviously older than that. She's less inclined to admit her age, though, so I won't give her away."

She said that last with a slight smile but it was strained. And the way she'd started with her parents then corrected to say her mother had his instincts rising. Something there. But for a later conversation. If they had another conversation after this.

And the fact that they were even having this conversation, when she didn't owe him any of this information, felt like a small miracle.

"I'm closing in on sixty," he offered.

"No mid-life crisis setting in?" Again she tried to joke.

But he could tell, from her scent as well as her body language, she was nervous. The musky punch of her nerves threading through her scent made him want to reassure her. "Not yet. But there's still time."

He blinked. "Or, well, maybe I am in a mid-life crisis." Being without his pack might well count as one.

At her raised brows, he waved the comment away. "Nothing. Sorry. You were saying about your family?" Except she hadn't been talking about just her family. She'd been saying families. "Why do you refer to families instead of family?"

"There are seven Families. All tasked with hunting monsters."

"Why seven?"

"That's how many the god En created to protect humans from the monsters his brother, the demon god Ne, created more than sixteen thousand years ago."

"Sure."

She smiled, genuinely this time, at his deadpan response. Which made something clench in his chest. He liked making her smile.

"It's a lot. I know. For the record, Ne isn't a real technical demon god from a demon realm. He's a god from this realm. He just got the designation 'demon god' because of raising the Slain Heroes to create monsters."

"I have no idea what you're talking about, you know? None of this is anything I've heard of before. Never even come across gods named En and Ne."

"Their names were changed through the years. They got folded into and sometimes combined with other gods. Occasionally, multiple gods represented them. But in our Families' history, these are the earliest names for them. These are what they were called when we were created."

"To fight monsters?"

She nodded. "To protect humans."

But strangely, her gaze darted away from his then, and she turned her attention to her food. She'd eaten a few bites, some of the potatoes. But now she dug into the roast with her full focus, as if she hadn't just ducked away so she could hide whatever emotion had crossed her expression.

Her scent didn't help enlighten him. The nerves were still there. A spike just then, when she'd dropped her gaze. But there was more mixing with her earthy citrus scent. Again, he thought of that underlying wolf smell, so very faint under her natural scent signature. Despite the straightforward conversation, the way she answered his questions with seeming ease, she was still hiding something.

And he wasn't sure it was his place to dig into those secrets any deeper. Despite the fact that he wanted to. Desperately wanted those answers. He wanted to know everything there was to know about her. All of it. But…

She wasn't his to know. She'd be leaving soon. And none of this was his business. Whatever hints and clues and information she offered he'd take. Eagerly and gratefully. But digging for more. Demanding answers… No. Not his place.

She ate a few more bites of roast and groaned. "This is really good. Not just because I'm starving either. It's really really tasty."

Her compliment gave him a deep sense of pleasure completely out of proportion to the act of feeding her. "Glad you like it."

He watched her gobble up half the food on her plate then, and couldn't have been more pleased if she'd sat on his lap and kissed him. Or, well, that would please him more, but watching her appreciate the food he'd fed her was close.

The fact that he let the image of kissing her build too long and in too much detail sent him quickly back to his own meal. If her sense of smell was heightened, a detail he couldn't be certain of but it wasn't unreasonable to assume, she'd smell his desire. He didn't want to make her uncomfortable, so he forced his mind back to the conversation and his own plate.

"So." He cleared his throat. "Monsters. Seven families to kill them. Irgotoc running around the forest."

"Yes," she said, sounding and smelling a little nervous again.

Damn. He had to keep his attraction to himself better. She didn't need that from him.

"So. Anyway. Because it's our job to hunt monsters, we also have to study them. For a long time, we've thought the irgotocs were extinct. Which would have been nice." She sighed. "But obviously they're not. And…and I'm afraid they've been evolving. That one I killed had some new abilities irgotocs haven't had in the past."

"Like?"

"Like the fact that it regenerated limbs after they were cut off. Well, some of them. Others didn't regenerate. But none of them should have. That's a new trait."

"What else is new?" He met her gaze again, a thread of worry seeping into his blood.

She gestured at her leg, and he resisted the pull to follow that gesture with his gaze with a great deal of willpower. "The poison, from its tail spike… It's never had poison there before. Acid blood is the same. But never poison. And the fact that any monster has a poison that can slow my ability to heal is…"

"New?"

"And very bad," she said, her voice quiet.

He agreed. Watching her so sick, maybe even close to dying… That had been very bad.

"Knowing this, it's hard to say for sure if my knowledge of the irgotocs is still useful. It's possible there've been more changes. But if they haven't changed completely, if they've retained more than a few of their original characteristics, then… Then there's a second one out there somewhere."

His fork clattered against his plate.

A second one?

Fucking hell.

CHAPTER SIX

Becca held Adam's gaze for a long moment as she let the news sink in. She tried to focus on the potential crisis. On the fact that there was possibly still another monster out there somewhere and she was weak but she still had to go hunt it. This part of the Northern Cascades was pretty isolated, with very few humans wandering around. But that didn't matter to an irgotoc. If there were humans anywhere nearby, they'd find them and kill them. They were *made* to kill humans. She couldn't afford to let too much time pass and risk a second one out there, a second one that might find more human victims.

That was the important part of this conversation. At this moment anyway. Not the more personal side of things. That would have to wait.

But she had a very hard time *not* getting caught up in the way his scent filled her head the minute she'd stepped into the kitchen. Or the way his eyes had darkened, the blue deepening when he'd seen her. Or the way his scent had spiked with something like desire earlier.

Oh how she wanted to believe those hints that maybe, possibly, he felt some attraction to her. Just because he was her destiny, didn't mean he had to accept that role. He could walk away. He had to choose to stay with her of his own free will or her curse wouldn't be broken. But if he wanted her, if there was attraction between them to work with… Maybe the rest wouldn't be so difficult.

The fact that he'd fed her a gloriously simple, hearty meal—exactly what she needed—hadn't helped her concentration. Having him cook for her left her feeling all soft and sentimental. Also made her want to climb on his lap and thank him with a kiss. Which she was not going to do. Yet. Not yet. Not before she told him…more.

But it was tempting. Very very tempting.

First, though, she needed to go hunting. And she was in piss poor shape for the hunt.

"I haven't found any direct evidence of a second irgotoc," she said. "When I was hunting the first. But that doesn't necessarily mean much. If they are still moving in pairs, the male was the one I killed. The female will be somewhere in hiding."

He leaned on the table, his gaze intent. "Somewhere nearby?"

"They're territorial. So, if the male was in this area, the female is. But—" she raised a hand when he opened his mouth, "—I can't tell if they…or I guess I should say the one killed had already established a territory or not. It was moving over a large area, traveling, when evidence of its kills started turning up. The reports that brought me to the Cascades. What it might have been doing was looking to establish a territory." She winced. "Looking for a place with a lot of food."

"Heading into more populated areas?"

"Could. Eventually. Depends on what it finds to eat along the way." It had already been seen near human homes. So the risk of it settling in to eat near a town was real.

"The…female? How far would that one hide from the male? Could it be near the site of the first kills? Or would it follow the male?"

"If they haven't established a territory, it would follow. And also be killing along the way."

Adam dropped back against his seat and ran a hand through his hair. "Well this is…"

"Bad. Yes. It is. *If* they still travel in pairs. With the changes to the irgotoc I killed, I just can't know for sure." She leaned on the table now herself, but mostly for support. "Which means I have to go hunting again."

"You're in no shape yet. You nearly fell over getting out of bed."

"The meal helped."

He dropped his chin and gave her a look. "How much?"

She wanted to exaggerate her recovery, but didn't think lying to him would be a great way to start things off between them. At least about this. Plus, lying about her abilities right now could get her killed. She'd already come too damned close to that.

"I'm feeling better and stronger, but… No, I'm not back to full speed. Whatever the poison did to me, it fucked me up. And I'm still a little weak."

"Which means you can't hunt that thing yet. Definitely can't fight it."

"Well, that's the problem. I have to."

"You were nearly killed fighting the first one. When you were at full strength."

"Only because I was interrupted," she said, giving him a look this time.

He returned the look with raised brows. "You needed the distraction to get in under the monster's neck."

"Fine." She wanted to roll her eyes but resisted. "You helped. A little. But you also distracted me."

"I'll go with you to hunt the other one." He said this so abruptly they both straightened and blinked.

"No. That's not what I was… No. This is my job. This is what I do. My divine duty. You don't need to get involved with the hunts." She wanted him involved in her world, though, so she was careful of her wording. "I just wanted to let you know, so you could be careful. So you wouldn't assume you were safe yet."

"How long will it take you to fully heal?"

She shrugged. "No idea at the moment. With the poison. I…" There was a way she could speed things up. But she still wasn't ready to show him that yet. "I'd be guessing."

But maybe if she could get somewhere isolated, she could let her own wolf out safely. The transition always helped them heal. And she'd be able to hunt just as well, maybe better, inside the wolf.

"Look," she went on, "I'm not asking you to endanger yourself. I'll take care of the other monster. If there is one. I just need information, if you have any. Where you've seen the kills. What you've seen. You live in this area. Maybe you've noticed something strange? Anything you can give me that might point me in the right direction."

"This area isn't just where I live. It's my territory. Small as it is."

He muttered that last sentence so low she wasn't sure she was supposed to hear it.

"And I don't share my territory with monsters," he finished.

She tightened her jaw as he held her gaze. She didn't want him hunting with her. She wanted him safe and away from the monsters. But she also wanted to spend more time with him. Needed to spend as much time with him as she could. The threat of a second monster was real. But it also gave her an excuse to stay in the area. To stay near him.

The memory of that brief flare of potential attraction when she'd entered the kitchen warmed her. Since then, though, he'd been very careful. His scent wasn't giving her much. He'd barely glanced at her legs when she'd let the robe fall open a little when she sat down. If there was attraction there, either he didn't want to acknowledge it, or he was just being honorable.

She really hoped it was the second.

Letting him help her rubbed her the wrong way. But she was weak at the moment. She'd be able to hunt. But a fight would be difficult. She could barely put weight on her leg. He was a wolf shifter. He had strength and speed and his senses were as good if not better than hers. Having a second set of heightened senses during the hunt would be useful…

She dragged in a deep breath and let it out slowly. "Fine. I'll accept your help with the hunt. But once we find it, *if* we find it, please don't put yourself in danger." She wasn't sure what she'd do if he got hurt. Or killed. The idea was so horrible she nearly lost her appetite.

He grunted a reply that wasn't really an affirmation and turned his attention back to his plate.

Becca did the same, but her nerves jumped as she forced more food in. The meal was delicious and she needed the sustenance. She had to heal as fast as she could. If a fight was coming, she couldn't afford to be weak.

Not when her Nam-tar might be in danger.

She shifted gears to talk about mundane things for the rest of the meal. She wanted to get to know him better. Actually, she wanted to know everything about him. But that would take time so she'd take what she could get to start. Unfortunately, he didn't reveal much.

He didn't discuss why he was here alone, with no pack. He didn't talk about how long he'd been in this house, though he alluded to it being a couple of years but not very long. He made a living doing freelance bookkeeping and financials for small businesses, but when she'd asked more questions about his work, he'd answered with brief, conversation-stifling, one-word responses.

So she tried something else and asked about his family. That conversation got shut down so fast, with such a solid wall of silence, it made her head spin.

Okay. Not close to his family. Fair enough. Probably why he was out here on his own. Not everyone had close family like she did. Or even liked their blood relatives. She let the subject drop.

Instead, since it seemed to be a subject they were both keen on, she talked about food. That turned into a wide-ranging, and surprisingly interesting conversation that got them through the rest of his delicious meal without tense silences. She did discover the rather horrible truth that he thought pineapple on pizza was a good idea. But he was her Nam-tar, so she'd learned to accept this about him.

She helped him with the dishes afterward, though he protested and tried to make her go back to bed.

"I've been in bed for two days," she said. "I need to be up moving around. And dishes are easy." She smiled. "Plus, you cooked. I should clean."

"Not when you're a guest in my house."

She snorted. "Not exactly an invited guest."

"I brought you here voluntarily. That counts as an invitation."

She glanced at him, but he had his attention firmly on the pot she'd just handed him to dry. Could he tell his gruff reply had made her happy? She wasn't used to dealing with shifters, but her entire Family had heightened senses of smell. They could mostly scent each other's moods. Mostly. But, from what she understood, shifters were even better at that skill.

Which meant she'd have very few emotional secrets from him.

Given how much of her life she kept secret from others, that was a little disconcerting.

They finished the dishes then went to the living room to look at a map of the area—despite him trying to insist, again, that she go back to bed and rest.

"You'll be better able to hunt if you aren't exhausted," he said. "You've been out for two days. And you've admitted you're not healing as fast as you should. You shouldn't push yourself."

"Spoken from experience?" she asked, mainly as a distraction. But also she was curious.

"I've dealt with enough stubborn shifters over the years, yes, I'm speaking from experience."

"But I'm not a shifter," she pointed out as she sat on his couch.

The living room was a nice, cozy room. The couch large and comfortable, set across from a stone fireplace and taking up most of the narrow space in the room. There were side tables but no coffee table, landscape photos hung in simple black frames on the walls, and thick rugs covering the hardwood floor. Clean but not fancy. No specific decorative look either. Just a mix of muted blues and greens and browns. No knickknacks cluttering the mantel over the fireplace.

And no photos of any people.

The room was warm and smelled so much like him it was like wrapping herself up in a blanket, but the room also felt a little impersonal. Like the sort of cabin you might rent for a vacation. Not the sort of place someone had been living in for any length of time and called home.

Which was so interesting, she very nearly let herself get distracted. But she had to deal with the other irgotoc, had to at least find out if it was out there somewhere. Monsters first. Curiosity about her Nam-tar later.

He sat on the opposite side of the couch from her, leaving a great deal of space between them.

She sighed. Time, Becca. This would all take time.

He'd pulled a paper map of the area out of a drawer in one of the side tables and spread it over the expanse of couch between them.

"Paper?"

"Internet is bad up here," he said, his attention on the map. "Paper is more reliable."

She smiled. "Old school. I like it."

The Logans took full advantage of technological developments. Her brother Richard, who handled a lot of security for the Family, often used those advances, and her Sarah had taken to technology immediately, creating and inventing all manner of things both for the hunts and for fun.

But Becca found technology had its pitfalls and tried not to get too reliant on it. The Seven Families had been hunting monsters for millennia without GPS and internet search engines. She liked staying in practice using little to no tech on a hunt.

"I think this will be the best area for us to start," Adam said, pointing to a section of the map she was pretty sure was east of their location.

Although, she realized with a start, she didn't have any idea how far they were from the site of the irgotoc fight, which direction, even where they were on the map. "Where's your cabin?" she asked, frowning down at the topographical details.

He pointed to another spot. In the middle of an area of forest with no towns or cities nearby. Everything a drive away. Seattle would take a couple of hours to reach, but there were some smaller places between the cabin and there for him to get supplies and things.

But he was about as isolated as it was possible to be and still have things like internet. The nearest little town on the map was miles to the west.

He tapped the area east of his cabin again. "There's quite a lot of wildlife here, but very few humans. This is where I was coming across the dead deer, a few moose, and a couple of coyotes. One black bear. That's the reason I was looking for the monster, too. Although I didn't know it was a monster at the time."

"You'd been hunting it as well?" The terror that shot through her system almost left her faint. That surge of adrenaline so unexpected, she had to fist her hands to keep from showing him her response. If he'd found the monster first, before she'd reached it… He wouldn't have had any idea what he was fighting. How to kill it. What to be careful of.

He could have been killed. Before she reached him. He could have been killed.

"Hey…" Adam leaned over the map and set a hand to her cheek. "You okay? You just went really pale. You should get back to bed."

She shook her head, a move that rubbed her cheek against his palm, and she really wanted to lean into the touch. His hand was warm and large and a little rough. His fingertips callused. The thought struck her again that he could have died before she reached him, that she might never have known what his touch felt like. And the panic surged all over again.

"I'm okay," she tried to reassure him, even though she had no doubt he felt the fine tremor that went through her, probably smelled the sharp musk of her fear, too. "Honestly, I'm… I'm glad you didn't find the monster before me."

He rubbed his thumb over her cheek, but absently, like he wasn't paying attention to what his hand was doing while he frowned at her. "I'm capable of killing that…thing."

"But you wouldn't have known how. Did you have a knife or anything like it on you? You have to take a monster's head off. It's the only thing that kills them. And you saw, it was dangerous even after it was dead. You wouldn't have known any of that. Hell, I didn't know about the poison in the tail spikes. You didn't know it had acid blood…" She shivered and closed her eyes briefly. When she opened them, he'd tossed the map on the floor and was sitting right next to her, both hands on her face.

"I'm fine. You're fine. It's okay. Hey." He tilted her face up so she'd meet his gaze, and she found herself falling into those blue blue eyes. "It worked out. The monster is dead. No need to panic after the fact."

She swallowed, knowing he was right, but also very aware of what could have happened. How close she'd come to losing him before ever finding him. She tried to shake off her reaction, tried to let it go. He was right. They were both alive and well and sitting, very close now, in his cabin. Safe. Alive. And none of the horrible things running through her mind had come to pass.

She pressed her hands against his where they rested on her jaw. Then she took in several deep, long breaths. "Sorry about that," she murmured. "I… I've seen what monsters can do to people, and it's upsetting to think you could have walked into a situation you didn't understand and gotten yourself killed. I know… Shifters are strong fighters. But you didn't know what you were fighting."

"I do now," he said. So matter-of-fact she blinked. "I'm not going in blind. And I wouldn't have if I'd found the monster before I found you."

There was a little tensing around his eyes, something that moved through his expression. But so fast, she wasn't sure what she'd just seen.

"But I didn't find the monster first, and it's all okay now. It's dead and we're not." He held her gaze, his thumbs still stroking her cheeks in soothing circles. "We're fine."

She nodded again, her heartbeat calming as the panic subsided. She let his scent move into her, fill her with that reassurance even as his voice and touch calmed her pulse. The terror had risen so fast, so sharply. She'd never had anything like that happen to her before. She'd been fighting monsters for her entire life. She accepted all the risks. To herself. To her Family. She'd never had such a punch of panic and fear as she'd had at the mere thought of him getting killed.

He was so close now, his breath warm against her lips. When his gaze dropped briefly to her mouth, the dance of nerves in her stomach changed, altered into something that wasn't fear at all. But was just as desperate. She tightened her grip on his wrists, but what she wanted to do was lean forward and press her lips against his. The impulse overwhelmed her sense. She did soften forward just a little. Watched his eyes darken again.

Then as suddenly as he'd ended up in front of her, he jerked back. Off the couch. Standing several feet away in a blink.

"I'll get you some water."

He turned and hurried to the kitchen before she could say anything. Before she could even open her mouth.

Which was probably good. Because if he'd still been standing there, she wasn't sure she could have hidden her disappointment and hurt.

They'd only just met and were essentially strangers still, she reassured herself. She'd barely woken up from a two-day sleep. He was probably just taking all that into consideration. Being thoughtful. Not wanting to push her.

They had time. No reason to feel utterly rejected.

So long as they stayed alive, they had time.

CHAPTER SEVEN

When Adam returned from the kitchen, he handed her a glass of water, which Becca dutifully drank even though she wasn't particularly thirsty. Then he sat down on the opposite side of the couch again, replacing the map between them.

She tried very hard not to be disappointed. He was right to refocus them on the hunt. There might well be another monster out there and she couldn't afford to forget that. Lives were on the line, not just his and hers. She had a duty. And that came before everything else.

So she concentrated on the map and they worked out all the places they'd both spotted evidence of the irgotoc. Once she was oriented on the map to her current location, it was easier to get a visual of the area, where she'd been. Where the second monster could potentially hide.

There was a large red spot on the map north of Adam's cabin, a dot she didn't pay much attention to at first, thinking it marked one of the nearby towns. But as they finished setting out a search grid they'd use to hunt, she realized that red dot was settled over a section of the forest, not centered on a town.

"What's that?" she asked, giving the spot a little poke.

"Nothing." He pulled the map away and folded it back up, fast.

"We have our search area now. Do you want to start in the morning? Or do you need more time to recover?"

He didn't meet her gaze as he spoke, keeping his attention on the map he carefully refolded, hiding the red mark.

She narrowed her eyes. "We should start tomorrow. If there's a second monster, we don't have time to wait on my healing." In fact, too much time had already passed. She'd lost two days. They were starting this hunt from scratch. "Have you heard or come across any new carcasses?" she asked. "In the last two days?"

"I've been here the whole time," he said, his gaze still averted as he slipped the map back into the side table. "I haven't been out to look. But there hasn't been anything on the news."

Not that there would be necessarily. The area was isolated and dead deer and coyotes and even the occasional moose or bear wouldn't draw much attention up here. More missing humans would. But if he hadn't heard anything about that yet, hopefully that meant any possible monster still roaming the hills hadn't wandered into any populated places while she'd been unconscious.

That was a good bit of luck at least, and she'd take it.

Still without quite looking at her, he said, "I didn't find anything more than your backpack in the woods. Are you staying somewhere close by or were you camping…?"

"Camping," she said, which was sort of true.

What she'd done when she'd needed to stop and rest was transition so her wolf could comfortably sleep in the cold woods and her human body could rest and recover in its stasis form. In the middle of nowhere, someone coming across a stone statue in the middle of the woods was unlikely. And the wolf's form was easier to sleep in when she didn't have time to stop and build tents and fires and things to make her human form comfortable.

"I've been moving, couldn't really stop, so hotels would have been inconvenient."

He nodded.

Something about the conversation made Becca's stomach tight. Was he hinting that he wanted her out of his guest bedroom? He hadn't actually commented at all on her staying here or going. Just that he'd help her hunt for a potential second monster. That didn't necessarily translate into an invitation to continue living with him in this house.

She tried not to let that thought disappoint her. She was a stranger to him still. And he'd really done so much for her already. Was going to do more for her than she really even wanted him to. She should make the offer to go. Give him an option so he didn't feel obligated to keep hosting her.

But now that she'd found him, she didn't want to be away from him.

"You're welcome to stay here as long as you need to," he said, his gaze on the cold fireplace. "Until you recover." His mouth quirked at one side and he glanced at her from the corner of his eye. "No one else is clamoring to use the guest room." Then so quietly she was pretty sure she wasn't supposed to hear him, "Not even sure why I have one."

That was a loaded comment. Something she wanted to explore more in her quest to know everything about him. But she pretended she hadn't heard and instead said, "Thank you. I don't want to be an inconvenience." Her turn to smile. "I was going to say I don't want to be any trouble, but I think we're well past that stage."

"No trouble," he said softly.

Her stomach danced.

Silence fell and she wanted to fill it with conversation. His mood had shifted when she'd pointed to that red dot on the map. He'd… pulled away. That's what it felt like, though she wasn't sure that was the right description. But it felt like he was distancing himself from her in a way he hadn't been doing while they plotted out their search grid. She wanted that feeling of comradery back.

"Hopefully, we'll know in a few days if there's a second monster or not." Something to say, but not exactly what she wanted to talk about. She just didn't want the silence between them to drag on too long. "Shouldn't take long. I don't want to disrupt your life too much." A little desperately, she added, "I'll pay for the food and care."

"I don't charge guests." The growl in his voice surprised her. "Especially guests who are injured and in need of my help."

"Even uninvited ones?"

He scowled at the fireplace. "Already told you, you're officially invited."

Well, offending him hadn't been the plan. "I'm sorry. I didn't mean to imply… I just don't want to…"

"You're not causing me any trouble, and I can well afford to feed and house you for a few days."

"Sorry," she muttered again, feeling awkward and ridiculous. She had lived in this world for nearly two centuries. Yet she couldn't manage to talk reasonably to the one man who was really important to her without putting her foot in her mouth.

Because he was really important to her, of course. Something he didn't know yet. And which made all of this so very different.

She felt the heat in her cheeks but faced him anyway. "I am not trying to offend you. I'm just feeling…uncomfortable forcing myself into your life like this." Even though *in his life* was exactly where she needed and wanted to be. "And I don't want you to think I'm making assumptions—about your help or…or anything. I do appreciate everything you've done for me. I'm grateful for your help with looking for the second monster—"

"Even though you didn't want to accept that help."

"Even though. This isn't your duty. I don't want you hurt on my account. But that doesn't mean I don't appreciate the help."

He grunted, lifting his chin in a brief nod. But his shoulders relaxed. "You're welcome to stay here as long as you need to. I *want* to help. And I don't want your money. That cover everything?"

She nodded. What she really wanted to do, though, was to wrap her arms around him, nuzzle his neck to get his scent, find out what it would feel like to kiss him, what it would be like to have his hands on her again when she wasn't weak and unable to stand on her own.

She stayed on her side of the couch. Despite every instinct pushing her to close the distance, to ask permission to touch him. Kiss him. But they weren't there yet. This was too important to rush.

Even if she really wanted to.

Becca yawned abruptly and slapped a hand over her mouth. "Oh.

Guess I'm tired now." She chuckled. "You'd think after two days of sleeping I wouldn't want to sleep again for a week." In truth, she didn't want to go to sleep yet. She wanted to stay on this couch, in his living room, in front of a cold fireplace, with him for as long as she possibly could.

But she wouldn't be doing herself or him any favors in the coming hunt if she was too exhausted. The poison had taken its toll. And since she couldn't transition here, yet, she needed rest.

"You've probably pushed too long anyway," he said. "I'll walk you upstairs, make sure you have everything you need."

She followed him up the narrow stairs, trying not to ogle him too much, but it was hard not to take advantage of the opportunity to admire his wide shoulders and back, the way his muscles rippled beneath his t-shirt. The way he moved with a kind of easy predatory grace that made her heart thump and her stomach dance.

At the bedroom, he nodded to her backpack in a corner where she'd dropped it after she'd finished her bath. "If you need anything, a toothbrush or…anything, let me know."

"Thanks." She had one in her pack, which she'd taken advantage of after her bath, but it was kind of him to offer.

She stifled another yawn, her eyes heavy with exhaustion she should not be feeling. When she woke up again, if this exhaustion was still dragging at her, she intended on finding some solitude in the woods so she and her wolf could get out a bit and leave the human body to heal.

"Thanks for everything," she said, facing Adam fully. "From the bandaging, to the meal, to the bed, to the help. You've gone above and beyond." She smiled, but now that she was so close to a bed again, she wobbled a little.

"Woah." He stepped close enough to grab her around the waist. "You sure you're okay?"

"Just got hit with a wave of exhaustion. Still healing I guess." She shrugged, but the feel of his arm around her was distracting. The position, almost but not quite pressed against him, felt very natural. Like she was supposed to be right here.

"In to bed," he said. "You pushed too hard. If you need anything, my bedroom is just down the hall."

Mmm. That sounded tempting. If she weren't about to fall asleep standing, only still on her feet because he was holding her up. But maybe after a little sleep…

She blinked and swayed toward him, from tiredness but also just wanting to be closer to him. He was warm. And he smelled good. And the arm holding her upright was strong and firm at her back. And she really wanted to know what his lips would feel like against hers. He brushed his thumb over her cheekbone with his free hand and studied her face.

With a suddenness that surprised a gasp from her, he picked her up into his arms, cradling her against his chest as he carried her to the bed. Which wasn't something she intended on arguing over. She wasn't about to give up such a perfect excuse to lean into him and wrap her arms around his neck.

She did feel like she should put up a token protest. "You don't have to carry me with the bed only a few feet away."

He set her gently on the mattress. "Easier to pick you up while you're still standing than to scoop you up off the floor."

She chuckled. "Fair enough. The exhaustion is pretty weird."

"Not normal?"

"No more normal than my slow healing. Fucking monster poison. Can't believe I got hit with monster poison *after* it was dead."

"Not many poisonous monsters? Or you're just not used to be poisoned by a dead one?"

"The poison part depends on the monsters. Some of them are, though not all." She rolled her eyes. "I'm just usually more careful, even after the monsters are dead." She scooted down on the mattress so she could roll onto her side and settled her cheek against the pillow. He pulled a sheet up over her. So thoughtful. "Suppose that's what happens when I finally meet my—" Wow, she was exhausted. She'd nearly called him her Nam-tar out loud. And since that word required explanation she wasn't ready to give yet, she changed the end of her sentence to, "—when I finally meet a werewolf."

"I'm you're first, huh?"

The slight innuendo in his tone had her toes curling under the blanket. Oh, if only she wasn't so tired. "Usually avoid them. All shifters." She tapped her nose. "Your sense of smell is too good."

"When you're no longer half asleep, I'm going to remind you you said that and then ask what it means."

"Fair." She reached out and gripped his hand, tugging so he sat on the bed next to her. "We still have lots to talk about. But after I sleep."

"After you sleep," he murmured, his voice a deep rumble.

His thumb brushed over the side of her hand, sending a warm curl of pleasure through her. She loved his touch.

"Goodnight," she said and closed her eyes. "Stay until I fall asleep?"

"I'll stay."

Oh she really hoped he meant that.

CHAPTER EIGHT

Becca woke to a quiet room and a lot of sunshine streaming in through the curtains. Staring at the light pouring across the hardwood floor, she took a moment to assess how she felt. Better. The ache in her leg around the wound had lessened. She only realized the wound had been aching now that it wasn't so bad anymore. The exhaustion that had swept through her last night had abated. She felt well rested and awake. Not groggy. That had to be a good sign.

Pulling in a deep breath, she filled her lungs with the scent of Adam's home. Still hard to believe she was in the home of her Namtar. He was here. She hadn't dreamed him. She wasn't imagining all this.

And if she didn't have another potential monster out in the mountains, she'd be a lot happier.

She pushed herself up and sat at the edge of the bed to examine her wound, unwinding the bandage to get a look. Fuck. Still not completely healed. It was definitely healing. The jagged edges around the puncture had knitted back together completely. The area looked less red and swollen. Only really a lump of red healing tissue left. Nearly there.

But three days after getting injured, she shouldn't see any sign of the wound anymore. Not even a red mark indicating where it had been. All evidence of the fact that she'd been hurt should have vanished by now. That there was anything there at all was disturbing.

She didn't want there to be a second monster in the mountains. But if there was, she would try to get a sample of the tail spike and its poison. This was dangerous for her Family, something like this evolving in the monsters. They needed to study it.

She crawled out of bed and collected her clothes. She only had one change of clothes in her backpack. She'd gone to bed in Adam's robe because she liked having his scent wrapped around her. The pair of pants she'd been wearing during the irgotoc fight were ruined, so she had to wear the only other pair she had brought on the hunt with her. But she'd have preferred to put on cleaner clothes. Having to see her Nam-tar in stuff she'd had buried in the bottom of a backpack was not exactly the impression she'd have imagined.

Though, as she collected everything she needed, she realized she hadn't much thought about what she'd do, say, how she'd look, any of that. Not since she was very young. Finding one's destiny could take centuries. Thinking about it too much could be disheartening. With the curse always hanging over them, even as they fought monsters and risked death, thinking about what might be, or what might not ever happen, messed with the mind and made it more difficult to do their duty.

When that happened, a person either got careless in their fights, or turned their backs on their duty. Neither way ended well.

Thoughts of her cousin's betrayal seeped in, thoughts she'd been trying to keep out. It had been a year now. And Eric had taken care of the situation when he took over responsibility for the Logan Family.

Still, losing her father to a murder plot concocted by her cousin… That was never going to be something she could get over. She didn't know why Jason had betrayed them all. She wasn't sure Eric had ever found out either. But part of her had wondered if Jason had grown despondent. It happened. When centuries passed without sign of that one person who could end the curse. Jason wouldn't be the first Family member to betray everything when the hopelessness set in. Didn't excuse what had happened. Not even a little bit.

And in the end, Jason had died without finding his Nam-tar anyway.

Becca shook off the thoughts. Dark places she didn't want to go right now. Not with the scent of her own future surrounding her. She had hope now. She just had to convince him they were meant to be.

She looked at the pile of less-than-clean clothes in her hands and sighed. But he'd already seen her at her worst, had to watch her nearly die. Mildly pungent clothes couldn't be worse.

Her pride still poked at her, though, as she quietly opened the bedroom door and padded down the hall to the bathroom. She was delighted she could make that walk without assistance this morning. Less delighted by the fact that she no longer had an excuse to let Adam carry her. She'd rather enjoyed that.

No sign of him in the hall as she went to the bathroom. She couldn't hear him anywhere in the house either. He had either stepped outside or was being exceptionally silent. Or he was still asleep. She was tempted to get a little closer to his bedroom door and listen for him, but that felt like invading his privacy. She had to keep reminding herself she didn't have a right to all of him. Not yet.

A hot shower and a thorough teeth brushing went a long way toward finishing the process of feeling like herself again. The weakness and exhaustion from yesterday were so unusual, she was only just now realizing how horrible it had felt. This morning, rested and feeling much stronger—and the shock of finding her Nam-tar no longer so profound—she knew she was able for the hunt again.

She glanced down at the almost healed wound. At least she hoped she was. That evidence that she still wasn't back to herself dampened her confidence.

Her growling stomach drove her from the bathroom and down the stairs. Still no sign of Adam. Not in the narrow living room. Not in the kitchen. Though the coffee machine was on and held half a pot of coffee still. And there was a single clean mug left on the counter near the machine. She smiled at his thoughtfulness.

She poured herself a cup and inhaled deeply. The strong scent rich and heavy, just the way she liked her coffee. That had to be a good sign, right? There was milk in the fridge she helped herself to. Then with mug in hand, she stepped out the door from the kitchen and onto a back porch.

The tree line started a few yards away from the porch, leaving a decent sized clearing of mostly dirt and scrub grass behind the cabin. A sturdy, if well used, truck was parked to one side of the clearing. There was a significant stack of wood piled against the cabin wall, under the cover of the porch overhang. A single rocking chair in the opposite corner of the porch. No sign of a road through the trees, just a dirt track leading around the side of the house. So she assumed the road leading away from the property was at the front of the house. No fences or landscaping. Just a cabin and the trees.

She liked it. She liked the simplicity of it.

Sunshine warmed the clearing, tempting her off the porch. She wasn't sure where Adam had left her boots—they hadn't been in her bedroom—so she stepped back inside long enough to search the floor near the door. And sure enough, her boots were sitting neatly against the wall, next to a much larger pair of worn hiking boots. The softening in her chest made her feel silly. But the sight of their shoes next to each other, casually, like that's where they belonged… Yeah, that made her a little sentimental.

She slipped into her boots without tying the laces and went back outside, stepping into the clearing to soak up the sun. Her skin warmed and the light and heat soothed. There probably weren't too many more days like this left in the year. Winter was rolling in, and in the mountains, that meant the cold weather would set in sooner rather than later. So she enjoyed the sun, turning her closed eyes up to the bright light and savoring the warmth.

She heard him approaching well before he moved out of the trees, knew it was him without having to open her eyes.

"Good morning," she said, finally blinking her eyes open to look at him.

He was in his wolf form, which probably shouldn't have surprised her. He was a wolf shifter. Most shifters needed to spend time in their animal forms regularly.

"Out for a morning run?" she asked. "Hope it was nice." She lifted the coffee mug. "Thanks for this."

The wolf grunted as he moved farther out of the trees. The last time she'd seen his wolf it had been dark, so she hadn't had a chance to study this side of him. Now, as he ambled into the sunlight, she took in his wolf shape.

Not an ordinary wolf. She'd seen that even in the dark. There was no mistaking a werewolf for a real wolf. The beast was significantly larger than a real wolf, his body long and sinewy with muscle. His snout a bit longer, and there were definitely a whole lot of very sharp teeth in his mouth. His fur in this form was a dark, almost black color with swaths of brown and gray layered through. His eyes were luminous, shifter yellow instead of the blue of his human form. Tuffs of fur on the points of his ears twitched as he angled toward her.

"Do you need some privacy?" she asked. Shifters weren't shy when it came to nudity, but not all of them liked to move between their different forms in front of non-shifters. The process wasn't particularly pretty. And while he'd shifted in front of her once before, she didn't want to take anything for granted. "I could go back inside."

Another grunt. Then his body started to convulse, the fur covering him rippled, and bones and sinew and muscle popped and rearranged themselves. Since he didn't seem bothered by her watching his shift, she didn't turn away. She hadn't seen many in-person shifts over the years, outside of his the other night. Not the full process from start to finish. So she was more than a little fascinated.

Nothing like her own transition, of course. She and her wolf were…different.

The shift wasn't pretty, but she'd seen so much worse she didn't find it particularly unnerving either. It took less time than she'd thought it would, too. Again, her memory of the night they'd met, when he'd shifted that first time in front of her, was a little blurry and the time scale warped. She'd assumed he was fast that night, but wouldn't have sworn to it. Now, it was obvious he could shift quickly. In the shifter world, that was a sign of strength, wasn't it?

When he was finished, he stood in the sunshine, naked and seemingly unaware of that nudity, his blue eyes still holding a faint yellow glow from his wolf. "Coffee taste okay still?" he asked. "Wasn't sitting in the pot too long?"

His first words, and they were ensuring her coffee was good. That place in her chest that had softened seeing their boots lined up next to each other did a little flip now.

"Tastes great," she said. "Thanks."

She very consciously kept her focus on his face, careful not to let her curiosity move her gaze down. She wasn't precisely sure what the protocol was with shifters when they were just standing around without any clothes on after a shift. But he'd been so kind taking care of her, she wanted to be respectful.

And she wasn't sure she could ogle him *respectfully* at that moment.

Despite how much she really wanted to.

She took a sip of her coffee to hide her desperate attempts to keep her attention on his face and not take in the gloriousness of him without a stitch of clothing on. The warm sunshine and soft mountain breeze kissed her cheeks, cooling her heated skin.

"I wasn't sure if you were a coffee drinker," he said, walking toward her as if he wasn't naked and this wasn't an unusual way to carry on a conversation, "but just in case, I wanted you to have some when you woke up."

"Not quite the addict my youngest sister is, but I'm still a fan."

She lifted the mug again in a little solute of thanks even as her heartbeat pounded harder the closer he got. Her pulse fluttered and jumped. Her stomach tightened. Her breathing quickened. Just from having him approach. Granted, he was still very naked, and she was acutely aware of that even if she was keeping her gaze on his eyes.

The closer he got, the stronger his scent carried to her, too. Mixing with the surrounding pine and rich soil scent, the smell of her coffee. The blend of all those elements settled into her, teased her, left her skin tingling. And it took a great deal of effort not to lean into him. Not to brush up against him. Not to tangle her hand in his hair and pull his face down to hers for a kiss.

She took a big gulp of her drink. He had to know how she was feeling in that moment. Her scent was no doubt giving her away. But she couldn't read his expression at all. And his scent wasn't giving her much to go on.

"How did you sleep?" he asked, his voice low now that he was standing close.

"Good. Great." She wanted to fidget? Why was she feeling the need to fidget? "Thanks."

"And how do you feel this morning?"

"A lot better." She hoped that didn't mean he'd kick her out of his home just yet. But she wouldn't lie to him about her health, even if it meant he'd send her packing. She didn't want lies between them. Especially when there *were* truths she was already hiding.

"How's the wound?" he asked, his gaze dropping to her leg.

She wanted to follow his attention down to her own leg, but that would mean she might see more of him than was strictly polite, so she kept her attention on her coffee mug. "Mostly healed now. A lot better."

"Still not fully, though."

She sighed. "Not fully."

"Which means the poison is still affecting you."

"Not necessarily." She shrugged. "But maybe. No way to know for sure." His gaze rose back to hers. The slight yellow of his wolf still hadn't faded completely. Was that normal for him? "How was your run?" she asked because she didn't have answers for the poison.

"Fine." The response was more of a grunt. "Would it help if you could figure out what the poison was?"

"Of course. At least it would give us a place to start. But…" She didn't want to make him feel bad for doing the thing he *should* have done by burning the irgotoc's remains and burying them. That's what she would have done too if the monster hadn't managed to stab her after it was dead. And she was still embarrassed by that. "Until and if we find a second monster, there's no way to study it."

She shrugged, trying for casual. She was pretty sure she failed at that since he was still standing remarkably close and was still fully naked and he smelled so damned good and it was hard to focus on what they were talking about.

He frowned. "I forgot about this in the…when I got back and you'd taken a fever and… Well, before I burned and buried the monster, I cut off one of the tail spikes and saved it."

She straightened, her gaze snapping to his face from her mug. "Why?"

"In case you needed it. Or if you didn't, I wanted to know what the poison was, since I had no idea if there were more of those things in the area or not."

"You… have a way to analyze poison?"

"Not personally. I was going to try and find someone." He shrugged. "I don't know anyone who could right now. But I…" He shook his head, hard, and said, "Anyway, would it be useful to you? Do you know anyone who can analyze it?"

"I do." Her sister Judith was the Family biologist and chemist. She studied newer monsters and their evolving features. "One of my sisters can. Once we get it to her. I need to ensure there aren't any irgotocs left on this mountain first, but after…" She almost said *we can take it to her*. But the "we" part wasn't a forgone conclusion yet. Making any assumptions right now was dangerous.

"Good. Okay. Good."

Something in his tone made her look at him a little closer. His scent was a mix of things she couldn't really parse out. So she went the direct route. "What's wrong?"

He sighed and ran a hand through his hair. The move mussed his already shaggy hair, giving him a climbed-out-of-bed tousled look, which was a little unfair for her hormones. The gesture also drew her attention to the flex of his arm muscles and shoulders and chest and that made it harder to keep her focus on his face. Damn. He should probably put some clothes on soon. She was having a very difficult time being respectful.

"I was afraid you'd think…" He shook his head. "Doesn't matter."

"No. Please. Tell me." She took a step closer. And only realized what a mistake that was when he looked down at her and they were so close now her knuckles nearly brushed his chest. She gripped her mug tighter with both hands and kept very still.

"When I remembered I had the spike still, this morning, I thought…" He shrugged. "I was afraid you'd think I'd kept the fact that I had it from you on purpose."

"Why?"

"I…expect distrust and suspicion." He opened his mouth like he would say more, then snapped it shut and shrugged.

She wanted to dig into that more and immediately. She wanted to hear everything. And then she wanted to reassure him and tell him she trusted him completely. Except she shouldn't trust him yet because she barely knew him. He would think her assertion was just words. But she did trust him. He was her Nam-tar. The gods wouldn't have made him for her if she couldn't trust him. Right? But since he didn't know any of that, he wouldn't have any reason to trust *her*. Or her words.

"What sort of suspicions were you worried about?" she asked, hoping if she got him talking about it more, she could reassure him in a way he'd believe.

"There are people in the world that would have kept that spike, knowing it was dangerous, to use it. For lots of reasons. Power. Manipulation." He shrugged again, but he wouldn't meet her gaze. "I thought knowing what the poison was could save lives, but not everyone would have that sort of motivation. You don't know me. And I didn't mention the spike to you right away. It would only be natural for you to assume the worst."

She blinked a few times as that settled in. The bitterness in his tone, in his expression, in the punch of a burnt peppery flavor in his scent… Everything in her wanted to comfort him. Wipe away all that bitterness. She kept her hands carefully wrapped around her mug.

"Why didn't you tell me about the spike right away?"

"I honestly forgot it was there. With everything else happening. Coming home and finding you…" His jaw muscles clenched. She could practically hear his teeth grinding together.

"That's natural," she said. "I nearly died. And having someone die under your roof, or almost die, is distracting." She quirked her mouth, not quite a smile. "You forgetting the spike is understandable."

He blinked down at her. "You mean that, don't you?"

"Of course. I would have forgotten it to, if the circumstances were reversed." She wanted desperately to settle her hand against his cheek, on his chest, some physical contact to reassure him. That bitterness in his scent bothered her on a deep level, and her every instinct was to sooth and comfort him. It took a lot to keep her hands to herself.

He nodded, his expression going through a series of emotions she couldn't really decipher. "Thanks for not assuming the worst from me."

Oh. Her throat clogged with such a need to comfort, she finally gave in. She settled her palm against the side of his face, meeting his gaze. She wanted to say something. But wasn't sure what because none of it would make sense to him after they'd only known each other such a short period of time.

So she ran her thumb across his cheek, over the scruff of his morning beard, felt the muscle in his jaw flex with his swallow, and simply said, "I would never."

The moment stretched, with only the coffee mug between them keeping her from closing the remaining space so she could wrap her arms around him. Reassure him. Not just reassure. She wanted very much to kiss him. The desire coiled in her stomach, fluttered in her chest, leaving her breathless.

His eyes darkened, the blue overriding what was left of his wolf. Bright sunshine warmed his skin under her palm. Or maybe that was just how warm he was naturally. So warm she wanted to wrap herself around him, bask in all that heat. She rubbed her fingers over his skin, letting her hand drift down to his neck, his shoulder. He pulled in a deep breath, his chest expanding to brush against her knuckles where she still gripped the coffee mug. Rough hair, warm skin, strong muscles.

She leaned in, the hand on his shoulder flexing as if she might pull him closer.

And then he blinked and straightened away. Taking a step back so fast she almost fell forward. She caught herself and wrapped both hands around the mug again as the shock of suddenly cool air hit her. She gave herself a mental shake, trying to get her brain working again.

"You must be hungry," he said. "Give me a few minutes to get cleaned up and dressed. Then I'll make us some breakfast."

She opened her mouth, not sure what she wanted to say, but he was gone. Moving at shifter speed back into the house. So fast, the breeze from his movements ruffled the fine hairs on her brow that had escaped her braid.

Well. That hadn't gone well. There'd been desire there, she was sure of it. When she thought back and analyzed his scent, she knew he'd felt that same attraction she had. But he'd rejected the feeling.

And it was getting harder and harder for her not to feel rejected as well.

Too soon, she reassured herself. That was all. They still had to get to know each other more. He obviously didn't have a lot of experience with trust in his life. He probably didn't trust her. He didn't trust the attraction between them. That made sense. Wasn't personal.

She repeated that to herself, her gaze on the surrounding pines, blinking rapidly as she finished her cooling coffee.

CHAPTER NINE

Adam climbed out of the shower, still cursing himself. Becca was under his roof because she'd been severely injured and because she needed time to heal. She needed help looking for a monster. And she knew nothing about him or his past.

Kissing her, giving in to that desire, would have been a huge mistake.

He'd been painfully aware of her attraction, the flavor of it rich and thick in her scent. A heady sweet smell, like melting chocolate, that had made conversation difficult. She'd been so careful to keep her gaze on his face, though. A reminder she wasn't a shifter, even with that faint hint of wolf underneath her scent. That reminder had driven him a little closer to the brink. She didn't know his status was compromised. She didn't view him as a monster. And she wanted him.

Almost impossible to resist.

Her acceptance of his story about forgetting the spike, though... That's what had truly wrecked him. She hadn't assumed the worst, hadn't even been upset. In fact, the flare of gratitude in both her eyes and her scent had curled around his chest like a warm hug. How was he supposed to resist her after that?

But she didn't know him. It wouldn't be fair to her to drag her into his life, into something that couldn't go anywhere because of his past. When his present was still precarious.

The gathering pack north of here was a constant threat. He'd picked this house, this location because there were no werewolf packs in the area. But now, with a new one forming, establishing their territory so close to his…

That was a fight waiting to happen. One he couldn't win. And it would mean moving. Again.

He didn't want to risk Becca getting pulled into that mess. In any way. Letting her stay here this long probably wasn't a smart decision. But he couldn't just let her go back into the woods, hunting monsters while she still wasn't fully recovered from her last encounter with the same type of monster. He *had* to help her. His every instinct, his very insistent wolf, pushed him to help her.

His wolf also wanted to keep her.

But that was impossible and even his wolf recognized that on some level. The wolf was just more stubborn about not resisting the impossible.

He toweled off, got dressed, and tried to quiet his wolf. First, he had to feed Becca. Then they'd start searching the grid they'd mapped out last night. And if they found another monster, they'd take care of it. If they didn't, he'd let her go. Back to her life. Whatever that might be.

She was still outside when he came downstairs, though sitting on the steps of his porch now. Her attention was on the trees, the coffee mug still cradled in her hands.

He opened the back door, propping it open to let the cool morning air into the kitchen. "Would you like more coffee?" he asked.

She didn't turn to face him. "I just got a second cup, so I'm good. Thank you."

He wanted to say more, but the temptation to sit down next to her with his own coffee, stare at the trees with her, talk quietly about the day ahead… No. Couldn't do that. Not allowed that kind of life anymore.

"Eggs and bacon okay for breakfast?"

"You don't have to cook for me. I don't want to put you to too much trouble."

"You have to eat. You won't finish healing or be able to fight monsters on an empty stomach."

She shrugged. "Wouldn't be the first time I've had to."

A comment that begged for follow up questions. He resisted. His need to know everything about her would only get him into trouble. "Well as long as you're under my roof, you won't need to. Eggs and bacon? Do you like toast?"

"I'm easy going when it comes to food. Anything you make for yourself will be fine." She finally glanced over her shoulder at him and smiled. "Thanks."

He took one step toward her, and that smile, before he caught himself. "You're welcome."

He retreated into the kitchen, running through the ritual of breakfast, working hard not to think too much about Becca sitting right outside on his porch. Or the drive to ensure she ate and rested. The instinct to look after her and keep her safe. That was his wolf talking, the bastard, and he didn't want to acknowledge how desperately he wanted the *right* to take care of Becca.

When he had large plates full of scrambled eggs, crispy bacon, and toast ready, he called her inside. "Unless you want to eat on the porch?"

"Table is fine."

She set her coffee cup down and sat in the same seat she had last night. He only had two chairs at his table, and that only because he'd felt too pathetic with only one. Thankful he didn't have to drag in the rocking chair from the porch for her, he waited for her to take her first few bites before he started his own breakfast.

"This is excellent," she said, her eyes wide. "You're a really good cook."

He had to work hard not to puff up his chest and preen at the compliment. "It was either learn how to cook or eat food out of boxes. I like this better."

She smiled. "Me too. Though I'm not a very good cook. I can

scramble eggs if push comes to shove. But the bacon would have been beyond my skill set."

For some reason, that surprised him. She seemed so capable he'd just assumed she could do anything.

"I can bake a mean chocolate chip cookie, though," she said, her smile growing. "Maybe I can make you some. Pay you back for doing the cooking."

"You don't have to."

"It would be fun." Her smile dimmed a little. "If we have time." She scooped up more eggs and ate quietly for a few moments. Then, "Did you see any signs of a monster on your run?"

"Nothing in the immediate area." He frowned. "How did you know I was out scouting already?"

"This is your territory, right? I don't know a lot about shifters, but I assumed you'd want to check the area. Make sure nothing was happening too close to your home."

That she got that, despite not knowing much about shifters, did strange things to him. A settling and calming in his chest that he hadn't felt since leaving his pack. He wasn't even sure why her comment sparked that feeling.

"If you do come across signs of the other irgotoc while I'm not around," she said, her expression hesitant, "I'd ask that you not try to engage it without me. I know this is your territory to defend. I get that. But… Well, I'm the one who hunts monsters. It's what I do." She opened her mouth as if she wanted to say more, then closed it and shrugged.

"I won't fight the thing alone unless it attacks me first. Fair enough."

Her shoulders dropped with her exhale. "Thank you. Yes. That's… that's good." She winced. "I wasn't sure how you'd take that request."

"This irgotoc is the first thing like it I've ever come across. I don't mind deferring to an expert."

That earned him one of her huge smiles, which warmed his chest and almost, *almost* made him forget she wasn't his.

"So you know, if you do come across one while I'm not there, you have to remove its head. That's true with all monsters. If you don't remove the head, completely, they'll just keep coming. They can take a lot of damage, too. And as you saw with the irgotoc's acid blood, they have some pretty substantial defenses." She winced when she said, "The irgotoc aren't picky about what they eat. They'll devour anything they come across. But all monsters aim for humans. It's… It's why they were created."

"You said a god creating them?"

"Ne, yes."

"Why?"

"Retribution against his brother En for coming down on the side of humans against Ne when Ne wanted to destroy humanity. It pissed Ne off that his brother chose humans over him. Didn't help that En won the war against Ne when Ne initially tried to wipe humans off the earth." She waved a hand. "Long story."

"I'd like to hear it. These aren't stories I've heard before. Though, to be fair, I've never given any gods much thought. Not a big believer in them. Didn't consider any of them might really exist."

"Old gods exist. They were…are a pain in the ass, but they exist."

He chuckled. "You going to get into trouble for saying that?"

"No. They know they're a pain in the ass." She paused to crunch on some bacon and make happy sounds. Then, "Not that I've met an actual god. Not even the ones who created my Family, all the Families. But I believe the story of our origin."

"Why?"

She turned her attention back down to her food. "Part of that long story. But we can talk about that later. First, you need to remember the thing about removing a monster's head."

"Got it. Can I rip their heads off with my bare hands, or do I need to use a specific weapon?"

He half expected the blunt violence of his comment to give her pause. It didn't. She didn't even stop eating.

"No specific weapon for most of them. Swords are the easiest. Which is why I carry that and a dagger. Guns cause damage but aren't precise enough to remove the heads completely. And it has to be a complete severing. If that doesn't happen, you just end up with a pissed off monster." She frowned a little at her food. "There are some...beings that require specific weapons to kill them. But in general, with most of the monsters, you just have to get their heads off. Any way you can. Which isn't as easy as it sounds."

"It doesn't sound easy at all."

"Worse when the head isn't obvious."

"There are monsters without obvious heads?"

"Mm hmm. Tricky bastards."

All this made his own head spin. What a world she lived in. A world he hadn't even known existed. Was this what humans felt when they discovered werewolves were real? "What other things besides acid blood and poisoned tail spikes do I have to look out for with the irgotoc?"

"Their regenerating limbs. That's new. I mentioned that?"

He nodded.

"So you may or may not make progress toward decapitating them by removing the tentacles. It'll help a little, though. Just watch out for the blood. And the suction cups on their tentacles, those will attach to any bare skin they can reach and burn. Damned painful. The shock of it can kill as fast as their other deadly attributes. Especially since removing them once they attach can be so difficult." She narrowed her eyes. "Shifters heal fast. Do you heal faster when you change forms or does that make a difference?"

"Speeds things up. Why?"

"Makes sense," she mumbled. Like she was talking to herself. Then she gave herself a rough shake and looked up at him again. "If necessary, how often can you shift? It takes time for the process itself, but do you need...hours between shifts or can you go back and forth?"

"Depends on the shifter. Species and individual. The stronger the shifter, the faster and more often they can go between forms."

She nibbled her bottom lip and gave him a narrow-eyed look. He wasn't sure whether to laugh or be offended.

He settled on amusement. "You really want to ask me if I'm a strong shifter or not, don't you?" he said. And delighted when a wash of pink colored her cheeks.

"Well, I was trying not to. But yes. I do need to ask. It's important I know what you can and can't do on a hunt."

"You saw my shift earlier. And the other night. Those weren't my top speeds. I can shift faster if I have to. But those were comfortable for me."

If he had to, he could shift as fast as his brother, which was significantly faster than most of the rest of his former pack. Which was one of the reasons his brother was the alpha. But he didn't want to bring up his brother or his former pack so he didn't mention that out loud. Despite his wolf wanting to boast and impress her with his strength.

"And how often can you shift?"

"As often as I need to." Grudgingly, he admitted, "Too often, I will wear out, get exhausted. But I'd really have to push to reach that. I could easily go wolf again now. Then human again a few minutes later. And that wouldn't bother me."

She let out a long breath. "Oh that's good. Good. So if you get injured, you can shift and heal faster, no matter what form you're in."

Her relief at knowing he had a way to heal quickly if he got hurt in a fight left him feeling much too happy. That she might care if he got hurt, that she cared if he died, wasn't something he was used to anymore. Except for his brother and sister, any wolves he encountered now would actively want him dead.

But, he reminded himself again, she wasn't a shifter. Whatever that hint of wolf in her, she wasn't like him and didn't know wolf shifters well enough to understand where he stood in that world.

He winced inwardly and ran a hand up through his hair. While they were discussing strengths and weaknesses, he should warn her about that danger. If they ran across other werewolves, there'd be a fight. Especially since the new pack had moved into the area. But he didn't want to admit any of that to her. Didn't want to watch her acceptance fade and die. He liked her thinking well of him. And he wanted to keep that gift for just a little while longer.

She held his gaze for a moment before ducking her head and returning to what remained of her food. He only realized then how much and how fast she'd eaten. Like a shifter. What *was* she? So much about her reminded him of other shifters, and yet she wasn't one. So what was she exactly? What did that hint of wolf in her scent mean?

"Outside of acid blood, barbed limb spikes, suction cups that burn, and a mean attitude," she went back to the irgotoc, "the female will be larger than the male, and will have working wings. Or…at least they used to." She raised her hands in a little shrug. "I'm giving you what I know from the original species, but since they seem to have evolved…"

"Guess work."

"Guess work," she said with a slight nod. "It'll have to do. If there's a female, it'll likely have wings that work."

"Can it perch in trees? Will we have to worry about ambush from above?" His wolf instincts both appreciated that predator advantage and saw the dangers in it if he was the one being stalked.

"Should be too big. The females are…or were a lot larger than the males. It would take an awfully big tree with very strong branches to hold an adult female irgotoc."

"There are some huge spruce trees in this area," he pointed out. Not the largest in the world. That was over in the Olympics. But still, some pretty huge trees.

"When I say the female is larger than the male, I mean a *lot* larger. That monster the other day was tiny compared to a female irgotoc."

"Fucking hell." He blinked. The irgotoc she'd killed had been a pretty big beast, the size of a grizzly but with tentacles and a long tail. "How big, exactly?"

"Five, six times the size of the male."

Which would make the female the size of a yellow school bus. "With tentacles and talons and suction cups and a spiked tail and acid blood?"

"Plus the huge wings."

"How the hell can the female fly and the male, which is smaller, ended up with vestigial wings?"

"Got me. I didn't make them." She frowned, her brow creasing. "Ne has a weird sense of humor?"

The fact that she talked about a god like he might still be walking around was pretty terrifying. He sort of hoped this Ne had faded away with time or whatever happened when old gods died.

"The irgotocs were one of the earliest monsters Ne and the Slain Heroes—sort of monsters themselves—created. Not the worst. Not the very first. But it's a species that's been around for a long time."

"Not the worst?"

"No real intelligence. Just an all-consuming instinct for eating and killing. The smart monsters are the ones you really have to worry about. When En's Seven Families proved capable of destroying the instinct-driven monsters, Ne created smarter creatures, ones that could use reason and logic, and think their way toward killing better."

She said all this with a sort of distracted air, her gaze mostly turned inward like she was thinking of something other than the conversation.

"What's bothering you?" he asked.

She blinked and refocused on him. "Not sure. Something started nagging me when I said I hadn't created the irgotocs, but I'm not sure what's bothering me. Something about the fact that the irgotocs seem to have evolved, and evolved more deadly attributes…"

"Don't monsters normally evolve?"

"They do. Some of them. But a lot of them are exactly what they were when Ne and the Slain Heroes created them. Exactly. No changes or evolving at all. In fact, almost all the first few generations of monsters fell into that category. Only later monsters found ways to evolve." She shuddered. "Some of those ways are not pleasant."

"Do I want to know?"

"Probably not. Let's just say, the more intelligent ones learned how to…use humans to adapt their DNA and create new kinds of monsters."

None of that sounded even remotely good. Especially the "use humans" part. But she was right, he probably didn't want too many of those details. At least not this morning over the breakfast table.

"Anyway." She waved a hand, moving on. "Some monsters can

evolve but most don't. Not randomly. They are what they are. Evolution in a monster that's been unchanged for millennia is…strange."

"And bad?"

"In this case, yeah. But also suspicious."

"How so?"

She shrugged again and shook her head. "I can't put a finger on why this is bothering me. Except that it shouldn't have happened with this particular monster. So what's driving it? How is it happening? Why now?"

"Good questions. Anyone you can talk to about all this?"

"My oldest brother. He's head of the Logan Family now." There was a slight hitch in her voice when she said now, but she pushed past it so fast he almost missed the catch. "He'll need to know. And maybe he's heard something, too. He gets information from all our Family, as well as the other six Families. If someone's come across something like this before, he'll have heard about it."

"Can you tell me more about the Seven Families? Or does that violate some divine dictate?"

He didn't have any rights to her secrets, but she was talking so freely and openly with him, he hoped she'd tell him more. More about her. More about her life and this duty to hunt monsters. Just…everything.

Even though he knew there could be nothing between them, the desire to *know* her overrode his common sense. He'd be better off knowing as little about her as possible so that when she left, he'd have less to hang on to. He'd be able to let her go. The more he learned, the better he got to know her, the worse things would go for him when she did leave.

But his curiosity wiped out his self-preservation instincts.

She blinked at him a few times, and then smiled. The expression so bright he found himself blinking back.

"I keep forgetting you don't know…" She shook her head. "Never mind. I can tell you about the Families, but it's a long story. It'll take some time. And right now, we need to find out if there's a second monster or not. That has to take precedence."

That last she said almost to herself. Like a reminder.

"You don't have to if it's privileged information or anything," he said. "Wolf packs are pretty secretive. I understand if you'd rather not tell a stranger about all this."

"Are they?" she asked. "Wolf packs? I suppose they must be since I know so little about them."

She set her fork and empty plate aside and leaned back with a contented sigh. That she'd liked and appreciated the food he fed her made his wolf extremely happy.

"It's true we don't tell many about the Families," she continued. "We're obviously secretive too." Flash of a smile. "But I'll tell you." She opened her mouth. Closed it abruptly. Then, "I don't mind you knowing."

But that wasn't what she'd intended to say. He was certain of it. There was something in her scent he couldn't quite catch or interpret, but he read it as secrets, as her hiding something. And yet she'd just said she'd tell him about these families. Strange.

Becca Logan was a mystery on so many levels. A mystery he wanted to explore fully, until he knew every facet of it.

Shame that was a desire he'd have to forgo. Like so much else in his life at the moment, she was just one more thing he had to let go.

CHAPTER TEN

The initial search turned up nothing at all. No signs of irgotoc droppings, evidence of kills, potential nests where a female might hole up. No obvious evidence of a second monster at all.

"Is this good or bad?" Adam asked after shifting in the clearing just outside his back porch.

Becca was deep in thought, which meant it took a full thirty seconds before the fact that he was standing next to her naked hit her conscious mind. When it did, she made an effort to keep her attention on the house and not on him so she could respect his privacy. And maintain her sanity.

Despite turning up empty, the hunt had been so...seamless. Amazingly easy and natural to hunt with him. He'd shifted right away, padding out into the woods in his wolf form. They'd gone south and east first. Searching a grid that covered a significant amount of area for the morning. Because he was a shifter, they were able to move fast, too. Not at her top speed. Not at his either, she suspected. But faster than if she'd been working with humans.

And it was all so comfortable. Not a lot of talking required—so he stayed in wolf form most of the time. A grunt, a nod, a few words from her, and they'd continued throughout the morning without need for much more.

Hunting with Adam was almost like hunting with someone from one of the Families. Easier even. Like hunting with someone from *her* Family. Like he was meant to be there. Had always been meant to be there.

Which, technically, was true. He was her destiny and they were meant for each other. But for some reason, she hadn't really thought about what that would mean for her job. Most Nam-tar didn't hunt with their partners. They did other things within the Family, if they chose. But even that wasn't necessary. Many had their own work and focus, which wasn't monster hunting. All of that was welcomed. Nam-tars were precious, and treated so. Given what they needed, and provided all the room they needed to live as they saw fit within the Families. But it hadn't crossed her mind that hers might be a hunter, too. Just a slightly different sort of hunter. It hadn't occurred to her that her destiny might be someone she could also work beside.

The idea was thrilling and terrifying at once. She didn't want Adam in harm's way, of course. In fact, until that morning, the idea of him coming across a monster without her had terrified her. She'd wanted to keep him away from anything to do with the monsters. But he was so capable. So…perfectly suited to her life in so many ways. She could almost imagine what the future would be like, having him by her side, hunting monsters *with* her in partnership.

And it was a nicer view of her future than she'd expected.

Unfortunately, the ease of working with him hadn't translated into any actual results. Except, "We've eliminated a significant area. No sign of an irgotoc anywhere in that section of the woods means that's one less place we have to worry about." She tried to give the morning a positive spin. Really, not finding anything was good news. "There might not even be a second monster. Which would be the best outcome."

"Or the monster could be slipping by us," he said.

"Some might be able to do that, but not an irgotoc. Like I said, they're not one of the clever ones. All instinct and hunger. That sort of creature isn't subtle enough to avoid us so thoroughly." At least, she assumed that was still the case. She couldn't take her own knowledge for granted, though. Not with an irgotoc that had evolved.

And that evolution…

Their conversation at breakfast had been niggling at her. Irgotocs hadn't evolved in millennia. They weren't the sort of monsters who had ever found a way to change and evolve. It was possible it was happening naturally. Things changed. They'd been driven to near extinction by the Families, so maybe they had just *naturally* found a way to improve their chances of survival. But…

Something about that bothered her. Something about them only *now* evolving…

She couldn't place her finger on why that was bugging her so much. Some inner instinct waving a red flag. But why? And what did it mean?

She wasn't sure how to answer that question without finding the second monster—if there was one—so she set the worry to one side for the moment. "We'll assume that area is clear unless and until we find some evidence to say otherwise."

He grunted, not sounding particularly hopeful.

"There might not even be a second monster," she reminded him.

"I doubt I'm that lucky," he muttered under his breath. So quietly she assumed he hadn't meant her to hear the comment. Or maybe he had. He had to know by now she could hear better than the average human.

"We still have a lot of ground to cover," she said. "No point in assuming the worst." Yet. "At least we didn't find any kills."

And that really had been a relief. Irgotocs were voracious. Letting them get near a human population was always a disaster. The male had been spotted by humans on its way into this area, but fortunately, those had been isolated homes. Since it had moved up here into this more isolated area, she hoped, *if* there was a second one here, it was occupied with deer, and moose, and coyotes, and bears, and even cougars. Enough to keep it busy and not immediately go looking for humans.

The fact that they hadn't found *any* kills left her, if not hopeful, then at least confident the area they'd searched this morning was clear.

"Lunch and then another grid?" Adam asked. Then more abruptly, "Or do you need to rest? We aren't pushing you too hard, are we? How's your leg?"

His concern made her feel all warm and fuzzy inside. "I'm fine. My leg was a little stiff initially, but it's fine now."

Mostly. She still felt the tug on the healing skin around the wound, but it *was* almost healed up now, so she wasn't lying about her abilities.

A lesson she'd had to learn early in her years hunting monsters. She'd tried to push through a few times, when she wasn't at her best— too exhausted, needed food, hadn't had any rest at all in days and needed a few hours of sleep. Her body could put up with a lot of abuse. She could function well past what an ordinary human might be capable of. Sometimes she could push even farther if she used periods of transition and let her wolf out while her human body healed. She wasn't close to her edge right now. But she'd tested those limits in her early years. Enough to know the dangers of ignoring her needs for food and rest and recovery. Pushing to her limits was one thing. Pushing past them could get someone else killed.

"Food will be good," she said, to reassure him. "Then we can take the grid farther east. So long as you're still good? Need to rest yourself? Has the shifting been pushing you too much?"

"I'm good." He sounded a little annoyed so she risked glancing at him. His expression wasn't quite a scowl, but he wasn't smiling either.

"Did I offend your pride?" she asked with a smile.

He huffed. "A little," he admitted. "I keep forgetting you don't know what I'm capable of."

But she'd like to know. Very much. And in ways that didn't have anything to do with monsters. She kept those thoughts to herself, though. "I suppose we'll just have to learn each other's limits. And try not to get annoyed when we check in with each other?"

That earned her a grunt. And a reluctant smile.

His expression made her want to wrap her arms around him and sink into a kiss. Made her want to explore her unintended innuendo just to see how he'd react. Also reminded her sharply that he was still standing right next to her stark naked and that made concentrating extremely difficult.

She waved to the cabin. "You should get dressed. Why don't I make us lunch this time? I can manage cold cuts and bread if you've got the makings for sandwiches?"

"I don't mind cooking for you," he said. "I enjoy feeding you."

Her stomach flipped and warmth seeped through her. She couldn't seem to help herself. She swayed toward him. Not conscious effort. She was pulled to him, impossible to resist that pull. The warm fall sunshine danced through his shaggy hair, and it took a concerted effort to keep her hands to herself. Would his hair feel as thick and soft as it looked? How about his body? All hard muscle and strength. She leaned closer just to feel the heat of him.

His eyes darkened, his gaze dropped to her mouth. And her pulse sped.

The hunt, even an uneventful one, had left her adrenaline high, and it occurred to her that she and Adam might find a fun way to work off that adrenaline. A way that involved him staying just as he was and her getting rid of her own clothes. She was tempted enough by the idea she opened her mouth to suggest it.

Then snapped her mouth shut an instant later. They still had a lot of area to cover. If she allowed herself to give in to temptation, to try and seduce him, right now, she risked getting lost in him and forgetting what she was here to do. At least what she had to do *before* she focused on him and their potential future.

But the draw to him, the need for him was overwhelming.

"I'll be back downstairs in a minute," he said suddenly, straightening his shoulders.

She only realized then that he'd been leaning closer to her as well.

"We can argue over who makes lunch then." He smiled and his expression made her insides all quivery and hot. Then he walked away.

But not at shifter speed. This time he strolled into the house, a pace that gave her plenty of opportunity to admire his naked ass. Which she did. Despite her determination to respect his privacy. Really, if he'd wanted her *not* to look at his magnificent ass, he'd have gone into the house faster.

Her heart thudded hard even after he'd disappeared through the back door. The lust was surprisingly overwhelming. After almost two centuries, she'd thought she'd experienced more than enough lust to be familiar with the feel of it. She'd enjoyed the build of tension, and she'd thoroughly enjoyed the release of that tension many times over the years.

But with Adam…

She felt like she had very little control over her desire. Like she couldn't be next to him without putting her hands on him. So far, she'd kept that need in check, but he had to know how she felt. *She* could smell the spicy sweet flavor of her need. Even worse—or really better—she could scent his, too. A deep, rich, musky, earthy flavor that made her pulse race. And knowing he wanted her, maybe as much as she wanted him, made focus and concentration more difficult than it had ever been in her life.

The reactions had to be because he was her promised mate. Made sense intellectually—a long long lifetime together would go a lot more smoothly if there was affection and physical attraction and all the things that went into making a relationship strong and successful. Lust for her Nam-tar was predictable.

And still she hadn't been prepared. Not for the itchy, needy, greedy degree of it. Not for the overwhelm of it.

She had a potential monster to catch before it discovered any human towns. She had the mystery of the monster's evolution and what that meant. And she had to tread a delicate balance with her Nam-tar so she didn't scare him away. He *had* to stay of his own free will. Had to accept her and accept living in this world of hers, without force or manipulation.

But trying to keep her mind on any of that went out the window when Adam stood next to her, close enough for her to feel the heat of his sun-warmed skin, smelling like absolute heaven. When all she could think about was getting her hands on him, and keeping her hands on him for days.

To make it all more complicated, she got the impression he was hiding something from her. Something important. She couldn't blame him for that. They were still getting to know each other. Trust would have to be earned. But whatever he was hiding seemed to be the reason he was keeping his distance. The reason he kept walking away whenever she got overwhelmed by her own desire.

He wanted her. She was certain of that. But he was the one resisting the pull, more than her, and she got the feeling that resistance had to do with the secrets he was keeping.

Or, she thought with a sigh, maybe she was just making excuses so she didn't have to feel rejected.

She trudged into the house, determined to make him lunch, even with her poor food preparation skills, and tried very hard not to think about the future.

And how quickly it could fall apart if she wasn't careful.

CHAPTER ELEVEN

The afternoon grid search didn't turn up any signs of an irgotoc. But Adam did find signs that the wolves from the new pack had been moving down close to his territory.

The grid they hunted that afternoon was outside his territory, directly east of his house. And shouldn't have been far enough to the north to encounter any evidence of the pack. Yet, as he hunted in wolf form for signs of a monster, he caught the scent of werewolves, rubbed into some of the trees. And at least two deer carcasses that were definitely wolf kills.

He'd sniffed to make sure. Not the poisoned stench from the monster. The bodies ripped apart but not in the messy, ranging way the monster had killed its prey. And there was more bone and skin left at the wolf kills than there'd been at the monster's kills.

Because he was certain those kills were made by shifters and not the monster, he didn't point them out to Becca. In fact, he steered her away from them both times. He'd have had to shift to explain who was responsible for the kills. That would lead to a discussion of the pack gathering to the north. And he'd have to tell her why that was a bad thing.

He didn't want to. He couldn't bring himself to admit he was an outcast. Not to her. Not yet. The way she looked at him, the scent of her desire… He hadn't known how much he'd wanted that from someone. How much he'd needed to be seen for himself again. Not the brother who'd been tricked into a position of either challenging and killing his brother or leaving his pack for good. Not the failed beta.

Not the wolf who would slowly lose himself the longer he was outcast.

He'd managed to avoid the fate of most exiled wolves so far. But he had little doubt he'd eventually succumb. Everyone did eventually. It was why banishing a wolf from their pack was considered a harsher punishment than just killing them. Wolves didn't survive outside pack structure for long without losing their hold on their sanity and turning feral.

Adam had been without that structure for three and a half years. And he'd felt the madness tugging at him more and more in the last few months. The panics came on more often. Were harder to calm. So desperate for the security and structure of pack life, it choked him. The loneliness and despair of forced separation from his people slowly eroding his control.

Most lone wolves didn't survive long on their own. They physically needed the pack. A strange quirk of werewolves. Without that pack to keep them whole, most lost their minds. And had to be destroyed.

He'd lived within a pack his whole life. He was born a werewolf, not made one, and he'd never been abandoned and left outside the security of a pack like too many of the converted wolves. His pack had even made an effort to find and help the lone wolves they encountered. Bring them into the pack if they could. Put them out of their misery if they were too far down the path toward insanity. At least that had been the way when Doug Corwin had been alpha. When his son had taken over as alpha though, things hadn't worked in quite the same way. Chris had been less…diligent about keeping the pack safe.

After Gabriel took over, order had been restored. And efforts to rehabilitate lone wolves had started again—though not using the same methods as Doug had used.

Adam had never thought he'd be on the outside of a pack. Never once had he considered going rogue. Yet here he was, isolated and considered a scourge by most wolf shifters.

And it was all his own doing.

Having Becca learn of his disgrace, having her no longer look at him in quite the same way as she did now, her beautiful brown eyes accepting and open… He couldn't face that. Not yet. Not just yet. He wanted a little more time of just being himself with her. A little more time with her thinking well of him.

So he kept the wolf kills to himself. Even during the brief periods of time when he shifted to his human form so they could talk, when he might have explained. They didn't affect the search. They weren't the result of a monster—at least not her kind of monster—so she really didn't need to know about them.

An excuse he kept telling himself throughout the afternoon.

But the fact that the new pack had come this far south, and was leaving evidence of itself so close to his territory, was worrying. They had to know he was here now. Picked up his territorial markings. And they had to know he was a lone wolf.

It was only a matter of time before they showed up to challenge him. Or worse, try to kill him outright without the formal honor of a challenge. He wasn't sure how much time he had left before that happened. But the signs that the wolves had come so close to his home meant that time was significantly less than he'd hoped.

Those worries had him preoccupied when they finally got back to his cabin that night, well after the sun had set. He shifted to his human form and went into the house to dress with only a cursory, "I'll be right back," to Becca. He was too distracted to notice her silence, or the slight change in her scent.

Those only hit him when he came back downstairs. When he realized she was out on the porch instead of at the kitchen table where he'd expected to find her.

"Everything okay?" he asked when he stepped out through the screen door. She was sitting in the single rocking chair he had on his deck—didn't need two when he never had visitors—so he leaned against the low railing, crossing his arms over his chest as he faced her.

She didn't look at him directly.

"I'm…worried," she said after a moment.

"Because we aren't seeing any signs of another monster? That should be good news."

"You'd think, wouldn't you?" She tried a little smile but it flattened out quickly and the creases across her brow remained. "But it's not just that we aren't seeing a second monster where there should be one. It's that the irgotoc, this specific monster, has evolved. That the rules of its behavior and actions have changed. That's been bothering me a lot. And as the day's gone on, the worry has nagged more and more."

She leaned back in the chair, rocking it gently as she finally met his gaze. "The irgotoc is an eating machine. As basic as a monster can get. And it's been that way for thousands of years. So…how has it suddenly evolved? Why has it suddenly changed? And not just changed and become more deadly in general. It's developed a weapon—the poison —that can really damage someone like me. That feels…purposeful."

"You're the monster's only predator?"

She shrugged and nodded. "Ordinary humans, shifters, other beings can all kill them. If they know to remove their heads. As I said, despite our best efforts, some knowledge of us and the monsters has crept out into the world. So, technically, we're not their *only* predator. Just the ones most focused on destroying them when we find them. Sacred duty." She waved a hand in the air as if that last was all the explanation needed.

"Still, if you're their main predator, it makes sense they'd evolve responses directly related to you. That's how animals evolve."

"Except that they haven't done that in all these centuries. They haven't changed even a little before now. If they were going to develop a weapon specifically designed to target members of the Seven Families, why not at some point before this? Why not in increments that we would have noticed? Why this sudden leap?"

"Evolution takes time," he said. But he was starting to see her point. "I suppose the question is why now and not sooner?"

"Exactly. What's driven it to change *now*?"

"You nearly wiped it out."

Another half shrug, half nod. "Possible. Still, the change feels… I don't know. I've been thinking about this a lot." She flashed another little smile. "Probably too much. And I just can't get around the fact that the change happened so fast, just recently, and with so few of the monsters left that we thought they didn't exist anymore."

"Are you worried there are a lot more in hiding than you thought?" The idea of that was pretty horrifying. What if those things were crawling all over these mountains? And were so good at hiding now, they'd escaped the attention of both her hunter families *and* the shifters like him who made these mountains home.

He was in an isolated area for a wolf shifter—at least he had been until the new pack started forming—but there were other shifters here. All over these mountains. Bears in particular roamed through the woods and wouldn't be the sort of shifter to ignore another predator within their range. Someone would have noticed the monsters before now if there were truly a lot of them.

Wouldn't they?

"That's one of my worries," she said. "More of them out there than we thought. Or that they've found a way to hide so we can't detect them—that one worries me a lot right at the moment, since we haven't found any evidence of a second. But…" She scowled at that railing, not looking at him when she said, "I keep coming back to the suddenness and speed of the change. In a monster nearly extinct. I've been going around and around with that all day. And I'm worried… I'm worried something or someone has…"

"Has what?"

She huffed out a sharp breath. "I'm starting to worry someone is creating new monsters."

Adam went still, the way he might have if he sensed another predator about. He didn't change positions. Just went so still he knew, in wolf form in the woods, anything that didn't hunt with smell would look right past him.

The idea that someone was making *new* monsters like the one he'd burned and buried was absolutely horrifying.

No wonder she was upset.

"What got you to that idea?" he asked, hoping they could dismiss the notion with logic. Because he really didn't want to face the thought of someone *making* monsters. With modern scientific knowledge and genetic technology, it was possible, he supposed. He wasn't a biologist or geneticist. But it seemed possible in a way that maybe it hadn't been a few centuries ago. At least if you weren't a god.

"Partly, what I've said already," she answered. "About their not evolving in all the time they've existed. Partly, the specificity of one of their new weapons."

"That weapon would have poisoned and killed me, too," he pointed out. "It's probably what killed the carrion birds who ate the carcasses killed by the monster. The ones I came across stank of the poison. The dead animals, too. It's not necessarily aimed specifically at your families."

"Maybe," she allowed. "Maybe. But the fact that it slows down our healing, which gives the poison time to kill us, is not something I can see happening spontaneously. No other monster has come up with that kind of weapon. And some of them have…put effort into evolving."

One of the things he'd prefer not to think about too closely. "So it feels unlikely they'd evolve this poison naturally?"

"Yes. It's possible. Anything is possible. But it's not probable."

"And that's what's led you to think they've had help evolving?"

"One of the biggest factors."

"Who would do that? Why?"

"The why is easy. To eliminate the Families. At least that's part of the why. Why turn more deadly monsters loose onto the human world…?" She raised her hands, palms up, and shook her head. "No idea."

"Probably have to discover the who to get their specific why."

"And I'm not sure where to begin with that. Maybe… Maybe if we get the poison analyzed, there will be some hint there. Some clue we can follow. Or maybe if we find the second irgotoc—"

"If there is one," he cut in to point out.

"If there is one. If we find it, maybe we'll find another clue with it."

"Lot of ifs and unknowns," he murmured.

"Which is why I'm sitting on the porch brooding instead of eating, like I should be." She huffed out a soft sound, almost a laugh. "I'm sorry I've dragged you into all this, though."

Something in her expression changed a little, almost like a different sort of worry line replaced the previous ones on her brow. He wasn't quite sure how to read that new expression though, and her scent was just one big complex mix of worry. He couldn't tease out any specifics.

"I don't mind being here," he said quietly, hoping to sooth at least a little of her troubled thoughts. "I want to help you." And feed her, and hold her, and kiss her, and fuck her, and keep her. But he wasn't going to say any of that out loud.

He pushed away from the railing. "I'll get us some dinner going. Food will help. Food always helps."

She chuckled. A real laugh this time. "It does. Do you want a hand? I can…butter toast. Probably stir something without burning it."

Her cooking skills involved buttering toast and maybe not burning the thing she was stirring. Why did he find that so fucking charming?

Because it was her. And something about her called to him. To a very primitive part of him, an instinct that went beyond logic. Oh, he had a lot of very logical reasons to be attracted to her, not least was the fact that she was beautiful and extremely capable and he'd always had a soft spot for capable women. But this was more. Because he didn't *just* want to take her to bed and spend the night finding all the places on her body that made her moan. He wanted to keep her. Wanted to spend long nights in front of the fire with her. Wanted to learn more about her world and who and what she was. Wanted…all of it.

Wanted her to stay.

Which was not only not possible, given his current status, it was not anything he'd ever wanted before.

But he couldn't be sure if he was craving the companionship simply because he was lonely and isolated. Or because he wanted that companionship from Becca specifically because she was…well, who she was.

Probably a little of both, he conceded as he went into the house to get dinner ready. He was lonely. But he didn't think he'd be craving something more than sex from another random stranger to drop into his life just because he missed company. He had a feeling there was more…potential there with Becca.

And the possibility was as terrifying as the possibility that someone was making new monsters.

CHAPTER TWELVE

Another two days passed without any signs of another irgotoc. By that third day of hunting, Becca was truly worried. Nearly panicking. Frantic to keep searching until they found something. Which wasn't the normal reaction to finding *no signs* of a monster. Usually that was cause for rejoicing and happiness. No evidence of one meant no monster. Therefore, she should be content. Instead, she was on the verge of jumping out of her skin—metaphorically.

At the very least, they should have spotted some sign of it sniffing around where the male had died. Irgotocs came in pairs—or used to anyway—and those pairs were male and female and they traveled and ate together. And they mated once they'd fed enough. She was pretty sure she'd killed the male well before that could happen—it took a long long time before a male and female pair mated, a slow process which was one of the reasons the Families had been able to drive them so close to extinction—but the female should have at least investigated the absence of the male. Yet they'd revisited the sight several times over the last three days, and no sign of any disturbances or movement in that area. No broken branches in the surrounding trees or paths dragged through the undergrowth. No digging at the place where Adam had buried the monster.

Nothing.

Damn it. What the hell was going on?

Adam, for his part, was a solid and steady support throughout the process. He didn't try to talk her out of her worry, which would have backfired and just pissed her off. Instead, he listened to her fears, hunted with her every day and into the nights. And then ensured she ate and rested once they got back to his cabin.

The more they worked together, the more…in sync she felt with him. They could exchange information without words, just a few grunts and nods, while hunting. He hadn't even had to shift to his human form for the last day while they were in the woods because their communication had gotten so good.

When he finally encouraged her to stop and rest, after he made sure she ate, they'd sit on his couch in front of his fire and just…talk. Quietly. About nothing important. Music—they were both fond of classic 70s rock, though he leaned toward heavy metal and she leaned toward glam rock. Food—which, outside of the pineapple on pizza thing, they were in agreement with most food favorites. Movies— neither of them had been to one in a theater in a while but they both liked older black-and-white films, and she admitted her soft spot for musicals. Books—they both liked ridiculously over the top thrillers, but where he gravitated toward good mystery, she was more into science fiction. They talked about travel—she'd been everywhere, he'd spent his entire life on the west coast of the US, mostly in Colorado.

As if by mutual agreement, they avoided monsters and everything to do with monsters during those quiet conversations. They only discussed monsters during the day. And they didn't talk about his family or childhood or where he grew up. Ever. He avoided any details about his life before this cabin. When he hinted, she got the impression of a great deal of sorrow. She wanted desperately to ease that information out of him, the reason behind his sadness. But because she was still keeping some secrets herself, she didn't feel she had the right.

So she let him keep their conversations on more neutral topics. And every night, he walked her to the door of the guest bedroom to say goodnight.

Despite all her worries about the irgotocs, those moments at her door were worth everything. Torture and pleasure and the heat of wanting all at once.

That third night, when they paused outside her door and she turned to face him, she found herself breathless, her nerves dancing with anticipation and the need that never seemed to leave her. He'd stopped close, close enough she could feel the heat of his skin seeping into her. She loved that he wanted to be near her. She craved some sort of physical touch, but he was careful, always, to avoid even brushing against her. The restraint was starting to drive her a little mad. She wanted his hands on her, his mouth, and she wanted him in her bed so badly she ached. Her gaze dropped to his mouth.

She was starting to forget why she couldn't just pull his face down to hers and kiss him. She knew he wanted her, too. They couldn't hide this kind of lust from each other. Her scent mingled with his and the combination of flavors was like an elixir on her tongue, cedar and citrus and spice and earthiness. She could only imagine what it might be like to finally fuck him. To taste their scents mingling as she tasted his skin. To have that taste melding in her as she slid down onto him.

Her pulse thrummed a hard, unsteady beat, her breathing deepening as her imagination provided a lot of possibilities for the night ahead if she just gave in to the want.

He leaned closer, but still kept that space between them. And she wanted to scream at him to stop, to just kiss her. She didn't. When she could think again, she was sure she'd remember there was a reason she wasn't attempting to take him to bed right at this moment.

Even if she had no idea what that reason could possibly be.

His shaggy hair fell across his forehead as he looked down at her. Her fingers itched to brush that hair back, to run her fingers through that mass of thick brown and feel the texture against her palms. Against her face.

"We should finish the grids tomorrow," he murmured, his voice deep and a little gravely.

The sound danced down her spine, making her thighs clench. She loved the things his voice did to her. "Yes," she said. Sounding too breathless for the actual subject they were discussing.

"If we don't find anything?" He moved from one foot to another and the change in stance brought him just a little closer.

He was so fucking warm. So close. She had to drag her attention back to his question, replaying it in her head so she could remember what he'd said.

"If we don't find anything," she said, "we'll expand the search area. Or…well, I will. I don't want to assume—"

"I'll keep helping," he cut her off before she could stammer out any more.

For which she was grateful. She didn't feel particularly eloquent in that moment. Trying to talk while her brain was full of very very different thoughts, involving them a lot more naked and the bed just beyond the door at her back, proved beyond her multi-tasking capabilities.

"Thank you," she said. "I really appreciate everything you've done to help me. Especially with no evidence to prove my worries are justified."

"I believe in paying attention to your instincts," he said.

Did he? Because her instincts were telling her right now that she should drag him backward into her room and fuck him until the sun rose. Or maybe that was her lust rather than her instincts. Hard to tell in that moment.

She'd been trying to be careful about respecting his privacy when he shifted, trying not to stare, or even look. Too much. But she'd given in a few times. How could she not? And he was magnificent. Having those glimpses burned into her memory only fed her fantasies. Did nothing to calm her pulse. Not when the thought of stripping him naked and having her fill, having permission to admire and touch and taste, were so front and center in her imagination.

She was so *aware* of him. Every part of her yearned toward him. She could close her eyes and know exactly where he was, how close, the way his head was tilted, even where his hands were. That awareness was both overwhelming and welcome. But also just a little bit of torture.

Swallowing, hard, she said, "I still want you to know how much I appreciate all this."

Out of habit, she wanted to declare herself in his debt. Except instinct stopped her. She wasn't sure why. The words stuck in her throat and she didn't say them aloud. Something about the sentiment felt too business-like for what they were supposed to be for each other. Although, he didn't know what they were to each other yet. Which was why she was resisting wrapping herself around him—yes, that was the reason! Still, she couldn't bring herself to insert anything into their relationship that might imply distance.

Distance between them was the last thing she wanted.

"If we don't find anything tomorrow," he said, "we'll pull out the map again and plan out a new search area."

His voice was so deep and guttural now he might as well have been sliding his hands over her breasts. Just with his voice, he brought her to the brink. Gods, could he make her come just by talking? The way he sounded just then, she suspected it might be possible.

"Sounds good." She told herself to lean backward, to open the door and go inside and put that flimsy piece of wood between them so she didn't rush this. This was too important to rush. Too important to screw up.

Instead, she leaned toward him, so that there was barely enough space between them for air. A deep breath and she'd be brushing against him. The thought of rubbing her breasts against his chest sent a shiver of heat arrowing into her core. She'd never wanted another person so desperately in all her life.

His nostrils flared as he looked down at her, and his eyes were so dark now, she could barely see any of the blue, just a bright aura around his pupils. The spike of lust that filled his scent made her head spin.

Not for the first time, she wondered why he was resisting this pull between them. She had her reasons. But she wasn't the only one working hard not to give in—she'd have folded two days ago if he wasn't so hesitant. She watched his throat work as he swallowed. Could feel his hands flexing at his side because she was so acutely conscious of his every move. He wanted to touch her as badly as she wanted to be touched. She was sure of it.

Yet he didn't. His gaze locked on her mouth when she licked her lips. His breath rasped out between them, matching her own ragged breathing. And still he didn't touch her.

His restraint was starting to worry her. If he was so determined not to give in to this desire between them, maybe he wouldn't accept they were destined for each other. Maybe he'd learn the truth and run away.

If he didn't choose to stay...

She set that worry aside. Again. She'd deal with that if it happened. She'd have to. But until it did, she had hope.

He was her hope.

The moment dragged on long enough, her nerves felt stretched to breaking. So when he took a deliberate step back, suddenly, she swayed forward as if the thing holding her upright had suddenly vanished. She blinked and straightened, trying to ignore the crawl of heat in her cheeks.

"Goodnight," he said.

And once again hurried away. Disappearing into his room before she could blink.

Damn it. She knew this was for the best. But her body was roundly disappointed.

So was her heart.

CHAPTER THIRTEEN

They were miles from Adam's cabin, deep in the woods just north and west of his territory, in a location that would have been almost impossible for ordinary humans to reach without specialized equipment, when they stumbled across the bodies. Four of them. All mauled so badly, they were difficult to identify as human.

Becca closed her eyes and let out a resigned breath. Not only hadn't they found the second monster yet, they hadn't found it in time to prevent this.

"Fuck," she muttered.

Adam shifted to his human form next to her, the minutes it took him to shift felt like a time pause, like the world stood still while he changed.

"I'm sorry," he said, his voice so quiet it was barely sound on the breeze.

"How have we missed signs of the monster, and yet it was able to do this?" She shook her head. "Not even sure how humans made it this deep into the woods."

She scowled at the bodies. Trying to detach from the loss and horror. Trying to see through her sense of failure.

These weren't the first bodies she'd had the misfortune to discover

over the years. That was, more often than she wanted to accept, the reason they knew where a monster was—the bodies started to pile up. But she hated that she'd already been on the trail of the creature and hadn't been able to prevent more kills. That felt like a huge failure.

But…humans really would have had a nearly impossible time getting here. There were steep cliffs and sharp climbs. They'd have had to work at it for days and be very determined to reach an inaccessible location to have even attempted it. She supposed that was possible. Humans could be a remarkably determined lot, whether for good or ill, and adventurous to boot.

She studied the positions of the bodies. The…scatter.

"Something isn't quite right, is it?" she asked Adam, though she was also half talking to herself.

"What do you mean?"

There was a note in his tone she couldn't identify, but she was too caught up with studying the remains to really think about it.

She stared a bit longer. Moved around the edge of the site. Studied the position of the bodies. The blood on the dark soil. She sniffed the area too, taking in the details her eyes couldn't pick up. Which might have bothered a human so she was glad her companion was shifter. A wolf would default to smells to investigate this, too.

"The bodies were moved," she said after a while. "Dragged to this location. Or… No. Not dragged." She scanned the surrounding underbrush. "Carried. There aren't enough drag marks."

"One at a time then? Or is the irgotoc female really that large?"

"It'd be large enough to carry more than one body, but from the decomposition smells, which seem to be indicating different rates—can you tell?—I'm going to guess they were moved one at a time to this spot. Maybe piled up here over several days."

"I can smell the different levels of decomp, but couldn't say what it meant."

She glanced up at him. "Is this too much for you? You don't have to stay." He might be a werewolf, but that didn't mean he was used to dead human bodies, especially ones with parts scattered around like broken rag dolls.

He shook his head. "Not the first bodies I've seen."

"Pretty gruesome sight, this one, though."

"Seen as bad before. Maybe worse."

A statement she hoped he'd explain at some point, when he trusted her more. She held his gaze for a beat, then returned her attention to the scene. "Moved. Not enough blood. Different times. Carried, not dragged."

"Would the irgotoc drag the bodies?"

"The female wouldn't if it had any distance to go. It would carry them and fly here. If it still has wings." She sighed. She hated that she had to question her knowledge of the species and didn't know precisely what to expect anymore. "But these people were carried here, not dragged in, so I'm going to assume it still has wings." She sniffed for hints of the poison the male had had in its tail spikes. "Can you smell the poison? I can't."

But she hadn't smelled the spike he'd kept from the male. He'd sealed the clothe wrapped barb into a cooler to keep it separated from everything. And after some debate, they'd decided to leave it as is and not risk messing with it. They had moved the cooler to the back of his pantry closet, to keep the thing cool, and so it wasn't just sitting out in the open. But she hadn't even looked at the piece to see what he'd collected.

She really did have to contact her family soon, especially Eric. And she had to get that spike to her sister for analysis.

"Can't smell it either," Adam confirmed. "You think that means the female doesn't have poison spikes?"

"Or it just didn't use them on the humans. Depends. On where it found them and how easy they were to kill."

A quick glance around confirmed no carron birds, dead or otherwise, nearby. That was strange, but maybe the local birds had realized these weren't the sorts of carcasses they should clean? She sat on her haunches and studied the scene from a different angle. The position put her close enough to the ground to really pull in the putrid stench of decomp, though, and she had to take a moment to dial back her sense of smell.

"Let me know if the smell is getting too bad for you?" she said after a moment. "It's really gross."

He made a grunting noise she took as agreement.

"Could we be having trouble smelling the poison around the decomp?" he asked, reasonably.

"Possible." At least one of the bodies had been here for a while and was well into the process.

And if all of them had been there that long, she'd have assumed the female had moved on from this location, which was why they hadn't found any signs of it before finding the bodies. She could have assumed this was an older body dump, a place to store food for future use, and the female had abandoned it when it had moved.

But there was a fresher body in the group. There for only a few days maybe. The face was still recognizable as a man's face, though half his skull was missing. That newer body indicated the female was still using this site.

"Teeth markings are different," she muttered mainly to herself.

The marks on these bodies were different to the marks that had been on the animals killed by the male irgotoc. That wasn't surprising. The female would have a different bite, being so much larger, with bigger teeth and a wider mouth. The female's mouth had, in the past, also had a sort of beak-like structure for lips instead of fleshy lips under a snout like the males. So the female's bite had always had that additional poke and scrape element around the teeth marks.

But again, with the evolution of traits, she couldn't be certain the female still had that more beak-like material surrounding its mouth. She didn't see signs of that in these bite marks or scrapping on the bones, though. Just sharp teeth.

She stood and paced away from the bodies to study the surrounds more closely, looking for other clues. A female typically would have a few feathers on its wings although most of the wings were a more leathery flesh similar to a bat's, but thicker. The feathers decorated the leading edge of the wings, along the bones. And if the female still had those, the feathers might have shed and been left in the area.

No sign of them, though. No feathers. No scat. No clawed foot marks. No broken talons or long lines of scraped dirt from tentacles.

She did spot what looked like a human shoe print. Which was odd. She was certain none of the bodies had come here on foot and then been killed at this location. But maybe she'd gotten that wrong? She also came across a smudged animal print in some deeper soil, but the print was too smeared to identify. Too large to have been a coyote. Not a deer or elk or other hoofed animal. Could be a bear, but would have to be a grizzly and there weren't many of those in this part of the range.

If there were ordinary animals in this area that the irgotoc could eat, she wondered that they hadn't found animal remains mixed in with the human ones. Irgotocs weren't particular. They ate what they found to eat. Because they were Ne's monsters, they were designed to favor humans as a food source. But that had never stopped irgotocs from eating whatever they came across.

Maybe the female had just devoured every part of the animals it had caught? Impossible to say. But the evidence of ordinary animals was scarce, so maybe there hadn't been enough in this area for the monster to catch. Or the animals had moved on when the irgotoc showed up. The smudged footprint could have been there for a while, sheltered by its position next to a tree.

She hunted a wide arch around the nest of remains. But outside of the shoe print anomaly and the single animal footprint, she didn't turn up anything.

No signs at all of the irgotoc. Which meant she had no direction to start searching for it.

"Damn it," she huffed as she rejoined Adam.

He stood away from the bodies, but his gaze was steady on them, and his eyes were much more yellow than blue now, a sign that his wolf side was just under the surface.

"No luck?" he asked, without looking at her.

"No sign of the irgotoc that we can follow. At least at ground level." She looked up at the pines overhead. None of them had branches big and strong enough to hold an adult female irgotoc. But the trunks themselves were thick enough if the female used those, clinging to the side of the tree like a gargoyle instead of alighting on a branch like an oversized bird. "Not having wings of my own is pretty inconvenient at times like this," she muttered.

She thought of her youngest sister, Rea, and smiled. But Rea wasn't here now.

Becca considered one of the larger trees, eyes narrowed. She wasn't the best climber in the family. But she might be able to drag herself up far enough to see if there were any claw marks in the bark. She picked the largest tree because it was the one most likely to hold the weight of an irgotoc.

"Can you hold my sword?" she asked Adam.

"What are you going to do?"

"Climb as high as I can get and see if I can spot claw marks."

"I can shift and do that."

"Your wolf can climb trees?"

She wouldn't have expected that. Not with a werewolf, given their size. Her wolf was a little larger than an ordinary, mundane wolf, but nothing like the size of a werewolf. And her wolf had never climbed a tree. Leapt onto a stable branch, sure, but scaling the trunk of a tree using just claws? Never

"I can get up to one of the lower branches," Adam said.

"They'll never hold your weight."

"That one will. Long enough for me to look around." He pointed to a branch about twenty, twenty-five feet over their heads. It wasn't thick or strong enough for an irgotoc. But maybe his wolf wouldn't crack it instantly. Maybe.

"You sure?"

He gave her a look that she took to mean, "You doubt me?" Then he returned to his wolf form. When the process was complete, he gave himself an all-over body shake and trotted back a few steps to look up at the tree branch.

She looked between him and the branch dubiously. That branch wasn't going to hold for long.

"Just be careful," she said. She got another of those looks for her trouble, and even in wolf form, that look carried a lot of arrogance. She might have smiled if they weren't in such a horrible location.

Adam took a running leap, jumping smoothly up to the branch, landing near the trunk, and scrambling to hold on as the branch shook under his weight. She winced, but when the branch didn't crack right away, she let out a breath.

Once he had his back paws on the branch, he carefully climbed his front paws up the tree trunk, until he was stretched his full length, staring up into the higher points on the tree. His tail twitched a few times.

A cracking sound echoed through the clearing and Becca gasped. Before she could even shout a warning, though, Adam leapt clear of the branch, landing on his feet just a few feet from her, as the branch collapsed in a heap of sap and needles and bark.

Adam sat on his haunches and licked his front paw. Looking very unconcerned with his close call with potential disaster.

"You sure you're a wolf and not a cat?" she asked.

That earned her a snort and a low growl.

"Did you see anything?"

Head shake.

"Damn."

She had no idea what to think. There were mangled bodies. Brought to and left in a location that was pretty inaccessible to humans. And yet, outside of a single shoe print and that smudged animal print, there were no signs of *anything* being here except for the bodies. And the shoe print could easily belong to one of the people killed.

It had to have been the female irgotoc. What else in these woods would do something like this? None of the bodies showed signs of being killed by a human. No gun powder smells or knife wounds. Too many sharp teeth marks. But no evidence of mundane animals causing this either. She wasn't picking up the scent of any other kind of predator in the area. Just wolf from Adam. And most mundane animals would frankly have eaten more. Irgotocs devoured their prey, but the females did sometimes save and store food in a sort of nest for later use. This *looked* like a female's nest.

But no sign of the irgotoc. Which meant no way to track it.

Now that she was certain it had been killing humans, the imperative to find it beat at her. It wouldn't stop killing humans. It was designed to crave human flesh. She had to find it. Soon. Now. Or more people would die.

Frustrated, she paced deeper into the woods again, and started another search of the surroundings. The stench of death and gore from the bodies overwhelmed her sense of smell when she was too close to them. And even away from them, the smell and taste still coated her tongue. Not a great experience, even if it wasn't the first time. She always hated that smell. But once she was farther from the nest of bodies, she could open her senses more.

She tried a larger circuit of the area this time. Adam joined her, searching in his wolf form, stalking through the undergrowth, his nose close to the ground as he sniffed his way through the trees. They searched until the sun started to dipped low in the sky. Taking in wider and wider circles of forest.

Nothing.

Just the scent of wolf where Adam passed. At the farthest point in their circuit, she finally picked up the pungent smell of mountain goats and a small group of deer that had passed this way. There were a few places with broken branches and crushed undergrowth that could have been signs of a monster. But when she'd tried to follow those trails, they'd disappear and left her with no direction to go again.

Chasing a monster that could fly. Fucking frustrating.

Finally, when it was pitch dark, and she still couldn't find a trail to follow, she plopped down on a decaying tree trunk and let out a huff. "Shit," she muttered.

Adam shifted to his human form. He didn't sit on the tree trunk next to her, but stood close to her back. "Even with our night vision, we aren't likely to find the monster tonight. There aren't any signs of it."

"I suppose I could camp out at the nest and hope it comes back. But if it does, it'll be because the thing has killed another human." She shuddered. Failure. She was failing the humans in this area. Failure was not acceptable.

"You can't camp out there indefinitely anyway."

She waved that away. "If needs be, I could. To catch a monster. But I don't think that's the best course in this situation. There's no guarantee it would go back to that particular location anyway." The thought that it might have additional nests for dumping bodies just waiting for her to uncover was appalling. "I need to get back to your place and check the news for missing persons. Maybe if I can figure out where the female is killing, where it's been finding the humans, I can find a trail to follow."

She wasn't convinced that would work, but she had to try something. Without even a scent mark to follow, she could wander these woods all night and not get anywhere.

"You need food and rest, too," Adam said.

Another wave, but absently as she considered her options.

Adam's hands landed softly on her shoulders, the touch so unexpected, she gasped. His hold was warm, his palms large on her arms. And the physical contact sent a bolt of happiness through her blood. A sense of rightness that left her dizzy. He'd been so careful not to touch her, not to even brush against her, that having his hands on her now shocked her speechless.

He rubbed her shoulders gently and tipped her backward so he could look over her shoulder and into her face. "You need rest," he said. "And food. So you can hunt more tomorrow. You're more likely to miss something if you're exhausted. Not too many days ago, you nearly died. This isn't the time to push your endurance."

Her heart did a funny little flip in her chest and everything in her softened and melted. His care, his efforts to take care of *her*, turned her to absolute mush. The sensation offset her frustration and her need to keep pushing until she found the monster. He was right. She'd been close to death not even a week ago. She felt herself again. But there was no telling what aftereffects the poison might have on her. She wasn't even sure if she'd be able to heal quickly again, or if her healing ability was still compromised. She had no idea if any of her other usual strengths had been compromised either.

Better to ensure she had as much strength as possible before confronting the monster. And going back to eat and rest would also give her a chance to do some research. All of which was a lot smarter than wandering aimlessly through the woods with nothing more than hope to direct her.

"Fine," she said. "We'll go back and eat and rest."

"Thank you," he murmured. As if she'd just done him a favor by agreeing to let him take care of her.

She stared up into his eyes, faintly yellow in the darkness, even in his human form, and felt her heart do another of those funny little flips.

If she wasn't careful, she was going to fall head first in love with him before he learned the full truth. Before she had any idea if he'd stay with her willingly or not.

A great way to ensure heartbreak.

CHAPTER FOURTEEN

Adam let Becca have the run of his television and his laptop in the living room while he cooked dinner. He needed the time alone to think, and cooking gave his hands something to do while he considered what they'd discovered that day.

He was more than a little worried those bodies hadn't been left by the monster. At least not the monster Becca was tracking.

Something about the mauling, the violence of the torn bodies. The location—outside his territory, but not by a lot, and in the general direction of the new pack. He'd seen bodies left like that before. When a rogue wolf who'd lost control of his animal side went on a rampage.

In a healthy pack, the alpha kept the wolves in their care from attacking humans. While shifters might be stronger and faster, there were just a whole lot more humans in the world. And if they ever discovered shapeshifters really existed, their fear would drive them to try and eliminate the threat. A war wasn't something any of them wanted. So shifters of all species moved secretly through the human world, attempting to keep their existence hidden in myths and legends.

To maintain that secrecy, there couldn't be a lot of human bodies turning up with wolf teeth marks all over them. Especially with modern forensics. No one wanted evidence of shifter DNA in the hands of human scientists.

So in a healthy pack, wolves were prevented from doing anything that might endanger the pack by drawing it to the attention of the world, including killing humans. But outside of the pack structures and supports, when a lone wolf lost control and went feral, humans did get killed. And that brought the wrong kind of attention.

That was why packs didn't tolerate rogue wolves near their territories. Why they either killed them or drove them off. Couldn't risk the wolf bringing down disaster on the entire pack. His own pack had been unique in their efforts to rehabilitate the rogues. Most packs just eliminated the problem in the most efficient way possible.

He couldn't even blame them for that. The discovery of those bodies today had brought the problem into sharp relief for Adam. The deaths had been too obviously caused by something not mundane. Not even a grizzly would have left bodies like that.

The fact that the dead had been moved was the part that really bothered him, though. Moved from where? And why that specific location?

Close enough to his territory to feel like a threat.

Becca was convinced the deaths were the result of the irgotoc. She was used to thinking in terms of these nightmare monsters. And she might well be right. She'd told him irgotoc females made nests to store dead things for eating later. She'd assumed what they'd found was that kind of nest. But…

But what if she was wrong? What if this was something…else?

And if it was something else, if it was a threat to Adam from the pack, the danger it posed to Becca was intolerable.

He minced onions and sliced mushrooms for his creamy pasta sauce, the movements rote, as he considered the positions of the bodies today. Something about that also bothered him. The…parts, for lack of a better word, had been apparently scattered around at random. But when he'd leapt back down from the pine tree branch before it broke, he'd swear he saw a kind of pattern in the remains. An arrangement.

That glimpse of the nest from the higher angle kept resurfacing in his mind's eye.

The arrangement of the bodies hadn't looked quite so random from that height. The scene had looked…posed.

He couldn't explain that impression. From ground level, everything looked violently scattered about and messy. Just as if a vicious animal —or rogue wolf—had tossed the bodies around and left them where they fell. But that randomness felt purposeful when looked at from above. And he couldn't shake the idea.

That there'd been no blood trail or scuff marks or anything at all to indicate the bodies had been dragged there was another thing. The irgotoc flying them in was the most reasonable explanation.

But the foot print and animal print mark Becca had found still gave him pause.

And then there was the smell. Three of the four bodies had been decaying long enough that that stench overrode his ability to get too deep into the various scent elements. That part felt purposeful, too. Had the bodies been fresher, he might have been able to scent if there was wolf on them or irgotoc.

There *had* been an underlying hint of wolf. But he couldn't parse it out well enough to say if it had been werewolf or just ordinary mundane wolf stumbling briefly across the bodies weeks ago.

The memories of the nest, including of the smells, made cooking a complicated process in that moment. The smell of the rich white sauce he was making—specifically because it wasn't red and there wasn't beef involved—was a sharp contrast to the memories. But thinking about the details of the afternoon was starting to make his stomach turn. Even his wolf wasn't crazy about things that had been dead so long. So he pushed those thoughts aside.

Enough to recognize that the scene *might* have been more than one of Becca's monsters. He'd have to keep his eye out for any other suspicious signs. Anything else that might help him determine if he needed to worry about the pack to the north yet or not.

Or worse, if he had to worry about another rogue wolf nearby. One that could draw the attention of the pack to him. And through him…

To Becca.

He dumped thick fettuccini noodles into a large pot of boiling, salted water, trying not to think about harm coming to her because of him. Yes, she fought monsters, and they'd only met because she'd been injured during one of those fights. But after a week, spending so much time with her, getting to know her… The idea of her getting hurt again cause him actual physical pain. In his gut. Deep. And all that would feel infinitely worse if something *he* did got her hurt. His wolf rebelled at the idea so strongly, he wanted to wrap her up in soft soft cotton and keep her close so he could ensure she was always safe.

A weird and unreasonable desire. He recognized he wasn't being rational. She was a hunter. It's what she did, and, honestly, he admired the hell out of her for her work The rational part of his brain accepted the risks she took. They were necessary and important, and she was amazing. But the part of him that had been much too lonely for much too long didn't want anything to happen to her. Didn't want to risk her wellbeing even a little bit.

He'd been outside the pack too long. Maybe he was closer to the edge than he'd realized. Which made him desperate to hold on to the person who was easing his loneliness. Not just easing. He hadn't even had those periods of panic whenever he thought about being without a pack sweeping through him much this week. The knowledge of being outcast hadn't overwhelmed him in days. He knew he'd been thinking about the fact that he was a rogue, packless, because those were the things forcing him to keep some distance between him and Becca. But those thoughts weren't triggering the panicked need to claw his way back to the structure and companionship.

There was more there than just companionship between him and Becca, though. Leaving her at her door every night was getting more difficult with every passing moment. Especially since he could tell she wanted him as much as he wanted her. She wasn't trying to hide her feelings, even if she'd been able to.

It was difficult for shifters to lie to each other—their scents gave them away—but some of them could still disguise their scent and make parsing out their emotions more difficult. He'd had to learn that trick under Chris Corwin during Chris's tenure as alpha, because Chris had been too volatile and reactive. Not wise. Not patient. And Chris had viewed the Walsh siblings as threats from the start. So Adam, Gabriel, and Siobhan had all learned fast how to muddle their scents and make it impossible to figure out what they were thinking with just a single sniff.

Adam wasn't doing that with Becca. Part of him thought if she knew how badly he wanted her it might scare her off. And in the end, that would be for the best. He was rogue and under constant threat. He did not want to drag her into that.

But she wasn't hiding her feelings either. And the lust there was such a delicious mix, such a heady elixir, he could wallow in it and lap it up like water. He wanted to lap her up, too. All of her. Find every sensitive spot that would make her moan and spend all night ensuring she did. Until they collapsed into exhausted sleep. Then he wanted to wake her with his mouth just to see how she'd react.

The fantasies plagued him every night after leaving her at her door. The awareness that she was so close, with only flimsy wooden barriers between them. His sleep had been wrecked by that knowledge, and he couldn't even regret it. Frankly, he preferred the unrequited lust to the loneliness of the past few years. But the lust was leaving him in a state, and soon even the exertions of the hunt weren't going to be enough to force him to walk away from her. Different if she didn't want him. He'd be able to keep his distance then. But she did. And that was wearing down his resistance. Fast.

Becca pushed into the kitchen just as another of his frequent fantasies started, which created a strange sort of disorientation that the real world was mixing with his fantasies. One look at her expression, though, and he banked his needs.

"What's wrong?" he asked.

"Dinner smells good," she said as she dropped into her seat at the table.

Yes, he now thought of that as her seat. He'd likely think of that as her seat from now on. "Is that the problem, or was that an attempt to deflect from my question?"

She chuckled, a sound that made his wolf preen. "Deflecting," she admitted. "I'm frustrated and want to talk about food, not the utter lack of information I managed to dig up."

"Fair enough. The food will be ready in…" He glanced at the clock on his microwave. "Pasta should be done in another three minutes, if you don't mind al dente. Do you want garlic bread with this?"

"That sounds lovely, if it's not too much trouble."

Nothing was too much trouble for her, but he didn't think he should say that out loud. "You want a glass of wine? I had to open a bottle of white for the sauce." He picked up the bottle and looked at it. "A Zinfandel. Nothing fancy, but I had a sip before pouring it into the sauce. Tastes pretty good. And it's cold."

"Yeah. I think I could use some wine. Thanks." She smiled up at him, her eyes soft, as he placed a glass in front of her.

"Sorry I don't have any fancy wine glasses. The water glass will have to do."

"I like this. Feels rustic."

He snorted. "Rustic I've got a lot of."

"Thanks for cooking. Again."

"It's nice having someone else to cook for." He kept his back to her as he said this, afraid he'd give away too much. "I only have so much freezer space for left overs."

"I'm not used to having left overs."

When he raised his brows at her over his shoulder, she grinned.

"My youngest sister could devour the entire contents of a super-sized grocery story in an hour and then be hungry for more food two hours later."

"I'm assuming that's an exaggeration?"

"Not by much."

And he'd thought shifters ate a lot.

"We all learned to eat our fill in one sitting because if we took a break and expected to come back to our food, we'd been sorely disappointed. Nothing remains behind if Rea is around."

She spoke with such affection for her sister, it made something in Adam ache. He missed his brother and sister.

Shaking off the melancholy, he concentrated on melting butter and garlic together for the toast. Patiently waiting for her to either talk about what was bothering her or tell him more about her family. Or just sit quietly, enjoying the peace together. They did that comfortably, too. Which was…strangely unprecedented in his life. Sitting in comfortable silence with a woman he also wanted this desperately? He was certain that had never happened to him before. Not least because he wasn't sure he'd ever wanted another woman quite this desperately before.

He slid the butter-soaked toasts into the broiler, scooped the fettuccini into the white sauce to mix everything together, checked on the toasts, pulling them out just before they burned. All in a companionable silence that left him feeling remarkably content. Hard to believe they'd only met a week ago. And the first few of those days she'd been on the verge of dying.

God. The thought that she'd been so close to dying hit him hard now. Harder than it had at the time. He'd worried, of course. And he'd done his best to ensure she recovered. But the thought now, that he could have lost her before getting to know her, ripped at his insides like wolf claws tearing into his gut.

He had to concentrate on filling the pasta bowls, setting garlic bread on a plate for the table, getting out the parmesan from the fridge, all to keep his hands from shaking at the sudden burst of terror the thought of having nearly lost her sparked. He just hoped the strong garlic, butter, and cream smells covered his lapse.

After he placed her food in front of her and took his seat, she finally broke the silence.

"I came across a few missing people reports. But not enough. Not recently. And they're scattered all across the area. Nothing to indicate a pattern."

"They haven't disappeared from the same location? Same hiking path? Same small town?"

"Nope. Nothing consistent to indicate where we might start looking for the irgotoc." She sighed and took a bite of pasta. Her eyes widen. "Oh, Adam, this is delicious." She closed her eyes and hummed under her breath.

And Adam felt the power of her pleasure in his entire body. Heat seeped into his blood. Hunger for her definitely stronger than his need for food in that moment.

When she opened her eyes, the lids soft as she smiled at him, his pulse raced. The only thing that kept him on his side of the table was the knowledge that she needed food and rest after their hunt today. His need to care for her kept his need to fuck her in check. But only barely.

He cleared his throat. "Glad you like it."

"Definitely a good choice." Her voice sounded a little husky and breathy, too.

Since he hadn't bothered to hide that sharp leap of pleasure and lust her appreciation had sparked, he knew she'd read his reaction. That she was still just sitting there, not hiding from the undercurrent or running away, did something to him on a very deep level.

Food first, he warned himself. Lust… Well. He wasn't sure what to do with that yet. But he was getting closer and closer to ignoring all his common sense. The future and his sucky circumstances be damned. He wanted her. She wanted him. Shouldn't that be all that mattered?

Since both conversations about food, and that undercurrent of desire, were all a lot more pleasant than their find that afternoon and her frustrated search, they kept the rest of their dinner conversation to food with some more stories about her family sprinkled in.

And Adam continued to ignore all the warnings his conscience threw at him.

CHAPTER FIFTEEN

After dinner, Becca helped Adam with the dishes. Because he cooked, and was actual good at it, she'd tried to insist on doing the dishes every night. He'd argue against it. She was his guest—true enough. She was still recovering—less true since she was recovered. He liked washing dishes—she highly doubted that.

Finally, they'd compromise, and she'd helped. He didn't have a dishwasher, so she washed, he dried and put things away because he knew where everything went.

Given the frustration of the hunt, and the fact that they'd found human remains today, the routine of washing dishes after dinner was such a welcome reprieve from her own thoughts, she could have stood at the sink scrubbing plates all night.

Especially with Adam next to her.

Which was also a wonderful distraction. He was extremely careful not to touch her while they worked. A caution that was impossible to miss because there were a few moments when taking the dish or pot without touching her required some interesting contortions. But he stood close enough she felt his heat along one side of her. Close enough, she was surrounded by his scent mingling with the lemon smell of the dish soap.

The desire, the *want* in his scent was as delicious as the pasta he'd made. She wanted to lap up that flavor and spend the rest of the night savoring it. He wasn't even trying to stifle his reactions anymore. Letting her know how he felt, even if he continued to keep his physical distance. And she wasn't stifling her responses either.

Restless energy burned through her, anticipation and impatience making her fidget when she wasn't forearms deep in soapy water. Every time she glanced at him, that restlessness rose and she found herself leaning closer to him, trying to brush against him whenever he was near enough. She was on the verge of just grabbing him by the t-shirt and pulling him in for a kiss, but that little warning in the back of her head—a voice that sounded suspiciously like her mother's—kept her from rushing him. She couldn't force or manipulate him into staying with her. That wouldn't break her curse. She had to do this very carefully. Handle this right.

And she wanted to do this right. She wanted to ensure he came to her because he wanted *her*. No divine imperatives forcing his hand. She *liked* Adam. Yes, the sound of his voice and the heat of him standing near made her skin tingle and her thighs clench. But it was more than the lust. He…

He had her back. In the hunt. She'd never had that with anyone who wasn't a member of her Family. And there were so few monster hunters in the world, as often as not she hunted alone. Having Adam with her was… She wasn't sure how to describe it. Contentment. Satisfaction. Security. Those words sort of worked. But it was even more than that. A sort of rightness she hadn't experienced before.

The rightness of having him by her side did more to her than just about anything else. She didn't want to lose this now by making a wrong move. By rushing things or, worse, making him think she considered this all a passing moment. She couldn't force him to stay with her, but she could ensure he understood that's what she wanted.

How to do that without freaking him out was the real question, though?

Especially since he was the one keeping his distance and resisting the pull between them.

She'd spent dinner regaling him with stories about her Family—monsters they'd fought, but also just the silly things large, long-lived families got up to—and she'd seen the longing and sadness that occasionally swept through him. Something about families? The bittersweet flavor in his scent got strongest when she talked about her siblings. Which always drove her to want to ask more about his family. Did he have siblings? Where did they live? Or—and this was her worry—had he once had siblings who'd died? That bittersweet nostalgia had a flavor of grief in it. If he'd lost a close sibling, his reluctance to talk about his own family made a lot of sense.

She wanted him to open up to her, hoped he'd trust her soon enough to do that, but she also didn't want to push against his grief. She understood, only too well, the complicated pain of losing a beloved family member. Her father's death was recent enough to still cut deep. She'd been avoiding the Family home in New York for the last year because of the memories it held—good ones she didn't want to hurt through. She'd handled the grief by diving into the hunt and staying away from most of her Family as much as she could. Not because they wouldn't be supportive—and understanding since they were all grieving—but because she couldn't take in that much of everyone else's feelings yet. She needed to deal with her father's death on her own. That was just how her grief was working.

Most of the stories she'd told Adam about her family were about her siblings, with only passing mentions of her parents. She loved her father so much. And he hadn't just died of old age. He'd been murdered, with the help of her own cousin. That left the whole conversation about his death a lot more sensitive for her. She couldn't discuss that with Adam yet. Especially without discussing more of the specifics of how the Seven Families worked.

So she understood why he wouldn't discuss his own grief with her yet. And maybe that would take a while. Maybe he'd never be able to fully discuss it. But she hoped he'd trust her enough with at least some explanation one day soon.

She handed him the last plate and then leaned against the sink, drying her hands as she watched him finish. The simple movements of him drying a plate and putting it away drew her attention to his hands. Adam had very good hands. Long fingers, wide palms. He had excellent forearms too, sinewy with corded muscles, dusted with dark hair. He needed a shave, which had her wondering how often shapeshifters had to shave. Could they just…shift and have less hair, or more, if they wanted? Or did they have to manage their body hair in human form the way humans did?

It was startling to realize how little she knew about wolf shifters, at the level of ordinary day-to-day activity. She knew the big stuff—heightened sense of smell, super fast, shifted whenever they wanted, not driven by the moon like myth claimed, lived in packs most of the time but not always. But there were a lot of small things, like the shaving question, she'd never had cause to consider.

With all the monsters they had to study and hunt, she supposed it made sense they didn't learn much about other beings who were, at best, peripheral to what the Families did. But she couldn't have been the only one over all the millennia who discovered their Nam-tar amongst the other beings that inhabited the planet. Not *all* Nam-tar were humans. There had to have been some from the shifter communities. Yet she knew significantly more about humans than she did about the mundane aspects of being a shifter.

"Do you shave?" she asked, when he turned back to her after putting the plate away.

He frowned. "Why is my beard getting too unruly?"

She chuckled. "I was just realizing how little I know about shifters. Simple things like if you have to shave or can just…shift the hair away." She felt her cheeks heating at that admission but she didn't turn away when he stepped closer.

"You didn't notice the razor and shaving cream in the bathroom?"

Now she was really embarrassed. "I haven't been snooping through your bathroom cabinets." Did that sound defensive? That had sounded defensive.

His crooked grin did nothing to ease her embarrassment, but it did shoot lust through her so hard she wobbled and had to brace herself against the counter.

He rubbed his face, the sound of his skin scrapping against his beard scruff teasing her until she wanted to replace his hands with her own, just to see what that scruff actually felt like against her finger tips.

"Suppose I do need a shave," he commented, though his attention was focused on her. "And yes, I do have to shave. When I remember to."

"Ever consider growing a beard?"

"Too itchy." He eased a little closer, also leaning against the counter.

"What happens when you shift? Does the beard just…come back when you return to human form?"

He nodded. His gaze dropped to her mouth. "Have to get my hair cut, shave, all those ordinary things when I'm in my human form. Shift doesn't change those things." He shrugged. "Does erase tattoos."

Her brows rose. "You can't get a tattoo?"

"Oh, I could get one. But it would be a waste. First shift to wolf and back and the damned thing would be gone."

"Shame." He'd probably look really sexy with a tattoo or two. She'd never considered tattoos one way or the other, really. She liked body art. But she didn't pay much attention to the inherent sexiness or not-sexiness of it. With Adam, though, she fell on the side of body art being sexy. Though she suspected that was because everything about Adam was sexy to her.

"You think I should get a tattoo?" His brows rose, his expression making her thighs clench.

"Only if you wanted one. But, yeah, it would be a little pointless, huh?"

"Little bit."

His attention was so focused on her mouth, now, she could hardly breath. Or maybe she was breathing too hard. Her heartbeat was certainly pounding too hard. Her skin nearly vibrated from awareness of him, standing so close, in her space, so so easy to just reach out and touch.

What the hell were they talking about again? She couldn't think enough to concentrate on conversation. She had a feeling the conversation they were having was silly anyway. But for the life of her, she couldn't remember because she was just too damned *aware* of him. Every part of her yearned toward him.

And the need to get her hands on him soon left her edgy and restless.

He leaned down, just a little, as if he couldn't resist the pull either. She wanted to scream at him to stop resisting and just kiss her. She wanted to scream at herself to not rush him by wrapping herself around him like a blanket and devouring him at the kitchen sink.

Mostly, though, she just wanted to feel his big, thick body against hers and couldn't think enough to worry about the rest.

"Becca," he murmured her name, his voice rough, deep.

The sound danced along her skin, lighting her up until she thought she might melt. She swallowed, and realized she was nodding. Though she wasn't sure why. Was she telling him she understood what he meant with that single word? That she was desperate, too. That he could kiss her and she'd welcome him.

All of that was true.

Hard to tell who leaned closer first. They seemed to flow together as one. He bent down, she rose up. Their breaths mingled. The need to have him, to taste him, wiped out all other thoughts. Everything. Gone. Except for Adam.

She whispered a quiet word. A simple, "Yes."

And their lips finally met. A single gentle brush, almost like they were testing each other. A test they both passed because in the next instant, she was in his arms, flush against his chest, her arms tight around his neck, and the kiss exploded into all the heat and need she'd been holding in for eternity.

CHAPTER SIXTEEN

Becca sank into the kiss, a desperation unlike anything she'd experienced before swept through her as she melted into him. Adam's arms tightened around her waist, his hands fisted against her lower back, as if he couldn't quite trust his hands even as he devoured her with his mouth. She wanted to tell him to touch her, she was desperate for his hands on her. But she didn't want to pull her mouth from his long enough to speak. Instead, she used her own hands on him, tangling her fingers in his hair to keep him in place as she kissed him even deeper. Rubbing against him because she couldn't feel enough of him at once.

None of it was enough, and yet it was everything. His kiss deep and overpowering, taking as much as giving. His scent wrapped around her, mingling with the smells of dish soap and the lingering hint of garlic. The flavor of him on her tongue, just a bit of wine and garlic there too. And the strength of his arms around her, bracketing her in all those glorious muscles.

He rolled to one side so he was leaning back against the counter and she collapsed against him, her full body, thighs to breasts, tight against the solid wall of him, letting him take most of her weight. He still wouldn't unfist his hands, though, which was starting to drive her a little crazy.

She untangled her fingers from his hair, and gave in to her need to explore, sliding her palms across his chest, over his shoulders, down his arms, up the sides of his waist. His muscles tightened wherever her hands traveled, a thrilling reaction she started to crave. She slid her hands along his back, brushing her fingers up his spine, dragging her nails gently over the cotton of his t-shirt. Having that thin bit of material between her and his skin was maddening.

She tugged at his shirt, waiting for permission to move it, not sure he'd let her. And when he lifted his head from her, took his mouth off hers, she thought she'd gone too far and he'd run away again.

He leaned back, she prepared for the excuses, but instead, he wordlessly stripped off his t-shirt and then pulled her back into his arms again. This time, his hands open and gripping her own shirt as she settled against the heat of his chest. And oh gods was that the exact perfect place to be. She didn't want to be anywhere else. Just right here, with his arms around her, his hands on her lower back, his hot skin under her palms. She ran her fingers through his chest hair, groaned when he tugged her so tight to him her hands were briefly trapped. Internally, she was chanted, *yes, yes, yes*. But she was too busy kissing him to get those words out.

Every inch of skin she could reach was warm, and solid, and delicious. Suddenly his mouth wasn't enough. She wanted to kiss him everywhere. All over. Explore each inch. She ran her hands along his waist and he sucked in a breath. When she did it again, he grabbed her hands and pressed them tighter against his skin.

"Ticklish," he muttered against her mouth. "Touch me harder."

She grinned. But she followed his instruction eagerly, dragging her hands over him roughly, scrapping her nails along his lower back, kneading his muscles as she tried to fit herself even closer to him.

And now that he'd stopped trying *not* to touch her, his hands were exploring as well. Over her back, down her waist, across her hips, to her ass, tugging her up hard against him. He leaned against the counter and widened his stance, settling her into the v of his thighs so she could feel him everywhere, feel the hard line of his cock against her lower stomach. That thick bulge drove her, knowing he wanted her, knowing she wasn't the only one swept up in this heat and madness.

He slid his hands up her back again, sweeping against her spine in a long glide that made her arch against him and moan. Gods he felt good. She rubbed her breasts against his bare chest, resenting the material of her shirt and bra. She wanted the feel of that crisp hair and solid muscle against her skin.

She wiggled against him as she reached for her shirt, his growl firing her blood. With barely a break in the kiss, they ripped her shirt off over her head—actually ripped it, she suspected, since she heard a tear. Her bra hit the floor, and she sank into him again, so relieved to feel him against her bare skin she shivered.

Any space between them felt like an insult now, but she couldn't seem to get close enough. She wanted him over her, under her, all around her. She wanted his scent sinking into her skin and wanted to wallow in all that heat. She needed friction, and sweat, and *him.*

"Bed or counter," she said against his mouth, too desperate for pretty words or coyness. Gods, she couldn't remember what coyness even meant at this point. She couldn't remember why she should be careful. Why this was important beyond the moment. She could barely remember her name, except how much she loved when he groaned it. That sound she savored. That sound she'd remember. The world outside him and this moment? Not so much.

"Bed," he muttered, his mouth dragging down her throat, his hands back to clenching her ass so tight she was up on her toes against him.

To her surprise and delight, he stood away from the counter and lifted her off her feet in a single swift movement. Breathlessly, she wrapped her legs around his waist, never taking her mouth from his skin as he carried her through the living room and up the stairs.

She licked a long line over his throat, bit gently at the base of his neck, taking a great deal of pleasure in the way he hissed in a breath and his hands tightened on her ass. "Love the way you taste," she said against his shoulder, grazing her teeth over his hot skin. "Want more."

"You can have everything," he muttered, his voice deep and rough, a delicious scrape against her nerves. "But save some of that until I get up these stairs so I don't trip."

She laughed and moaned at once. "Hurry."

They reached the top of the stairs in an instant when he put on a burst of shifter speed. She clung tighter to him, happy beyond measure with him, grateful for the speed, and squealing a little at the unexpected leap.

He didn't bother with turning on lights or even asking which direction. He took her to his room, a place she hadn't been yet. She hadn't wanted to invade his privacy—curious though she'd been—by peeking into his bedroom. And now, she was too caught up in him to look around. She noticed the cool darkness, cool enough she shivered and snuggled closer to Adam's warmth. She noticed the scent of him everywhere, permeating the small space. And she noticed the large bed. But only when he dropped her on it, tumbling onto the thick mattress with her in a tangle of arms and legs and hot hot kisses.

Stripping out of the rest of their clothes took less time than getting up the stairs. And even then she was impatient to have those last vestiges of material gone. To have him naked and this time able to fill her gaze with him, feel her hands and mouth with him. Despite the many times he'd stood right next to her without clothes, this was the first time she'd felt free to really worship and savor that thick, glorious body of his. He really was magnificent. Muscled and sinewy and strong. The hair on his chest thick and crisp. Thick thighs that she just wanted to wrap herself around.

She dragged her teeth over his neck, her fingernails down his chest, and thrilled at his moan. There was freedom too in needing to be rough, in him wanted her touch to be hard, because she wasn't feeling gentle in that moment. She was too hungry. She didn't want him to be gentle with her either.

He kissed his way over her shoulder, his bread scruff scrapping her skin. She hadn't thought she'd be grateful for bread scruff before, but here she was, grateful he had to shave and that he hadn't and now she got the glorious sensation of feeling that scruff against her neck, scrapping over her chest, nuzzling her sensitive nipple just before he took her into his mouth. He sucked at her breast hard enough to make her arch into him. Bit her just hard enough to send electricity arching through her.

So much sensation she didn't know what to do with herself. She was all restlessness and need and hungry movements. Digging her fingers into his hair, wrapping a leg around his thigh to pull him closer. Panting and exploring and crying out whenever he licked or sucked or gripped a sensitive part of her. He found the place on her hip that made her see stars. And when he settled between her legs, spreading them wide, and licked into her pussy, she lost all sense. She was a nerve ending, a pulsing bud of sensation, all of her centered on the wet, hot slide of his tongue over her clit, through her folds, driving her crazy with his beard scruff scrapping her inner thighs as he devoured her.

She came so fast and hard, she screamed in a shattering burst of breathless extasy. Trembling and overwhelmed as the orgasm shook through her. Jumped when he nipped her inner thigh. So sensitized, the rub of his chest hair across her stomach and breasts as he rose over her was almost too much. Almost. But not so much that she stopped him. In fact, she rubbed harder against him as he settled over her and kissed her on the mouth, needing to both feel him everywhere and settle her nerves.

"More," she said against his mouth, sinking deep into his kiss. Surfacing only long enough, to murmur, "I want more of you."

"You have all of me," he said, and sank into their kiss again, his hands gliding over her neck and up to cup her face.

She took him at his word, explored, filling her hands with him. When she cupped the thick weight of his cock, he sucked in a breath and pumped into her hand, as if he couldn't help himself. Which fired her blood. Having him as helpless to this hunger as she was. Knowing he was just as swept away. She stroked him, using the moisture at the tip of his cock to slick and smooth her movements, gripping him hard and gliding her hand up and down until he was panting, his forehead resting against hers, his jaw tight. She loved it. Every moment. Watching his control slip away.

She bit his shoulder, hard, and then said, "I want you inside me.

Now."

"Yes." So guttural a groan it was barely a word.

He pulled away from her long enough to slip on a condom, and then he was covering her, pressing her into the warm mattress, the weight of him so perfect she wanted to live just like that. This was all she needed. No air or food would ever be more important than having Adam's weight on her, hot and strong, his scent filling her head, mingling with hers until she started to think of that combination as a single scent. Their scent. *Them.*

The feel of him sliding into her, slowly, stretching her, the friction of finally finally having him sent her reeling again, her nerves lighting up, and her body tightening, coiling.

"So good," she muttered. Or maybe that was him. She'd lost track. Didn't matter. Having him inside her was everything. Perfect.

And the hard, pounding thrusts as he fucked her were perfect, too. So fucking perfect. She ground up against him, wrapped her legs around his waist to angle her hips better, and when he sank even deeper, she gasped.

"Again."

"More."

Yes, yes, yes!

The rub of his hair, the slap of skin against skin, the hard thick thrusts of his cock inside her, all of it overwhelmed her, filled her, and sent her once against tumbling over a sharp, shocking edge that left her entire body vibrating with sensation and satisfaction. Even more satisfaction when he pulsed inside her, when he shook, when he groaned her name as his own orgasm took him.

And when he collapsed against her, holding her in a tight hug that felt so real and solid and forever, she knew the greatest contentment she'd ever experienced in her life.

This was what perfect felt like, she thought as she slipped into a contented drowsiness, hugging him back even as her muscles and bones felt like jelly. This was what they were made for. What their future could be.

So long as she could convince him to stay.

CHAPTER SEVENTEEN

Adam woke to the scent of Becca everywhere. On his skin, in his sheets, on his pillow. The scent of her in his room, filling the space and mingling with his own ordinary scent…those two together made up something new and unique and utterly perfect.

And he had no idea how he'd ever be able to walk away from her now.

He'd have to. Sooner rather than later. He was a rogue wolf with no pack and no stability and no safety to offer. Even his home was likely something he'd have to abandon soon because of the pack to the north. He could never keep her in his life when he had so little to offer her.

But he wanted to. He wanted to keep her forever.

She rolled against him, in the cocoon they'd made of his blankets, and his arms came around her instinctively, before he was awake enough to think consciously about that need to hold her close. She was soft and warm, mussed from their night and from sleep. When he looked down into her face, the quiet beauty of her made his throat tight. And his arms tightened reflexively, pulling her even closer.

He nuzzled her messy hair, soaking in her scent and warm softness, wishing he could live the rest of his life in this moment.

Wishing reality would remain at bay for just a little bit longer.

By some miracle he didn't think he deserved, reality did hold out a bit longer. She woke with a sleepy smile, looking up at him with her beautiful brown eyes soft. And without a word, pushed up to kiss him. A gentle brush of the lips. But it was the *familiarity* of it that shook him to his bones. The sense that this was a regular morning ritual for them. They did this all the time. Waking in each other's arms and kissing good morning.

He didn't want just a gentle kiss this morning, though. He wanted their familiar mornings to involve more. So he nudged her over onto her back and kissed her, slow but deep. Her answering passion sparked something hot and sharp in his chest. Something possessive. Too possessive for their situation. But he didn't care. Not just then. With her soft and naked and warm beneath him, she was *his*, he was *hers*, and this was a moment they could have.

Gliding his lips down her jaw, over her neck, he bit the skin where her shoulder and neck met, an area that made her shiver and moan. He scrapped his morning beard over her chest, then down across her breast, her peaked nipple. And her moan deepened.

"I love the feel of your scruff on my skin," she murmured.

He was amused those were her first words this morning. "I noticed. I may never shave again."

She chuckled, a sound that dropped into a gasp when he took her nipple into his mouth, sucking her hard, teasing her with his tongue. Her hips rolled under him, seeking, and knowing she wanted him, so easily, so quickly, left him hungrier for her. He slid down her body, licking and nipping his way to her hipbone, and that sensitive spot in the hollow just above her thigh. She actually whined when he licked her there, a whimper of need and impatience. He could probably survive for a week on that sound alone.

But he liked the sound of her panting and keening toward an orgasm more.

Shouldering her legs wide, he settled between her thighs and looked his fill. Not sure how long he'd have her, he wanted to savor every single second. He gently rubbed his cheek against her inner thigh, watched her stomach muscles tremble, felt her thigh muscles clench against his arms. Wetness between her folds drew him, demanding he taste. And taste he did. Feasting. On her. On her flavor, like an explosion of perfect salty sweet against his tongue. Loving the way she gripped his hair with one hand, the sheets with the other, the way her body trembled and thrashed as she sought relief. He kissed her, sucked her, tongued her until she tightened like a bow, called his name, and came with a keening cry that imprinted itself on him.

That sound became a part of him, something he would never be free of. Didn't even want to be free. His. All his.

She softened, jerking a little when he brushed his lips over her sensitized flesh. Before he could do more than kiss her inner thigh again, she launched up and shoved his shoulders. Pushed until she'd rolled him onto his own back. And then her mouth was on him, sliding over his chest, down his waist. Mindful of how sensitive his skin was, she was rough with her touch and her mouth, biting him none too gently, scraping his skin with her nails and teeth. His turn to shiver, to pant, to groan.

Her mouth closed around his straining cock, just the very tip, her lips wet and soft, her mouth hot and tight. She fisted the base of him and then slid her lips down, taking him into her wet heat, sucking him gently at first as she learned the length and girth of him. Then taking him harder, using her fist and mouth. And god but it felt so good. So fucking right. New and familiar and everything.

She took him right to the edge of coming, right to the point when his control teetered on a fine edge, his muscles shivering, his jaw tight. The sheets clenched in his fists tore under the strain. He had more sheets. When the strain got one blink from beyond his control, he reached down to pull her up and over him, burying his hands in her hair where it tumbled in soft messy waves around her face, kissing her like she was his very air.

He only released her long enough to slide on a condom and then he rolled her over him again, letting her straddle him, thrusting up when she gripped his cock and guided him inside. When she dropped fully, hard, taking in the full length of him, he lost the last shreds of control. He thrust up against her again, watching her beautiful breasts bounce with the impact, watching the color rise up over her chest, across her cheeks. He gripped her hips tight, probably too tight, and held her as she rode him, rolling her pelvis until she found just the right rhythm. Until they were both desperately dancing together.

He kept his eyes open to watch her face, watch where they joined. Seeing her slide over his cock left him nearly feral with that possessive need. *His*. His wolf growled in his head. Wolf shifters didn't have destined mates like some shifters. But in that moment, he could almost believe in them, almost think…

The thought washed away in the next instant as she started to pant and grinding harder against him. He set a thumb to her clit, gentle pressure, a few firm rubs. And she exploded in a body shaking groan that pulled him right over the edge with her. He came so hard he had to close his eyes, the sensation dragging everything from him until he felt drained, rung dry.

Happy.

She curled down and wrapped herself around him, his own personal weighted blanket of warmth and femininity. Their scents melded together again, along with the scent of sex and sweat. Her arms came up limply around his neck, holding him close. And he never wanted to be anywhere else. Not ever.

He hadn't had a real home in years, since he'd been forced to leave his pack. Hadn't had a place he felt like he belonged. Settled. With her arms around him, her gentle breath on his neck, her weight and warmth as she clung to him… He felt home. This was his home.

She was his home.

The thought of having to leave this place of safety and connectedness, the idea that he'd have to let this home go too, punched him with such a sharp arrow of dread and pain he nearly gasped aloud.

He must have made some sound, because she pushed up enough to smile at him. "Am I too heavy?"

"Not even a little," he said, patting her ass. "Stay here all day if you like."

She purred and rubbed against him, her breasts scrapping over his chest so that he felt the hard little nubs of her nipples. "Oh I could," she murmured. "I wish I could." She sighed and settled her head into the crook of his neck, clinging to him tighter. "Wish the real world wasn't quite so…intrusive at the moment."

He couldn't agree more. If they didn't have to worry about the outside world, they could stay just like this. At least for a little longer.

Her stomach growled.

Or at least until they needed to eat.

She rose up to give him an embarrassed look and rolled her eyes at herself. "I guess I need food after all that. And probably a shower." She frowned.

He cupped her cheek. "What's that expression about?"

Her shy shrug tugged at his heart like nothing he'd ever experienced. "I like the way our scents mixed together. Don't really want to let that go yet."

Ah, Becca. If she only knew what she'd just done to him with that comment. He pulled her in for a kiss, because he didn't have the right words to offer. So he let her know with his mouth that he agreed, and he felt the exact same way.

The call to feed her, to ensure she was taken care of, was the only thing that could drag him away from her in that moment. "Tell you what," he said, pushing her hair back away from her face so he could savor the sight of her beautiful eyes. "I'll go downstairs and get us some food and we'll have breakfast in bed. We can stall on all the real-world stuff for a little longer that way."

"Oh yes, please. That sounds perfect." She snuggled against him. Hugging him tight.

And Adam accepted that he was a goner. This was going to hurt in the end. Maybe even more than when he'd walked away from his pack. But he'd deal with that pain later. Right now, he intended on making the time he had with her as memorable, as perfect as he could. So she'd remember him when she left.

Because he'd never forget her.

CHAPTER EIGHTEEN

Breakfast in bed proved as delicious as anything Becca had ever tasted. The food, of course, was good—Adam made a yummy omelet for them with bacon and vegetables and enough toast to feed a small army. But sharing food in bed with Adam, surrounded by their mingled scents as they talked about things that had nothing to do with monsters was heavenly.

The shower together after was pretty glorious, too. Especially because that somehow kept their scents mingled, even after they got out. And Becca was absolutely certain that was her new favorite smell, having their scents mixed together into this one uniquely them smell. The entire morning was like floating on a cloud of contentment and possibilities. They could have this. All the time. This life could be theirs.

So long as he stayed.

So long as she didn't fuck things up.

Underneath the contentment, she was painfully aware of all the things she hadn't told him yet. She'd been as honest about her family, about the Seven Families, as she'd felt capable. And she'd really only left out the little part about the curse and how he was her destined mate and the one person who could break her curse. Oh and also the fact that she carried a wolf spirit in her that could leave her body, taking her human spirt with it, which left her human form encased in stone until the wolf returned. Other than those two little things, she'd revealed most everything else to him.

She also couldn't shake the feeling that he was hiding something about his past, too. Well, of course he was because he never talked about his past. Never talked about his family, his life in Colorado. She got the impression he'd only admitted to living in Colorado because he'd slipped when they were talking about travel. She knew there were things he was keeping from her. So she wasn't the only one who hadn't revealed all yet.

She would, though. She'd have to. And she hoped he would as well. They could lay out all their histories, make the decision to stay together in full knowledge of the implications.

All very logical and straightforward.

So long as whatever he was hiding didn't throw a wrench into that logic. And so long as her last secrets didn't send him running away.

Lot of "so long as"s left to worry about.

When they finally made their way downstairs and she spotted all the maps she'd left scattered across his couch last night, she remembered the other thing she had to worry about. They still had a monster killing humans somewhere out there in the woods.

She paused next to the couch and ran a hand through her damp hair, looking down at the maps. She'd used a pencil to circle the location of the nest with the four bodies. And then tried to find information about missing persons, marking them on the map too. But as she'd told Adam, there was no pattern. She tried to see it again this morning, but it just wasn't there. The missing people were from scattered locations as far away as Seattle, none of them consistently taken from one town or location.

If any of them were victims of the monster, it meant the monster was traveling all over the area looking for its next meal. And yes, if it was the female, it could fly to those places. But in the past, irgotocs would find a source of food and stick with it until they either ran out or a hunter caught up to them and put an end to the killings.

"This moving all over the mountain isn't typical behavior," she said aloud. And was grateful Adam made the leap with her thinking and didn't need clarification.

"Part of its changes? Or not the monster?"

"Those are the questions." She sighed. "And until we find it, I can't answer them." Tracking something whose behavior she didn't know anymore was a lot more complicated that she'd have liked. "I need to call my brother."

Eric was the head of the Logan Family now and the one to whom all the information about everything flowed. He'd known if there was any information on irgotocs evolving and what their new behavior entailed—if anyone else had come across them. Since she'd still assumed them extinct right before this hunt, it was possible no one else had encountered them either. Which left her exactly where she was now.

"The cell service is spotty but better outside in the clearing," Adam said. "I'll go for a run, check the perimeter of my territory."

She glanced at him, eyebrows raised in question.

"To give you privacy," he said and tapped his ears. He blinked and said, "I suppose you're used to extremely good hearing, though, aren't you?"

"Among my Family, yes." She smiled. "But I do appreciate the thoughtfulness. I don't need the privacy, though." She had no intention of discussing the fact that she'd found her Nam-tar with Eric yet. The last thing she needed was advice from her big brother about all this. What did he know about it anyway? If she wanted *helpful* advice about her love life, she'd call their mother or their sister Judith who'd found her Nam-tar already.

"I need to check the perimeter anyway," he said, his gaze dancing away from hers as he did. "Do you need anything before I go?"

She shook her head. Frowning after him as he left through the back door. She followed to the porch a few minutes later, after going over the map one last time. She found Adam's clothes neatly folded on the single rocking chair on the porch and no other sign of him. A ridiculous impulse to sniff his clothes, to drag in more of his scent and reassure herself he was real, drove her off the porch to pace around the clearing between his cabin and the tree line.

No one had warned her about this fear and obsessiveness that developed when finally meeting her Nam-tar. She got itchy and nervous when he wasn't close by. Restless. Worried about his safety. Worried she'd made the whole thing up and he wasn't here after all.

Absolutely ridiculous since she was quite literally staying in his home and her body still felt the physical imprint of their night—and morning—together. He was real. She shook her head at herself and made her call.

Which proved enlightening on a bunch of levels.

"You found your Nam-tar?" she nearly shouted down the phone at Eric when he admitted as much to her. "What's her name? When did you meet her? What does she do?" She peppered him with more questions before she finally took a breath so he could actually answer.

Except that he didn't, the bastard. "We can discuss that some other time," he said. "You need to know we have a problem. With the Elementals."

That got her attention. She straightened and blinked at the pines.

Elementals didn't normally get involved in the fight between the Families and the monsters. They were neutral. Things of nature that were quite literally immortal. They *were* the elements—water, air, fire, earth—and would exist as long as this planet existed in a form that allowed for their element. Earth and fire would survive even after the rest of the planet was scorched clean. Air would last until the atmosphere evaporated. Water… A little harder. Eventually, though, all the elements be destroyed when it finally came to the end of the Earth in a few billion years. But until then, Elementals weren't beings that could be killed. They generally considered themselves "above" the machinations of living creatures with their finite lives. Even more uninvolved than the gods.

But sometimes, every once in a while, an Elemental sided with either the monsters or the Families.

And when they sided with the monsters, it always spelled deadly disaster.

She listened carefully to Eric's story of the Water Elemental working with monsters on and around their Family estate in upstate New York, the creatures breaking into their home, nearly killing their little sister Rea—which was an impressive and horrifying feat—and then hinting at a larger conspiracy.

"Whatever the Water was talking about," Eric said, his voice sounding harsh and deep even over the cellphone, "we're going to have to keep our eyes open for anything strange happening in the monster world. There's something going on and we need to find out what."

She had a lot of questions for him, about the sided-Elemental, and how it had been dispatched, but first, she had to tell him… "I've already come across something strange in the monster world. That's why I'm calling."

She explained about the irgotoc she'd killed, the changes, the fact that they couldn't find a female but they had found a nest of human remains. The way the poison had slowed her healing and she'd nearly died.

Eric's one word response when she mentioned almost dying was, "Fuck."

Which, from her big brother, was kind of gratifying. She was positive he'd be upset if she died. But it was nice to know for sure he cared.

They all accepted that death was part of the job. That it could happen at any time. And mostly, none of them thought about the possibility much. But for all of the Logans, the murder of their patriarch, their beloved father, had been a wake-up call. Alexander Logan had found is Nam-tar centuries ago—Becca's mother, Laksana—and so her father had had an ordinary death. Still. He'd been murdered. By someone he should have been able to trust. And it had changed the calculus, at least for Becca, on the possibilities of death. She got the impression it had done the same for Eric.

"The…person who's helping me, who saved my life, he kept one of the irgotoc's tail spikes. So we'll be able to analyze it as soon as I can get it to Judith. Hopefully find an antidote before anyone else comes across an evolved irgotoc."

"This person who's helping you," Eric said, cutting to the very subject she wasn't ready to discuss with him. Any more than he'd been willing to discuss his newly found Nam-tar yet. "You can trust him?"

"Yes," she said without hesitation. Even though there was so much about his past she didn't know. She realized she probably shouldn't trust Adam as much as she did. Didn't change the facts. Everything he'd done so far involved helping her, seeing to her comfort. He'd jumped into the irgotoc fight to help her, even though he hadn't known what he was getting into. Hell, he'd saved her life when he didn't even know who she was. Those weren't the actions of someone she couldn't trust to have her back in this.

"Anything else I should know?" Eric asked. She could tell by his tone he was asking about more than the monsters.

She didn't take the bait. "I called to see if anyone else had heard anything about evolved irgotocs. I need to find the female. But I can't trust my knowledge of their behavior anymore."

"Irgotocs," Eric grunted. "Of all the monsters to suddenly show up and evolve."

"Especially with something that works against hunters more effectively than any of their previous weapons," she said. "Monster evolution hasn't worked that way in the past."

"No," he agreed. "It hasn't."

"I've been thinking…wondering… What if the monsters had…help evolving? What if someone was building better monsters?"

"That would be pretty fucking horrible."

She agreed. "I don't want to make a leap here," she said slowly. "But this, coupled with what the Elemental said, seems too coincidental to be just a happy accident for the irgotocs."

"Yes, it does," he said.

"You don't suppose the sided-Elementals are not only trying to help the monsters destroy humans but are maybe…"

"Helping the monsters evolve to make that effort easier?" His growly sigh was obvious even over the phone. "I'm afraid of just that."

"Well that's not good."

"No. And it means we've got our work cut out for us."

She frowned at the dirt, kicking at a rock absently, as she considered her most recent hunt. "I tracked the male irgotoc over two days, after I picked up the strange series of animal killings just over the mountains. It didn't start killing in the Cascades. It started killing on the eastern side of the mountain, lower near the plateau." She squinted up at the trees, still too deep in thought to see the woods. "If I...go back to the start. Try to trace the monster to its origin... Maybe I can find something?"

"A place to start," Eric said. "Good suggestion. But I'll see if any of the other Family are available to start tracking the creatures from their origin. I want you to concentrate on finding the female first."

She snorted. "No, I thought I'd leave it to roam around killing people instead of tracking it down and destroying it as I'm bound to do by divine edict."

She could practically hear him rolling his eyes at her smart-ass comment, and his long-suffering sigh carried clearly through the phone. Which was gratifying for a little sister.

"Your sarcasm aside," he said, "do you need help with the female?"

"If I can find it, I'll be fine killing it. It's finding it that's proving impossible. I may have to go back to the beginning, anyway, just to pick up its trail if I can't locate it in the area soon. I was hoping you'd have some useful information about these newer versions of irgotocs."

"Not specifically. Sorry about that."

"It was a long shot." She shrugged even though he couldn't see her. "I'll keep you updated on the hunt. And if I come across anything...suspicious."

"Check in regularly. Every couple of days. With everything that's been going on, I want everyone touching base more often."

Everything meaning the sided-Elemental as well as what had happened to their father a year ago. Eric took his new role as head of the Family very seriously. And she appreciated his attention to all their safety—even if, as his younger sister, his attitude sometimes felt overbearing and annoying.

"Please," he added begrudgingly at the end.

Which made her grin. "That nod to politeness the influence of your Nam-tar?" she asked.

"I'm not talking about that right now. Especially not over the phone."

"Fine, fine." She bit her bottom lip. She probably should tell him she'd found her Nam-tar too. But... Not yet. She wasn't ready yet. Especially, as he'd pointed out, over the phone. Their cellphones were secured. They had the money and resources to get the very best equipment. But even the most secured phones could still be compromised. And she didn't want to risk Adam's life by bringing his importance to the attention of enemies.

The possibility of something as terrifyingly deadly and impossible to kill as an Elemental coming after Adam left her breathless. She nearly dropped to her knees at the sudden, horrifying thought.

"Becca?" Eric's voice, too alert to her silence. "You okay?"

"Fine," she repeated. "Good. Just need to get going. I'll call again in a few days. Text me if you get any information about irgotocs that I might need."

"I will. You sure you're okay?"

"Grand. Fine. Perfect. No worries." She winced. Well if that didn't sound sketchy as hell.

Fortunately, her brother didn't push. "Stay safe," he said. "I'll be in touch."

After they'd disconnected, Becca took a moment to consider the scary realization she'd just had. Adam was her future. Her way out of the age-old curse that haunted all the Families. But he was also her weakness. Killing him to get to her would be...diabolically effective. On so many levels.

That it hadn't occurred to her before left her stunned. If they had sided-Elementals to worry about, those beings knew and understood what Nam-tar were and what they represented. Going after her Nam-tar would not only destroy her, it would be an excellent distraction.

Suddenly, keeping Adam's existence, and his importance to her, a secret from the outside world felt imperative. At least until she could ensure he was safe from this current enemy.

The thought that he could be in danger left her desperate to have him close again, to assure herself he was well. She wanted to race out into the trees and track him down, find him. Stick to his side always so she'd know he was safe.

Instead, she took a deep breath and sat on the back porch steps to wait for him. She might be driven to never leave his side, but until he understood their bond, her clinging and desperation weren't likely to endear her to him.

She needed to come clean. Tell him everything. And soon.

Because it might be the only way to keep him safe.

CHAPTER NINETEEN

Adam padded through the trees in his territory, letting his wolf senses guide him and hunt for any disturbances while his brain focused on other things. On last night with Becca. And the reality that came crashing in with the new day.

The reality that he'd been dishonest with her. And he had to fix that. Sooner rather than later. He had to tell her the truth. About his past. About his status. He'd been selfish, keeping that to himself and thinking he could still have her, for this short period of time, without revealing who and what he really was.

But she needed to know the truth.

He was stalling, though. Leaving to patrol while she made her call. Stalling because he wanted a few more minutes, another hour, of her thinking well of him. Just a little longer of having her look at him with those gorgeous brown eyes, seeing *him* and not his fallen circumstances.

For the first time since making the choice to leave his pack, he really resented the position he'd been forced into. Resented it in his bones.

Though, he had to admit, if he hadn't been here in these mountains, he might not have met her. They might have continued on never knowing each other. A true tragedy. Didn't make his current predicament any better or easier, but at least he'd had the chance to know her.

On his last circuit of his territory, at the very edge of the northern border, a scent brought him up short. He stilled and sniffed the air. Faint. But there. Too close.

The smell of another wolf.

Fuck. They knew he was here, for sure now, and they were coming close to his land. Which meant a challenge. Soon. The fact that they'd left enough of themselves behind for him to detect their presence meant they didn't care if he knew about them. They wanted him to know he was on their radar.

He followed the faint scent of wolf until he found the marked tree where the werewolf had purposefully left their scent—not with the usual piss but by rubbing against the bark, leaving a slightly different, much fainter mark. Harder to find, actually. But not impossible.

A fucking test? To see if he could pick it up? To test his strength? Probably. He had two choices now. Leave his own scent behind, prove he'd found theirs. Or pretend he hadn't. Pretend he wasn't aware of the near encroachment. Let them think he was a weaker shifter, one they could ignore as harmless.

Except that wasn't how most packs would think. There was no such thing as a harmless rogue wolf. A weak shifter meant the plunge into insanity hit faster. The stronger the shifter, the longer they could survive without a pack. He'd gone for three and a half years already. A long time for any werewolf, even a born one and not a converted one. But the new pack would be worried about his stability, whether he was dangerous to them or not. Proving he'd found the spy's scent might reassure them he wasn't a dangerous rogue. Yet. Might push off the confrontation. At least until he and Becca found the second monster. A fight with the new pack while there was still a monster roaming the mountains, killing humans, would only complicate things.

If there was a monster. If that nest of remains they'd found yesterday belonged to the monster and wasn't…something else.

He considered the scent of that wolf on the tree. Sniffed a little deeper, trying to parse out something nudging at his instincts.

The faint scent of wolf around the remains. The shoe and smudged animal print Becca had found. The possibility he'd considered yesterday.

A human shoe. A faint wolf scent.

Same scent. Same wolf as he was smelling now.

Son of a bitch.

He'd worried about the nest, worried it hadn't been the monster who'd been killing humans. If it wasn't, if it was this wolf... What did that mean?

Another rogue? A pack with a murderer in their midst?

With the site of those bodies close to but outside his territory, and the scent of this same wolf there as well as near the border of his territory... None of that could be a coincidence. But what did it mean?

A threat. It was definitely a threat. He just wasn't sure what kind.

His lip lifted in a snarl he couldn't control, a low growl leaking from him. The undefined threat had the hair along his back standing up.

Ignoring the strange wolf's scent mark now was impossible. Only one choice.

He rubbed his fur along the far side of the tree, just enough to leave a faint hint of his scent signature. Enough that if the wolf was a strong enough shifter, they'd find it. A weaker wolf wouldn't notice it as any different to the first mark. In fact, a weak wolf wouldn't notice either mark until they were right on top of them.

But Adam was certain the wolf who'd left the mark wasn't weak. Whatever else, this was a dangerous shifter, strong enough to keep their presence subtle. Patient enough to make a threat without even showing their snout. Able to sneak around this close to Adam's lands without getting caught except as they wanted.

Very, very dangerous.

And he'd left Becca at his house without knowing this threat existed.

The sudden punch of panicked adrenaline sent him racing back toward his cabin at his fastest speed, without even stopping to consider the instinct. She was a hunter, she fought monsters, she could fend off a dangerous werewolf… If she knew to expect an attack.

Anyone could be taken by surprised. Anyone could be caught off guard by a threat they weren't anticipating.

The thought of his fierce and strong Becca being hurt because he'd hidden his past from her nearly closed his throat. He pushed faster, moving at the top edge of his speed to reach her, so fast he'd be nothing but a blur to any humans watching. Middle of the day, moving like this was a risk. But he didn't care. He had to get to her, warn her. Now.

He never even questioned the instinct.

He hit the edge of the tree line near his cabin and skidded to a stop. Scented the air. Becca. Coffee. No wolves.

Panting, he allowed himself to sink into the loamy dirt for a few moments to calm his racing heartbeat. She was safe. There were no wolves in the immediate area.

But then another scent hit him. Something…familiar. Not wolf, but…

Fuck.

He shifted at his quickest rate, a speed that left him a little breathless and achy when he reached his human form. He rolled his neck as he crossed the small clearing to his back porch. No sign of her outside, so he assumed Becca was done with her call. He paused on the porch to slip into his jeans, sniffed the air again. Harder in his human form to pick out the faint, subtle scent, but it was still there. Just at the edge of his senses.

Death.

That hadn't been there earlier on his patrol. The scent of a dead body, of decay, that was new. Something that had happened while he was at the farther end of his territory.

Near the other wolf's scent mark.

Not Becca, though. He was certain of that. He'd felt a moment of panic, an instant hit of terror, when he caught the scent. But the decay was too strong. Whatever the dead thing was, it had been dead longer than an hour, longer than the time he'd been away from her. So not Becca.

That knowledge was the only thing that calmed his raging wolf and kept him from slamming into his house like a madman to find her.

Making an effort to keep his hands from shaking, he opened the back door and called her name as he entered the kitchen. She wasn't there, but the smell of fresh coffee in the coffee pot warmed the room. He hurried to the living room. Not there either. But a still steaming mug sat on one of the side tables next to the couch, and the maps she'd been studying for days were spread out on the floor and couch.

"Becca?" he called again, working to keep his worry and fear at bay. She was fine. She was fine. Here. Probably just in the bedroom or bathroom. He started up the stairs, looked up…

And there she was on the landing, frowning down at him. "Hey. Everything okay?"

He reached the landing in a single leap and pulled her into his arms. He couldn't help himself, couldn't have stopped the impulsive move if he'd tried. She hesitated for a brief beat, then wrapped her arms around his waist and held tight.

"You're not okay," she murmured. "What happened? What's going on?"

He buried his nose in her neck, pulling in her scent to calm himself. That familiar, beloved smell went a long way toward settling his raging, panicked wolf. When he could bare it, he lifted his head and looked down at her. A frown creased her brow, tugging the lush line of her mouth downward. He kissed her, because he had to, a gentle brush of his lips against that frown, before he straightened again. But he didn't let her go. He couldn't just yet.

"We need to talk," he said. "But first, I think there's another body. Somewhere close. Human, not animal. It wasn't there when I went out. But I found something at the north end of my territory, came back to tell you…about everything. And caught the scent."

"Another body? You're sure it's human?"

He nodded. That part of the scent at least had been unmistakable.

She closed her eyes and winced. "Shit. And this close to your cabin? What the hell is the monster doing?"

"That's what we have to talk about." He gripped her tighter, afraid to let her go, afraid she'd run away the minute he started his explanation. "I have reason to think it's not the monster."

"What, then? Who?"

"I can't be certain about the other bodies, but this one... I'm... I think it might be another werewolf."

CHAPTER TWENTY

Becca studied Adam's face. His wolf was near the surface, his eyes glowing yellow in the dim landing light, blocking all signs of the blue. He was only dressed in his jeans, so he hadn't taken the time to slip into the rest of his clothes when he'd shifted back to human form. His hair was mussed, his cheeks reddened, and sweat trickled down his temple. Under her palm, his heart pounded hard, like he'd just run a marathon.

"Another werewolf?" she asked, carefully, keeping her tone calm and even.

Because his scent was a chaotic blend of fear and panic and just a little anger, and she couldn't understand why another werewolf would provoke that kind of reaction from him. The dead body wasn't great news. It was pretty horrible news, actually. But his panic didn't seem to directly relate to that. Hard to tell, though. There was a lot in his scent and she couldn't pick it all apart to work out what he was thinking. So she had to resort to a more straightforward approach.

He let out a rough sigh and ran a hand up through his hair, mussing it further. He kept his other arm locked around her waist, keeping her tightly pressed against him. Since she didn't want to be anywhere else, she didn't mind that hold. But his agitation and worry sparked her own fears.

"How much do you know about wolf shifter packs?" he asked.

"Like I've said, not much at all really. Less than I even realized until I met you." She tried to smile but he didn't smile back. A trickle of fear moved into her blood. She snuggled closer to him and his arm at her back tightened. "What are you trying to tell me?"

"Werewolves need packs," he said, his tone abrupt. "Whether born or made, all wolf shifters have to have a pack. They…they *need* that structure."

"Okay." She hadn't heard that before but she supposed it made sense. Her own wolf leaned toward an attachment to family groups and loyalty. It was one of the reasons her cousin's betrayal to the Family had hit so hard.

"It's a driving, biological need to be within the structure of a pack," Adam said again, meeting her gaze. "Wolves outside packs… They don't last long."

"What happens to them?" She realized even as she asked that Adam was, at least outwardly, alone here. There wasn't a pack he'd ever referenced. Wasn't one she'd seen. Or scented. No other wolves but him in this territory. Territory he called "his" not "his pack's." The point of what he was trying to tell her slowly sank in.

"Most," he said, "go insane in a short period of time and have to be killed. For everyone's safety. Without pack structure, wolf shifters lose control of their wolf side and go feral. They start killing with abandon. Dangerous for any nearby pack. Dangerous for all shifters. Risks exposure to the human world."

She pressed her lips together as she took all this in, nodded slowly even as she studied his face. "How long do most wolves survive without a pack?"

"Months. A year or two if they have a degree of control. If they were made werewolves, not born to it, and abandoned by their maker outside the pack, even less time. They usual go feral almost immediately and have to be put down."

"How long have you been alone?" she asked quietly.

He let out a long, slow breath, and a muscle along his jawline jumped. "I was born a werewolf and born into a pack, so I had a firm base, and a lot of control over my nature. I was with a pack for most of my life. So that helped."

"How long?"

"It's been three and a half years."

She gasped. More than three years, without the structure he was telling her he needed. For someone who'd seen a hundred and ninety years, three years didn't feel like a long time. But given what he'd just told her, three years seemed like an eternity.

"You haven't gone feral," she said. Not asked. He was obviously in full control of his wolf. If he wasn't, being around the dead bodies yesterday would have trigger something in him. Something more than disgust. She'd dealt with feral animals in her life. She'd dealt with all kinds of beasts. She knew Adam was still well in control of himself.

"I haven't," he said with a short, jerky nod. "Yet. But…it's out there. A thing I keep waiting for. Fighting against."

She opened her mouth to ask if there was something she could do to help, some way she could fix this for him. But having that conversation required her to explain what Nam-tar were, and she didn't want to derail what he was telling her.

Next, though. Once he'd told her all he needed to. She'd tell him everything, too. She'd waited too long as it was.

"But the thing is," he continued, "because of the way packs will respond to any lone wolf in their vicinity, I moved here because there were no other werewolves around. No packs claimed any territories close enough for them to even notice me. I could live quietly under the radar with no one the wiser." His jaw tightened before he said, "But in the last few months, a new pack has moved in north of here, started to form and grow. Well outside my territory. That red dot on my map? That's them. I was hoping to go under their radar. Based on what I found today, I haven't."

"Tell me."

He explained about the faint scent of wolf, purposefully marked, just at the edge of his territory. Too obvious to have been an accident or mean nothing, but subtle enough a weaker shifter might have missed it. He told her he'd been suspicious at the nest because of the scent of wolf there, the animal print and shoe print. He couldn't explain why he'd thought of the werewolves when they were at that site, but he had. And while she still thought that had been the work of the irgotoc, she had to take this new information into consideration. If this had all been wolf shifters, there might not even *be* another irgotoc.

In some ways, that was a relief. No impossible-to-track monster out killing people. But it also meant her chances of tracing where the original irgotoc had come from were going to be a little more difficult. She still had to find where it had come from, see if she could trace its origins. Something she realized she hadn't discussed with Adam yet. Again, she waited, though. His information first.

"Then when I raced back here to make sure you were okay," he said, "I smelled the dead body. Inside my territory this time. Too close to miss. But it hadn't been there when I started my patrol."

"It wasn't there while I was outside talking to my brother either," she said. "I would have picked it up. Whoever put the body there must have done it in the last…twenty minutes maybe. I haven't been back inside for long."

"Which means whoever it was, they were probably watching us close enough to monitor our movements."

"Or they just got lucky with the timing. You would have picked up some evidence of them. I would have. In the last week while we were hunting for the monster. We would have found…something." A scent. A marking. Something. They'd been literally hunting and paying attention to everything in their surroundings for the last week. If there'd been a wolf shifter close enough to spy on them, they would have picked that up.

Then something else in his sentence really hit her and she felt her heart speed up for a new reason. "You raced back here for me? To make sure I was safe?"

He settled a hand on her cheek, holding her gaze, his thumb brushing softly against her cheekbone. "You didn't know there could be trouble. You didn't know about the wolves and the chance of them attacking. Even the best fighter can be taken off guard if they don't have all the information."

"You were worried the wolves would come for me?"

"Because of me." His hand at the base of her spine flexed and flattened against her. "And because I'd kept all this from you, you were vulnerable."

"Why *did* you keep this from me?" Not that she blamed him. She'd kept things from him too. With every intention of telling him everything. She had to tell him everything. But she'd made excuses not to reveal all just yet. All the excuses had made sense at the time. The more he revealed, the less those excuses held much water, though.

"I didn't want you to know I was disgraced. An outcast. A potential threat. I'm not a danger to you. At the moment." He sighed. "But I didn't want you to look at me differently when you found out I didn't have a pack."

"You said you were born into a pack. What made you leave?" She got the feeling *that*, more than the actual fact of him being a lone wolf, was the reason he'd kept most of this to himself. "If you don't feel like you can tell me that, it's okay."

Though she really hoped he'd trust her enough to explain. But she had to keep reminding herself, even after last night, they were still getting to know each other and she still had a long way to go to earn his trust.

"It's… It's a long story."

"Okay. It's okay. I don't need to know." She *wanted* to know because she wanted to know everything about him. But if he wasn't ready to talk about it yet, she had to respect that. "We should go investigate the body. See if it is a wolf killing or a monster killing. That will probably help decide what we do next."

"If it was one of the wolves, leaving a body in my territory is a sign. A message to me."

"Of what? And why a human and not just a deer or something like that?"

"Human… I'm not entirely sure. The message… They know I'm

here. Exactly where I am. And they don't intend on letting me just live here quietly."

She frowned. "They've killed a human, though. Maybe more if the remains from yesterday were actually their responsibility and not the irgotoc's. Isn't that the kind of thing a pack is supposed to prevent? To help maintain secrecy? The whole reason they kill lone wolves who might kill humans."

"It is. Which is the other thing I'm worried about. If it's just a message from the new pack, they could have used any animal. Yet the remains have been human. That feels deliberate. And if it is, it's… possible there could be another rogue wolf in the area."

"We need to go see the body," she said. "We need to determine if it's a monster kill or a wolf kill."

"Yes." He looked down at her again, and to Becca's surprise, swooped in for a hard, solid kiss. His arms wrapped around her, his mouth firm, his scent filled with a strange sort of desperation.

And then he stepped away from her. Completely releasing his hold. She missed the physical contact immediately. It took an act of will not to walk into his arms again. He obviously needed the space for what was to come. She'd give him that.

But she didn't like it.

"I'll get my sword. Meet you downstairs."

He was gone in a blink, moving at that speed that made his form blur.

She hurriedly retrieved her sword from the guest room and dropped the scabbard strap over her head on the way down the stairs, ensuring the strap was angled across her chest so she could easily reach up and withdraw the weapon. She also made sure to slip her dagger into the ankle scabbard inside her boot.

Whether they were hunting wolves or monsters, the weaponry was the same. And she didn't dare go without all of it.

Given how upset Adam seemed, the implications of what this might mean for him, she realized as she reached the back door that this was the first time in her life she was actually hoping the trouble was caused by a monster.

CHAPTER TWENTY-ONE

Adam waited on the porch, still in his human form, agitated and unable to stay still. She hadn't sent him packing, hadn't even put distance between them, when she'd learned he was a rogue. She wasn't rejecting him. At least not yet. And he was going to take that glimmer of hope.

A mean little voice whispered that she didn't really understand yet. That when she thought about all this, really understood what he'd been telling her, she'd leave. Why wouldn't she? Why would any woman stay with an outcast who could go insane at any moment?

But she hadn't left yet. She wasn't rejecting him yet. In fact, she seemed determined to help him. She'd said "we" went talking about investigating the new body.

So fuck the mean little voice. He'd take the hope.

He'd never been so relieved in his life as he had seeing her safe and unharmed in his house. No matter what happened between them after this, he had to make sure she stayed safe. That felt like an imperative to his wolf, and in this, he and his wolf were in complete agreement.

She came out onto the porch with her sword already strapped on, her head lifting as she scented the air.

Someday soon, if she didn't leave, he wanted to ask her about that hint of wolf he got from her. The way she so often approached the hunt almost like a shifter—using scent and senses significantly better than a human's. Sometimes he had to remind himself she wasn't a shifter, because so much about her *felt* like one to him.

She groaned and shook her head. "I'm picking the smell up now. Yeah, that wasn't there when I was out here talking to Eric. Definitely not there until after I went inside."

She stepped off the porch, heading directly toward the smell of death. He followed, padding along barefoot but still in human form.

She glanced at him. "You're not going to shift?"

"If I need to. I want to be able to talk with you right now, though."

She smiled, and the soft expression made his chest tight. What was he going to do when she stopped looking at him like that?

If, he reminded himself, *if* she stopped. He was supposed to be holding onto the hope.

Without having to discuss it, they hit the tree line at a slow, loping jog that covered the fern strewn ground fast but more carefully than a full run.

The body hadn't been left that far away. Far enough the scent wouldn't have been picked up by a human, but close enough to be a definite calling card to a shifter.

Except…he couldn't smell wolf in the area.

"I can't smell anyone but you," Becca said. "I mean, not on the body." She gave her head a little shake. "I'm trying to say I can't smell another wolf's scent anywhere around here."

"Yeah, me neither." He scowled. She was right. Nothing but his own scent in the area. "And I can't smell the monster either." Which was the other real possibility for the dead human at their feet.

He moved a little closer, squatting beside the body without touching it, attempting to keep his sense of smell tapped down because the kill was not fresh. A man, dressed in jeans and a flannel shirt, his head ripped off completely. No evidence of the head anywhere nearby. There were also no claw marks on him, like Adam might expect from a shifter kill. But no teeth scrapes, suction cup burns, or puncture wounds from spikes, like he might have expected from the irgotoc. He couldn't even really tell how the head had been removed. Not a sharp weapon, like a sword, he didn't think. The neck wound was too rough. But other than that, he couldn't be certain.

"No obvious signs the monster killed him," Becca murmured. "But honestly, if it had been the irgotoc, it would have…eaten more. There'd be less body here. And if this was a body it wanted to store for later feeding, it would have brought it back to the nest not just abandoned it here."

"If that nest belongs to the irgotoc," he said absently.

"Fair point." She squatted next to him. She didn't cover her nose, but he noticed she flexed her nostrils, as if trying to smell less. "This poor man has been dead for a while, though not as long as at the oldest body in the nest. From the smell, he's been dead long enough he could have been one of the first two humans who disappeared, the two I suspect were killed by the irgotoc."

"Maybe." Adam wanted to search the body for identification, which he doubted was even there, but it seemed natural to look for some way to identify the poor man. He resisted touching the body yet, though. "We might have to call the human authorities."

"If it's the monster they won't be able to do anything about this. If it's the wolves, do you really want to draw them to human attention?" She winced and glanced at him. "And it's possible they'll put you into the suspect category. Me too. That will hamper our ability to find the female irgotoc." She shrugged. "If it exists."

"We can't just leave him here. Outside everything else, this is my territory. I don't want a dead human body here." He snarled at the idea. The fact that he could still be disgusted and horrified by the sight of a murdered human was probably a good sign. A rogue wolf on the edge of turning feral probably wouldn't see the body as a dead human anymore. A feral wolf would only see food.

"The body has already been moved," she said with a sigh. "It's not like this was the original crime scene. We could move it again. Move it to the location of the others? Eventually, once we've caught the monster, we can anonymously send the human authorities to that location so they can give closure to these deaths."

The sadness in her voice had him looking at her.

She sighed. "I've seen too much death and devastation in my lifetime. What the monsters can do, obviously, but also what humans do to other humans. It's never easy."

"Don't think it's supposed to be, though, is it? If it was easy, wouldn't we be different beings? The moment you lose empathy for humans is the moment you get too close to becoming one of the monsters."

Her turn to give him a look, and a little smile. "That's exactly what my father used to tell us all the time."

That was the first time she'd spoken of her father to him. She'd mentioned her mother numerous times but stopped short every time she started to speak about her other parent. That was something Adam wanted to ask more about. But not here.

"If we move the body, we'll risk leaving evidence of ourselves on it," he said, returning to the more pragmatic part of the conversation. "We can't even wrap him in anything from my house if we're going to eventually let the human authorities know where the bodies are."

She made a face and glanced around the area. "There are mundane wolves in these woods?"

"Some. Not a lot in this immediate area. But they exist in these mountains. Why?"

A slight wince. Then, "I have an idea of how we can move this poor man without leaving…shifter or human evidence."

"How?" Something in her tone, her wince had him leaning back on his haunches and frowning at her.

She stood and moved away from the body, motioning him to follow as she stepped back into the woods. When they were out of sight of the body, she said, "There's a lot about me I haven't told you yet. Aspects of…what I am. How I can do the things I do, on the hunt."

"Like the way you use scent the way a shifter does but aren't a shifter?"

"Exactly. The Families aren't just humans made strong enough to hunt monsters. We've been given additional… Gifts, I suppose you'd call them." She turned her gaze inward and shrugged. "Yes. Gifts will do. Each Family is associated with a specific animal. My Family, the Logans in modern times, are associated with the wolf."

"I can smell just a little wolf on you, but it's really faint. I've been wondering about it."

She nodded, not quite meeting his gaze. "Since you shared something very personal with me, about how packs work for werewolves and how you aren't part of one anymore, I'm going to reciprocate and show you something very few outside the Families have ever seen."

He opened his mouth to ask questions, but stopped when she raised her hand.

"It's okay for you to know. I would have shown you this eventually anyway."

A statement that begged even more questions. Why would she share something personal, something restricted to her family, with him? A strange twist in his chest that felt suspiciously like pleasure only confused the issue, so he ignored it.

"Don't panic," she said, her chin down as she looked up at him through her lashes. "This might be…difficult at first. But it's perfectly normal for me. Natural. It doesn't hurt."

"You sound like a shifter explaining the shift to a human."

"Similar idea." She took another few steps from him and glanced around. Then she took a seat on the ground, near the base of a tree, leaning against the tree and letting the large ferns around it lap over her a bit. If someone wasn't looking, she'd be difficult to see. She glanced at him, holding his gaze. "Remember, this is normal for me. And…try not to freak out. Or run away. Or…anything else."

His frown only deepened. What the hell was going on? What was she talking about?

She closed her eyes, and for a long moment, nothing seemed to happen. She just sat there, quietly, her eyes closed, her body still. Then he noticed a faint creep of gray over skin. Hard to see at first, but there.

And in the next instant, a wolf leapt from her chest. A full-grown, adult wolf, leapt from her. At first an insubstantial thing, like a spirt rising from her body, but as the wolf moved forward, its body because more solid, the farther it got from Becca's chest. As it moved, Becca's body also changed, becoming all over gray, like she was fading, like the color was being leeched from her.

The whole thing happened fast, and it took several moments for his mind to catch up to his eyes, to translate the process he'd just witnessed. By the time he realized he'd seen a wolf literally leap from the center of Becca's chest, going from a non-corporeal thing to a corporeal thing, he blinked and there was an actual wolf standing a few feet away.

And Becca was…

"What the hell?" What remained in the place Becca had been sitting was a stone statue that looked just like her, was posed just as she'd sat. Solid stone. A statue made of light gray, nearly white marble. He blinked at the statue several times before he looked back at the wolf.

The animal sat and gazed up at him, a soft whine coming out when he stared directly at it. The wolf didn't turn its gaze away, though, or duck its head.

He looked between the wolf and the statue. "What the hell just happened?" He glanced back at the wolf. "Is Becca okay?"

The wolf nodded. Whined a little. Continued to stare up at him with huge dark brown eyes.

Eyes he realized suddenly that looked…familiar. Not Becca's eyes, exactly, but something like them. Something very close. Something in those large brown eyes that reminded him of her.

"Becca?" he asked, looking right at the wolf.

The wolf nodded.

"You're the wolf?"

A nod and then a head shake.

He sighed. "Impossible to have a conversation this way. Why I didn't shift yet."

He wondered if they could communicate better if he did shift, in the non-word-based use of scent and soft growls that a pack used. But she wasn't a shifter, so maybe not. In fact, despite looking at a wolf, and Becca obviously part of that wolf, he had no idea what he was *actually* looking at.

"What am I looking at?" he asked aloud, glancing between the wolf and the statue.

The wolf rose and padded close, nudging his thigh a little. He didn't flinch away. In fact, he held very still, as he might with a werewolf as he and the wolf showed they trusted each other enough to allow touch without attack. The fact that this was Becca, even though he didn't understand what was happening, meant he didn't want to hurt her by flinching away. But he didn't want to trigger this strange wolf's attack instincts either.

After that brief nudge, the wolf trotted to stand several feet away. Then it ran toward the statue, so fast, it nearly blurred. It leapt right into the statue's chest…

And seemed to merge with the statue, becoming insubstantial as it melted back into the body. As it went, the gray stone that made up the statue retreated, moving away from the spot the wolf entered the stone, leaving color and flesh behind.

Again the process happened quickly. Too fast for his brain to really take in the transition until after the fact. What he saw, when his brain could finally translate it, was the wolf disappearing back into the statue, the statue's stone melting away like ice, and then Becca, as her ordinary self again, sitting there blinking up at him.

For the first time in his life, Adam had seen something so different to anything he'd ever experienced, he had no idea how to react. How to even ask the questions pummeling him. The whole thing was so very weird. In the end, he just blinked and stared.

She stared back. Not saying anything for a long moment.

Finally, he let out a grunt of confusion and dropped abruptly to the ground a few feet from her, sitting cross-legged and running his hands up through his hair.

"That's going to need some explaining," he said.

CHAPTER TWENTY-TWO

Becca held Adam's gaze as she tried to gage his mood, his reaction to what she'd just shown him. The woods around them were quiet, the ferns she'd settled around herself before the transition tickled her skin now that the wolf had returned. Pine sap at her back offset the stench of the body several hundred yards away.

The Families were unique. Her transition wasn't something a shifter would have come across before. No one outside the Families knew about this aspect of their nature. Except for the monsters, of course.

And because the monsters knew, there were steps they had to take to disguise themselves during the transition.

"Obviously, I'm not a shifter," she said slowly, watching him closely as she spoke.

"Obviously."

"But I do have a wolf."

The pervasive smell of the body nearby wasn't helping this conversation. She'd have preferred doing this in a more comfortable and private location. But they needed to move the body from his territory—and not least because she worried the human authorities would get involved and give her more humans she'd have to protect from the irgotoc she still suspected was around here somewhere.

She was also worried he could be right—that this wasn't the monster. If it was a warning or message from the new shifters, she was very worried about what that message meant.

"What…" He shook his head. "How does…?" He rolled his eyes. "I don't even know the questions to ask. Just, please explain what that wolf was, how it can jump in and out of you. Why the hell your body turned to stone."

The hint of fear in his scent at that last made her wince. "The turning to stone thing is actually good. Protects the body. Allows it to heal faster." She shrugged. "All the Families have an associated animal. There are seven. Seven different animals. The Logans are the wolf Family. En, the god who made us, gave us the spirit of this animal to live with us in a symbiotic relationship. The wolf spirit gives us strength, heightened senses, better hunting instincts. The human gives the wolf logic and dexterity and an ability to speak. We are two different beings, inhabiting the same body. When the wolf leaves the human body, the human spirit goes with it. That basically leaves the human body an empty shell. Which is why En made it so the body turned to stone. To protect it."

"Stone can be crushed with a sledge hammer," Adam pointed out, his expression carefully neutral. But a muscle in his jaw jumped.

"Sixteen thousand years ago, sledge hammers weren't an issue. Mostly had to worry about erosion." She tried to smile, but when he didn't, she dropped the patently bad attempt at humor and said, "We've developed ways of dealing with that…flaw in an otherwise pretty good plan. Every Family has an artist, a sculptor who makes lots and lots of Family statues, in different poses. We keep those statues everywhere. It creates a kind of camouflage for us. The monsters don't know which statue is an empty human body and which is just a statue."

"They could just go on a rampage and crush them all."

"Some have tried. We usually won't transition around those monsters."

"Transition? That's what you call it?"

"I do. Some of us do. Not everyone." She shrugged. "The word works for me."

He nodded. "Does it hurt?"

"No. Not at all."

"The body turning to stone, that's not…disturbing?"

"Disorienting. Feels a little cold while it's happening. But I've done this since I was small, so not disturbing. It's part of me. Like the shift is for you. Born to it. Like you." She sort of hoped the comparisons would help this sink in for him, help lessen the shock.

"The Families have been around for sixteen thousand years and no one has ever figured out to destroy all the stone statues?"

"Well, obviously, we don't let humans know. And humans make a lot of statues too, as you'll recall, especially back in the day. It's a lot easier to hide with all those decoys around."

He nodded. "The way shifters can hide among humans in their human shape if they're careful."

"Exactly." She wanted to smile again, but he didn't look ready. His jaw was so tight she was worried he'd crack teeth. And his hands kept flexing and relaxing in his lap. She held very still so she wouldn't trigger his flight instincts, but he very much looked like he wanted to run away. And she didn't think sitting on the ground would slow him down even a little if he did decide to take off.

"So your…spirit was in the wolf when it left your body? You're two different beings? Not a single aspect of one being, like a shifter."

"Yes."

"And your body is…empty when it's stone?"

"Yes."

"What happens if the body is destroyed while it's empty? You stay wolf?"

This part moved them into some tricky territory. She really really didn't want to tell him about the Nam-tar and the curse while they were still so close to a dead body and had things to do and he already looked like he wanted to run.

But she needed to be honest with him. So she tried to give as truthful an answer as she could, for as far as it went. "If the body is destroyed while the wolf is outside the body, the wolf will eventually die, too. The animal spirit isn't meant to remain corporeal indefinitely. It requires the human body. And obviously the human body requires the animal spirit. If the animal is killed while it's outside the body, it takes the human spirit with it, they both die, and the body remains in stone."

Of all the possible ways she could die before meeting her Nam-tar, that seemed the least horrible. But before Nam-tar, even that death wasn't…pleasant. Well, she imagined no death was technically pleasant, per se. But no matter where the two spirits were residing—in animal form or human—death while still under Ne's curse involved a painful, torturous passing with the guest spirit trying to rip its way out of the corporeal body as that body turned to stone.

A shiver crawled along her spine, though she tried to suppress her reaction so Adam didn't misinterpret it. That death was the stuff of nightmares for all the Families. Painful, inevitable, no way to stop it. And as internally violent as Ne could make it. His brother's promised salvation, the Nam-tar, broke the curse and allowed their deaths to be less…violent. Even if she were killed by a monster, it wouldn't be as horrible a passing as under the curse.

But to break that curse, she had to convinced her Nam-tar to stay with her voluntarily.

A topic for a different setting.

"Anything in particular needed to kill you? The way silver works to poison and weaken a werewolf?" His tone was flat and even, emotionless. Though his scent was chaotic with emotions she couldn't read.

"Funnily enough, each Family has a weakness like that. And for wolves it's also silver. Silver works like a poison for us, kills us faster if it's part of the weapon that's used against us."

And that was considered a blessing. Killing a member of the wolf Family with a silver-based weapon so they went through that painfully horrible death faster was considered mercy.

The weaknesses weren't part of Ne's curse, but something En had initially worked into them when creating the Families. Because even their benevolent creator god acknowledge the possibility of the Families growing too powerful without any weakness. Maybe even joining the monsters to destroy humans.

That's how her father had been killed—by a cousin joining the monsters, arranging for her father's murder, all in a quest to destroy humans. Eric had taken care of their cousin, but that was the very reason En had worked a weakness into his creations instead of making them all-powerful. And frankly, until she'd met Adam, Becca had been very grateful for that small glimmer of…well, not exactly hope. She hoped to survive long enough to meet her destined mate and break her curse. But if she'd had to die before meeting him, she'd hoped to be killed by silver.

Adam nodded, but his gaze turned inward so that he wasn't really looking at her. His shoulders were stiff, his hands flexed one more time as she watched him warily, and there was a faint yellow glow in his eyes, his own wolf barely below the surface.

After several quiet moments, he said, "We have things to do. A body to move. Is that all or is there more?"

She sighed. "There's more. But this is the important stuff." For now. "And as you might guess, it means I won't leave evidence of either human or shifter on the body. In wolf form, I can move the poor man, and if there's anything found at all, it will be ordinary wolf DNA and hair."

"Your wolf doesn't show differences at that level from the mundane animals?"

"No. The…differences are in a realm humans haven't got the technology to identify yet."

While member of the Families didn't go to human doctors or the hospitals when they were injured—mainly because they'd heal up on their own just by transitioning for a while—there was nothing in their human DNA to indicate they were anything but human. Unlike Adam, who's DNA would mark him as *not* human if it ever landed into the hands of human forensic experts. Another advantage for the Families.

"Your wolf is strong enough?" he asked. "To move the body, I mean."

"Stronger than a similar mundane animal, even though we're closer to the same size as a regular wolf than…" She gestured at him.

"Okay." He climbed back to his feet, towering over her. "Let's take care of this poor guy now. Then we'll go back to my cabin. And talk more."

She nodded, but leerily. He looked like he was barely holding on to his temper. She couldn't tell much else beyond that. Just that he didn't seem to be taking any of this well. And if he couldn't accept this part…

What hope did she have of him accepting the rest?

CHAPTER TWENTY-THREE

Becca agreed to return to Adam's cabin before transitioning again, leaving her stone body safely inside his house while they collected the body. He wasn't sure why, but the idea of leaving her vulnerable in that way raised his hackles. When he wasn't sure what threat the pack to the north were making, he didn't trust them not to destroy the statue if they found it. Which would kill Becca.

And that would push him over an edge he'd only barely been holding onto before her.

He would turn into the very killing machine all wolf packs feared, the very thing he'd been afraid of becoming. Though his focus wouldn't be humans. He'd kill whoever harmed Becca. Anyone and anything that tried to take her away from him.

An instinct that, frankly, scared the shit out of him.

He'd lived with violence, in the pack certainly, but also since leaving. He wasn't naïve. He knew his own nature, even when he was fully in control of it, was violent. But the sheer raging blood-thirstiness of his instinct to destroy anyone who harmed Becca took his breath away.

Now that he knew one of her weaknesses, that instinct had only gotten worse. All things he'd have to consider, later, when he could be alone and quiet. For now, though, he had to acknowledge that his own sanity hung on a thread that was linked directly to her, and that meant he had to ensure she remained safe. Safe, in this case, meant no one found the vulnerable stone statue until she could return to that body.

Moving the dead human's remains proved unpleasant but not as difficult as he'd feared. He shifted too, so they could move through the woods easier, and he could better protect her back while she was burdened with the body. She'd been right about her strength in that form, though. Unlike a normal wolf who would have had to drag a grown human, she was able to carry the body on her back, after a little maneuvering to get it into place securely. They moved at a measured pace, no racing through the trees at top speed, but they were able to get to the location with the other bodies before nightfall.

She gently set the man's remains down at the edge of the others, in a clear spot. Whining softly as she looked at the horrible site again. And then she raced back into the trees, so fast, Adam was caught off guard.

He flew after her, following her scent until he caught up to her, and then ran at her side through the undergrowth.

The feeling of having her in wolf form beside him was almost as shocking as finding out she could do this. Because it was so settling. Exhilarating and calming at once. Like… Almost like being in a pack again. Like being home.

He nearly tripped when that realization hit him and only the dexterity of his wolf form kept him from plowing into a tree.

But the realization followed him all the way back to his cabin. She was *wolf* too. Not a werewolf. Not a shifter. But still *wolf*. Running with her in that form settled his own wolf the way pack structure and security did. The panics he'd been living with for more than three years, that had started to fade since she arrived in his life, they didn't rise at all when he thought about pack now. He hadn't felt anything like this in so long, it left him shaken. He almost forgot there were still other wolves and a possible monster to worry about.

Becca could be his pack. Becca could be his home.

Those thoughts repeated over and over again in his head as they reached his back porch. The joy of them. The exhilaration. The hope.

They just had one problem. She was still keeping secrets from him.

The fear that those secrets might drive them apart was a physical thing in his chest as he shifted back to human form, while she went inside to return to her human body. There were things she still hadn't told him. And to be fair, he hadn't explained everything to her yet either—especially the reason he'd left his pack—but he was more worried that whatever her secrets were, they would be the wedge between them. The thing he couldn't overcome or defeat to keep her.

And here he'd assumed she'd run away when she realized what being a rogue wolf meant.

She still might, he reminded himself sternly. She still might leave because she didn't want to be with a man who might lose control of his animal at any moment. They still had an awful lot to work through.

The fact that he *wanted* to work through those issues so she would stay was astonishing.

When he finished his shift, he slipped back into his clothes and, still barefoot, padded into the kitchen to put on a pot of coffee. He wanted to clear the lingering scent of death from his nostrils. And he and Becca had a lot to discuss.

He heard her moving around in the living room, and then up the stairs. A few minutes later, he heard the shower turn on. He couldn't blame her. He could do with a shower too after their afternoon's work.

The idea of joining her in the shower crossed his mind. He glanced up at the ceiling, memories of their time in the shower that morning teasing his imagination. She probably wouldn't kick him out. She might even welcome him. The thought of losing himself in her, in bringing her pleasure was beyond tempting. But he dismissed the idea. For now. Mind-blowing orgasms wouldn't solve any of the problems they had to deal with.

A large bowl of rice and fajita chicken wouldn't solve all their problems either, but it would solve one. His stomach was hollow from hunger. She seemed to need as much food as he did—and now he better understood why if she was hosting another whole entity in her body!—so he had to assume she'd be hungry when she came down.

Dinner it was. Then they'd talk.

And maybe she'd open up about her other secrets.

He was nearly done with dinner by the time she came down again. He didn't turn to look at her immediately, because he was finishing the chicken and couldn't look away yet without burning it.

"Good shower?" he asked.

"Great. Needed it."

"Wash off the scent," he said, with a nod.

"Sort of. My human body didn't carry the scent, remember? So once I was back inside, it wasn't there anymore. But…well, residual memory and all that."

Huh. He hadn't considered that. "You said your body heals faster when you… What do you call it again?"

"Transition."

"Transition."

"It does." Quiet for a moment, then, "I probably should have done that after I woke up from the monster poisoning. I would have healed quicker."

"But I didn't know about that yet, and I was a stranger. I understand."

"You shifted in front of a stranger."

"We'd just fought and killed a monster together. And you figured out I was a werewolf. No point in not shifting then." He glanced back. "I didn't know the Families existed. You had every reason to keep that a secret."

He got caught on the way she was looking at the table, not at him, picking at a spot in the wood. And the fact that she wasn't dressed. Just wearing his robe again.

A low growl caught in his throat. See her in his robe trigger a primal possessiveness in him. Knowing his scent was on her skin. Knowing that mingling of flavors from last night was now covering her. He had to force his attention back to finishing the chicken, but his hands clenched tighter around the spatula and pan handle. Tight enough he heard the pan handle crack.

"You're mad, though," she said softly. "Bothered."

"No." He was trying to keep his attention on finishing dinner and not abandoning everything to go bend her over the table. "Not by what you revealed."

She fell silent, and even over the cumin and pepper spices he'd used on the chicken, he could scent her uneasiness, a touch of disbelief. Sadness.

The sadness was what nearly did him in. It took an act of will not to just toss dinner into the sink and go to her, take her into his arms, hold her until she wasn't sad anymore.

And if he hadn't heard her stomach growl, he might well have done just that.

She made a huffing noise. "Guess all the activity has me a little hungry."

He smiled, though his back was still to her. "Figured it might. I'm almost done here. Chicken fajita rice bowls. Good?"

"Perfect." She paused. "I noticed you haven't made anything with beef in it the last couple of nights."

"After what we've dealt with, the bodies…" He shrugged. "Figured you wouldn't be keen on red meat." He risked a glance at her again. "And frankly, I didn't want you to know I wasn't turned off red meat after all that."

He held her gaze. Those big dark eyes looking right into his soul. She needed to understand his nature as much as he wanted to understand hers. He desperately wanted her, wanted her to stay, but not under false pretenses. He was what he was, who he was, and she needed to understand all that.

"You're a wolf. Meat is meat." She shrugged. "I could have eaten beef. But…it was very thoughtful to consider I might not want to and making food that didn't use it. Actually, it's very thoughtful of you to keep cooking for me. I do appreciate that."

He grunted something vaguely resembling "it's nothing" and faced the food again because what he wanted to do was pull her into his arms for a kiss and assure her he'd cook for her for the rest of their lives if she wanted him to. Which wouldn't get this particular meal finished. And she was hungry.

The drive to take care of her seemed to have gotten worse in the last twenty-four hours. Which he hadn't thought possible. Knowing she could be his pack had broken something open in him. A deep need to do everything he could to make her happy. To keep her safe. More even than his loyalty to the pack and to ensuring his people were safe. This was a much more powerful drive.

A terrifying drive. Because if she chose not to stay with him, he wasn't sure where that would leave him.

He shook off the fear. Getting ahead of himself. Dinner first.

He used large pasta bowls to serve up the rice and chicken, and after a hunt through his pantry, turned up a bag of tortilla chips he poured into another bowl and set on the table between them.

"You're going to run out of food," she said, smiling at her dinner.

The smile was tentative, a little tense around the edges. And he could still scent her uncertainty. That bothered him.

"I keep the freezer and pantry well stocked. We're good."

He limited his trips to town, because while being around humans helped ease some of his isolation, he also risked drawing attention to himself from any shifter who happened to be passing through. He spent a great deal of time trying to avoid calling the attention of any other shifters. So he stocked up his large freezer and walk-in closet-sized pantry once a month with enough food to keep him and his wolf satisfied for several months—in case he couldn't make the trip down one month for some reason. He was stocked with enough food to keep his high metabolism satisfied. He had enough for her metabolism for another month at least.

The idea of shopping for food to feed her was weirdly satisfying.

"Smells delicious," she said. Looking up at him hesitantly from under her lashes. "You have more questions, I take it."

"I do. But eat first." He waved at the food, and when she continued to hesitate, he started on his own dinner.

His shoulders relaxed when she started eating. Her groan of

appreciation did the opposite of relaxing him, but for different reasons. The robe she wore, his robe, gapped open across her chest, giving him a delectable glimpse of her cleavage, and suddenly his own food seemed secondary to getting his mouth on her skin.

He blinked and refocused on his rice bowl.

He waited until she was halfway through her dinner before he spoke. "The wolf pack is going to be a problem for me."

She looked up at him. "That's…not where I thought we'd start this conversation, but okay. Is there something I can do to help with that? Some way to get them to leave you alone?"

"That's not how it will work. As far as they're concerned, I'm a threat. They don't know how long… How long I can remain isolated without losing control. They've been testing my territory. And if that body was planted by them as a message to me, I don't have much time before they'll confront me."

"That assumes it wasn't a monster kill. We couldn't tell either way."

"Which means I have to assume it was the pack. If I don't, I risk…" He risked them hurting Becca because he wasn't prepared for them. "It's just better that I prepare for a confrontation with them. One way or the other there's going to be one."

"Why leave a body as a message to you, though? I still don't understand that. Why a *human* body?"

He'd been considering that question all afternoon—when he wasn't thinking about Becca's unique nature—especially after she'd pointed out that a wolf killing humans was the very thing they destroyed rogue wolves for. To avoid drawing attention to the pack. If the wolves were murdering humans, they risked the very thing they'd kill him to avoid. It didn't make sense.

If the body wasn't the monster's kill, if the wolves were responsible for it, for leaving it in that location… Why? Why would they plant it on his territory? What message were they sending?

The only explanation he could come up with was, "To prove I'm killing humans and have to be eliminated."

"You think that's the message they were sending? Trying to set you up?"

"It's possible. Unless it *was* another rogue wolf. But that's pretty unlikely. A feral wolf wouldn't have the kind of control necessary to hide evidence of themselves. And the body would have been in a lot worse shape."

"So we can safely eliminate the possibility of another rogue. But we still have the possibility that the new pack is trying to frame you for murder."

He nodded.

"They'll confront you?"

"They'll try to kill me."

She frowned. "No."

He shrugged. "That's how rogues are dealt with. Especially rogues who've already started killing humans."

"No." She straightened. "No. They won't kill you. I won't allow it. So…what do we do?"

He liked the "we" in that last sentence. And he liked the way she refused the inevitability of his death. "We might be able to stall for a little while. I could try to arrange a meeting with the alpha to have a conversation that doesn't start with a fight. But… No pack will let me stay here. Especially when there are bodies piling up."

"Those could still be the monster," she said.

"Even if the monster killed the human and then abandoned the body, it's most likely the wolves moved it into my territory. A monster would have no reason to do that. The wolves would have every reason to want to 'show evidence' I've lost my mind and am murdering people."

She huffed out a frustrated breath. "So what does this mean?"

"That I'll need to move soon."

"We have to ensure there's no second monster first. Those bodies came from somewhere. Those people were killed by someone or something and then brought to that nest. We have to find out who, or what, first. If it's a monster, I need to kill it."

"Divine duty," he murmured.

"Exactly," she said without hesitance.

"The wolves are escalating. Trying to force a confrontation, one way or the other. If they confront me, and I'm lucky, they'll offer a challenge."

"Why would that be lucky?"

"A show of respect. If I'm not lucky, they'll just go right for the kill. But even with a challenge…" He sighed. "Challenges are to the death. And once offered, I won't be able to refuse it."

"What happens if you kill your opponent?"

"They send in another opponent. And another. Until I'm dead. Or their entire pack is. But…" He shook his head. "No one wolf can fight an entire pack and survive. Even my…" He closed his mouth abruptly, the thought of his brother, of the things he'd lost catching his throat.

"Even your?" she asked, again quietly, her gaze steady on him.

He pulled in a deep breath. "The reason I'm rogue, the reason I left my pack… It's complicated. A lot of history." He leaned back in his seat and ran his hands through his hair.

Becca sat silently, waiting him out.

Finally, he said, "We had a good alpha, for a while. We thought he was a good alpha anyway. He actually tried to rehabilitate rogue wolves. Had a lot of success. Or so it seemed. When he died, his son took over. And Chris Corwin was…not a good alpha. Greedy. Weaker than his father. More vicious. He didn't want to hide from humans. He was a bully. And he wasn't strong enough to hold the pack on his own. So he gathered the rogue wolves that had been brought into our pack around him to strengthen and shore up his position. For a while, we dealt with that. Accepted it. The pack was better off together with a weakish leader than none at all. Or so we thought."

He dropped his gaze to the table, picked at the edge as memories swept over him. "I haven't talked about this in years."

"You don't have to now if you don't want to." Her voice was soft and soothing.

He glanced up. Those beautiful dark eyes of hers dragged him under. He wanted to tell her all this. Wanted to lay his soul bare for her.

Because he wanted her to trust him enough to do the same for him.

"I want to. The…background is important for why I'll leave here rather than challenge the pack. I was here first. Even if I weren't rogue, I'd have the right to defend this territory from them. But I won't. I'll leave first. I think it's important you understand why."

She nodded, but didn't say more.

So he continued. "There were rumblings, under the surface, during Chris's reign… He overspent, drove the pack into financial difficulties. Then tried to solve the problem by shaking down the people in one of the human towns inside our territory." He sighed. "That led to a chain of events that… My brother, my younger sister, and I were all strong enough to beat Chris in a challenge. To take over the pack. Become alpha. My sister, Siobhan, just wanted to make clothes and didn't want anything to do with running a pack. I never wanted leadership either. Still don't. But my brother was the type of wolf to make a great leader. Smart. Strong. The right combination of sympathy and ruthlessness. You need that to control a pack of wolf shifters."

He started picking at the edge of the table again. "He didn't want to be the alpha, but… The nudges from the others in the pack to challenge Chris never impacted me or Siobhan, but they pushed Gabriel's sense of duty. He was considering issuing the challenge. But as I said, challenges are to the death. And he didn't want to kill our beloved alpha's son. Even if the son was an asshole."

"Loyalty is good. Most of the time."

He snorted. "Anyway, the asshole got himself into a tangle with a tiger shifter of all things. Made a big mistake thinking he could mess with the Chernikov brothers."

"Who?"

Adam waved that away. "All of that's another long story. And tangential to what happened for the pack. Chris's fuck ups finally pushed Gabriel into challenging him. Gabriel won."

"He killed the other wolf?"

"He did. And for a while, things were okay with the pack. A lot of the other wolves wanted Gabriel to be alpha anyway. I served as his beta—a sort of second to help mitigate between the pack and the alpha —and we worked our asses off to get the pack out of the financial bind

Chris had left us in. Even worked with the tigers to make some of that happen. For a while, that was enough. The pack was stable."

"What changed?"

He glanced at her, then back at the table. "The rogues, the ones who'd supported Chris? They weren't happy with Gabriel taking over because he insisted they follow the rules, wouldn't let them run wild the way Chris had. They weren't happy to have lost their alpha, definitely not happy to be muzzled, but more importantly, they hated that Chris had been replaced by a supporter of his father's."

She frowned. "But…they were brought in by the father, right? Given a pack when others would have just killed them?"

"Yes. But there was a lot of resentment in *how* Doug Corwin went about that process. A lot of anger." He shook his head. "I don't want to go into details. When I found out the way Doug had…tamed rogues… Well, it was way too late to change anything. Except that we didn't go about 'taming' rogues in that way anymore."

The cabin in the woods near Eirene. The silver chains. Memories of that cabin still occasionally haunted Adam's nightmares. Doug had kept rogues chained there, in pain, tortured by the silver, until they could prove they were calm enough, reasonable enough, to be brought into the pack. If they didn't, Doug killed them without any hesitance. And none of the others in the pack knew this was what he'd been doing. Except the rogues he'd "tamed." The rogues who didn't necessarily want to be tamed.

But saying all that aloud made bile rise in his throat. He'd supported and respected Doug Corwin. Considered him a good man, a good alpha. Learning the truth had shaken a lot of Adam's foundational beliefs. And he still hadn't come to terms with that.

"I'll tell you that whole story some time," he promised. "Just… Not yet."

She nodded. "That's fine. You don't need to tell me anything you don't want to, anything you can't discuss. Even if you don't want to tell me any more about your brother, that's fine."

"I need you to know why I'm not in my pack now."

"Why?"

He frowned a question at her.

"Why do you want me to know?" she asked quietly.

So many reasons, he almost said aloud. Mostly because he wanted her to know him, to trust him, to stay with him. But these things would hang over any future they might have. So he needed her to know what had happened, from him, before someone else made her doubt him.

That last was the explanation he went with. "If…when the pack to the north confronts me, they'll likely say…a lot. I want you to know what they'll throw at me. If they have any idea who I am, they'll know what happened in my pack. Werewolves are secretive with others, but gossipy amongst ourselves. Word of the Walsh brother wandering around rogue somewhere along the west coast will definitely have carried to other packs after all these years."

"You're worried about what they'll say in a confrontation?"

"Worried if I don't tell you first, you'll believe what they say."

"I believe *you*," she said. Without any hesitation. Without even a blink or pause.

Her faith in him left him breathless. Staying on his side of the table got infinitely harder. He flexed his hands against his thighs so he wouldn't reach for her. He did manage a rough sounding, "Thank you."

But inside, she'd just sealed something for him. Something he was sure would remain for the rest of his life. She'd sealed his loyalty. He was hers. He wasn't sure how else to say it, even to himself. He was hers.

Whatever it took. Whatever he had to do.

He was hers.

CHAPTER TWENTY-FOUR

Adam took a shaky breath as his realization sank in. He still had a lot to tell her. But knowing she would believe him made the telling easier. Their dinner was nothing but empty bowls and a half bowl of tortilla chips at that stage. He wanted to do something with his hands—that didn't involve getting distracted by putting them on Becca—so he started clearing the table as he continued his story.

"The angry rogues in the pack caused a lot of trouble for my brother. A lot of disruptions that threw the pack into inner turmoil. Caused some serious trouble again with the humans in Eirene and with the tiger shifters there that didn't end well for the wolf involved. Gabriel and I were able to reestablish some order after he took over, but the rogues kept upending all our efforts."

She sat quietly at the table while he moved around putting dishes in the sink, chips away, the things he'd used to make their dinner. Giving him space and not crowding him or offering to help. Her instincts to give him space while he spoke, to let him do the clean up so he could keep his hands busy, were good. And once again he found himself awed by her ability to just…trust him.

"As beta of the pack," he continued, "I ran interference with the people in Eirene, with the humans and the tigers. I took care of the pack's finances, which were such a mess when Gabriel took over. I did whatever he needed me to do while he was attempting to impose structure and stability on a group of wolves who weren't happy about that structure and stability."

"Why didn't the unhappy wolves just leave?"

"Where would they go? They *needed* pack structure, even if they resented it. If they left together to form their own pack—which my brother wouldn't have objected to—they didn't have any one individual wolf strong enough to serve as alpha. That's also why none of them directly challenged Gabriel. They'd have lost. Badly. Been killed. And to what end? Without a strong alpha, a werewolf pack ends up the pray of other packs. They don't survive a lot longer than a lone wolf outside a pack."

He put away the spices and got some water into the rice pot to let it soak. But his mind was back in those days when he'd been trying to help Gabriel shore up the pack. And at every turn, they'd been undermined. Even by some of the wolves they thought they could trust.

"My brother hadn't really *wanted* to be the alpha. He'd just felt more duty-bound to take up the position than either my sister or I. Before taking over the pack, he'd worked for the local Search and Rescue group. With humans who didn't know he was a shifter. He enjoyed the work. He was always the kind to want to save people." Adam snorted, the sound bitter even to his own ears. His brother didn't deserve that bitterness. But his altruism was one of the things that got them into trouble.

Busying himself wiping down the countertop, Adam tried to refocus on the story. The parts Becca needed to know. The details were overwhelming him, though. He needed to get this out, get it over with. He'd been avoiding these memories for more than three years now, at least when he was awake—they sometimes haunted his dreams. Time to get them out, like ripping off a band-aid. Fast to minimize the pain. Only he'd never needed to use a band-aid. He had no idea if there was any truth to that saying.

He was about to find out.

"Because my brother and I are about equal in strength, the adopted rogues concocted a plan. They started spreading rumors, stories about Gabriel's weakness as an alpha. About how he needed to face a proper challenge fight—Chris hadn't been strong enough to really put up a challenge. To rule the pack, Gabriel needed to *prove* he could beat all comers. He didn't deserve to be alpha without that. He couldn't remain in that position unless someone else challenged him. Someone stronger. Someone who'd put up an actual fight. Gabriel had to be challenged or they would all be killed. Other packs would come in and take over, because he wasn't strong enough because he hadn't gone through the gauntlet of proving himself."

Adam pulled in a shaky breath. Rubbed at an invisible spot on the counter. "Lots of this repeated over and over again, until even the wolves who'd supported Gabriel were no longer so certain of their opinion. The supportive wolves were also the ones who'd urged Gabriel to challenge Chris originally. When he'd refused for so long, they tried to push me into that position. They stopped nagging me once Gabriel took over. But once the rogues started circulating those rumors of Gabriel being weak without another challenge... The nagging started again."

"They wanted you to fight your own brother?"

"They'd started to believe we were a weaker pack, that we were vulnerable, because the alpha hadn't been challenged enough when he took over. The big problem... There were no other wolves in our pack who could have challenged Gabriel and survived. Not even our sister."

"Except you."

He hung his head, his back to her, his shoulders tight. "Except me."

He still couldn't believe he and Gabriel hadn't seen this coming, hadn't prepared some sort of contingency plan. They'd ignored the rumors and innuendo. Tried to use calm reassurance and reason. But reason had faltered in the face of fears, real fears born of already having lived through a bad alpha. None of them had wanted to take any chances. And the rogues played that fear perfectly.

Adam finally turned to face Becca, crossing his arms over his chest and leaning against the sink. He couldn't bring himself to sit down again. But he'd at least face her when he admitted this last part.

"We didn't see the trap forming around us until too late," he said. "Or, really, we thought we could talk our way out of the trap the rogues were trying to set. We couldn't. And finally, Gabriel's hand was forced. He had to issue a challenge to me—the only wolf who could rival him —or his life would have been forfeit. The pack would have killed him. Would have tried anyway. And then there would have been a fight to see who the next alpha would be. Winner take all. I think some of the rogues figured they were capable, but not quite strong enough to beat Gabriel. Or me."

"If they thought they were strong enough to lead your pack, they could have just left and formed their own pack."

"Like I said, establishing a new pack with a weak alpha is difficult, nearly impossible. But that's different to a semi-weak alpha taking over an established pack. The established pack will definitely last longer. The established pack has money and territory and treaties already worked out. And thanks to me and Gabriel, we'd put most of the mess Chris had left the pack in back to rights. We were in good shape, getting there anyway, both financially and strategically among the other packs in the region. Taking over that would have been a lot easier than trying to establish a new group with a weak alpha."

She straightened a little, frowning. "Do you suppose the new pack to the north has a strong enough alpha?"

"No idea. Couldn't even tell you if the wolf I scented at the edge of my territory was the alpha or not."

"Something we should probably look into," she murmured.

There was that "we" again. His heart beat harder when she said things like that. "It could be useful information. Maybe. But not likely to change anything for me. I'm still a dangerous rogue." He hit the dangerous part a little heavy with sarcasm.

But Becca didn't react to his tone. "If they challenge you, and you're strong enough to beat their alpha, that does change things. You were strong enough to beat your brother in a fight?"

"Neither one of us wanted to find out. The alpha challenge is to the death. Whatever arguments and sibling rivalry we might have had, I love my brother and I didn't want to kill him. He felt the same. I wasn't sure I'd survive long if I did have to kill him. And I suspect that was the real plan. Gabriel and I were close, had always been close. Forcing one of us to kill the other would have destroyed the surviving brother. Made them weaker. There was no way to do what the pack insisted we do without it destroying both of us."

"So you left," she said quietly. "You gave up everything. To save your brother."

Something moved through her expression. Hard to read. Sadness, he thought, based on her scent. But also a surprising amount of rage. The bitter tang of her rage on his tongue was so strong he wanted to doubt his senses. Her anger, on his behalf, overwhelmed him.

She understood. That rage meant she understood exactly what the cost had been for him and his brother.

Her understanding left him so relieved his hands shook. And that relief made it impossible for him to remain so far away from her. He crossed to the table, held out his hand for her. Frowning slightly, she set her fingers in his palm, and he pulled her to her feet. Then into his arms.

For a long long moment, all he could do was hug her. Just hold her and breath in her scent and the way his own scent was on her skin from wearing his robe and how her arms felt so tight around him when she hugged him back. Fierce and strong and trusting.

All of it left him overwhelmed. Left him undone.

Hers.

He found her mouth, willing and open, kissing her like the lifeline she'd just thrown him, like he'd drown without her and he needed her for his next breath. She didn't hesitate here either. Returning his kiss with such fierce passion his head spun.

Where had she come from? How had he earned such a gift? He wasn't worthy of her, but damned if he wasn't going to try.

He poured all those unspoken emotions into his kiss. All the passion, all the relief, all the need and hunger. He couldn't taste her enough, get close enough, feel enough of her skin. He pushed the oversized robe down off her shoulders because he had to get his hands on her skin. Her soft moan, the way she ground against him… God, he loved doing that to her.

Him. This was for him. He could taste that in her scent. All this need and passion, her grasping hands, her soft sounds, the dance of her tongue against his… All for *him*.

And he wanted more. All of her. Everything she had. But he'd give all of himself in return.

Shoving the robe down farther, he skimmed his hands over her warm skin, trailing a line over her spine and up her neck. Her shudder fired his blood.

"More," he murmured against her throat as he tasted the skin there, sliding his lips down her neck, greedily drinking in her gasp. One side of the robe fell down to her wrist, leaving her upper body mostly bare. He tasted his way over her shoulder as he eased her back against the table until she was half sitting on it. Though he wasn't entirely sure the furniture was sturdy enough for this, he didn't care. He'd get a new table.

"Been thinking about you like this since that first day," he said, his voice harsh as he tasted the salty freshness of her skin. "When you wore my robe the first time." He growled against her neck, nipping the skin. Her gasp went right to his cock. "Been wanting to spread this robe and taste you."

She arched into him when he lowered to her breast, taking her nipple into his mouth, sucking hard. She dropped one hand to the table for balance, gripped his hair with her other, and wrapped one leg around his hip.

"Fuck I want you," he said. And moved to her other breast. She was panting, and her scent was full of musky lust and the faint citrus that was her. "More," he muttered. "I want more."

"Yes, yes, yes, yes."

Her chant drove him crazy. So much acceptance was going to kill him. He didn't care.

He leaned back enough to push the rest of the robe down her arms, pinning bother her hands on the table, the robe tie still around her stomach but otherwise spread wide. Nearly naked, on his table, she was the most delicious thing he'd ever had here. He dropped to his knees, spread her thighs wide and shoulder between them, breathing her in. She was wet already, the moisture glistening around her folds, peaking past her dark curls. That only made him hungrier.

He bit her thigh, none too gently, and she bucked. The movement made the table groan. He licked the bite to sooth it, and her thighs tightened against his shoulders. Then he gripped her hips, holding her in place as he licked into her. Ah, the explosion of flavor, the mix of her scent and salty taste, the way she moaned and leaned back farther on the table. He licked, suck…ate her like she was his only meal for months. And loved watching her lose control. Watching her fall apart.

For him.

She bucked against his mouth, panted and groaned, gasped when he focused on her clit. She trembled and shook and one hand went back and forth between gripping his hair and balancing against the table.

"Adam!"

God he loved hearing her say his name. Just like that. All passion and heat as she fell apart. He growled into her as he sucked her clit and pushed her over an edge that made her scream. He licked up her shuddering, gasping release, the way her hips lifted off the table was she came. The way she collapsed forward, breathing hard and trembling everywhere.

Perfect.

He nibbled her inner thigh again, soothing her shuddering reaction with his hands as he drank her in. She was flushed pink, the robe all askew, her hair a tousled mass hanging over her face as she curled toward him.

"Beautiful," he murmured. And rose up, taking her mouth in a fierce kiss as he stood.

She followed the kiss, wrapping around him until he held more of her weight than the table—which had survived. So far—her legs around his hips, her arms locked around his neck. "More," she murmured against his mouth.

And nearly broke him. "Yes," he growled. His turn to accept. He balanced her on the table again, gently easing her arms from around his neck. "Don't move."

He flashed upstairs for a condom and back, moving at his top speed, giving her no time to even notice the cool air. She startled and then giggled when he appeared in front of her. Ah, he loved that sound. Glorious. He wanted her to laugh more.

But right now, he wanted to make her moan again.

He kissed her, bending her backward until they were nearly lying on the table. The less-than-sturdy wood groaned in warning. He pulled them both upright again, setting her on her feet, then turned her around, pushing the robe to one side so he could admire her curvy, beautiful ass. She arched her back as he smoothed his hands over her skin, letting his gaze drink her in.

"Thought about this a lot," he muttered. "Too often. Bending you over my table. Fucking you like this."

"Fuck," she murmured. "Yes."

His cock pulsed, so tight against the fly of his jeans now it hurt. He wasn't sure he'd ever been this hard before. And when she looked over her shoulder at him, her hair falling across one eye, her lips swollen and red from his kisses, he lost his last strained grip on control.

Not that he had much control with her anyway. Not that he cared about control with her.

He carefully unbuttoned and pushed his jeans down enough to free his cock. Gripped his length and pumped his fist up and down once as she watched, her gaze bright and focused. The flush in her face spread over her body, her ass pink and pretty. Without urging, she spread her legs farther, steadying herself against the table. The welcome was all he needed.

He slipped on the condom, then he slid into her wet heat, groaning at the tightness and friction, letting her feel him stretch and fill her slowly, fully. She arched her back on a moan, pulling him deeper, gripping him tighter. Breaking his attempt to go slow. He pulled back and slammed forward, hard enough to bring her up onto her toes. She moaned and arched again. His hands tightened on her hips and he rocked into again, another hard thrust. And again. And again. And again. Until she called out his name.

"Wanted this for forever," he muttered, fucking her hard and steady, holding her in place to keep her on her feet. "Wanted you forever."

"Yes. Oh, gods, yes."

She rose higher on her hands, and he leaned forward to cup one breast, pinching her nipple while his other hand on her hip held her steady. He fucked her until she was panting again, her body trembling. And when her breathing turned desperate, he reached around between her legs and pressed his finger against her clit, giving it just enough pressure to send her spinning out over that edge again, her body gripping his cock so hard he saw spots. As she trembled, before she'd fully come back down, he gripped both her hips again and thrust into her hard until his own orgasm ripped through him, tearing him apart. Leaving him empty, overwhelmed…to be filled back up by her.

Their scents twinned together, mixed with sweat and sex as they both panted. He wanted that scent on his skin for the rest of his life. When his limbs stopped trembling, he wrapped his arms around her waist and pulled her upright, her back to his chest, cradling her close. The change meant his softening cock slipped out of her, and he missed her heat, but he wanted her in his arms more.

She leaned into him, so trusting, hugging his arms, her breathing slowly calming. He found himself unconsciously matching his breaths to hers, trying to match his heartbeat to hers as they both came slowly back to earth. And his wolf growled in his head. In approval.

This was home. She was his home.

Now he just had to convince her of that.

CHAPTER TWENTY-FIVE

Becca woke the next morning with Adam's arms tight around her, in his bed, their scents blended together and surrounding them in a cocoon of perfect harmony. Her heart did a happy dance in her chest, the contentment so thorough, she sighed.

A contentment that dimmed, just a little, as the dawn crept in past his closed curtains, lining across the hardwood floor. She'd never gotten the chance to tell him about Nam-tar and their significance to the Families last night. She'd meant to. But then… Well, he'd kissed her, and she'd lost her mind, and then he'd been all she could think about. She'd forgotten everything else but greedily fucking him half the night until they both collapsed exhausted into bed. She remembered that part.

But she'd forgotten she was going to tell him the rest of her secrets. That one last thing she needed to tell him. The choice to stay was his. She couldn't force him. That was the rule. He had to be willing to spend his life with her. The only way to break her curse.

Though, the more she was with him, the better she got to know him, the less she cared about him staying to break her curse. Even if she remained cursed, faced that horrible death for the remainder of her years, she'd still want Adam to stay. With her. For her.

She squeezed his arm, where it lay heavy against her waist. Afraid to disturb the peaceful moment and break this bubble of contentment. Wanting to just hide in his cabin and let the rest of the world roll past without them.

Unfortunately, there might still be a monster out there—even though, with Adam's revelations yesterday, she was starting to doubt her own confidence in that. No sign of another irgotoc, not obvious signs anyway. And the bodies could, unfortunately, also be the victims of the werewolves. Though, if they'd killed humans, they'd seriously endangered themselves, risked calling the attention of the human authorities. Irrational and illogical. Why? Why do all that just to taunt a lone werewolf? Even to set him up? From what Adam had told her, his mere presence was enough to give the wolves an excuse to come after him. They didn't need to kill people and leave bodies around to instigate a confrontation. Why not just confront Adam directly?

Not that she wanted Adam to face this pack who would want him dead. But she'd be at his side. And at least they'd have their cards on the table.

For all her job required a great deal of secrecy, she was actually pretty crap at subterfuge. Which was why, during all the human wars she and the Families had been sucked into over the last century and a half, she'd never pretended to be a spy. Like Eric, she'd worked as a nurse-medic, and kept most of her assistance in the background. They continued to hunt and kill monsters during those wars—wars brought monsters out in large numbers and the Families always had their hands full in those chaotic years—but her cover story, and efforts, in those wars were entirely behind the scenes and required no actual attempt at anything like spycraft. She'd have failed that assignment spectacularly.

She snuggled back into Adam's heat, smiling when his big arm tightened to keep her close. She really didn't want to leave this cocoon. He was so warm, almost hot, in his sleep, like having a warm fire at her back. And that heat seeped into her in such a satisfying way, she never wanted to move back into the cold air again.

He hadn't run away when she'd shown him what she could do.

She was still a little in awe of that. She'd leerily watched him all afternoon, all through dinner, terrified he'd reject her after he'd learned what she really was. And yet, instead of asking her questions about that, instead of bringing it up at all, he'd revealed his own vulnerability. His own secret. She ached for him, for the decision he'd been forced to make. She couldn't imagine being forced to leave her family like that. They were rarely in the same city anymore, often not even in the same country, but her family was close and tightknit. It would kill her to have to break that bond.

And she was even more in awe of him now, that he'd managed for three and a half years not only alone and outside a pack, but without his family, because it was the only way to save his brother.

Her instincts screamed to wrap herself around him and keep him safe and secure from now on. To give him the home he'd lost. Be his family. And, if he accepted, she *could* be that for him. They were destined by ancient god and divine promise to be together. If he accepted. She wasn't a werewolf. She couldn't replace his pack, and the structure and security he apparently got from being part of one. But she could give him family. She could give him that closeness he'd gone without for years. And while she wasn't a shifter, her own wolf could run with his whenever he needed that.

There had been something so utterly satisfying and right about them working side-by-side in their wolf forms. She inside her wolf, her spirit along for the ride and providing a level a logic to her animal half. Him in his wolf from—still himself but the beast half. Different from being with her Family when they were moving around inside their animals. But different in a way that still felt right.

Would it be enough for him? Could he accept her offer of family and something like structure, even though they weren't technically a werewolf pack?

Would he even want that?

So many questions she was afraid to ask. Because she didn't want to poke a hole in her bubble of peace.

His arm tightened around her again, and he stretched along her back. She felt the nudge of his erection against her ass and smiled as his lips glided across her shoulder in a lazy good-morning kiss. Maybe she could hold this bubble a little longer. Just a little longer before she came clean and told him the rest.

She rolled into him, or started to, but he held her in place, with her back to his front, kissing along her shoulder and up to her neck, nuzzling a sensitive spot on her throat. She moaned softly, dipping her head farther into the pillow to give him better access. She loved the scratch of his beard stubble against her skin. Like little shots of electricity through her nerves. She loved the way that stubble felt against her inner thighs, too. And the memory of that rough scratch, had her moving restlessly against him, her hips grinding back into his.

His low growl vibrated along her skin, making her shiver. She loved that sound so much. And the way his scent spiked with his desire, a sharp taste of sweet and salty musk.

He slid his hand down her stomach, down until he cupped her pussy, his big hand covering her thoroughly. Brushing his middle finger ever so gently against her folds. She melted against him, letting her thighs fall open, lifting her top leg and wrapping it back over his thighs so he had better access. That appreciative growl against her ear again. He slipped between her folds with his middle finger, teasing her, spreading the moisture that had already pooled there. She rubbed her hand down his arm, curling her fingers over his, holding him in place and gently guiding him at the same time, until her breath came in sharp pants. Her hips bucked against his palm when he finally gave her clit the attention it so desperately wanted.

"Hungry," he said against her ear. "For me."

"Yes." She shook, trembled when he bit her neck none to gently this time. "Yes!"

"Play with your breast, pinch your nipple. Let me see how you like to be touched."

She did, releasing her hold on his wrist and cupping her breast, squeezing and tugging at her peaked nipple. The contrast of his finger rubbing her clit and her own on her breast felt delicious and perfect. She ground back against him again, feeling the length of his hard cock against her ass, knowing that was for her. Desperate for all of him. Everything all at once.

Ah and his groan, his own desperate growl. She wanted more of that too. Watching him lose control, watching him fall apart for her made her come as hard as his hands and mouth. She abandoned her breast to grip his cock, holding his length tight in her fist, squeezing and releasing. Her orgasm was too close for her to do more. Lost in the sensations, the build and tension and grasping desperation. He bit her again, his teeth on her shoulder, as he fingered her clit. She would swear she saw stars behind her closed eyes as he pushed her, as she hit that tipping point… And came. Hard. The release shuddering through her in a jerky wave of extasy that left her limp and breathless and utterly content.

Adam hugged her back against him while she settled, holding her close, his hand gliding up over her hip, up to gently cup her breast. She was very aware of his hot, hard cock in her hand still and began to gently stroke up and down as she slowly returned to earth. The way his breathing hitched, the sound of him sucking in air through his nose, had her smiling. She loved the way he reacted to her touch. To her. And all this in the warm heat of his body wrapped around hers, her leg still draped over his thigh.

"Minute," he mumbled into her hair and pulled away, long enough to get a condom and slip it on. Then he was against her back again, all heat and hunger, nudging her leg over his again and pulling her hips back. He adjusted their bodies until his cock nudged her entrance. "Guide me in," he said, his fingers tight on her hip.

She reached down to take him, guide him in, settling back as he pushed slowly up into her. The friction had her head dropping back against his shoulder. The angle made her so very aware of every inch of him, of the tightness of her channel gripping him. She rocked back, her ass against his lower abdomen, taking more of him. His chest hair rubbed against her back as he slipped one arm beneath her neck so he could hold her closer, his other hand cupped her breast this time, squeezing and kneading her as she'd done to herself just a few minutes earlier. She was surrounded by him, filled by him, her senses overwhelmed by him. Only him. Her world was this moment, as he rocked into her, slow, steady, hard, taking her back up, higher and higher.

The bed shook when he slammed harder up into her, making her gasp. And that only drove him harder. Harder. He moved his hand from her breast back to her clit, already so sensitive she wasn't sure she could take the touch. He proved her wrong. His finger rested gently against her swollen bud, just a light brush. And that was all it took to send her careening again, blowing her apart.

"God, Becca," he said, his voice harsh against her hair. He held her tighter, pumped up into her a few more strokes, and then he shuddered, shook, his arms flexing tightly.

Wrapping her arms around his, holding him in place as he folded around her… There was nowhere she wanted to be more in the entire world than in this exact place, with this exact man, held by him in just this way. So warm and content. The bubble of pleasure and peace holding them just a little while longer.

That bubble of contentment and post-sex bliss actually lasted all the way through breakfast. By silent mutual agreement, they didn't talk about monsters, her nature, or the werewolf pack to the north. Not in the shower together before coming downstairs. Not while he cooked eggs and bacon for them. Not as they ate. Not even as she sipped her last cup of coffee after breakfast. They only talked about nonsense and inconsequential things.

Right up until the shout from the back of the house shattered their peace.

"Come on out rogue," a deep feminine voice shouted. "Time to talk."

CHAPTER TWENTY-SIX

Adam went rigid in his seat, all sense of settled contentment vanished in a flash. He didn't know the voice. But he didn't need to.

Werewolves couldn't *sense* their kind, the way say a tiger shifter might, and with the door closed and the scents of coffee and Becca filling his head, he hadn't picked up any scent clues ahead of time either. But he didn't need any of that. He knew exactly who stood outside his back door.

He met Becca's gaze over the kitchen table. She held his, her beautiful dark eyes serious and steady. She was dressed in the same pants she'd been wearing since arriving, but was wearing one of his t-shirts this morning, and the satisfaction that filled him when she wore something of his against her skin still surprised him. She'd left her hair loose after the shower, but she pulled it back now into a low ponytail as her gaze moved to the back door. The soft, sexy, sleepy woman he'd woken up with was quickly replaced by the hunter who stalked monsters through the forest.

A fierce sense of...some strong emotion he wasn't prepared to name yet filled his chest. Watching her prepared to fight. For him. With him. He couldn't imagine anything that could make him adore her more, but that shift to warrior for his sake did. If she hadn't already captured his emotions, his loyalty, she would have in that moment.

Without a word, she rose and snatched up her sword, pulling it free of the scabbard where it leaned near the back door, not even bothering to drop the scabbard strap over her head.

He got between her and the door before she could open it, though, and whispered against her ear—because the shifters outside could hear them talking, even through the closed door—"I'll go out first. There will be more than the one we just heard."

"I'll guard your back, don't worry," she whispered, her voice barely a breath in his ear. "They might have circled the house. How many would they have brought?"

"Not less than five. Depends on how worried they are about me."

She nodded. Then met his gaze. "I've got your back," she repeated, mostly just mouthing the words.

He gripped her waist, pulling her into a hug he needed more than his next breath. It was on the tip of his tongue to confess to emotions he hadn't even admitted to himself yet. He couldn't speak at all, though, just hug her to convey how much her support meant to him. She wasn't going to abandon him because he was a packless rogue. She had his back.

The tumble of his emotions was too much to parse through in that moment. He'd have to face that excess and chaos later. Right now, he had a hostile pack of werewolves to confront.

"Stay safe," he muttered against her lips, kissing her quickly. Then he stepped outside before he did something reckless, like try to scoop her up and run away as fast as he could go so she wouldn't be in danger. Because of him.

The wolves arrayed between his back porch and the tree line were mostly what he would have expected. There were four of them. Three standing just a step back from their leader. A couple of men and a woman, all dressed in ordinary jeans and t-shirts. None of them acknowledging the cooler autumn weather with coats or jackets or even flannel shirts. Shifter metabolisms meant they weren't cold in these mild temperatures, any more than he was, and there were no humans around to fool.

The two men, one white, one Hispanic, were tall enough, maybe six-foot. A little shorter than him but not by much. The woman was taller than Adam, closer to six-foot-five if she was an inch. An Asian woman who had her black hair wound into a tightly braided bun on top of her head. All of them were leanly muscled, wiry-looking, like they could pounce at any moment. And all their eyes glowed faintly yellow in the morning sunshine.

The woman standing in front of the other three was shorter, more compact than her companions. She was a Black woman, with curly dark brown hair cut short, the sides shaved close to her skull and with a swirl pattern over her ears, giving the remaining puff on top a sort of mohawk appearance. Her eyes weren't yellow, no wolf showing in the dark brown depths. Yet. But she held herself with that kind of cocky arrogance Adam had seen a lot over the years. An alpha who wasn't fully settled in her place as head of the pack yet, and had to ensure everyone around her remembered who she was.

She certainly emanated enough power to be an alpha. He had no doubt her wolf was strong. A sharp pepper flavor mixed with more earthy elements in her scent, and she made no attempt to disguise any of her emotions or strengths.

Not entirely secure in her place in the pack. But definitely sure of her power, and her ability to rule as alpha.

Adam kept most of his attention on the alpha. And because she was, and he was without a pack at his back, he acknowledged her position with an eye-lowered nod. He'd grown up playing pack politics. He knew how to play the game.

Except he wasn't entirely sure if they did or not.

New packs were…tricky. They hadn't established all the rules and order and traditions yet. Which meant there was often room for confusion and instability. Instability in a pack was always dangerous. More so if the alpha wasn't quite strong enough to hold them all together. He couldn't say for sure if this alpha was. Time would tell. He didn't want to be in the middle of the chaos if she wasn't, though.

The alpha's gaze shifted briefly to Becca, standing behind Adam with her sword in hand, then settled back on Adam. She smiled. "You have a friend. A bodyguard." There was a subtle question in that last comment.

He ignored it. "What do you want here? You entered my territory without permission or provocation. You'll need a reason." He spoke without anger, putting as much matter-of-fact as he could into his tone, an accountant explaining why a deduction won't work.

"A rogue near *our* territory is provocation enough," she said, with the first signs of anger, a slight lifting of her lip in a snarl.

"I was here and established before your pack formed."

"You can't hide from us," this from one of the men behind the alpha. "We know who you are."

That man held Adam's gaze, his eyes very yellow as he smirked at Adam. He wasn't the sort of man who stood out in a crowd of humans. Six-foot, white, short dark hair, neither handsome nor obviously unattractive. Ordinary. Adam wouldn't have noticed him if he'd passed him on the street.

Except for his scent. That…

Adam recognized that scent.

This was the wolf who'd subtly marked the tree just outside Adam's territory, on the very same day they'd found a headless body in the woods too close to Adam's cabin.

"Wasn't hiding here," Adam said, holding the man's gaze. "I marked my territory clearly."

The man's lip jumped, whether a snarl or smile though, Adam wasn't sure. His scent spiked with a sharp charge of adrenaline and hunger. No fear. A lot of anger.

"Rogues don't get territory," the man said. "Adam Walsh."

The very tall woman hissed and snarled at him. Which was a pretty extreme reaction to his name. Especially since he didn't know her. Now he had to wonder what they'd heard about him. Had the story of him being forced from his pack evolved?

"What do you think you know about me?" he asked, genuinely curious to hear what stories they'd picked up. And if any of them even remotely resembled reality at this point.

"You tried to overthrow your alpha and were banished," this alpha said, speaking before any of the three behind her could.

A muscle in the jaw of the man with the familiar scent jumped, and his lip twitched again. But he held silent.

"Not quite what happened," Adam said. He had his attention split between the alpha and the man behind her.

"We don't need your lies," the tall Asian woman said. "You're rogue. Packless. That's all we need to know."

"Pretty upset about all this for someone not involved," he commented.

"Rogues are dangerous to us all," the man with the familiar scent said, quietly though, his gaze hard on Adam.

"Can be," Adam admitted. "My former pack made an effort to bring rogues in, help them reintegrate into pack structure."

The alpha snorted. "You think you'll get into my pack by asking?"

"Wasn't asking. Don't want into your pack. Just stating something about my old pack." And stalling for time as he took everyone's measure and tried to pick up the location of any other wolves around his home. He was pretty sure he caught the scent of at least one more, but they were being smart, staying upwind, so he couldn't be sure.

He doubted the alpha only brought three other wolves with her, though. Given the stories they thought they knew about Adam. There would be more wolves around his house. He was sure of it.

All here to ensure he died.

"This is our territory now," the alpha said. "If you don't leave, you die."

Always the same. "I've been here longer."

"Doesn't mattered. The pack has laid claim."

"Is that a formal challenge?" A challenge meant he'd have to fight the alpha to the death. And if he killed her, that would bring the entire pack down on his head. He didn't want to challenge the her. He wanted to be left the fuck alone.

And he didn't want any of this shit spilling onto Becca. She didn't deserve to be caught up in his fight.

Having her there, sword at the ready, was…more gratifying, more of a relief, than he'd admit out loud. It felt right. Her having his back against the other wolves. Like…pack of his own. But he also desperately didn't want her hurt, or killed, because of his past and the mess it had made of his future.

The alpha lifted her lip, an expression both snarl and smile. "I don't have to *challenge* a rogue to take his territory. You can't stop me. Not alone."

"But you don't need my territory so we could always come to an arrangement." He knew this wouldn't work. But damned him if he wouldn't at least try to negotiate. A negotiated truce would allow him to stay here at least. Not move. Again. This was the place he'd managed to settle the longest, the place that felt most like…well, home might have been a stretch. Without his brother and sister, without his pack, no place felt quite like home.

Until Becca that was.

"Arrangement?" the alpha said through narrowed eyes.

"A truce. I stay here, out of your hair. We don't cross paths. You don't have to worry about me."

"We always have to worry about rogues," the tall woman snarled. "They kill and draw attention to us. You're too fucking dangerous to leave here."

The alpha, very subtly, flinched at the tall woman calling him dangerous. What was that flinch for?

"Rogues always bring down death and chaos," the alpha said, hiding the flinch well in a firm, hard tone. "There is no *leaving* a rogue so near our territory. Not going to happen."

"You're forcing a fight that doesn't have to happen," he tried again.

But this time he let his wolf rise. Let the strength he normally disguised around other wolves show. Not a challenge so much as a revealing of cards. He didn't want to kill the alpha. He didn't want control of their pack. And he didn't want to fight the entire pack. But he wasn't prepared to let them walk over him. He wouldn't lay down and die. And if they wanted a fight, it wouldn't go well for any of them.

The man whose scent was familiar issued a low growl. The other man gave his companion a narrow-eyed look. That quieted the man, somewhat. But he still snarled at Adam.

The alpha, on the other hand, gave him a more curious once over. "I expected you to want a fight."

"Why?" An honest question. "I haven't come near your territory. I haven't challenged you. I've actively avoided you. Why would I want a fight?"

"Rogues kill and slaughter and can't be left alone," the tall woman hissed, this time to her alpha.

The alpha made a sound, like a grunt, and the tall woman dropped her head in submission, though her lip still lifted in a slight snarl.

Good control of her people. A good sign she could hold the pack together over the long term.

"I haven't killed anyone," Adam said, trying again for diplomacy. "I've lived here more than two years. No undue human attention because of a lot of wolf killings in the area. You're here because there's a lot of room and no overt threats. We can establish a truce and live next to each other without trouble."

"You might be in control now," the alpha said, sounding thoughtful rather than challenging now. "And you're obviously strong enough to have stayed in control this long. But outcasts always break. Always. Eventually, you will, too. And that will bring a shit ton of trouble onto our heads. I can't allow that."

"He hasn't gone this long without breaking," the wolf with the familiar scent said, his voice a hiss to his alpha. "He broke. He's killed. He's lying to you."

Adam held perfectly still. His hands loose at his sides. His scent as controlled as he could manage in that moment, with his wolf so near the surface. But the man's claims set off a chain of anger and suspicion. And Becca's quiet exhale behind him only confirmed those suspicions were grounded.

"Why do you say that?" he asked, keeping his gaze on the man, his tone empty of emotion.

"Check the area," the man said to his alpha without answering Adam. "You'll find bodies. There are human bodies not far from here. Torn to pieces."

"In his territory?" the alpha asked, her gaze narrowed on Adam.

"Outside. But there's one nearby. Inside his territory. The others have probably found it by now."

Confirming there were more than these four wolves in his territory.

Also confirming the man with the familiar scent was trying to set him up.

"Not sure what you're talking about," Adam said.

The man snarled. "Liar. I know rogues. They kill. You've killed." He faced his alpha again. "Trust me. There are bodies out there."

Adam felt Becca move closer to his back. She didn't say anything. Didn't even gasp or grunt. She just took up a place behind him, in a position that left her sword arm unobstructed.

The alpha tilted her head to consider Adam. "He's right. Rogues kill. He would know."

And what exactly did that mean?

"Maybe you haven't maintained your control all this time," she murmured. "In which case, it's my responsibility to destroy you. To protect my people."

"You won't find any bodies on my territory," he said. "Not with my scent on them. Not that I've killed." That last just in case the man had managed to hide a body somewhere Adam hadn't located already. Even if they found the site with the other human remains, none of the bodies would have Adam's scent on them.

But he did have to wonder who was killing so many humans. Was the man just using monster kills to set Adam up to look like a murderer because the man hated rogues? Did he honestly think Adam had killed all those people, maybe wanted to ensure his alpha followed through with killing Adam?

Or...had those people actually been killed by a werewolf?

How to determine which without giving away too much himself?

"He's lying," the man said. "You can smell it."

The alpha's frown deepened. Because Adam wasn't lying. There weren't any bodies in his territory, that he knew of, and that sincerity came through in his scent. The man who'd claimed to smell his lies had to know better. Had to know the alpha would know better.

Adam noticed the tall wolf also frowned at her packmate, a sharp look. And a hint of confusion hit her scent before she covered it with anger again. There was a lot of anger in that one's scent, enough to keep him from knowing for sure what was going on. Most of that anger directed at him, at rogues in general. The man with the familiar scent also had a lot of rage in his scent. Bitter and sharp like gasoline. The anger made it hard for Adam to pick up anything more from them.

The alpha, however, had turned thoughtful again. She knew Adam wasn't lying. She likely didn't know what to think now.

That worked to Adam's advantage.

The second man, who'd so far been quiet, moved up to the alpha and murmured in her ear, talking so low Adam couldn't hear. There was a familiarity there between the alpha and the man whispering to her, a flavor in their scents, that made clear they were mates. Adam gave the man a more thorough inspection. He was strong, kept his wolf well controlled, hadn't reacted much to the other two wolves' anger. His eyes were only faintly yellow, and that yellow dimmed more to reveal the brown underneath as he spoke to his mate. He didn't touch her, but even from a distance, their scents mingled and blended in an unmistakable harmony. As often happened with mates well-suited to each other.

That thought made him think of the way his and Becca's scents mixed and mingled so well together. How he could live in that blend of flavors for the rest of his life.

He forced out the thought for the moment. He had to focus on them both surviving this confrontation. But the reminder of what mates could be together had him…considering.

The alpha leaned into her mate when he spoke, not touching him either, but close enough they could talk without being overheard. She kept her gaze on Adam the entire time.

Finally, her mate stepped back. The alpha considered Adam. "If we find bodies in your territory, you know I won't be able to leave you alive."

"I know. But you won't find any with my scent in my territory."

"You're being very specific about any bodies not having your scent on them."

His gaze jumped to the man who may or may not be setting him up. "I am."

"Why?"

"Ask your packmate."

Her gaze narrowed, but she didn't turn to look at the other wolf, even as he cursed and snarled at Adam.

"He's a killer," the man said. "You have to destroy him." The vitriol, the violence in his tone, brought the attention of the tall woman and the alpha's mate to him. Both frowning. Even the tall woman's anger couldn't cover her confusion in that moment.

"I haven't killed anyone," Adam said, very seriously, his gaze on the alpha, letting his scent show his sincerity. "I don't want trouble. From anyone."

"Adam," Becca's quiet but urgent voice behind him.

He half turned toward her, without taking his gaze from the alpha.

"We have a problem," Becca said. Her tone so low he knew it wouldn't carry to the others.

"I know," he said back in that same very low voice. "The man with the anger management issues is setting me up."

"No, not that. I mean, yes, he is, but…" She touched his shoulder. "Take a deep breath. Smell that?"

He did as she'd instructed. He'd been so focused on the scents of the wolves arrayed around him, nothing else had gotten through. But at her urging, he let in more, filling his senses with as much as he could.

And there…

Just at the edge of his sense of smell. Something putrid. Something bitter.

Something horribly familiar.

"Fuck me," he muttered. "Is that…?"

"The female monster," Becca confirmed. "And it's approaching fast."

CHAPTER TWENTY-SEVEN

"You have to leave," Becca said to the arrayed werewolves, her tone no-nonsense. No anger. No fear. Just blunt and straightforward.

The alpha's gaze finally touched on her. After her first cursory glance, the alpha hadn't paid much attention to Becca during the confrontation. Becca hadn't taken that personally. This was werewolf politics and she wasn't a werewolf. The lack of attention had given Becca space to study the wolves as well as study the surroundings for other wolves. The alpha had confirmed there were more out there. Becca had been hunting for signs of them when she picked up the first hints of the approaching irgotoc.

"Get the rest of your people and go," Becca said, her gaze on the tree line, the sky. "Hurry. You don't want any part of what's coming."

"Are you threatening me?" the alpha asked, her tone low and carefully controlled.

"You're here threating my…" Becca almost called him her Namtar. But since none of them—including Adam—would understand that word or its significance, she finished with, "friend. It'd be within my rights to threaten back. But this isn't about your wolf fight. You need to leave. For your own safety. Now."

She didn't want to tell them about the irgotoc approaching. Fast. Because she hoped they'd go the rest of their days not knowing these kinds of monsters existed. Unfortunately, they weren't moving. At all nonetheless fast enough. And there were still unaccounted for wolves in the surrounding woods.

"You have to hurry," she tried again. "Go. Get your people and get out. Before it's too late."

She raised her sword. She could hear the approaching monster now, at the edge of her range, but there. Leathery wings beating the air. She noticed the alpha's mate was also studying the sky, frowning. And the tall woman who'd been so full of anger toward Adam earlier was now looking between the sky and Becca, her frown creasing her brow, worry in her scent.

The man who'd likely tried to frame Adam as a murderer hissed. "Liars. They're trying to distract us. Kill them both."

"What's happening?" the alpha asked.

"Something you don't want to deal with is approaching," Adam said. He was staring at the sky, where Becca was staring. He'd moved a little away from her, giving her room. "Get everyone out of here, fast, before it's too late."

A scream cut through the air, loud and piercing and cut off abruptly in a sickening sharpness.

"Too late," Becca said under her breath. She started toward that horrible sound, toward the monster who'd already found one of the wolves.

The alpha blocked her way. "What's going on? What just happened?"

"A monster unlike anything you've seen has just killed one of your people. If you don't want to lose any more, get the rest out of the area."

She shoved past the werewolf and took off at a fast run through the trees, swerving around obstacles, stretching to reach the monster as fast as she could. If they were lucky, it would be occupied with its victim and she'd be able to stop it before it went airborne again.

The fact that it had killed again, before she'd found and stopped it, dug deep furrows of guilt and failure into her gut. Damn it. Where the fuck had that thing been hiding?

She realized Adam was keeping pace beside her after a few moments. And part of her wanted to shout at him to go back, to get the other wolves out of here. To stay safe. Another part of her wanted to burst apart with all the love filling her, knowing he had her back as she'd had his with the wolves.

Love. There it was. She loved him. And she didn't even have time to savor that realization.

In fact, a deeper well of panic set in as they approached the monster. She couldn't lose him now. Not now.

They found the monster in a small clearing, and the sight brought them both up short.

The creature was easily five times the size of the male. Its wings thick and leathery, folded along its back. A dozen long tentacles flailed from its body, some covered in feathers, others in scales, all lined with the suction cups that would burn on contact. There were spikes on the tentacles with scales. And a long thick, scale-covered tail with more barbed spikes. Its legs were similar to the male's, short and stubby and alligator-like, though significantly larger than any modern-day alligator. Where the male had had a pig-like snout over its teeth-filled mouth, the female had a beak for a mouth, a more pronounced beak structure than on any irgotoc Becca had ever seen. A beak currently covered in blood as it dug into its victim.

Becca had to swallow down her disgust and shame at having let it kill again. She didn't have time for recriminations. She had to destroy the thing.

"What the fuck is that?" a high, pinched voice from behind them.

Becca cursed, glancing briefly over her shoulder to see all of the werewolves had followed. "What did I tell you?" she barked. "Get the fuck out of here. Now!"

She charged the monster before anyone else could move. Her sword up, going right for the head.

The monster lifted its head at that moment and filled the clearing with an ear-shattering screech. Over the sound, Becca heard the wolves behind her curse and shout in pain. She didn't have time to worry about them.

She dove under a flail of huge tentacle, skidding along the pine strewn dirt and coming to a standing position just inside the monster's reach, near its head. She slashed across its face, but had to dive away from the tentacles again before she got its neck.

Fucking tentacles. Why the hell did they always have to have tentacles.

She rolled and stood again, slashing at the tentacle coming for her, lopping it off and letting the thick, huge limb drop to the ground. Acid blood spurted out, forcing her to dive away again so she wouldn't be hit.

The limb didn't regenerate, thank the gods. One of the ones with scales and spikes on it. She had to assume those spikes had poison.

The irgotoc swung away from her, screeching again, and to her horror, Becca saw one of the wolves had grabbed at a tentacle with spikes.

"Acid blood," she shouted. "Spikes with poison. Careful!"

Adam, in human form, grabbed a tentacle reaching for the alpha and jerked hard. The move pulled the irgotoc a few feet in one direction, throwing it off balance. Becca took the opening and stabbed her sword into the monster's side, dragging her sword along the scaly hide.

The wound made the irgotoc screech again and swing around to face her. She lopped off another tentacle as it tried to bat her away. More acid blood sank into the soil, sizzling the dark earth and pine needles.

Another wolf, in wolf form, dove at the monster's feat. Grabbing the giant ankle area with teeth and jerking hard to one side.

The irgotoc spread its wings and lifted off the ground with one heavy stroke.

Shit.

"We can't let it get airborne," she shouted.

Noise filled the clearing. The irgotoc's screech. Wolves growling. Voices shouting. A black wolf grabbed another one of the monster's alligator legs, lending weight to the first wolf. Still not enough to pull the irgotoc back to the ground, but the weight of two huge werewolves kept it from getting too far into the air.

Becca used the monster's distraction. She launched off a nearby tree, high into the air, moving over the top of the irgotoc to drag her sword through one wing, taking it at the joint near the shoulder, her weapon cutting through bone like butter.

She hit the ground hard on the other side of the monster, rolling to take the fall, and came up on her feet in time to see the creature drop hard to the ground, the wolves still under it. Adam dove in to pull at tentacles, dragging the monster to the side to free the werewolves beneath. And the tall woman, who hadn't shifted to wolf form, joined him, both of them grabbing hold of tentacles in both hands and jerking hard against the screeching, struggling monster.

Those tentacles had poisoned spikes, though, and seeing both Adam and the woman so close to the spikes sent an adrenaline-fueled punch of fear through Becca. She rushed toward the monster's head again.

The wolves caught under the creature when it dropped pulled free of the body, but one of them limped away.

Becca reached the head and slid low under the monster to try and drag her sword across its neck. A scream that made her skin go cold with fear tore through the clearing. A male scream.

She shoved her sword up into the monster's throat, piercing rather than slicing, pushing her blade deep. Acid blood drip down, catching her on the arm and hand. She ignored the burning sizzle and stood. Pushed the monster upward with all her strength. Shoving the sword deeper and lifting the beast at the same time.

More acid blood squirted, hitting her chest, the burn sizzling holes in her shirt. She felt the heat and pain as the acid ate at her skin. Ignored that, too.

Another scream. This one a howl of a wolf in pain.

She cried out herself. Held the monster over her head as it screeched and flailed. Then she flung the whole creature to one side, ripping her sword sideways through its throat. She dove in the opposite direction at the same time. Acid still caught her thigh, her foot.

She gritted her teeth through the pain, but a hiss of it seeped out. No time for pain. She stumbled to her feet, sword held low so the acid on it dripped into the dirt instead of getting more on her hand.

The monster sprawled on the ground, its head barely attached to its neck. But it still flailed, tentacles swinging around it, an impossible screech leaving its beaked mouth.

Her attention completely on the monster now, she barely heard the sound of someone calling her name. The voice seeped in, though. Adam. Still alive.

Relief warred with her anger, but her anger won out. The monster was still alive, too. She snarled. Had to take its head. Kill it fully. End this. She pushed upward, jumping over a tentacle that swung toward her legs. The jump didn't have a lot of height on it, thanks to her injured leg and foot. But it was enough.

She came down just inside all the slapping tentacles, avoided the swing of the still intact wing. And brought her sword down hard through the remaining piece of the monster's neck. Cutting through bone and muscle, even with a sword as finely honed as hers, jolted through her shoulders. More acid blood spilled into the ground.

And the irgotoc's head rolled a foot away from its body.

Having learned her lesson the first time, Becca hurried away from the still flailing limbs, ensuring there was plenty of room between herself and the tail and tentacles. She searched the area, the trees.

Before she spotted Adam, though, her legs gave out from under her, dropping her hard onto the ground, startling her. She looked down and realized blood leaked from parts of her where the monster's blood had coated her. Her skin sizzled still, continuing to burn. And the pain, now that she felt more of it, made her head dizzy.

Fuck. She had to transition. Her body wouldn't heal fast enough like this. She could already barely lift her sword, everything weak and limp. She wouldn't be able to make the jump soon. She could feel her wolf, pushing up against her skin. And there was pain there, too.

Like the wolf was pushing to get out and couldn't. Like it was going to corporealize inside her. Before it got out.

She blinked as a panic she'd never felt before sunk in. Her gaze darkened. Spots of white light danced in the darkness. The sharp edge of Ne's curse taunting her.

Oh no.

CHAPTER TWENTY-EIGHT

Adam skidded to the ground beside Becca when he finally found her. She was leaning against a tree trunk, her sword limp at her side. Blood everywhere. Her skin burnt. He could smell the acid, acrid and horrible, mixing with her blood and burnt skin. And he'd never felt so fucking helpless in his life.

"Becca," he said, cupping her face.

"Acid," she mumbled, but the sound came out a gasp, full of pain. "Will burn you."

"No." She didn't have any on her cheeks. Across her neck, though. And her chest. Her leg. Her arm and hand. God, she was burning alive from that shit. What could he do? What did he do? He'd never dealt with this kind of injury among the pack before.

If she'd been a werewolf, he'd tell her to shift. To let the shift heal the damage. But she couldn't shift.

She couldn't shift. But she could do that other thing. Let her wolf out. Transition she'd called it. Her wounded body in stone. It would heal like that.

"You have to jump," he said against her ear. "I know there are others around. I'll take care of your statue. You have to…transition. Now. Please, love. You have to."

She whimpered a little, a sound that cut through his heart. Might as well have been covered in acid himself.

"Please. Please. Becca. You have to. You have to survive. You won't live like this for long. There's no other help nearby. I don't know what to do. Please."

He kept up the stream of quiet begging in her ear, and when her skin started to turn a faint gray, his heart lurched with relief. But…

But when he looked down, no wolf was emerging from her. No spirit wolf leaping and become substantial as it went.

Under his hands, her skin started to lose the pliant feeling of living flesh and take on a texture like stone. Something pushed against his hand. He looked to see a wolf snout pushing at the skin. The wolf. Trying to get out. But it wasn't.

Fuck. Fuck. What was wrong? What was happening?

Again against her ear, he whispered, "Becca, I don't know what to do. You have to live. Please. I love you. You have to live. Tell me what to do."

He lost track of the actual words coming out of his mouth. Panic overwhelmed him and nothing else, not even the sound of his own voice, got past that panic. He couldn't lose her. Not now. He'd just found her. She could be his home. They could have so much together. They needed time. More time. He couldn't lose her, couldn't let her go now.

"Stay with me," he begged. "Don't leave me. Stay with me. If you'll have me, I'll stay with you until my last breath. Just…Please don't go. Stay."

She gasped, a sound sharp and abrupt. Her skin went momentarily soft and pink again where it wasn't bloodied and damaged. He lifted away from her enough to see her eyes, beautiful and brown, staring up at him, shimmering in the dappled light under the pines. He started to smile.

And then the gray spread through her, fast this time, charging across her skin in a rush that took her human flesh to stone in seconds. Her eyes turned to stone, her face, her neck. The sweep of it happened with such an abruptness, he gasped and jerked his hands away. Only to grab at her again.

No! This couldn't happen. He couldn't lose her. Not now.

He could feel his own wolf tearing at his insides as his heart burst apart, his chest exploding with a pain he'd never felt. Not even when he'd been forced from his pack. Nothing had ever hurt this much. The monster might as well have torn him apart. Because that was happening now anyway.

He wouldn't survive this. How could he survive this?

He collapsed back onto his haunches, moisture leaking over his cheeks. His body trembled, but he was too lost to move. He stared at her face. Stone now. Completely stone. He couldn't even look at the rest of her, to see her wounded body become a statue.

He'd lost her. How had he lost her after only just finding her? How was this possibly real? This couldn't be real. She couldn't be gone.

He let his gaze finally move over her body. The statue lay sprawled out, just as he'd found her. The sword even still loosely griped in a solid marble hand.

A soft whine from behind him leaked into his awareness. One of the werewolves. Probably blaming him for this. If they wanted to kill him, he wasn't sure he had the will to fight them. Not now. Not in this moment.

A gentle nudge of a wet nose against his bare arm. Were they actually trying to comfort him? A rogue. A rogue who couldn't even keep the woman he loved from dying?

He glanced at the wolf as it nudged his arm again. Several long moments passed before he realized the wolf's eyes were brown. Not yellow. And that it was significantly smaller than the werewolves. Closer to the size of a mundane wolf.

Another heartbeat passed, before the significance of all that sank in. He blinked. Straightened and half turned to face the wolf.

Soft dark fur. Brown, familiar eyes. The wolf nudged him with her nose again, darting in quickly, then sitting back on her haunches and whining softly.

"Becca?" he breathed, hardly daring to hope. He hadn't seen the wolf leap free. He hadn't seen her make that transition like she had in the woods before. She'd just suddenly become a statue. He had to be imagining this. Grief had broken his brain.

But at his quiet question, the wolf whined again softly and batted at him with her paw. Then she nodded.

"Becca, that's you?"

She nodded again.

Relief swamped him. So hard and so fast, he saw spots. He ignored the rush of darkness edging his vision from all the blood rushing back to his head, and pulled the wolf in close, wrapping his arms around her neck. She settled her head on his shoulder, her long nose dropping against his back in a canine hug. He buried his fingers in soft fur and squeezed, gently but with an intensity that left him trembling.

"I didn't see you leap free," he murmured for her ears only. "I thought… I thought I'd lost you."

A soft sound, half whine, half huff, almost like a canine sneeze, and her chin tightened on his shoulder.

He wanted to laugh. He wanted to scream. He wanted to shout out his relief.

All he could manage for a long long time was holding her tight, her soft fur in his fingers as he gripped the loose skin over her sinewy muscles and breathed in her scent. Even in wolf form, her scent was all Becca—though the hint of wolf wasn't a hint when she was like this. The canine musk was definitely strong and present. But every other part of it was her. Citrus and earthy spice and perfect.

The rest of the world rushed back in when someone cleared their throat.

Reluctantly, he lifted his head. The alpha stood there in her human form. Naked now since she'd shifted without taking off her clothes. Behind her stood the tall woman holding a wounded wolf in her arms. Adam couldn't be certain, but the wolf seemed to be missing a limb. One leg was wrapped in the tall woman's t-shirt, a rough bandage that hid the injury. From the smell of the wolf, Adam realized that was the alpha's mate.

"We have a lot to talk about still," the alpha said, looking down at

Adam and Becca's wolf, her gaze narrowing slightly, but that was the only sign of her thoughts. "But my mate is seriously injured. I have to get him back to the pack doctor."

Adam nodded, glanced behind the tall woman. "Your other wolf?"

"He was killed. We'll be talking about that, too."

"The other ones in the woods around my house?"

"Two others killed besides the one we found…" She gestured vaguely behind her in the direction of the monster. Toward the one they'd found the monster eating. "The other two sent back to the pack because of their injuries."

Nine werewolves all together. Four dead. Several seriously injured. Fuck. "If they were poisoned by the spikes on the tentacles," he said, "a shift will help. But they may be slow to heal over the next week."

The alpha nodded.

He hadn't been paying close enough attention to the wolves as he'd raced with Becca to reach the monster. He wasn't sure when they'd had time to find their other people, send the wounded ones back. They'd joined the fight not long after he and Becca had engaged the irgotoc. But the whole fight was a blur of movement and anger and fear now. He'd probably remember it all more clearly later, when he wasn't so overwhelmed by relief and the rawness of having almost lost Becca.

"Get your mate the help he needs," Adam said. "Come back when you've recovered."

"Your mate…?" The alpha nodded to Becca's statue form. Then her gaze danced to the wolf and back to Adam.

He felt the wolf's soft growl rumble through her body. Soothing with a gentling hand over her neck and the back of her head, he said, "I'll take care of this. And disposing of the monster. It has to be burned and buried. Get your mate help. We'll talk later."

The alpha looked like she wanted to say more. But the tall woman behind her murmured something, a name Adam didn't catch. The alpha's no doubt.

She gave a sharp nod, and the tall woman raced into the trees with the wounded wolf. The alpha shifted back to her wolf for with impressive speed. Gave him one more look in that form, her yellow eyes glowing in the uneven sunlight. Then she followed her wolves, disappearing into the woods so fast, her form blurred.

"This is going to be an issue once she and her people have a chance to regroup."

The wolf still resting her head against his nodded. Then she rubbed her soft, fur-covered face against his cheek, and he let his worry about the future confrontation with the alpha go for now. That was a meeting for another day.

He faced the wolf that was Becca. "I'll get you and your body back to the house. Then come back with the stuff I need to burn and bury the monster."

She nudged his arm. He wasn't sure what that meant, but there was a flavor in her scent that spoke to stubbornness.

"You want me to burn the monster now? I don't have any way to do that."

She shook her head and nudged him again.

He frowned. Communicating when he could speak and she couldn't was tricky because everything they needed to say to each other now required more than scent and instinct and a few meaningful nudges. They needed words.

"How long do you need to stay outside your human body for it to heal?"

She huffed out a snort and pawed the ground twelve times.

"Twelve minutes?"

Headshake.

"Twelve days?" he widened his eyes.

Another headshake.

"Weeks?"

An irritated huff.

"Don't get mad at me. Twelve could be anything. I don't know how long it takes you to heal from something like this. The poison took you days. This was worse. Weeks isn't an unreasonable guess."

A soft whine and a nose bump mollified him.

"Sorry I snapped. I was scared and I just want you better. Let's try again. Twelve hours?"

A nod. And a nose nuzzle against his cheek.

He let out a slow breath. "Okay. Twelve hours for you to heal. That's fine. I would have waited twelve days. Even twelve weeks." He brushed his hand over the wolf's face, letting his fingers burrow through the soft fur over her neck. "I'll wait as long as you need."

Another soft whine, and then she wrapped her chin over his shoulder again, giving him another one of those canine hugs.

He hugged her back, for a few minutes, just letting the relief of having her alive sink into his bones. When they finally broke apart, he stood and gently lifted the stone statue into his arms. He considered her sword but decided that would require too much juggling so he'd come back for it when he came back to destroy the monster's remains.

Carrying the statue that was Becca's body through the trees and over the uneven ground proved awkward. God help him, he didn't want to drop it! He wasn't even sure what would happen if he broke off one of the statue's arms on accident, and he didn't want to find out. The stone was heavy, too heavy for a human to have carried on their own. He'd never been so grateful for his shifter strength. Everything in him urged him to get this statue to safety, away from anything that could harm it, so Becca would have a safe place to return to when she healed.

And until then, he'd look after her wolf. Ensure she ate and slept as well.

Everything else, even disposing of the monster's remains, took a secondary place. Taking care of the woman he loved came first.

And when she was able to hold a conversation with words again, they were going to talk about all this.

Especially the part about him asking her to stay with him.

CHAPTER TWENTY-NINE

Becca spent the next few hours talking herself out of rushing the return to her body. Unlike a stab wound or other similar injury, with only one part of her body to heal, the acid had caused a lot of damage over several parts of her human form. And, she'd realized as death came to whisper in her ear, there was poison in the acid blood as well as the spikes on the tail and tentacles.

She really wished she hadn't had to find that out the hard way.

But the female irgotoc was dead. Worth the pain of her injuries. Though she still felt the guilt of not having found it before more people died.

Where the hell had it been hiding this whole time? A problem she needed to solve when she got back to her body. Because even though irgotocs used to only traveled in pairs, she couldn't take anything for granted. Not anymore. Not with the other changes.

From her wolf form, she watched Adam leave to dispose of the body. When she'd tried to go with him, so she could have his back in case the werewolves returned, he'd insisted she stay behind. The worry and fear in his scent had gotten to her, despite the fact that she desperately wanted to stay with him. So she reluctantly agreed to remain in the cabin. But she paced the living room and whined softly until he returned. It was well after dark, close to midnight before he got back, and she greeted him by rushing him before he'd even gotten through the back door, stopping at the last second so she didn't run him over, and instead bumping her head gently against his thigh in greeting.

He looked weary as he smiled down at her, so tired he might drop soon.

"All done," he said. "And no, the wolves didn't come back. So I didn't have any trouble with burning the monster and burying it. I tried my best to burn the blood too, or bury it. I have a feeling the trees in the area aren't going to do well over the next few years.

She whined quietly, her only way to answer while she was stuck inside her wolf. Her wolf was content, because the body was being healed and her Nam-tar was nearby now. But Becca wanted back into her body where she could actually speak with Adam.

They had so so much to talk about.

He went upstairs to the bathroom and she waited outside the door for him, laying on the ground with her head resting on her forepaws, the wolf's patience and ability to live in the moment instead of worrying about the future helped calm her human spirit. Somewhat.

She wondered how he felt when he was in his wolf form. He wasn't riding around in another being, the way she was at that moment. The wolf was the wolf. She was just a guest inside its body. While they were symbiotes, they were different entities. He was the same being as his wolf. Two sides of the same coin. Did that make him feel more comfortable inside his wolf form? Still himself? Or did he ever have this sense of disconnect from himself, the way she did sometimes in this form?

She mulled all those questions until she heard the door click. Then she jumped to her feet and moved out of his way so he could get out of the bathroom without tripping on her.

Following him to the bedroom, her wolf wanted to instantly go inside with him. Her wolf didn't want to leave his side. But the human part of Becca inhabiting the wolf hesitated. He'd said he'd stay with her. He'd even said he loved her. But...

He still didn't know what that meant, that he'd *voluntarily* agreed to stay with her.

Even if he was desperate and didn't understand the repercussions at the time, apparently, the curse didn't count that as a cheat. Because she'd been dying. The acid combined with its poison had been working on her faster than she could heal, the poison slowing down the healing, and despite wanting to make the transition, she been too close to death. Her wolf had started to solidify, become corporeal, *inside* her. She'd been dying. The painful, horrible, cursed death promised to her people by a vengeful god.

And then he'd agreed to stay with her forever.

She'd *felt* the curse break. Felt the moment it had shattered with an almost audible hiss of anger. Like the old god Ne himself had objected to having his revenge taken away at the very last second. The pain of her injuries alone crowded in after that. No longer the pain of her wolf corporealizing inside her. But so much pain and slow healing, she would still have died. Just not under the curse. Her only hope had been a fast transition. Too fast to explain any of this to Adam before she'd jumped. So she'd hurried into her wolf as her wolf leapt free from the injured body. All of it faster than she'd ever transitioned before. Even the sense of cold that swept her during the leap didn't have time to set in.

Adam had no idea what had happened or how. And she couldn't explain it to him until she could return to her human body. The delay was driving her to distraction.

The wolf, on the other hand, was too content with the situation to show that distraction, now that Adam was back in the house. The wolf laid down just inside his bedroom door to wait for him while he got dressed. The wolf followed him back downstairs as he got food ready and waited patiently for him to do whatever he intended on doing next.

Inside, Becca's spirit was restlessly counting seconds.

She'd told him twelve hours. She was a little afraid it would take longer than that, though, thanks to the fucking poison. She really hated the new irgotoc poison.

"I kept another spike," Adam said, as if reading her human spirit's restless thoughts. "Can't know whether or not there are differences between the male and female so I figured it was good to have a sample of each."

She let out a quiet sound she hoped he took as thanks.

He glanced at her from the stove. He was apparently making another pasta meal, but there was steak involved. Her wolf liked the idea of steak. Even cooked steak, though the wolf preferred raw. After the fight, the wolf was fine with any sort of sustenance.

"Your stomach is growling. Can you eat raw meat like that? The way a shifter can?"

It was like he'd read her mind. And her wolf's mind. If the breaking of the curse hadn't proved to her beyond all doubt he was her destined mate, his ability to know what she needed would have. She nodded to his thankfully simple yes/no question.

He lifted one of the four steaks he had sitting on a plate on the counter with a fork and put it on a serving plate, then set it down gently in front of her. He didn't touch her, hadn't since he'd returned. She wasn't sure she liked that. Her wolf definitely didn't. But since they had a lot to discuss still, she supposed boundaries were to be expected.

She ate the raw steak quickly, no ceremony or neatness. The wolf was a lot more basic that way. And since he was used to werewolves, she assumed Adam wouldn't care about neatness or manners when it came to food after a battle. He was hungry too. In his scent and the sound of his own stomach rumbling. But he took his time making the meal, not rushing just to get food in. She'd have rushed just to get food in.

He wordlessly set a second raw steak down for her. And she hurriedly ate it. Two steaks filled the stomach-clenching need for sustenance enough for her wolf to settle again. She was still hungry. Between the fight, the injuries, the near death, and the transition, she could have eaten a whole cow and still had a few twinges of hunger. But the steaks were enough to take the edge off.

Her wolf went back to silently sitting and watching him. Content just to be in the same space as him.

The contentment was...surprising. She wasn't sure why. The

settled feeling wasn't something her wolf had experienced before. Not ever, she realized now, in hindsight. Her wolf had always been a little restless, a little edgy. But that was how things had been for Becca's entire life, so it hadn't occurred to her there could be a difference. There was a difference now. A definite settling.

Seemed having her Nam-tar agree to spend his live with her did more than just break her curse.

His scent made her nose twitch, though. There was so much they had to say and discuss. And she could smell that in his scent. The mix of relief and confusion, some anger and fear still there, churning beneath the surface, a bit of insecurity and hesitance. Maybe even some regrets. In this form, her wolf picked up a lot more of the subtilties, and was able to parse out more of those mixed emotions. But she didn't have the words for it all. Beyond complex. And that complexity created a very low level of tension in both Becca and her wolf, enough to keep the wolf from completely relaxing. Though she was still more settled than Becca.

"Will you eat pasta when you're like that?" Adam asked, his attention on moving spaghetti noodles into the large pan with the red sauce he'd made and then flipping the remaining two steaks on the stovetop grill pan.

She made a grunt noise, and when he glanced at her, she nodded.

"I know we have an awful lot to talk about," he said as he used a pasta scooper to dump the pasta and sauce into two large bowls. "But I don't want you trying to rush the healing. You said twelve hours. But if you need more, take your time." He gave her a level look. "I mean that. I'm not just stalling our conversation. I want you healthy again. Watching you nearly die took several decades off my life. I won't be able to think about anything else until I know you're fully recovered. Okay? So just…if you can, stay that way as long as you need. I'll take care of you."

The last he said with his back to her, his attention on the steaks. But she hoped he could scent her sharp leap of emotion at his words, the spike of love and gratitude. If he knew how she felt, their upcoming conversation would probably go a lot more smoothly. At least, she hoped it would.

He set down the bowl of pasta and another steak, one of the cooked ones, for her. She whined a little and gently tried to nudge the steak back to him. He stopped her with a look. "I'll eat enough, don't worry. You need the protein."

And he brooked no refusals. So she ate the full meal he gave her, both of them enjoying the delicious garlic laden food in silence.

By the time she was full and he was satisfied he'd fed her enough, her wolf's eyes were drooping, sleep sweeping through her. Though the wolf's form was fresh and hadn't taken the brunt of the fight and injuries, she still wanted to nap now that her stomach was full. The urge overwhelmed almost everything else but her need to stay near Adam.

He gave her a look, and then without a word led her upstairs, into his room. "If you're comfortable sleeping in here," he said, "I'd like you to. So I know you're safe."

He'd gently placed her stone body in the guest bedroom, on the bed. She'd even watched him debate covering the body with a blanket, which was so sweet, she'd nearly exploded from the love filling her. With the stone statue in that bed, though, there was only one left in the house. And the couch. She could sleep on the couch, but then she'd be too far away from him.

She curled herself into a comfortable ball in one corner of his bedroom in answer to his request. She didn't need a bed in this form anyway. And she didn't want to be anywhere else.

Before he could comment, or do more bring her a pillow, she was asleep. The turmoil of the day taking a toil even on her wolf.

She slept more peacefully than she ever had in her life. The sounds of Adam's breathing in the same room a soothing background noise that followed her through her dreams.

CHAPTER THIRTY

When Becca and her wolf woke, sunshine streamed in through open curtains. The open curtains were a little surprising. Adam usually kept them closed. The sunshine rained down on her through the window, warming her skin through her fur in a way that left her wanting to purr. If she'd had the right vocal cords for it. She did make a contented sound that vibrated through the wolf's throat. Both of them happy for the heat.

After a moment, though, she stood and stretched, letting her bones and muscles ease after the long rest. Glancing around, it was clear Adam was gone, but listening closely, she picked him up downstairs moving around. The clock on his bedside table said it was after noon. Wow, she'd slept a long time.

She padded to the guest bedroom and considered her human body. But the wolf whined in her head about leaping back. That gave her pause. Her wolf usually went back willingly because being outside the human body for too long felt…abnormal. The wolf wasn't meant to remain corporeal for weeks at a time. Hours. Occasionally days while the body healed from a serious injury. The whine meant the wolf didn't think the body had fully healed yet.

Becca analyzed the scent of her stone body through the wolf's senses. There wasn't much there. If their real bodies could be given away so easily just by scent, all the efforts of creating statues to camouflage themselves would be pointless. The monsters would just sniff them out. But under the ordinary smell of stone and dust that usually marked her human body when it was like this, Becca caught a hint of the poison.

Damn. Her body needed more time. Twelve hours wasn't enough. The poison was slowing things down. She'd been afraid of that.

She was tempted to leap back into her body anyway. She and Adam needed to talk and she couldn't do that from this form. But rushing back and still being visibly injured and in pain probably wouldn't help either of them concentrate on the necessary conversation. Still, she butted her nose against the body, vaguely hoping the wolf's sense of smell was wrong. It was not. Still that hint of poison. Her body, even encased in marble, was healing slower and it was taking time to clear out the poison.

Which mean she needed to stay inside the wolf a little longer.

The wolf didn't seem bothered by this. Probably because, to the wolf, all the conversation stuff was peripheral. Adam had agreed to stay. The curse was broken. Her Nam-tar loved her. All was right in the wolf's world. The wolf didn't understand why the talking was even necessary. But that's why En had combined humans with an animal spirit. The animal spirit needed the human logic as much as the human needed the heightened animal senses. And they both needed the other's strength.

With an internal huff, Becca resigned herself to going downstairs still inside the wolf. It would make things awkward for a bit longer, but at least she'd heal.

She found Adam in the kitchen, sitting at the kitchen table, staring at the back door as he sipped a coffee. She let out a little whine to alert him to her presence.

"Body isn't healed yet?" he asked, without looking at her.

The fact that he wasn't looking at her opened up something hollow in her gut. She made a sound she hoped he'd take for a yes, then sat on the floor next to the table, looking up at him. He kept his gaze on the back door.

"Do you need or want coffee when you're like that? My wolf doesn't like the flavor when I'm shifted, but I don't fully know how this works." He waved vaguely at her.

She didn't need coffee at the moment so she shook her head and let out a sneeze that passed for a no.

"Hungry?" he asked.

He still had his full attention on the door, which had her more than a little edgy now. She redirected her attention to the door. Was he avoiding looking at her, or was there something else happening? She couldn't sense anything outside, and she wasn't able to smell anything that signaled danger. No monster scents. No werewolves.

So maybe he was just avoiding looking at here.

She whined softly, hoping he'd at least glance at her so she could read his expression. His scent wasn't given her anything. The same chaotic mix from last night was still there. A lot of swirling emotions that made it hard to parse out his mood. Lot of anger and fear still there. Even this morning. And she had no way to reassure him that she was going to be fine. The healing was just taking longer thanks to the poison. She wasn't sure if the anger was directed at her or the wolves or the now dead monster or the universe at large. She couldn't tell if the low level of panic still occasionally sending trickles of adrenaline into his blood was about her or the werewolves or the monsters either. And he wasn't telling her out loud what the issues were so she couldn't help. Not that she'd be able to help much while still inside the wolf. There was only so much she could communicate by scent and the various noises a wolf could make.

He didn't glance at her when she whined, but his shoulders drooped into a little shrug. "I'll get you some food. You ate everything last night, so I assume raw or cooked won't be an issue?"

She released another sneeze-sound to represent no since a headshake would have gone unnoticed.

"You'll probably feel better eating raw. I'll get you some meat."

Her wolf did prefer uncooked food most of the time, but frankly, in either form, they'd eat whatever was put in front of them. Her and her wolf wholeheartedly agreed on eating being a good thing.

Adam left his coffee mug cooling on the table while he got her some cuts of beef and a couple of whole salmon, all of which the wolf devoured happily. Becca hadn't really noticed the emptiness in her stomach until that moment. The food did more than satisfy her growling stomach, too. It helped sooth her ruffled fur and allowed her senses to sharpen.

Because she'd barely finished eating, when she sensed something approaching outside, and the first hint of werewolf finally reached her.

Her lips lifted in an almost involuntary snarl as she stared at the door and moved between it and Adam instinctively. He brushed his fingers through the hair on her head as he moved past to the door, the gesture soothing and helping to lower her hackles. It was the first time he'd touched her since they'd returned to the house last night, which also helped sooth her.

But the scent of werewolf kept her on alert as she followed him out to the back porch, and she once again put herself between him and the surrounding woods.

Only one wolf this time. The woman. The alpha. She stepped out of the trees in her human form.

"You got my message," she called, keeping her distance.

Adam nodded. "A phone call or text rather than a note left on my porch would probably be better next time. Don't like having strange wolves here."

"I didn't have your number." Her gaze danced over Becca before she looked up at Adam again. "Wolf is still around, I see."

"She is. How is your mate?"

They spoke across the clearing, neither moving closer to one another. Becca still placed herself more solidly between Adam and the other werewolf. She didn't trust the alpha, even a little bit.

"He'll survive. We have a good doctor in the pack. He won't have an arm when he can finally shift again, but he'll survive." The alpha's gaze moved over Becca's wolf again. "I assume this is why she's still…" She gestured vaguely in Becca's direction. "She's healing or…something?"

"Why are you here?" Adam asked without so much as hinting about Becca's status, and for that she was grateful. The less a strange and hostile wolf knew about her, the better.

"I told you. We have things to discuss."

"One of your wolves tried to set me up. Dropped a body into my territory to frame me for murder. I haven't murdered anyone."

"The monster was responsible." Not quite a question, though the slight uptick at the end of the last word turned the statement into an almost question.

"Probably."

"You knew there was a body on your territory when we confronted you yesterday?"

"Why are you here again?" Still avoiding direct confirmation.

Becca did like the way he was dealing with the alpha.

"Parlay," the alpha said.

Adam raised his brows. "Are we pirates now?"

"I like a good pirate movie." She dropped to the ground, sitting cross-legged, staring patiently back at Adam.

Even Becca's non-werewolf wolf recognized that move as a peace offering. A way of showing she wasn't here for a fight.

Adam hesitated for several long moments, then he stepped off the porch and sat on the rough dirt, crossing his legs as well. He and the alpha remained fifty yards apart, but in positions that didn't lend themselves to a fight.

Becca studied both for a long moment. Then she sat down on her haunches beside Adam. She didn't lay down—she could leap up and react fast if the alpha attacked—but she made a show of relaxing her muscles. The wolf was content with Adam being so far away from the other wolf, so that helped keep her hackles settled.

"What do you want to talk about?" Adam asked after they'd stared at each other for a long time.

"My name's Josephine. My pack calls me Jo."

"Josephine," Adam greeted, pointedly. "I'm Adam."

"Yes," she said sardonically. They all knew she knew *his* name already. "The story of the wayward Walsh brother is not unknown to me."

"You knew who I was even before you brought your pack into this part of the Cascades." Adam wasn't asking, but Becca was curious enough she hoped the alpha elaborated.

"I did."

"You thought you could kill me and take my territory?"

Well. That was the question wasn't it. Becca's hackles rose and settled in a wave, and her wolf let out a very low growl at the thought of someone trying to kill her Nam-tar.

Josephine's gaze flicked to her before settling back on Adam. Adam ran a hand over her head, a gesture that helped the wolf calm. The fact that he was touching her again settled Becca's human spirit as well.

"You're strong enough to have been the alpha of your pack," Josephine said. "Why didn't you take it?"

"I love my brother."

She nodded. "Most wolves think you weren't strong enough to beat him and that's why you were banished."

"Figured."

"You don't care?"

"Why would I? I'm not part of a pack now. Pack gossip doesn't impact me."

"It impacts you." She let that statement hang in the air for a moment. Then, "If we fought, it would be close, the winner."

"I don't want your pack." There was something in his tone that caught Becca's attention, but she didn't have a chance to analyze it.

"I don't intend on giving up my pack," Josephine said. "That…creature?"

"It's called an irgotoc, apparently. From what I've seen, they're best avoided."

"It was responsible for the body, the one Tim left in your territory?"

"Could have been." He hesitated, then, "There's an area a few miles from here, inaccessible to most humans, where a number of human bodies have been dumped." He let that hang in the air, his gaze steady on the alpha.

"Not my pack. No one in my pack would kill a human."

"You're sure?"

"If they did, I'd kill them."

"What about Tim? He moved a body into my territory. He wanted you to kill me pretty badly. And the other wolf, the tall woman who carried your mate to help? She was pretty adamant you kill me, too."

Josephine sighed and waved her hand in the air in a sort of frustrated gesture. "Tim and Vera… They lost a lot of their original pack to a rogue wolf. Most of my pack is made up of the scraps of former packs. We came together because we had nowhere else to go. Short of becoming…" She trailed off but the word "rogue" hung in the air as if she'd spoken it. "Most of them wouldn't have survived long like that. Not like you. They'd have gone feral in months."

Adam nodded. "It's not…" He swallowed audibly. "Not a life I'd recommend to any wolf."

Josephine nodded as well, and a contemplative silence fell between them for a few moments.

Josephine was the first to speak again. "I'm not sure if Tim killed the human to frame you, or if that monster did it, and Tim just found the body. He might even have thought you were responsible. Given his history with rogues. He'd have had more reason to suspect you than a nightmare monster none of us knew existed."

The alpha paused. But when Adam didn't respond or elaborate on the monster, she continued. "Vera was the closest person to Tim in our pack, and she isn't telling me anything one way or another. I'm not sure she knows what Tim did or didn't do. But I can guarantee that none of my wolves will kill humans in this territory. I've made that clear. If… If Tim was responsible for any of the deaths, it's too late to ask him."

"We're going to send the human authorities to the dead. So the humans will get some closure and peace," Adam said. "I hope you're right that none of your wolves were responsible."

The alpha's jaw muscle twitched. But she didn't argue with Adam. "Are there more of that monster around here? Or was that the only one?"

"There was another. She killed it already." He nodded to Becca. "Historically, they've come in pairs, so that should be the last of them. But…"

Becca blinked and faced the side of his head. He turned to look at her. She couldn't read his expression but his scent filled with uncertainty.

Gods she wished she could speak with him in that moment. Use human words to communicate. Her wolf found the inability to put all this stuff into words through the human mouth oddly frustrating, too.

Adam faced the alpha again. "But I intend to ensure there aren't any more in this area. We're going to try tracking the…origin. Where they're coming from."

Becca sat up straighter. She hadn't discussed doing that with him yet. With everything else happening, she'd never gotten around to telling him about her conversation with her brother. The fact that he was already thinking along the lines of tracking the monster's origins left her a little stunned. The fact that he'd said "we" left her wolf very happy. It implied that future she hoped they'd have.

Josephine narrowed her dark eyes. "Where they're coming from?"

"I'm not sure I can explain. I just want to make sure there aren't any more anywhere near these mountains."

Josephine let out a snort and nodded her head. "That's one thing we can agree on." She studied Adam again, for another silent moment. Then said, "You have the help of my pack if you need it. Tracking down…what was it? Irgotoc? And ensuring there are none left in the area seems prudent to both our interests."

Adam's shoulder muscles seemed to relax. A subtle release of tension. And again Becca wondered at that. Was he glad to have the alpha's help? Werewolf senses on the hunt, a full pack of them, would make any search faster. She wouldn't turn down the help, though she did intend to make sure they didn't get involved in another monster fight. That was her duty. Not theirs. If she needed help in the fight…

Well, she had a whole Family full of people trained specifically to this task. No more innocent victims like Tim, the other werewolves, or the humans. She might not have liked Tim for what he was trying to do to Adam, but she still felt like she'd failed him by not getting to the monster sooner. She wouldn't tolerate any more of their pack lost that way.

Again, all things she couldn't say out loud yet. Her wolf sighed and she leaned her chin on Adam's shoulder. He didn't flinch or move away. In fact, he reached up and wrapped his hand over the top of her head, running his fingers over her fur in another gentling gesture. The wolf saw this as a natural state of affairs, but Becca breathed a sigh of relief that he wasn't pulling away from physical contact with her.

"Your pack will…not like that you're not kicking me out of this territory," Adam said.

The comment clicked a lightbulb with Becca. Why he'd been so tense. He'd been essentially telling the alpha he had no intention of moving away from this place. That he was sticking around. He'd issued a sort of challenge Becca hadn't even recognized. She really needed to study more about werewolf politics since she was going to be spending the rest of her life with one.

If, she corrected, even though her wolf bristled. *If*. They still had a lot to discuss.

"My pack will follow my orders and do as I say," Josephine said. "Or else."

Becca wanted to ask, "Or else what?" But maybe it was better she didn't know.

"The one…Vera? She'll be especially unhappy, given what happened to her pack."

"She will. And I'll deal with that with her." Josephine pursed her lips and studied the clearing, the surrounding pines, the cabin behind Adam. "This isn't so very close to our territory. No real reason to deal with you." She flicked a glance to Becca. "And it seems like you might have…something to keep you from going feral now." There was definitely a question in that statement.

Adam ignored the question. "If the pack objects enough to overthrow you?"

"There's no one strong enough in my pack to challenge me." Her mouth lifted in a slight, self-deprecating smile. "You might have been able to. So I hope we've come to the understanding that you won't try. I'd hate to kill you after all this."

Adam nodded. "I don't want your pack," he repeated. "I have… other interests."

Josephine's gaze flicked to Becca again. But Becca only caught the gesture from the corner of her eye, because her entire focus was on Adam and what he'd just said. The swell of hope and anticipation that filled her made her want to whoop and also shiver. What if she wasn't reading him right? What if he meant something else?

Josephine nodded and then gave Adam a look. They rose to their feet at the exact same moment, neither getting up quicker or earlier than the other. The move was so well coordinated, and instigated with just a look, Becca was once again a little awed by how much she didn't understand werewolves, despite her own wolf.

She scrambled to her feet and her wolf moved to stand next to, but not in front of, Adam this time. She might not get the subtleties of werewolf machinations, but her wolf did get some of the broader strokes. Knowing there'd been a sort of truce negotiated in those clipped and brief sentences between Adam and Josephine meant the alpha wasn't an immediate threat. That might change. But for now, there was an understanding in place.

"We're going to be patrolling the area around our territory," Josephine said, "looking for more of those…things."

"We'll start searching tomorrow," Adam said, without explaining further. "We can coordinate efforts then. But you might want to avoid the area where the dead humans are. I'm alerting the authorities to that spot today."

Josephine nodded. "I may take a look myself. I want to know if that was the monster or…" She trailed off, but the implication was obvious to all of them. She wanted to make sure none of her wolves were responsible for the murders. That there was no evidence of werewolf on the bodies.

"It'll take the humans time to get back into that area. Not very accessible. You should have time."

Adam set his hand gently on Becca's head, just behind her ears, and she only realized then she'd bristled and was letting out a low growl. The memory of the dead, too many humans lost, bothered her wolf on a deep level. The wolf's response was different to Becca's in some ways. The blood and destruction weren't as disgusting to the wolf as they were to Becca. But they both felt a sense of profound failure. The deaths weren't anything Becca could have reasonably prevented. Almost all the bodies they'd encountered had been killed before she'd reached these mountains, before she'd even identified a threat in the area. Still, the sense of failing them was real.

Not a novel feeling. She'd experienced this before. She always experienced this when the monsters got to humans before the Families could get to the monsters. Divine duty carried a heavy weight.

"Until tomorrow, then," Josephine said, her gaze once again dancing over Becca and back up to Adam. Without the yellow glow of her animal being close to the surface, her dark brown eyes were more human looking. And the curiosity was obvious there, even if it hadn't been in her scent.

"Tomorrow," Adam said, his tone neutral.

The alpha shrugged and stepped back into the trees without turning her back on Adam until she was under the pines.

Then a blur of movement and she was gone.

CHAPTER THIRTY-ONE

Adam remained where he was, staring into the pines for several long moments after Josephine had vanished, his hand resting lightly on the back of Becca's head. He hadn't done that consciously. His hands just seemed to gravitate toward her. *Not* touching her took a conscious effort. Touching her felt like the most natural thing in the world.

The meeting with the alpha hadn't gone as he'd expected. The truce was useful, though. A relief. One less thing he'd have to worry about. At least for the next few weeks. Maybe longer if she could control her pack's natural reaction to having a rogue wolf living this close to them.

He wasn't sure how much time he needed yet, if months were even necessary. He was glad for at least a few weeks reprieve, though. And the help ensuring no more monsters roamed the mountain would be good, too. They'd be able to cover a lot more ground. He also wouldn't have to worry about accidentally crossing too close to the pack's lands.

He glanced down at Becca. She hadn't returned to her human body. That worried him. The healing was slower than she'd expected again. Which mean there'd probably been poison in the acid blood. He would have smelled it at the time, but he'd been too desperate and panicked, watching her die and not being able to do anything about it.

She hadn't died, though. Something had changed.

They had a lot to talk about.

But how much longer did her body need to stay encased in stone to heal? The poison had taken days to metabolize and stop making her sick before. But then, she hadn't done this transition thing that first time. This shouldn't take days. At least he hoped it didn't.

Until she could get back to that body, though, he was surprised by how remarkably content he was having her in wolf form, puttering around his house. Just having her near. The scent of wolf filling his bedroom—a wolf other than himself—had momentarily baffled him when he woke that morning. The sense of ease, of peace, of being settled. Of belonging. He hadn't felt anything like that since leaving his own pack. Being surrounded by the scent of wolf again filled him with a strange sort of hope he didn't want to examine too closely.

He didn't know how she would react to his declaration when she returned to herself. Didn't know if she'd even heard him confess his feelings. And the not knowing left him leery. So odd to be both settled by her presence and on edge near her because he wasn't sure how much longer she'd stay. If she'd stay.

A truce with the local pack didn't change what he was to werewolves. What he'd face any time he encountered other werewolves. Even those from his own pack. Was that the kind of life Becca could deal with? Did she even want to?

So much to discuss. Impossible to do safely for hours, maybe days yet. And he worried he might take advantage of the fact that she couldn't say anything to confess all his deepest fears and worries and feelings in one big deluge. Didn't seem fair when she couldn't respond with words and questions and interruptions. Still, the idea was tempting.

Instead of spilling his guts, though, he said, "I'm going to call Search and Rescue for the bodies. They have the equipment to reach that location, and they'll be able to better explain to the police what they've found. Hopefully, that'll put a barrier between the authorities and the call. Keep us out of things."

Becca nodded, staring up at him with her soft brown wolf eyes. Patient and waiting.

"After, I thought, since we have some time before you can return to your human body… You want to watch old movies and eat popcorn?"

She actually did a little jump and spun in a circle like a small dog and let her tongue hang out of her mouth in the canine equivalent of a smile. The quick, light, happy gestures made him smile. The first time he'd been able to relax since she came down the stairs still in wolf form that afternoon.

"Not exactly the way I pictured our first date," he said, heading back into the house with her. "But it'll due."

She let out a sound halfway between a sneeze and a snort, a noise that sounded suspiciously like laughter.

That she wanted to spend time with him, just sitting around watching movies, did as much to ease his tension as the meeting with Josephine had done.

Maybe everything would be all right. Maybe this would work after all. Maybe he hadn't destroyed what they'd been starting to build by confessing his feelings too soon.

Maybe they had a chance.

Adam fell asleep on the couch with Becca curled up on the edge of the sofa next to him, after spending most of the night watching old black-and-white films from his DVD collection—streaming was out of the question with his spotty internet, and his satellite dish service's movie selection was limited at best. They'd only argued once over which movie to watch next, though argue was maybe a strong word for her stepping on the DVD she didn't want him to put into the player and refusing to budge until he picked something else. Apparently, she wasn't a fan of *The Maltese Falcon*. But she'd leapt at *Casablanca* and *The African Queen*, so he knew it wasn't a Bogart issue. Thankfully. He loved Humphrey Bogart. He'd be very disappointed if she couldn't at least tolerate a Bogie film.

She'd also done a little dance when he pulled out *Bringing Up Baby* and *Some Like It Hot*. He filed away those preferences in his mental list of "things Becca liked" for future reference.

He'd made them dinner—roasted chicken he suspected her wolf would like, and roast vegetables he was surprised her wolf ate. In wolf form, he didn't always appreciate cooked vegetables. They tasted weird to him through his wolf's senses—and they ate on the couch with just the flickering light of golden age drama rolling over them.

Sometime in the early hours of the morning, in the middle of their first foray into color film—*Singing in the Rain*—he'd drifted off. Falling asleep with her close, with the scent of her filling his head, had resulted in some of the deepest, most satisfying sleep of his life, even though he'd slept sitting up and had a crick in his neck to show for it.

But when he woke, rubbing his sore neck, Becca was no longer on the couch with him.

He launched up and spun around, the immediate adrenaline rush of fear hitting him before his logic had a chance to kick in. When it did, finally, he took a deep breath and listened for her. Heard her clearly moving around upstairs.

Shaking his head at his own jumpiness, he debated heading up to check on her. He should probably give her some privacy. She'd be back downstairs when she was ready. She knew where he was.

Still, he headed toward the stairs instead of the kitchen, justifying himself by deciding he needed to clean up, change clothes, brush his teeth… Not coming up here to check on her and reassure himself she was still around.

The door to the guest bedroom was closed when he reached the landing. He hesitated, his hands fisting and relaxing at his side. With a rough head shake, he shut himself into the bathroom. When she was ready to talk, she'd come out. He couldn't push her. Even if he was a little desperate to be near her again.

When he came back out of the bathroom, the guestroom door was open, but Becca was nowhere in sight. He hesitated, then checked in the room. The statue that had been her human body wasn't on the bed anymore. That was good, right? His heart started pounding harder. She was okay, right? She hadn't rushed the process?

He heard noise from downstairs so hurried down, only checking his speed and slowing to a more human pace when he hit the bottom of the steps.

Becca was in the kitchen, her back to the door, in her human form again, pouring a cup of coffee from a freshly brewed pot. She didn't turn to face him immediately and so he had a chance to just drink her in. Her hair was brushed and pulled back into a long tail. She stood straight, and she didn't smell like acid and blood anymore. He nearly collapsed against the doorjamb when he realized that. She was also wearing one of his t-shirts—the few clothes she'd had in her pack had been through the wringer during their monster hunts and the one that she'd been wearing after the last irgotoc fight had been destroyed. He loved that she wore his t-shirts. He'd given her a few to use over the last few weeks, and the fact that she had one on now left his heart about to explode with…relief? Yeah. That was relief.

Watching her take her first sip of her coffee, her back still to him, he suddenly found it wrong that she wouldn't turn, that she wasn't looking at him. *Turn around. Let me make sure you're okay*. He knew she was, of course. Her scent filled the room and there was nothing worrying in it. Everything was all earthy citrus, the faint hint of her wolf, and Becca now. But, now that he'd calmed enough to analyze things, he realized there was something under the surface. Not bad. But something that struck him as a wrong note, made him want to sneeze like he'd got a hint of pepper up his nose.

What was that?

She finally turned to face him, her smile hesitant.

Just seeing her safe and whole, even with that hesitant expression, left him breathless. She was okay. He swept his gaze across her body, reassuring himself there were no lingering injuries. Nothing he could see around her clothes.

Still, the first words out of his mouth were, "You're okay now, right? No more burns? No more poison? You didn't rush back?"

The hesitance in her expression dropped, replaced by a more genuine smile. "I didn't rush back. Even though I wanted to." That sentence muttered. "But no, no more injuries. All healed now. The poison that was mixed in with the acid is gone too." She shrugged. "I can still feel the side-effects. The lingering grogginess of it. It definitely slowed things down. But the worst is over."

He did lean against the doorjamb then, letting his relief wash through him.

"I think we have some things to talk about now, though, don't we?" she murmured.

"Yeah." He didn't want to talk yet. He wanted to pull her into his arms and spend the next few hours just reassuring himself she was recovered. He wanted to take her face in his hands and kiss her until they both forgot their own names.

But she stood all the way across the kitchen, hesitating, fidgeting with her coffee mug. So he hesitated, too. Not sure how to approach her. He wasn't even sure she'd remember what he said to her after the monster fight. If she'd even heard him. But if she had, if she'd heard his declaration and was still hesitating across the room from him…

Did that mean she didn't feel the same way? Was she going to tell him she couldn't be his pack and that this had all just been temporary? She'd apologize, because she was a kind woman, and then she'd leave. And he'd have to figure out how to not go feral without her.

He shook his head, hard, and pushed away from the doorframe. "Thanks for making coffee." He pulled out a mug, his every nerve ending *aware* of her, standing so close. She didn't move away when he stopped to pour himself a cup, which seemed like a good sign. But she also didn't set her mug aside and throw herself into his arms, which is what he wanted to happen.

"Thought we might need it," she said. Then shrugged. "And it helps when I come back into this body after staying out of it for longer than a few hours."

"Have to do that often?"

"Not too often. But sometimes."

"When you almost die?"

Her expression tightened. "When I almost die." She looked down into her mug instead of at him. "It was close there."

"Too close. I still haven't recovered."

She nodded. Her expression turned inward as he watched, her brow creased, her jaw tense. The fact that he'd admitted to being shaken by her near-death and her response was to frown… That probably didn't bode well for this conversation.

"We should sit," he said. "Couch or table?"

"Table is fine," she said absently, still deep in thought. She blinked back to her surroundings and forced a smile. "Closer to the coffee machine."

He hated that forced smile. He wanted genuine smiles and less of this distance between them. She even looked stiffly awkward when she moved to the table. Like she held herself tightly. He almost asked if she was okay, if she was stiff from the…transition. But he realized that would reveal just how closely he was watching her and decided he didn't want to admit that part out loud.

They sat, her cradling her steaming mug between her hands, her gaze on the table. He tried not to stare at her, but his gaze didn't want to land anywhere else. He didn't want to look anywhere else but at her. She was okay. She was alive. Even if she destroyed him now by leaving, he'd still be so overwhelmed with gratitude that she was alive, he'd want to soak up the sight of her.

He forced his gaze down to his own mug, twisting the ceramic between his palms. Waiting for her to start.

"The alpha," Becca finally said, "Josephine. Things will be okay now with the pack? There were some undercurrents in the discussion I wasn't quite sure I picked up."

"Things will be fine as long as she remains alpha. If she's overthrown…" He shrugged. "That's a worry for another day."

"But it means, for now at least, you won't have to leave here?"

"I can stay."

"And she'll help make sure the mountain is clear of any other monsters."

He nodded. "Do you think there will be anymore?"

"Hard to say for sure." She shrugged. "But I think the female was the last one. In this area. They're only supposed to come in pairs. We didn't see any signs of any others."

"We didn't see any signs of the female until it was too late either."

She winced. The gesture might as well have stabbed him with a hot poker. He'd hurt her, even without meaning to. The thread of her guilt wove through her scent like a pinch of burnt pepper, bitter to the taste.

"That wasn't an accusation," he said.

"I'd like to find where the female was hiding," she said, ignoring his comment, her tone strained. "But I think we won't find any other of that monster here." She flicked a brief glance up at him before focusing on her mug again. "I do need to try and track the origin of the beast. See if I can find where it came from. My brother was going to send another member of the Family to start that search, but I'll need to help once we're sure the mountain is clear. We need to understand how the irgotocs evolved, and if there are more of them."

He nodded. He'd told Josephine he and Becca would need to track the monsters' origins because that had seemed like their next logical step. But now it felt presumptuous that he'd be helping Becca with that. "Where will you go?"

A very slight wince. "I'll start where the first animal deaths occurred. I assume that's where it came out of hiding."

"Hiding?"

"They hide from hunters for long periods of time, creeping into the human world to eat when they think they're safe."

"Like hibernating?"

"A bit." She frowned.

"What's with the frown?"

She glanced up, her expression clearing as if she hadn't realized she was frowning. Giving herself a shake, she said, "I'll get it figured out."

She kept saying "I" as if he wouldn't be right by her side during all this. As if she intended on leaving him behind. No more "we" when she spoke of the future.

He wanted to offer his help. To tell her he'd go with her. He'd never leave her again if she'd have him. But he kept that to himself. She clearly had things she needed to discuss first.

"So… I'm stalling," she said slowly. "But I did want to make sure the situation with Josephine and the pack was settled."

"As it can be. For now."

She nodded. Took a sip of her coffee. Set the cup down gently on the table. Spun it in a slow circle between her palms.

"Still stalling?" he asked.

She huffed out a breath and rolled her eyes. He hid his smile in his coffee mug.

"I'm not entirely sure where to start," she said. "And I'm… nervous. About this part."

The honesty hit him even as the fear of what she had to say tightened his chest. "Take your time, then." Even though he wanted to leap over the table and pull her into his arms and tell her everything would be okay if she just let him love her. He wasn't going to do that. But it was tempting.

"A little background maybe…" She let out a groan. "Or maybe I'll just say that I nearly died after the monster fight. I was…dying."

"Yes." He swallowed. Hard. And gripped his mug so his hands wouldn't shake. She was safe and fine and sitting right across the table from him. But what had *almost* happened still left him shaken to the core.

"You…" She shook her head. "Okay, yes, we need the background. I told you about the god En making us to fight the monsters his brother Ne created."

He nodded.

"Ne got pissed at his brother for continually taking the side of humans against him, so he… He cursed the Families. A curse En couldn't break."

The hairs on the back of his neck lifted. "What does this curse do?"

"When we die, it's… There's no way for us to die without it being a torturous journey of pain and horror."

"That sounds bad." Was ever there a more stupendous understatement uttered? "What does that mean?"

"You watched me nearly die. What was happening was…the human body was becoming stone as the wolf corporealized inside this body. Normally, we…cohabitate and the wolf only becomes corporeal when it leaps out of the human body. But when we die, we get…stuck together. The wolf becomes a solid thing inside us, as the human body turns to stone. The wolf can't leap free, though it tries, and that…tears us up inside. While we turn to stone, slowly, aware and in pain and unable to change what's happening. Whatever else the injury, or cause of death, the process of death is always a torture. That was Ne's curse. That we'd never have peace, even in death."

"You're not…trapped after death? Your soul…" God, he wasn't even sure he believed in souls. Everything she'd just told him sounded horrible on its own. What happened if she was then trapped like that? The thought made him physically sick.

She raised a gentling hand, palm facing him. "When we're finally dead, we're dead and gone. I don't know what happens after since I've never died before, but we aren't trapped in the statues made of our deaths."

"You're sure?"

"According to En. Well, according to the Family histories that describe the knowledge he passed on."

Adam could only hope those histories held truth. "Jesus, if that's how you die, why do you bother to kill monsters and not just…go in hiding and never die?"

"We're not immortal." She tried to force a smile, but it vanished quickly. "We'll die eventually anyway. Like most things. But…En gave us an out. A way to break the curse."

"I thought you said he couldn't do that?"

"He couldn't stop us from being cursed. He could give us a way to break it. Eventually."

"Which keeps you fighting monsters? You have to in order to *earn* this out from the curse?"

She shrugged. "I guess you could put it that way."

"How was this the 'good guy' god in these stories?" The whole thing sounded pretty fucked up to him. Manipulative and cruel. But then, he'd always thought most things passed down by the old gods sounded cruel and manipulative so what did he know. And as a werewolf, who'd had to sacrifice his family to werewolf politics, he probably wasn't one to talk.

"Fighting monsters and defending humans isn't a bad way to live," she said softly. "I would do this even without the promise of an out from the curse."

"Because you're a good an honorable person," he said. "I doubt everyone in all seven Families feels the same way."

"Some don't. My cousin didn't."

"What happened with your cousin?"

She let out a long, slow exhale. "My cousin decided our duty wasn't his duty anymore. He… He sided with the monsters. And with them, arranged… They murdered the head of the Logan Family. My father."

"Fuck." He closed his eyes briefly. "I'm so sorry, Becca. When?"

"A year ago. And no, I'm still not okay. But life continues."

He still wanted to kick himself for bringing up such a sensitive topic. His parents had died more than twenty years ago and he still missed them. But they hadn't been murdered. "What happen to your cousin?"

"Eric took over as head of the Family. Then he hunted down and killed our cousin. Justice of a sort." She shrugged. "But Jason died still under the curse. His betrayal… I'm not sure it was worth the cost for him in the end."

"Your father?"

"His curse had been broke years before. Centuries. When he met my mother."

Adam narrowed his eyes. "How did meeting your mother break his curse?"

She sucked in a deep breath and a lovely flush of pink colored her cheeks. The blush fascinated him. Why was she blushing? What was happening?

"En's solution to the curse," she said, her gaze on the table, "was to promise us one day we'd meet our…our Nam-tar. Our destiny. The love of our life. The one person who could break our curse."

Love of their life? "How does this person break your curse?"

She picked at a spot on the wooden table, refusing to look up. "By…by loving us enough to stay with us. Voluntarily."

He blinked. "Say again?"

She let out a huff. "Our Nam-tar are our…destined mates. The person fated to love us and break our curse. If we can earn their love. If they agree to stay with us voluntarily. If that happens, our curse breaks, and we no longer have to worry about that horrible death."

"Lot of 'if's in that statement," he said.

She still wouldn't look up at him.

"I thought fighting monsters was the way to earn your freedom from the curse. You still have to earn someone's love on top of fighting monsters? Sounds like a crock to me."

Her mouth flattened, but he couldn't tell if she wanted to laugh or if she was upset. Her scent was too chaotic for him to sort out which mood prompted the facial tic.

"Maybe. I never thought about it that way. It's a free will thing, I think. Our Nam-tar is our destiny, but they have the free will to meet that destiny or deny it. Gods have to account for free will in these things."

"Doesn't give you any free will, though."

"We have free will. We can reject all of this. Like my cousin did."

"And die in excruciating pain."

She sighed. "Yes. But, honestly, after all I've seen, the myriad ways humans die and kill each other… Dying in pain is…not as unique as all that. Some are willing to take that chance to deny our Family destiny. And not all of them do so for the reasons my cousin did. Not all of them give up and turn against the Families to join the monsters like Jason. A lot of the ones who give up just…go away and live quiet lives until they die."

He nodded, but he was still pretty pissed off at the way these gods from millennia ago had manipulated so much. Old gods were assholes.

"So…" Becca said. "Anyway, En promised us our destined loves, and if our Nam-tar agrees willingly to stay with us, our curse is broken. Whether it's a good or fair situation isn't really the point. It is what it is."

She finally glanced up and met his gaze. "And I think you might be missing my inferences here, with all the other stuff, so I'm just going to say this outright. Adam. You're my Nam-tar."

CHAPTER THIRTY-TWO

The clicking of the coffee machine turning off marked the only sound in the kitchen following Becca's statement. Adam stared at her, but couldn't quite make the words she'd spoken and the image of her casually sitting in his kitchen, twisting her cooling coffee mug between her hands sync up.

He must have misheard her. Had to have. Because, if he hadn't, she was saying he was her…

Her destiny?

The idea probably should have sent Adam screaming into the morning sunshine. Or, well, cloud cover he realized. A storm was apparently rolling in as the sky darkened and clouds converged overhead, changing the light in the kitchen. Dimming things. Which felt really strange.

Because everything in him was exploding in bright lights and hope and joy and terror. All of that mixing together into a mess of feelings that left him breathless. And unable to speak. Which was probably bad in that moment. She looked nervous. Uncomfortable. Her scent spiked with…was that disappointment? Why was she disappointed? In him? That he was her…what was the word? Nam Tar. Her destiny. Did she not want him? Was that the problem?

He cleared his throat. He needed to say something here. This was important and he had to fill this increasingly awkward silence with actual words that would convey how he felt. A task that might have been easier if he actually *knew* how he felt. He did know the thought of some ancient asshole god deciding Becca was made for him and he was made for Becca was one of the only decent things the old asshole god might have ever done. To be fair, creating warriors to fight monsters was decent, too. But there were a lot of less-than-decent parts to that deal beyond just the brother god's curse.

But the creation of a destined love…? Well, he would have scoffed at the idea of something like that for himself just two months ago. Werewolves didn't have destined mates. A few species of shifters did, like leopard shifters. But werewolves definitely didn't do destined mates. And the fact that somehow, of all the wolves, an outcast like him had ended up with one who wasn't a werewolf but *was* still a wolf was…unbelievable.

And glorious.

And terrifying.

"Wait, you're saying I'll be responsible for breaking your curse?" He winced. Not exactly the first words he'd meant to say. Something more like, "Well that's good since I love you and want to stay with you, and would have been pissed if there was another someone out there meant to be your forever when I really want to be your forever, but I would have dealt with that to make you happy, but still, I'm glad I'm the one and not some other asshole." All of which would probably have sent *her* screaming into the dim morning light. So maybe it was best he'd started with the less emotion-ladened part of the conversation.

Maybe. Her brow creased and her mouth tightened into a flat line. Something moved through her expression he couldn't read. And there was no help from her scent because too much was happening there. A lot of her citrus and earthy scent seemed to be buried under a sharper flavor like a bitter burnt sugar. That part of her scent had his wolf's hackles bristling. Though he wasn't entirely sure why.

"So, this is where it gets interesting," she said, not meeting his gaze. "You *already* broke my curse."

"I…" He swallowed. What? "When?"

"When I nearly died. I was dying. I would have died. But you said…" She rolled her lips into her mouth, made a popping sound when she released them. "You said you'd stay with me. You asked me to stay and said you'd stay with me. And that broke the curse and my wolf was able to break free and we survived. Because of you. Because of what you said."

She flicked a glance up at him, then back down at her coffee mug.

He narrowed his eyes because he couldn't judge her mood and it was driving him crazy. "That was…a good thing."

"It was. Of course it was. I…" She huffed out a breath. "But I hadn't told you about the Nam-tar stuff yet. So, you didn't know what you were signing up for. A life with a monster hunter who might always be in danger and who might keep getting you into danger and who isn't a werewolf so I can't actually be your pack, but—"

"But you are wolf so you actually can be," he said, stopping her ramble.

She did look up then. Her dark eyes wide and uncertain. She swallowed, visibly, and said, "I would be your pack. If you wanted me to be."

"Was the part where I said I'd stay the only thing you heard or remember?" He kept his voice very quiet, but still those words felt like they reverberated through the otherwise silent kitchen.

She didn't look away again, but she hesitated before saying, "No. I remember… I remember…"

"That I told you I love you."

She swallowed hard again. "Yes."

"Does that… Are you unhappy about that?"

She straightened. "What? No. No. Not unhappy at all. The opposite. I mean…" She pushed out a long stream of air through pursed lips. "I thought, maybe after learning everything, you might change your mind about…well, everything. Including that part." She shrugged. "I can't coerce you into staying. That's not how it all works."

"I'm not being coerced."

Her nod was jerky. "No. But now that you know everything…"

"You think I'll change my mind."

Another awkwardly jerky nod. "And that's your right. I won't hold you to something said in a desperate moment. You saved my life. I'm so grateful for that."

"Do you not want me?" he asked quietly. The real crux of the matter for him.

Her expression broke his heart, a mix of pain and hope that wrapped like a fist around his chest. Filled him with similar hope. And a lot of fear.

"Adam," she murmured. "I love you. I want you. But more than that, I want you to be happy. And if I'm not… If my life isn't something you want to be a part of, I will honor that. I'll walk away."

"If you tried to walk away, I'd follow," he said. "And I will do whatever it takes to convince you I want to be in your life and I love you and even the old gods and their stupid fucking curses couldn't keep me from loving you and being with you. The only question for me now, or ever, is what do you want? If you want me, I'm yours."

A tear slipped over her cheek, but it was accompanied by the most beautiful smile he'd ever seen in his life. And he couldn't stay on the opposite side of the table anymore.

She met him halfway, coming out of her seat and stepping into his wide-open arms in a rush that brought her momentarily off her feet. She laughed, and wrapped her arms around his neck, kissing him soundly. The feel of her in his arms, warm, alive, and *his* was almost unbelievable, almost too much to be real.

And she loved him. She wanted him in her life.

She wanted to be his pack.

The sense of coming home, of settling and allowing all his tension and guard to relax… Only with her. Not even in his pack had he felt so himself, so at ease. And so loved.

He wasn't even sure how to put all that into words, how much having her in his arms felt like home and belonging and peace. So he poured it all into his kiss, all the passion and love and forever he could muster.

Their scents mingled in that way that felt so right. A scent uniquely their own. A flavor he would now always and forever think of as…

Home.

EPILOGUE

After weeks of scouring the mountains for miles around, between the pack and Becca and Adam's efforts, the search turned up no signs of any more irgotocs, and no more dead. Thankfully. They did find the female's hiding spot finally, many miles away from the site of the nest with the remains. The small, shallow cave still had the stink of irgotoc filling it, which kept most of the local wildlife away. There were no signs of recent irgotoc activity when they reached the cave, though. And no sign of eggs.

Becca had been pretty sure it was too soon for the irgotocs to have reproduced, but the confirmation of no little monsters about to hatch had been a huge relief.

A relief nearly as strong as her relief at learning Adam hadn't changed his mind about loving her.

Still hadn't changed his mind. Even after more than a month. Something that continued to awe and humble her. He loved her. She loved him. They weren't just destined to be together. They *wanted* to be together. She loved being with him, watching old movies, hunting the woods, just…being with him. And that made everything else okay. Everything else manageable.

Even the lingering worries weren't as horrible as they'd seemed before him.

And at least one of those worries was close to a solution. She'd taken one day away from the hunt to send her sister Judith the two irgotoc spikes Adam had kept, mailing them by special delivery to her sister's lab west of Toronto. Judith had managed to isolate the poison, and with that, she was currently working on an antidote. She was hopeful she'd have something for the Families soon.

Not having to worry about anyone else in her Family going through what she had, had only added to Becca's relief and happiness of the last few weeks.

Unfortunately, there was less progress being made on the hunt for the irgotocs' origins. Which was frustrating. Now that she was sure the surrounding mountains were clear, though, she'd be able to help with that.

But doing so meant she had to leave the haven in the woods that Adam's cabin had become. She'd be away for a while, too. Not just a few days. Her Family had been hunting for a month now with no answers. Unless they got very very lucky, finding the origin of the irgotocs and any hints to how they'd managed to evolve so suddenly was going to take time.

She didn't want to ask Adam to leave his home behind for that long. Especially when he was still on delicate footing with the werewolves. She also didn't want to be away from him for months after they'd only just found each other.

She brought it up after dinner the night after they'd declared the mountain and immediate territory free of monsters.

"I'll go with you," he said, without hesitance as he put away the plate he'd just finished drying.

"You don't have to. This is my job. Not yours. And this will probably take a while. What if the wolves decide you leaving for that long is a sign they can take over this area?"

He shrugged, taking the next plate she handed him and drying it in quick, efficient swipes. "They won't. Josephine and I have an understanding. But even if they did, I don't really care anymore."

She turned a little from the soapy sink to study him. "Why not?"

He gave her a look, his head tilted to one side. "You're my home now. Wherever you are, I'm home. The house and location are just…places."

A familiar and yet brand new feeling of gratitude and love rushed through her. She let the cup she'd been washing drop gently back into the soap suds, gave her hands a pat on a dry towel, and then wrapped her arms around his neck. "I love you," she murmured. "Thank you for being my home, too."

His arms tightened around her as he held her gaze. "You saved me," he said quietly. "I know the Nam-tar thing is supposed to be me breaking your curse, but… You saved me. I don't have to worry about going feral anymore. No more panics when I think of being without a pack. I feel whole for the first time in years. Settled. Content. Even my wolf is content and that bastard never relaxes."

She chuckled.

"I need you to know that no matter where you go, no matter what you have to do, I'm with you. Always and forever. I'm with you."

"With you too," she whispered and kissed him because that kiss felt more important in that moment than anything else in her life.

She surfaced, a little breathless, and was about to suggest they forget the dishes for a while, when a knock on the front door had them both stilling. No one every knocked on that door. No one was expected. No one who might come to see them went to the front of the house.

Adam's head came up suddenly, his body going tight, his muscles clenching.

Adrenaline shot through Becca and her gaze jumped between the front of the house and Adam, his jaw tight. "What is it? What's wrong?"

He shook his head, his gaze narrowed, a frown causing his brow to crease. "Stay behind me," he murmured as he headed toward the front door.

She grabbed her sword where it was leaning against the back wall and followed him, keeping her steps silent as she pulled her sword from the leather scabbard, dropping the scabbard onto the couch as they passed.

He hesitated at the door, his hand hovering over the knob for a long moment. Becca waited at the ready, her sword at her side, but her body coiled and prepared to pounce if necessary.

"Open the door, Adam," a deep voice said through the thick wood. "I'm not here to fight."

Not any of the werewolves Becca had met. Who the hell was that?

Adam let out a resigned sigh, his head drooping forward. "You're not supposed to be here," he said, still not settling his hand on the knob.

"No one knows I'm here. Are we really going to have this conversation through the door?"

Adam cursed quietly under his breath, then flung the door open. "This will only cause trouble if the others find out," he snarled.

The man on the porch was about the same height as Adam, black hair, blue eyes, a little leaner. But the family resemblance was unmistakable. The newcomer's features were a little longer maybe, but there was no missing that the two men were family.

"Why are you here?" Adam asked, staring hard at the man.

"My brother tells me he's having trouble with a new pack, I help." The man faced Becca. "I'm Gabriel Walsh," he introduced himself. "You must be Rebecca Logan."

Becca blinked a few times, then turned a look on Adam.

He sighed. "Becca, my brother Gabriel. Gabriel, my mate Becca." The introductions were almost comically delivered in his irritated tone.

Becca tried not to let the delighted butterflies in her stomach when Adam called her his mate show in her expression. But she was pretty sure her scent gave her away. She nodded a greeting at Gabriel. "I thought you two didn't… Weren't supposed to see each other."

"We're not." Adam turned on his brother. "And things with the new pack are settled. Which I told you already. Weeks ago. Why are you here?"

The fact that Adam talked to his brother often enough to have given him her name, and to have explained the situation with

Josephine's pack left Becca a little stunned. She'd just assumed all this time they never talked, never communicated. *Couldn't* communicate.

Gabriel sighed and lifted his big shoulders in a shrug. "I wanted to make sure you were okay. In person. And Siobhan was worried."

"How's her boutique doing?"

Becca narrowed her eyes. That sounded like a subject change.

"Fine. As always."

"Good. Now leave before you start trouble you don't need."

"No one knows I'm here except Siobhan, and she's not telling on me." Gabriel's expression warmed as he faced Becca again and noticed her sword. "Guess I don't need to worry about who has my brother's back now, though, do I?"

"No. You don't." She flicked a glance to Adam, then met Gabriel's gaze again. "We're pack now."

"Gonna explain the scent of wolf on a person who's not a werewolf?" he asked.

"No." But she relented a little with, "Maybe when I'm sure I can trust you."

"Adam knows?"

"Adam knows."

"Adam is also standing right here and can answer these questions," Adam said, his mouth flat as he shook his head at his older brother.

"Adam has been avoiding answering my questions for weeks," Gabriel responded without missing a beat. "I was hoping your mate might help clarify things."

"The best I can do for you," Becca said, "is tell you he's got a home now and is safe." She winced inwardly. Her life, her world wasn't exactly *safe*. But Adam didn't have to worry about going feral anymore.

"And that's all you're going to get for now," Adam said. He looked his brother over, and finally relented. "You want to come in for a coffee before you get back on the road?"

"Gee, such hospitality. After I've come all this way to check on you."

"Shut up. You want the coffee or not?"

Gabriel's expression turned to a smile and his shoulders relaxed. "Coffee would be good. Siobhan is going to want all the details. If I go back without anything more than a 'you're fine,' she will kill me."

Adam stepped aside, letting Gabriel into the house, and motioned him toward the kitchen. Becca hung back as Gabriel proceeded them, taking in the cabin as he went.

She slipped her sword back into its scabbard and leaned in to Adam. "Is this okay?" she whispered for his ears only.

"You suddenly meeting my brother when I wasn't expecting to see him? You tell me."

"I love being able to meet him. I wasn't sure that would happen, given everything."

Adam stared at the open doorway into the kitchen. "I can't believe he came. I'm not sure…" He swallowed. "The pack won't like it if they find out, but…"

"But you're glad he's here?"

"I'm glad I get to introduce him to you." He turned and took her in his arms. "One day, when it's safe, I want you to meet my sister, too. I think you'll like her."

"I'd love that. When you're ready. Family is important." Not always easy. Not always the family of your blood. But Becca knew very well how important family was. And she'd ached for Adam losing his the way he had. If there was hope, even a little, that one day they could bridge that gap, she'd take it.

"Family is important," he said. "And I'm very grateful to have found my new family. In you."

Her heart pounding, she rose onto her toes to kiss him, once again letting her kiss and her scent tell him what she had trouble putting into words. He was hers. She was his. And the rest…would work out.

"Come on," she said, leaning back and patting his chest. "Let's make sure your brother takes home reassurances for your sister."

"I love you," he whispered against her mouth.

"Love you too," she whispered back.

A love that would see them through anything.

THANK YOU

Thank you for reading REDEMPTION IN STONE. I hope you enjoyed the second novel in the Seven Families: Wolf series. Keep reading for an excerpt from Book 3 in the series, FATED IN STONE, which will be out May 2023.

If you'd like to try more of my Paranormal Romance, don't miss my Tiger Shifters series, the first book of which, ONCE UPON A TIGER, is available for free. For those among you who are curious, the stories Adam refers to about the Chernikov brothers and the tigers shifters in Eirene are told in two books from the Tiger Shifters series: HER TIGER TO TAKE and WHAT A TIGER WANTS. Those are books 4 and 8 of the series, and they will reference things that happen in other books, but both can still mostly be read as standalones. Adam and Gabriel Walsh even make on-page appearances in both books.

I also have a standalone novel, ROMANCING THE LEOPARD, which is a crossover between the Tiger Shifters world and my urban fantasy Cary Redmond world. Most of my paranormal and urban fantasy worlds are specifically written to take place in the same "universe." So there's also a Cary Redmond story that references the Seven Families—*Dinner with the Joneses*. I love a good crossover universe.

For more on my books, upcoming releases, and a couple of exclusive stories, please consider signing up for my newsletter at https://bit.ly/KatSimonsNewsletter. You can also follow my author page at BookBub or at your favorite vendor, or go to my website.

Thanks again for reading!

~Kat

FATED IN STONE
EXCERPT

A Seven Families Novel
Wolf Family
Book 3

CHAPTER ONE

Benjamin Logan remained deep in the woods as he watched the woman, staying far enough into the shadows to avoid her sensing him in any way as she studied the house. It was just after sunset, but even in the dark, he wouldn't have had trouble seeing her clearly.

She was a pretty average looking woman. Not too tall but not short. Dark blond hair cut into a short, loose style. Pale skin. Cargo pants, hiking boots, and a t-shirt. No jacket. It was still early enough in spring to be cold in the woods after dark. It wasn't freezing, yet, but as the night progressed, it would get too cold for a human woman.

She was too far away for him to see details, like eye color, but his general impression was one of efficient movements and watchfulness. He was upwind of her so couldn't catch her scent, which would have made figuring out what side of all this she was on a lot easier.

The way she scanned the area, slowly, taking in the house, the surrounding trees. She didn't approach the place like she belonged here. She stuck close to the tree line as she studied things, not moving out into the narrow clearing circling the house. She hadn't come in a car. He'd have heard that. So she must have walked in from somewhere. Which hinted that she didn't want anyone to know she was approaching.

There were two SUVs outside the house, parked against one side of the building. If she'd belonged here, wouldn't she have just driven up and parked with the other cars?

When she finally moved toward the house, she did so carefully, slowly, furtively. Her gaze continually scanning the surroundings as she headed for the side of the building instead of the front door.

The others went in through the front.

She wasn't with the others, then. Not one of the Elemental's humans.

So what was she doing here?

He started toward the house, only to stop in place again when something else caught his attention. A movement through the trees. A flickering of…something. Something gray.

A scent reached him.

Monster.

Without pausing to think, Ben raced toward the house. The woman was still on the side of the house, approaching carefully. He moved too fast for her to see, and reached the back door before she got around the side of the building. With a hard twist, he turned the handle, breaking the lock. A lock designed to keep humans in and out, not someone like him.

An oversight by the Elemental's people.

He edged inside, keeping his senses alert. The myriad of crates, like a maze, making the interior of the house more storage unit than anything. He used the cover of those crates and headed in the direction of the single light source at the center of it all. Toward the smells of reagents and cleaners and human sweat.

He heard the woman ease inside the building moments later. But his focus was on the people ahead. The geneticist.

A monster was approaching the house.

He had to extricate the geneticist before the monster got him.

* * *

ELLE BARKER STUDIED THE HOUSE FROM JUST INSIDE THE TREE LINE. IT wasn't what she'd been expecting. Especially since it wasn't a real house.

From the outside, the building—roughly the size of a three-bedroom, single story ranch—looked a little rundown, maybe not used for a few years. The surrounding northern Michigan woods moved in close, encroaching on any yard space. There was some room at the front of the house, with two black SUVs parked along the side, and a little clearing between the back of the house and the woods. A boxy building with a slate roof and worn walls in desperate need of a paint.

But that was where the resemblance to a home ended. No windows. No light leaking out of the wooden slate sides, though it was dark now and if there were people inside, there should be some light. But, most telling, was the steel front door that looked more solid than the walls. No way to confuse this for a slightly rundown family home.

The door being more solid than the walls was interesting, and it nearly threw her off the scent. The look of the place from the outside made her distrust her information. How could *this* be the place?

She'd seen places like this in her years of tracking people. Especially in the early days, when she'd specialized in finding men that were like her father. Back then she'd been working with various law enforcement agencies. Now she worked for herself, and she went looking for who she wanted, when she wanted. No more hunting down budding domestic terrorists. Now she found people whose families actually wanted them back.

She liked this work better. Much better.

But being back in the Michigan woods and seeing this particular building brought her back to those early years and made her doubt her instincts, her information, and her skills. This couldn't possibly be where the professor was being kept.

Circling the outside of the house, she took note of the generators, humming quietly, that kept the building in electricity but off the grid. And there was a small hole in the wall, high, hear the roof, that leaked some faint light. That hole was interesting. An anomaly, like walls that weren't as strong as the steel door in the front of the building. Or the steel door in the back of the house.

That was open.

Her tracking sense started to tingle. This was the place. This had to be the place.

Finding lost things, specifically lost people—even if they were "lost" because they wanted to be unfindable—was a skill she'd had for as long as she could remember. She'd been ten years old before she realized not everyone had that particular sense of *where* things and people were.

But Elle didn't rely on her unique talent for finding things when she worked. She did her research. She used more conventional methods. Especially when she'd worked with law enforcement because she had to ensure she could *explain* how she'd tracked someone, could provide information that went onto official records and sometimes got introduced into court cases. She rarely had to go to court these days. That was for the lawyers and cops and federal agents. But she did sometimes have to give testimony or be deposed, sometimes file a police report, and she needed an understandable and legitimate record of the things she'd done and used to track her targets. Telling a skeptical judge or lawyer that she'd "just known" didn't go over well. Telling *anyone* she had a psychic sense that helped her track people was not going to happen.

Those conventional methods reassured *her* as well, most of the time. She trusted that other sense…to a degree. Because it had always worked for her. But she worried that one day, it wouldn't, and she'd be unable to find someone who was the light and life of the people looking for them. Failure wasn't an option in those cases. So she ensured she used every skill at her disposal to find the people she was hired to find.

In this case, a beloved father. Kidnapped from his university office more than a year ago. His family were desperate. They knew he was still alive. He was allowed to call once a month and speak to his wife and kids. No one ever asked them for money—which they didn't have enough of to pay a huge ransom, but they would have found it among friends and associates if they had to—and there was no sign of the professor being returned. The police had put the case onto a backburner because nothing had changed and the man was still alive.

After talking to the officer in charge of the case, Elle realized why they'd backburnered things. They were convinced the man had left his family, of his own volition, and just wasn't ready to admit it to them yet. The police assumed the professor was living with a mistress or second family or something and faking the whole "kidnapped" thing for shits and giggles.

Elle knew better. The minute Sherry Arron had walked into her Detroit office, Elle had known the truth. But with no help from the police, Sherry was desperate. She'd come to Elle. And Elle had promised to find her husband.

A search which had led Elle to this seemingly old and abandoned house in the middle of the northern woods in Michigan.

The open door had alarm klaxons screaming in her head, though. It wasn't wide open. Just enough to look like someone had either forgotten to close it fully or had purposefully left it ajar. Just enough to get back out without making noise, but not so open as to be obvious.

Whatever the reason, that open door gave Elle her way inside.

She slid past the heavy steel door, quietly, studying her surroundings, ensuring no one had seen her enter. Just inside, she paused. The building felt very large on the inside. A lot larger than it had looked from the outside. Even the roof felt higher, peaked and with no attic or anything to lower the ceiling. The building was one big open space, as far as she could tell. Turned into a maze by stacks and stacks of wooden crates that piled almost to, but not quite as high as, the roof. More like a warehouse than a home.

There wasn't much light either. Without windows, the shadows beneath the crates were deep enough she could have used a flashlight. She wasn't going to turn one on, but it would have helped. There seemed to be a single light source coming from somewhere in the middle of the maze, which gave just enough illumination throughout the building she could see to navigate. That light source also gave her a direction to head.

She made her way silently through the maze of crates, pausing often to listen. A faint hint of something dripping. A medicinal smell like strong bleach softened by lemons. She didn't have much of a sense of smell, but she thought she caught a hint of something burning? Not like a campfire, or fire in a fireplace, or even a gas stove. Something a little more… She wasn't sure. She wanted to say metallic, like metal was burning.

The soft whirring sounds of a machine of some kind guided her through the maze. She squinted at a few of the wood crates as she went past, looking for hints as to what they held. But they were either plain with no writing on them, or the marks were things she didn't understand and the language used one she didn't know.

As she neared the source of light, she saw a single bulb hanging from an unadorned wire dropping down from the roof. Except for the slow drip of some liquid and the soft whirring of a machine, the house was silent. A silence that made her nerves jangle. Once again, she might have doubted her information and her instincts. If that back door hadn't been open. That opened door set off all her tracking instincts. She was in the right place.

But she was a little worried she was going to find a body instead of a living man.

Her heart hammered hard, way beyond the effort it had taken her to hike up to this house from where she'd parked her car. She steadied her breathing, carefully controlled the rush of adrenaline that whispered she had to hurry. Eased through the boxes, her hiking boots quiet on the scuffed wooden floor.

A sound. A creak of wood and a whoosh. Behind her.

She spun, prepared to dive for cover. But nothing appeared in the shadows. No movement. She stared into the dimness back the way she'd come. No one rushed her. No strange glints, like the light hitting metal on a gun. No shadows changed sizes.

She scanned the tops of the stacked crates. Nothing up there either.

Releasing a slow, calming breath, she faced the light bulb and the machine noise again. The hairs on the back of her neck prickled.

She was almost to the part of the maze where she could see what the light bulb illuminated when she finally heard voices.

"Hurry." A man, his voice deep and urgent.

"I'm doing the best I can. You didn't give me any warning. If I leave this…everything will be lost." Another man. A nice tenor rumble to his voice. A crisp clip of vowels. The second man sounded only a little less panicked than the first.

"We don't have time to worry about that," the first man said. "You'll just have to redo everything."

"I have been working on this for eight months. I can't just *redo everything*. Not in the timeline I've been given."

"You don't, professor, you die. So I suggest you figure it out. But not now. Once we get to the next location."

"I can't work like this," the second man muttered. The "professor."

That was her target. Sherry Arron's husband. Professor Gabe Arron.

Elle eased forward, careful of her steps so she didn't make the wooden floor creak, careful of her breathing so she didn't give herself away in the mostly quiet building. The high ceiling ensured sound carried, echoed. Like the voices ahead of her.

"Stop that," the second man snapped. Professor Arron. "You'll destroy it. That won't make your boss happy."

"The boss wants you in a new location immediately. That'll make the boss happy. Move it."

The sound of footsteps. Heavy and thudding. From the direction of the front door. "We gotta move," a third voice. Yet another man. "Someone's here."

Shit. She must have left a footprint or something that a scout had found. She'd tried to be careful. But it had rained two days ago and there were still muddy spots in places under the trees.

A rush of fear froze her in place. What did she do now? If they ran, she was too far away from her car to follow immediately. She'd have to hurry back to her car and pick up the trail from there. More time. More chance the ones holding Professor Arron would panic and kill him. Not a chance she wanted to take.

But there were at least two men ahead guarding the professor, and there could be more in here who just hadn't spoken yet. She was one unarmed person. If the guards had guns…

She shook her head. She'd worry about that when she spotted the guns. For the moment, she needed to get closer, see what she was working with. See exactly how much danger the professor was in.

And how much trouble she was in.

* * *

Out May 2023
FATED IN STONE
The Seven Families: Wolf
Book 3

BOOKS BY KAT SIMONS

The Seven Families Series

Wolf Family

Darkness in Stone

Redemption in Stone

Fated in Stone

Tiger Shifters Series

* Once Upon a Tiger * Along Came a Tiger * Here There Be Tigers * Her Tiger To Take * To Tempt a Tiger * Down Will Come Tiger * To Catch a Tiger * What a Tiger Wants * Taming Her Tiger

Tiger Shifters Series Vol 1 (Books 1 - 3)

Tiger Shifters Series Vol 2 (Books 4 - 6)

Romancing the Leopard: A Tiger Shifters-Cary Redmond Crossover Novel

The Cary Redmond Series

* The Trouble Black Cats and Demons * The Trouble with Ghouls and Serial Killers * The Trouble with Leopard Queens and Shifter Wars * The Trouble with Baby Gods and Vampires * The Trouble with Magic and Faery Curses * The Trouble with Wizards and Old Enemies * The Trouble with Death and Demon Gods

The Cary Redmond Series Box Set Books 1-3

Cary Redmond Short Stories

* When Cary Met Jaxer * When Cary Met Pickles * When Cary Met Marianne * When Cary Met Lucy * When Cary Met Angie * Cary and Deacon (Try to) Go on a Date * Date Night Take Two * Third Date's the

Charm * Cary vs the Goblin King * Dinner with the Joneses * Cary and the Cursed Jack-O'-Lantern * Cary and the Demon Witch * Cary Goes to Hawaii * Cary Holidays * Cary and Dragons and Goblins * Cary's Galentine's Day * Cary at the Haunt and Howl * Cary's Leprechaun Troubles

When Cary Met the Good Guys (Collection 1)

Dates, Dinners, and Other Disasters (Collection 2)

Witches and Weavers and Ghosts, Oh Boy (Collection 3)

A Very Cary Holiday (Collection 4)

Demon Witch Series

* Howling Dreadful * Moonlit Strange

* Bone Lantern Witch * Spiderweb Witch

Joan of Kerry Series

Joan of Kerry: Joan and the Abhartach

Joan and the Leprechaun

Joan and the Kraken

Haunts and Howls Collections

Haunts and Howls and Guardian Spells

Haunts and Howls Where Demons Dwell

*Tombstone Wizard * The Unshattered Sword * Destiny Through the Cats Eyes * Going Out of Business: Everything's for Sale

ABOUT THE AUTHOR

Kat Simons earned her Ph.D. in animal behavior, working with animals as diverse as dolphins and deer. She brought her experience and knowledge of biology to her paranormal romance and urban fantasy fiction, where she delights in taking nature and turning it on its ear. She writes urban fantasy, contemporary fantasy, and paranormal romance in series which combine action adventure, the otherworldly, and a frequent dose of sexy romance.

DARKNESS IN STONE, launches the newest paranormal romance series for Kat, following the exploits and loves of the Seven Families of monster hunters. The first trilogy follows the Wolf Family, as our heroes and heroines struggle to win their fated mates while fending off deadly monsters bent on destroying the world.

The latest book in her bestselling romantic urban fantasy series about Protector Cary Redmond, THE TROUBLE WITH DEATH AND DEMON GODS, is also out now. As are the newest stories in the romantic urban fantasy Demon Witch series, including the first "meet cute" for Angie and her demon hunter boyfriend Sebastian in the novella HOWLING DREADFUL.

For something a little different, Kat also publishes fantasy, science fiction, and the occasional hockey romance under the name Isabo Kelly (https://www.isabokelly.com).

After traveling the world, living in places like Hawaii, Germany, and Ireland, Kat now lives in New York City with her family and a library's worth of books.

For more on Kat and her future books

Website: https://www.katsimons.com
Newsletter: https://bit.ly/KatSimonsNewsletter

Kat Simons Books Bookstore
https://tanddpublishingbookstore.com/

Socials
Facebook Page: https://www.facebook.com/KatSimonsAuthor
BookBub: https://www.bookbub.com/authors/kat-simons
Instagram: https://www.instagram.com/isabokelly/
Twitter: https://twitter.com/IsaboKelly

KAT'S NEWSLETTER

Don't miss the latest Kat Simons

news, updates, excerpts, cover reveals, and more!

All new subscribers get two free stories.

* * *

Mate Run

A Tiger Shifters Paranormal Romance short story

and

When Cary Met Ariel

A Cary Redmond Urban Fantasy novella

* * *

Join Now!

https://bit.ly/KatSimonsNewsletter